Cannons for the Cause

A Novel of the American Revolution

Martin R. Ganzglass

To Jodie &
Barry
all the best
Marty

ALSO BY MARTIN R. GANZGLASS

Fiction

The Orange Tree

Somalia: Short Fiction

Non-Fiction

The Penal Code of the Somali Democratic Republic
(Cases, Commentary and Examples)

The Restoration of the Somali Justice System, Learning From Somalia,
The Lessons of Armed Humanitarian Intervention,
Clarke & Herbst, Editors

The Forty-Eight Hour Rule, One Hand Does Not Catch a Buffalo,
A. Barlow, Editor

For David

Cannons for the Cause
A Peace Corps Writers Book,
An imprint of Peace Corps Worldwide

Printed in the United States of America
by Peace Corps Writers of Oakland, California.

For more information, contact peacecorpsworldwide@gmail.com
Peace Corps Writers and the Peace Corps Writers colophon are
trademarks of PeaceCorpsWorldwide.org

This novel is a work of fiction. The historical figures and actual
events described are used fictiously. All other names, characters,
places and incidents are products of the author's imagination.
Any resemblance to living persons is purely coincidental.

ISBN 978-1-935925-38-5
Library of Congress Control Number 2014934074

First Peace Corps Writers Edition, March 2014

A PEACE CORPS WRITERS BOOK

I never intended to serve the entire war in General Knox's artillery. I did, though, not as a levy but as a teamster and Continental. I first made the General's acquaintance when he was still a civilian on an important mission for General Washington. I was only fifteen years of age. I look back, from the vantage point of my Seventy One years, on the splendid panorama of the great events in which I participated and am amazed, not that I survived the War for Independence, in which I had many a close call, but that in each armed encounter I acquitted myself with honor. I stood up when the time came. I was not a coward.

Today, I am not one of those who, sitting before a warm fire on a cold winter night, or on a stone bench in the Village Commons on a fragrant spring day, dwell upon his duty to our Nation, making himself more zealous and faithful, and his actions more heroic and crucial to the cause. Nor am I one of those current pretenders who claim to have been motivated to leave farm and family for the Sacred Cause of Liberty embodied in the now mythical Spirit of '76, when all was supposed to be universal patriotism. In fact, if these present-day patriots served at all, they deserted before their enlistment was up, or did not tarry one day beyond their term, or perpetually flew between military camp and farm, being more farmers with muskets then true disciplined soldiers. I saw enough of these militiamen to know.

Indeed, I myself admit I was drawn into the conflict by accident, protected by a Beneficent God and treated as a son by General Henry

Knox, one of the finest men who ever walked this earth. He had the misfortune, after enduring all the risks and hardships of the War, to die choking on a chicken bone in the peaceful tranquility of a dinner among friends. I attended his funeral, but that is another story.

Mine begins, like the lives of all men, from the humblest individual to the greatest prince, with my birth. I suppose, as my wife would gently remind me, and as Mrs. Knox would assertively interpose, it is also true for the lives of women.

I was born in 1760 in Schoharie, a town near Albany. My father, George Stoner, a farmer of independent circumstances, accumulated more of his wealth by shrewdly making as much money as possible from the public till, than from tilling crops. Although he did drive a hard bargain for those as well.

He was a wagoner during the French and Indian War, hauling supplies from Albany to the head of Lake George and, on occasion, bringing bodies of Officers back for burial in the city. Unlike others in this trade, my father, sensing the opportunity brought on by the necessity of supplying the army with victuals, tents and blankets, horses and wagons, of which there were too few to meet the need, had bought up horses that were definitely not in prime condition, and constructed wagons that would not have lasted more than five miles on the roads of those days. He signed up with Colonel Bradstreet with four wagons, each pulled by two teams of these spindly-legged, swaybacked nags. In the first week out, as was the custom, all of the wagoners turned the horses out for forage. My father pretended all but three were lost and ostensibly went to look for them, leaving a young hired lad to continue on the arduous journey north with but a team of two. Father then returned to the farm, harvested his crops and when his time was nearly run for the period he had been engaged, presented himself at headquarters in Albany and received the full amount of his stipulated wages and handsome payment in compensation for his "lost" horses. He was that type of man.

He smelled another such opportunity in November 1775, when there was talk rife in Albany of the need for teamsters to haul cannons from Fort Ticonderoga, recently captured from the British by Ethan Allen and his Green Mountain Boys, to General Washington, who was investing General Howe and the British Army in Boston. General Knox, then a private citizen awaiting his Colonel's Commission, arrived in Albany on December 1st. His presence and purse and his association with General Philip Schuyler, a much respected and prominent person in our locality, gave confirmation to what had simply been tavern talk and speculation.

Knox's agent, an experienced Quartermaster and formerly the Manager of General Schuyler's estates, could not be fooled by nags and shoddily built slapdash carts. My father presented himself, two well-made sleds and a wagon, ten horses accustomed to farm work and quite sturdy in their frame, and me, Willem Stoner, for hire on this grand expedition.

My father received a better than fair price, knowing of the unavailability of sleds, wagons and teams. Reluctantly, the agent agreed to a bit above the normal pay, one-half paid in advance in British pound sterling, the other half payable upon completion of the journey. Our engagement was to travel empty from Albany to Ft. George with a return trip heavily loaded past Albany, across the Hudson and through the mountains to the border with the Province of Massachusetts. The cannons, fifty-nine in number, ranging from one to eleven feet in length and one hundred to more than 5,000 pounds, together with flint, shot and balls were ferried by boat down the Lake from Ft. Ticonderoga to our meeting place at Ft. George.

My father's natural greed and Divine Providence intervened, so that I continued on with the expedition to Boston, while my father returned to Schoharie and the farm. I never saw him again. He died in 1781, caught alone by Tories and marauding Indians in the woods near Saratoga. What he was doing there I do not know. My stepmother buried his scalped body on our farm. My brother Johan, originally apprenticed to a dry goods merchant in Boston, never returned to Schoharie. He eventually sailed to London and died there. The less said about him the better.

As for me, I was given up for dead. When my stepmother remarried, her new husband, Andrew Ten Broek inherited our farm and all the appurtenanced property. After the War, I could have proferred my claim as the sole surviving son but I surmised it would have been futile. Ten Broek was well connected with the landed Aristocracy, and Justice likely would have been rendered in his Favor. Thus, did our War for Independence fulfill for me the fine words of the great Declaration that all men are created equal. However, I had learned much in General Knox's service. His friendship opened doors of opportunity for me in the mercantile trade, enabling me, after the War, to prosper and support my family in New York City. That too is another story.

I have in common with many garrulous men of a certain age to digress from the tale at hand. The best course is to begin at the beginning and tell it chronologically from what is now known as the great trek of the Noble Train of Artillery from Fort George to Cambridge in the bitter cold winter of December 1775 to late January 1776, and to let the subsequent retreats, battles, defeats and victories fall into their appointed places. As I said, I was fifteen years old when my father signed his name to the roster Colonel Knox kept to transport the cannons down from Fort George to the Massachusetts border. From there, others were to bring them to menace the powerful British fleet lying in Boston Harbor.

Over the past two years, recognizing that my time on this earth is surely coming to an end, I have told my story to my grandson, William Stoner II, who has the good fortune to be formally educated at Princeton, a place I know well from the bloody action there in which I participated. He has faithfully copied down the details as I have related them. He is an intelligent young man and I do not say that because he is my grandson. In the course of relating my adventures, he has asked many probing questions, compelling me to reveal much of what I had kept hidden in the deep recesses of my mind.

However, he has some concept, acquired at college from reading the great authors, to present my life, not as a memoir, as I intended, but as a Novel. My grandson fancies himself a writer and affirms he will be precise as to the events I participated in, and my feelings as he knows them to be. He promises to add other characters only after the most thorough research and verification as to their actions and the events as they witnessed them. Since he is my only grandson and my namesake, I am inclined to indulge him.

I am familiar with novels, having been given my first one on the

Great Trek by Colonel Knox himself. I have read many in my time and enjoyed some more than others. However, I find it difficult to distinguish what is true about the actions described in them and what originated in the author's imagination. I hope you find that my grandson has scrupulously depicted the historical facts and that your reading is not burdened by fictitious or exaggerated events.

While I do not approve of my grandson's diversion from my original intent to write a memoir, he has my blessing to proceed as he wishes, provided that his Novel is not published in my lifetime.

Therefore, Dear Reader, as you turn this page and begin this book, handsomely bound I hope, you know I am in the Great Beyond, together with my Beloved Wife, dining with General and Mrs. Knox, followed by a game of cards, Mrs. Knox being greatly addicted to such diversions, and occasionally, between hands, looking down on you with bemused curiosity as you read my grandson's account of my youthful adventures and the War which brought you Your Independence.

Willem Stoner, May 16, 1831

"The route will be from Fort George to Kinderhook, from thence to Great Barrington, and down to Springfield. From Saratoga, trusting that we shall have a fine fall of snow, which will enable us to proceed further, and make the carriage easy. If that shall be the case, I hope in sixteen or seventeen days' time to be able to present to your Excellency a noble train of artillery."

Colonel Henry Knox at Fort George, New York to
General George Washington, Cambridge, Massachusetts,

December 17, 1775

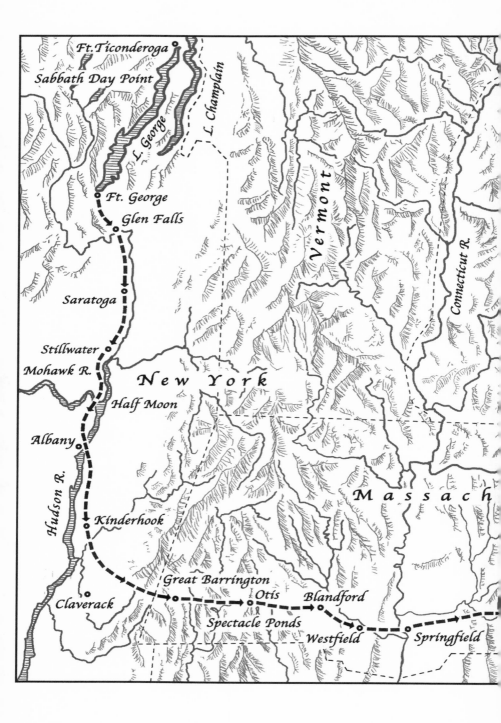

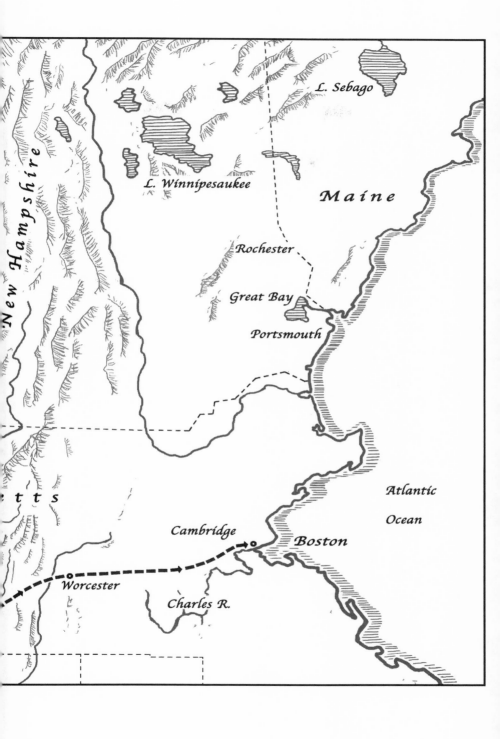

The large flat-bottomed scow was beginning to founder. Strong winds blowing toward them from the southern end of Lake George whipped the icy waters over the gunnels. The ungainly vessel, already low in the water with its load of twenty-three cannons, some weighing more than a ton, was turning sideways.

Ensign Nathaniel Holmes silently cursed the contrary winds, which had made their two sails useless. He cursed the inept and clumsy Continentals from Fort Ticonderoga, weak and thin-as-rail soldiers he had been compelled to use as rowers for the voyage down Lake George. If he just had four Marblehead Mariners from his Regiment, experienced fishermen who could bring a dory through any nor'easter, he could have kept the boat steady and rowed until the winds had ceased. No sense wishing for what he did not have.

They were more than one hundred yards off the promontory jutting out into the menacing waves. If they sank closer to shore it was possible to save the cannons. He tied down the tiller. The rudder was as worthless now as the sails. Jumping up on the narrow walkway, he grabbed the twelve-foot-long sweep oar from the nearest soldier on the starboard side.

"Go forward and double up with the one rowing ahead of you," he yelled over the wind. "And tell the one ahead to do the same, up to the prow." The soldier looked at him bewildered.

"Two of you on each oar all along the walkway," he shouted.

"Hurry, or this scow will break apart and we will drown." Fear will make them put their backs into it, he thought.

His plan was to strengthen the rowers on the starboard side and keep the prow pointed forward as much as possible. The soldiers rowing on the left side would barely help to steady the craft. He hoped the action of the waves would push the scow toward shore. The race between their rowing and the amount of water they were taking on would determine whether the boat sank in deep water or closer to the shoreline.

Nathaniel looked at the promontory, called Sabbath Day Point. The rocky granite finger with low scrub pines seemed nearer, maybe less than fifty yards away. Still too far, he concluded, using the sweep oar to probe the depth. If we sink here, it will be too deep to easily raise the cannons. They would lose more than a third of the artillery Colonel Knox had selected from Fort Ticonderoga- cannons urgently needed by General Washington to drive the British army from Boston.

He planted his feet and leaned his broad shoulder into the oar, timing his stroke to the pair in front of him. The poor fools did not even know how to pull together. Better for him to do two to every one of theirs. Nathaniel glanced at the water sloshing around the lashed-down cannons. The scow was riding lower and becoming more unmanageable. A series of waves crashed over the gunnels and drove the wallowing craft sideways. Nathaniel plunged his oar straight down. It struck bottom. Less than twelve feet deep. He ran to the other side of the scow.

"Use your oars as poles to push us toward shore," he shouted, motioning for the soldiers on the starboard side to join him. One man leaned too far out as he thrust against his oar, lost his footing on the slippery walkway and fell into the water. Two others dropped their oars and leaned over to pull their comrade out. The oars quickly disappeared in the roiling white caps. The waves continued to drive the scow sideways closer to the Point.

Nathaniel judged them to be near enough and ordered them all to jump from the starboard side.

"With your haversacks," he shouted, throwing one after a soldier who was already in the water, thrashing about like a frightened calf although his feet had touched bottom.

The men waded through the frigid, chest-deep water, crunched through the thin layer of ice at the shoreline and collapsed on the gravel beach. The scow lay less than fifteen feet off shore, its gunnels above water. Nat knew they needed to build a fire to survive the cold December night.

"Sergeant," Nathaniel called to a soldier leaning exhausted on one knee with his head bowed. "Organize your men into work parties."

The Sergeant laboriously hauled himself up. He walked slowly, almost insolently so and when he was close, he bent his tall lanky frame forward. Nat could smell the rum on his breath.

"We are on land now, Mr. Ensign Holmes. You are no longer in command," he snarled. He rubbed his chest under his dripping wet jacket and brazenly dropped his right arm to his waist. His fingers curled around the bone handle of a large sheathed hunting knife.

Nathaniel resisted the urge to smash the Sergeant in the mouth and knock out his brown stubs of teeth. He looked at the darkening sky and glanced at some of the soldiers greedily emptying their canteens. In another hour they would be drunk on rum and unable to stand. He needed them in the morning to bail out the scow. Then, if necessary he could sail it by himself to Fort George.

"I say the men rest, and rest they shall," the Sergeant said, daring Nathaniel to contradict him. " Tis fourteen to one."

"We need to build fires for all to keep warm," Holmes replied calmly. "They can rest later around the bonfires. The work will keep them from freezing until then." Nathaniel pointed at some of the soldiers curled up where they had fallen. "I have seen men, soaked from the ocean, succumb to numbing, comforting sleep, never to awake again. Is that how you want them to die?"

The Sergeant turned back toward the exhausted, wet men lying in frozen heaps on the beach. Nathaniel did not wait. He walked to the edge of the pine forest carrying one of the few axes they had. Two other soldiers soon joined him.

"Fell the shorter trees first," he said, gesturing to the low scrub pines. The sooner they got any fire going and the men felt its warmth, the better they would understand the necessity to cut more trees.

Several soldiers fanned out through the woods searching for kindling on the ground. Others trimmed the branches from the downed trees with their bayonets and knives. They quickly started two small fires, the bright dancing flames guiding those in the woods back to their pitiful encampment on the shore.

Two hours later, Nathaniel was the only one still wielding an axe. The others had retired to the large bonfires, standing in front of them, turning this way and that, to warm their bodies and dry their uniforms. He chopped down three more trees and strode back to the beach.

"Have your men bring those trees in, lop off the limbs and top them off," he said to the Sergeant. "With these three, we should have enough wood to last us through the night." The Sergeant pointed at five men closest to one fire. The men groaned in protest. Sullenly, they left the heat of the bonfire, stumbling and slipping on the ice-coated rocks and disappeared into the woods.

"And what then," one of the soldiers shouted from the far side of the fire. "How do get off this God-forsaken place?"

"The same way we arrived. By boat," Nathaniel answered, leaving them to puzzle it out.

"We should wait here for those ahead to return and rescue us," one said loudly. Others grunted their agreement. "Why does the bloody sailor decide?" someone grumbled from the shadows, in a slurred voice.

Holmes ignored their continued muttering. He sat down on his knapsack, ate some hard biscuit, washed it down with a swallow of cider and stared into the flames. The soldiers would not dare to attack him at night, he thought. But rum could encourage the most cowardly. If it didn't make them drowsy first. He decided to move away from the rocky beach and keep his axe nearby. When he thought most of them were asleep, he quietly rose, and walked away from the fire. He found a broad tree trunk to rest against, pulled his cloak up behind his neck and, with his knees against his chest, fell asleep his right hand grasping the axe handle.

He awoke numb and stiff before sunrise to a clearing sky. The wind was now gusting briskly from the northeast. Chilly but most welcome, Nat thought. It would fill the sails and take them to Fort George at the southern end of the lake. The two large bonfires had burned down to glowing red embers. He scraped the hot coals together with a stick and flames leaped up. After throwing the remaining brush and a few roughly cut logs on the fires, he awoke the Sergeant. They would have to move quickly to take advantage of the limited hours of winter daylight.

"The wind is favorable. Rouse your men. We must get to work."

At first, the men didn't understand. When it was clear they had to wade back into the frigid lake waters and bail the scow out, they rebelled. Nathaniel's original plan was to have all of them working at the same time and be on their way in a few hours. He was forced to concede in the face of their protests.

"There are buckets for swabbing the cannons, more than enough for all of us to use. However, we will work in shifts, seven men in the boat bailing, seven on shore keeping the fires going." Despite the grumbling and muttering, the soldiers divided into two seven-man squads.

With Nat in the lead, the first shift waded out to the scow. Nat gritted his teeth as the icy waters soaked his canvas breeches and rose up to his armpits. He hauled himself over the gunnel and helped the soldier closest to him. Pulling the slip knots that tied the buckets to the gun carriages, he handed one to each man. The soldiers began bailing, at first in a disorganized frenzy of activity, as if they would empty the scow in a rush.

"Set a pace," Nat commanded. "We will be at this for a while. Watch me and bail when I do." Soon he had them working steadily and complaining loudly about their frozen fingers and numb legs and feet. After an hour, when the second squad of men, led by the Sergeant, came out, the level of water was lower but still almost waist-high in the hold. By noon, Nathaniel determined they had bailed enough for the sails to do their work. He let loose the bowline, which drifted back toward shore, untied the tiller and directed the raising of their two sails.

The dirty square canvas billowed out full and the masts creaked with the strain from the strong following wind. The soldiers cheered as the scow headed out into the wide lake. Once they found there was no place for them to escape the blustery gusts, they fell silent. Several of them, still wet and shivering, sought shelter among the gun carriages.

Most took refuge in the remaining rum in their canteens.

Nat did not care if they became drunk and useless now. He would bring the vessel and its cargo of cannons to Fort George and report to Colonel Knox, who would be anxious at their delayed arrival. From the Fort it was three hundred thirty miles overland to General Washington's headquarters in Cambridge. There, he would be reunited with his Regiment. With these cannons, the Army under General Washington would attack and force the Redcoats out of Boston.

He dreaded the upcoming long trek on poor roads made worse by winter blizzards, the mountains they would have to cross, and whatever other difficulties they would encounter. This would be his last time on open waters for a long time. He leaned comfortably against the oak tiller, pulled his cloak collar up and breathed in the fresh air. High above the two tattered sails a hawk soared swiftly on the wind toward Fort George. [1]

Horses can see ghosts. He knew it for certain. The de Ruyter boy, on the next farm over, had been thrown from his horse near the ruins of Adril's mill. His horse must have seen the ghost of old man Adril, killed by Indians, scalped and worse, while he was still alive. His mill burned to the ground during the French and Indian War.

Will Stoner sat up straight on the wooden plank of the sled's seat. The wagon train was approaching Bloody Pond. Many men had died in the woods off this old military road leading south from Lake George. [1] It was a place filled with their ghosts. Horses can see ghosts, he repeated aloud to reassure himself.

He leaned forward, as if by being closer he could pierce the cold December night. The reins were slack in his frozen hands. Ahead, the darkness seemed to be peopled with the dead spirits of the slaughtered soldiers. He peered ahead, barely able to distinguish the low hanging dark boughs of the evergreens from the dreary gloom of the forest.

Everyone north of Albany knew about Bloody Pond. It happened during the French and Indian War. British Colonials, many of them militia from New York, had caught French and Canadian troops and their Indian allies resting by the water. It was late on a balmy autumn afternoon in September 1755. They shot, stabbed and tomahawked more than two hundred of them, and dumped their bodies in the water. The Colonials crossed the pond using the backs of the corpses as stepping stones, in pursuit of the fleeing survivors. Will had heard this from a man his father had once invited home for dinner. He said he was a veteran of that war and had the scars to prove it. [2]

The sky was clear but the slim quarter moon gave little light to see by. He passed the end of the open rolling snow-covered fields and entered the forest. He was seized by a terrible fear of the unknown. The coldness he felt in his body was nothing compared to the terror that froze his mind. The cedar and fir tree branches, bent down like icy fingers, reaching to pluck him off of his seat. Will listened anxiously for the comfort of human sounds. Behind him, after what seemed an interminable silence, he could hear noises from the main body of the wagon train, the creak of axles, the snuffling of horses and oxen, a man's voice, the occasional crack of a whip. The sounds reached him faintly through the gloomy air of the bitter cold night. There were more than eighty wagons and sleds and over two hundred horses and oxen pulling the cannons, barrels of shot and lead, and boxes of flint, accompanied by a small detachment of Continentals. The entire disorganized train was spread out for miles on barely passable roads through the sparsely populated wintry countryside.

Will was in the lead of a group of teamsters pulling the heavy guns. His small sled was loaded with bags of oats and feed for the horses. Enough weight to smooth out the rutted road for the wagons and sleds behind but not so heavy as to get bogged down in the slush. He had been glad to get away from his father when they had first set out. Now he reproached himself for being so far ahead.

The nighttime silence and isolation of the woods were in stark contrast to the noisy tumult and confusion at Fort George earlier that morning. He had never seen so many teamsters, horses and oxen in one place. The men boisterous and good humored at the money to be made. Seven pounds sterling per ton for every sixty-two miles, or twelve shillings per day for each span of horses. They stood stamping their feet, waiting for the cannons to be loaded, telling stories and passing around a jug of rum. The oxen stoically rooted in place and yoked in tandem, stared disinterestedly in front of them. The horses, more intelligent and hobbled nearby, sensed the excitement and raised their heads, their ears pointed forward at every strange noise, before pawing the snow to find some bit of grass beneath.

Once the guns were securely tied down on a sled or wagon, the teamsters left quickly, whipping their animals on, hoping to reach Glen Falls and a warm inn or barn before nightfall. By early afternoon it was George Stoner's turn.

Will carefully checked the harnesses on each of the four pairs of horses and then attached the traces. He brought the eight horses around to the large sled with the thick ash runners to hitch them to the worn wooden tongue.

"Wilhelm," his father shouted at him from the seat of the sled. The long wait and rum had put him in a vile temper. "The bay and the dun mare are foremost. Not third. And you paired the roan with the grey. That one pulls better with our white spotted plow horse." He let loose a string of curses. "Now we will be camping out in a snowy field tonight. Make it right and be quick about it."

Will was certain he had paired the eight horses as his father had instructed. It would do no good to tell him so. Resentfully, he rearranged the spans and hitched the horses to the sled. His father made him walk the half mile to the flat pasture adjacent to the beach. It was the loading area for the cannons brought down by boat from Fort Ticonderoga.

The frenzy of activity and tumult made Will forget his anger and humiliation. Men strained on ropes, pulling cannons over freshly cut log rollers up from the waterline. Others wrestled to lift the smaller pieces, the three and six pounders, weighing between four and six hundred pounds each, on to waiting sleds and wagons. He watched the men tie ropes around a large fortification gun. It was the cannon for his father's sled. They ran the thick cord back to a double block and tackle hanging from the apex of a ten foot high A frame of roughly hewn oak tree trunks.

A squad of soldiers from Fort George strained and grunted on the ropes. The gun rose slowly off its temporary bed of logs and swung up in the air, a few feet off the ground but high enough to clear the lip of their sled.

"Wilhelm," his father yelled from his wagon seat. "Stop your woolgathering and pay attention. Hold the team steady," he commanded, pulling back on the reins. "Worthless boy," he said to no one in particular, shaking his head in disgust. Will firmly grabbed the bridles of the two lead horses. He kept their heads down so they would not rear at the unexpected noise.

The gun came down on the oak planks of the sled with a loud crunch. "You have cracked my sled you whore-faced assbags," George Stoner shouted, seeing his chance to earn sterling gone if the planks were splintered. He jumped down from the sled seat, cursed the soldiers again for their clumsiness and went to assess the damage. With the gun resting on the sled, the soldiers no longer needed to hold on to the ropes. A few of them stepped from around the scaffolding and advanced on Stoner. Will's father looked quickly for an officer to intercede.

"Not the loudmouth now, you dickweed farmer," one of the soldiers said, holding a large wooden mallet in one hand. Two others followed him, one with a stout club, another with an iron pry bar. Will saw his father glance desperately around for help. The other teamsters were either too far away or preoccupied with getting their own sleds loaded.

"You there, Sergeant," a man yelled. "Get your men back to work. Knock those pegs out and take down the frame. We have more cannons still to be put on sleds." He ducked under the ropes dangling from the block and tackle and came over to examine Stoner's sled. He was young, with enough flesh on his frame to indicate he ate well and frequently. He wore a wool dark blue great coat, opened in front to reveal a simple hunting shirt with a brocaded waist coat underneath.

"Your name, sir," he asked Will's father.

"George Stoner. This is my sled and team of eight, duly hired by Colonel Knox himself to haul this cannon. If the sled is smashed by those oafs, I will demand my full payment from Colonel Knox as promised. And who be you?" He stood with his hands on his hips in front of the man.

The man didn't answer but smiled slightly, amused as if privy to a secret joke. He walked around Stoner, stepped on to the sled, knelt down and examined the planks. The heavy cannon's breach rested at the front, and because it was far thicker than the muzzle at the rear, the gun was on an angle with space beneath revealing the sled's floor.

"The flooring is sound," he declared, after running his hand along the planks up to the breach. "A crew will come and lash this gun down. Then you had better be on your way, Mr. Stoner." He stood up and pushed back his shoulder cape that had fallen forward.

The man walked the length of the four span, noting the strength of the horses and checking the traces. He smiled at Will, still holding the lead pair's bridles. He turned to Will's father who had followed closely behind.

"I am William Knox. Fortunately, Mr. Stoner," he said, before returning to supervise the dismantling of the A frame, "you will not have to contend with my brother for your claim for compensation. I am certain he would have denied it, and had you thrown in the brig at Fort George for demanding it. He does not take kindly to war profiteering."

A few of the teamsters who had approached, hoping to profit from George Stoner's ill fortune if his sled were ruined, snickered enjoying his discomfort.

Will knew his father. He would not let this public rebuke go unanswered. He would wait for the opportune time to make the Colonel pay for his brother's demeaning words.

In some way, Will was certain it had been by wheedling or trickery, his father had been assigned the transport of the largest of the guns, the iron fortification cannons, weighing more than 5,000 pounds. George Stoner had shrewdly calculated more weight and slower going, with the possibility of being delayed by either thawed out muddy roads or snow covered impassable ones, meant more money for him.

Instead of being satisfied with getting the heaviest of the guns, as he had wanted, his father had left Fort George angry and fuming at everyone and everything. If his father were still in his evil mood he would take it out on him that night. But for now, Will was more concerned about the ghosts of the slaughtered French and their Indian allies, waiting for him in the forest.

Big Red, the horse Will depended on to keep the grey mare calm, shied to the left, ears alert, exhaling warm air from his nostrils like twin puffs of smoke. Will tightened his grip on the reins, wrapping the cold leather around his knuckles. He stood up to urge Big Red forward. The horse refused to move, pawing at the ground and snorting. He lifted his great head and shook it from side to side. The grey, in harness next to him, lowered her neck and rubbed her shoulder against Big Red.

Will had been handling teams since he was eight. At fifteen, he was tall and rangy with shoulders too wide for his long, narrow torso. He was still growing into his body, his feet too large and his neck a bit too long, like a colt whose conformation indicated the horse he would become. He had strength in his arms though. He pulled back firmly on the reins to get the horses' heads up and snapped the straps smartly on their haunches. The team responded and pulled the sled forward down the narrow dark road and further into the murky forest. Suddenly, on his right he heard a crunching sound, like someone or something walking on the frozen crust and moving toward the road. Big Red halted, his ears pointing up, his nostrils flaring to catch the scent.

Will reached for the whip and lashed at both horses forcing them forward. The crunching was louder, accompanied by a soft moan. To Will, it was the sound a soldier would make as a tomahawk bit into the flesh of his back before striking bone. In his mind, he saw the bloody blade raised again, splitting a man's skull, the brains spilling out between the gaping white of shattered bone.

Big Red whinnied and reared up. Will whipped both horses again. The team leaped over something in front of them. Will pulled back on the reins but the two horses, blinded by fear, were too strong for him. They bolted off the road. The short sled bounced over fallen trees and rocks covered by snow and ice, hit a boulder and upended. Will was thrown against a tree, his breath knocked out of him. He got up quickly, still more afraid of the ghosts of dead Frenchmen than the wrath of his father for losing control of the sled.

He secured the reins to a small cedar before unhitching the team. He patted Big Red on the neck, making soothing sounds, more to calm himself than the horse. He shouted back to the wagons and sleds following on the road and was relieved to hear his halloos answered by human voices, the creak of wagons, the snuffling of horses and the deeper, lower snorts of oxen. Some men emerged from the darkness and righted the sled. One remained to help him reload the bags of grain.

"I would rather be in a dory in a nor'easter than riding a wagon on this accursed road," the young man said, easily lifting one of the bags onto his shoulder and hoisting another under his arm. "These ruts have jarred my very vitals."

Will followed him, carrying only one sack on his right shoulder, steadying it with his left hand. The snow was deep with just enough crust to hold his weight momentarily before he sank in up to his calves. The wetness numbed his skin through his thin stockings. He stumbled, and winced with pain. He must have bruised his left side when he fell. He dropped his sack on the sled.

"Nathaniel Holmes, from Massachusetts," his companion introduced himself, barely puffing from the exertion. He was shorter and a few years older than Will, stocky, muscular and solidly built. He had a high forehead and prominent cheek bones, with reddish brown hair, curling forward at the temples. His thin lips formed a mouth that would have seemed grim except that it was dispelled by blue, clear eyes, showing pleasure at their meeting and amusement at their predicament.

"Will Stoner, from Schoharie, New York," he said, catching his breath.

Fortunately, most of the sacks that had fallen off were close to the sled. They made quick work of reloading them, moving faster on the paths they had already made in the snow.

"Wilhelm," his father shouted, striding from the road. "What have you done now? You idiot." He stomped through the snow in his knee high black boots, with his horse whip in hand. He glanced at the unhitched wagon and the rearranged pile of grain sacks.

"Held up the Colonel's train and embarrassed me in front of the others. That is what. You better not have lost any feed or there will be hell to pay."

"Nothing is spilled," Will said sullenly, his shoulders sagging under his father's tirade, as if he had been struck with the whip instead of lashed verbally. In the last year he had grown taller than his father and now stood slightly under six feet. Still, his father intimidated him.

"We have loaded the last of the sacks," he said, turning his back to his father as he led Big Red and the mare to the sled.

George Stoner noticed Nathaniel and introduced himself. "I appreciate your helping my idiot son, here." He pointed at Will with the whip handle. "His stupidity is from his mother's side. She was Dutch, passed away in childbirth, leaving me to raise this worthless one on my own." He noticed Nathaniel's dark blue cloak with the broad collar, the flat stiff broad-brimmed black hat and the thick canvas britches. "You are not a teamster from around here. A soldier from the Fort?"

"Hardly, sir" Nathaniel replied. "Ensign Nathaniel Holmes of the Marblehead Mariners. Colonel Knox brought me along to dismantle the artillery and supervise their passage to Boston."

George Stoner appraised Nathaniel in a new light, taking in the broad Massachusetts accent and calculating how he could turn the Ensign's acquaintance with the Colonel to his advantage.

"Come, ride with me on my sled. I am pulling one of the double fort cannons with a four-span team. Just as the Colonel specified," he said, affecting a greater familiarity with Knox than was warranted by the passing nod of acknowledgement from the Colonel at Fort George. "His brother himself, supervised its loading," he added, giving Will a venomous look to hold his tongue.

"Wilhelm. Haul your sled back on the road." He pointed with the whip handle through the trees as if Will didn't know where the road was. "When you find the first group of wagons, stop there. Make sure you feed our horses first before the others. Have three bags ready for my teams when I arrive," he shouted, as he walked away. "You bed down by yourself tonight. I will look for you on the morrow."

Will flicked his whip at Big Red, taking his anger at his father out on the horse. "Sorry," he said under his breath and clicked softly, encouraging the two horses to move forward. Since his mother's death, every time his father called him Wilhelm, he heard his mother's proud reprimand of her husband. "We are Dutch. My son's name is Willem. Wilhelm is German," she would say vehemently. His father would shrug as if it were all the same to him. He would wait until Will had done something wrong and deliberately call him "Willem," adding "you stupid Dutch boy" to demean his wife's heritage.

Will felt the stabbing needles of pain in his head, brought on by his raging, helpless fury. He hated his father. The man never missed an opportunity to belittle him in front of others. Deep inside, he had another reason, formed when he was much younger and unable to understand. After his mother had died, George Stoner had not waited a month before he let the word out among the local farmers and merchants around with eligible daughters that he was "in the intent of mind," as he put it, to take another wife.

Will was eight years old when his mother, Sarah Ryckman Stoner, had passed, dying while giving birth to a stillborn baby boy. His stepmother, Martha, an 18-year-old farmer's daughter when she married George Stoner, was nice enough to Will. He resented her because he saw Martha's face every day but couldn't remember his own mother's face at night before he fell asleep. Sometimes, he saw his mother's figure in his dreams, hanging clothes or feeding chickens in their yard, her face a blur or turned away from him. All that remained were his receding memories and the red wool scarf she had made for him one winter. Unconsciously, he burrowed his chin in it to protect against the cold night wind, feeling his warm breath blow back on his face.

When he thought about it at all, he recognized that his stepmother's life was not easy. Martha had lost her youthful spirit and exuberance after giving birth to two girls in quick succession, followed by a baby boy who had died within the month. They had buried him, unchristened, behind the house, his tiny grave marked by a flat stone no more than a foot in length. In the next two years, she gave birth to his half-brothers, Silas, who was now three, and Jacob who was two. When he had left with his father for Albany, Martha had looked worn and tired. She had given him a hug, and had stood waving goodbye as they drove the teams out of the barn and down the road past their hay fields.

Later, he discovered she had stuffed a small package of smoked venison, dried apples and a few potatoes into his leather rucksack. A wooden bowl, a pewter cup and a narrow-handled pewter spoon with a broad oval, good for eating stew or soup, made up the rest of his kit from home. His knife was tucked into his waistband. His hatchet, with the hickory handle he had carved by himself, was stowed in his leather bag for convenience.

His older brother, Johan, had taught him how to carve. He smiled at the memory, sitting in the barn one cold winter afternoon, almost a year before their mother had died, watching Johan finish making a sap funnel out of apple wood. His brother had found a hollow sycamore branch and showed Will how to make it into a wooden cup. Now Johan had it better, Will thought enviously.

Sarah had insisted both her boys be taught to read and do sums. Grandma Ryckman had educated them. Once they returned to the farm George Stoner had smelled a profitable opportunity. He apprenticed Johan to a merchant in Boston and required him to send home each fortnight whatever extra shillings he earned. That had been three years ago. At age twelve Will had assumed the additional burden of his older brother's share of the farm work.

Will thought of the many times since Johan had left, his father had hit him for not doing something right, for taking too long, for reading, for eating too much. Sometimes it seemed George Stoner hit him for existing or being in his sight.

After Will had distributed the feed to the encamped wagoners and fed his father's team of eight, hobbled together under a copse of firs, he bedded down on the sled, nestling among the sacks of oats for warmth. He stuck his hand inside his leather pouch and felt the worn hickory handle of his hatchet. I swear if he strikes me in front of the others, before this trek is over, I will smash his head with my hatchet. I will too, he said out loud to himself. That was his last thought before he fell asleep- hungry, angry, cold, defiant, and alone.

He awoke shivering under the brown homespun blanket he wore as a cloak during the day, shook the stiffness out of his legs, jumped off the sled and trudged a short distance down the flattened snowy track to relieve himself. In the early-morning winter darkness, he carried sacks of feed to the teamsters, homing in on the dying embers of their fires. Defiantly, he brought the oats to his father's teams last. He was confident his father would still be asleep, having stayed up late quaffing rum either by himself or with others. He quietly passed his father's figure, lying wrapped in a cloak, next to the sled's thick curved runners of ash, and made his way to a nearby campfire. Still angry from last night, he imagined the frozen ropes tearing loose and the cannon sliding off the sled and crushing his father into the frozen ground.

Nathaniel saw him coming and waved him over. His cheerful greeting instantly changed Will's mood.

"Come close to the fire and warm yourself if your bones are as chilled as mine," he said. Nat moved to make room for Will on the fallen log among the circle of men. Will shifted his leather bag to his back and held his hands out to the fire.

"Those clouds promise snow today," Nat said, pointing to the south, the direction they would be traveling. "The Colonel expects to reach Boston in sixteen days should the weather favor us. If we are granted, by Divine Providence, a decent snow not followed by an accursed thaw, we will deliver what Colonel Knox has promised to General Washington in good time"

One of the wagoners sniffed the air and shook his head. "Snow or not, today will be too warm to freeze the roads." He shrugged. "For me, I only care the damn Hudson be frozen until we cross and return. From there on, the thaw will be your problem, not those of us from around here," he said. "I am signed on only as far as Kinderhook," he explained. "Some of the others," he gestured at the teamsters around the circle, with a battered long handled claw hammer he was holding "They will be going to Claverack or beyond to Great Barrington and will leave the train there. I say good luck to you, the Colonel and his young brother crossing the mountains of Massachusetts."

The wagoner took a skillet of roasted coffee beans from the fire and put it down on the snow. A small cloud of steam rose around the hot pan like a halo, accompanied by a hiss, which quickly died down. He mashed the beans with his hammer and emptied the skillet's contents into a pot of hot water resting on two sturdy green branches over the fire. Will didn't particularly like coffee but held out his pewter cup for his share. He would drink anything hot this morning. He stretched out his feet toward the fire, feeling the heat through his wet, thin shoes.

"Though the weather has not been frigid enough to freeze the Hudson River for the ice to bear the heavy cannons, I am confident when the time comes we will all be able to cross," Nat said, holding his pewter cup of coffee with both hands. "The Colonel is a most able man, a careful man who plans well. On our outward journey, the Colonel made arrangements and has already hired other teamsters to take the cannons to Cambridge," Nat said, responding to the man with the hammer. He spoke loud enough for the others to hear. "They are to meet us at Great Barrington. Some of you have dispensation to leave us there and Massachusetts men will haul these cannons through those mountains you mentioned and on to General Washington." He retied his reddish brown hair back in a tail with a black ribbon and readjusted his Mariner's hat.

Will half-heard the bearded wagoner saying something about the strange happening last night. "Damn lucky for the drunken sod, he found the trail again. He would have frozen to death in the woods."

"No, most likely not," another said. "The pockey bastard had enough rum in him to keep him warm for hours yet." Several of them laughed. A few licked their lips as if savoring a swallow of rum with their morning biscuits.

So, the ghost of Bloody Pond had been a drunken soldier from Fort Ticonderoga, Will thought. He had fallen off the wagon on which he had been riding, stumbled off the road into the woods and gotten lost before eventually finding the train of artillery again. Big Red had simply shied at running over the man. Maybe there were no such things as ghosts. Will listened quietly to the conversation. At home he never talked much, afraid of his father's reaction both verbally and physically.

"They are a sorry lot of oddities, them soldiers from the fort," the teamster who had made the coffee continued. "Not enough flesh on them. They look like scarecrows in uniform. Probably not worth a damn in a fight."

"Worse," another wagoner said. "They will not be much help unstucking our wagons on the road. They lack the muscle or spirit to do the job. They do like their liquor though," he added. "Especially that one last night."

There was a thick band of lighter grey low in the eastern sky when George Stoner joined the group. His father motioned Will to get up and sat down next to Nathaniel. Will stood there unsure what to do, chewing on his last piece of coffee soaked bread.

Sitting next to Nat, it had tasted pleasant. Now it was bitter in his mouth.

"Good morning Ensign Holmes," George Stoner said amiably, making sure he was not crowding Nat. He looked up at Will, and feigned surprise he was still there.

"Go feed my team of eight. Do I have to tell you to do every simple task. Can you not think for yourself?" He dismissed Will with a wave of his hand.

Will stalked off through the muddy slush to his father's hungry team. When he returned to his own sled, still smarting from being embarrassed in front of the others, he found Nat waiting for him.

"I would prefer to ride with you, if that is acceptable," he said. Will nodded, eager to have his company.

He pointed to the train forming up behind them. "I will leave the block and tackle on the other wagon," he said, hoisting himself up on the sled. He threw one sack of oats on the seat for himself and another for Will. "They make a good cushion, as comfortable as a velvet seat in the Royal Governor's carriage," he said, winking. He patted the sack. "Of course, the Governor is not at liberty to go anywhere these days, with General Washington's army surrounding Boston. With these cannons, we will play a fiery tune for General Howe and the British Navy as well."

"My father would thrash me if he found me using the sacks as cushions," Will said.

"I do not need your father's permission," Nat responded, gesturing for Will to get the horses on their way.

Despite the peculiar way he spoke, with a broad flat A sound, and the use of strange words Will had never heard before, Nat proved a good companion and an excellent storyteller. During that day and the next few that followed, on the rough slog down from Glen Falls south to Saratoga, Will forgot the cold biting wind that always seemed to be before them, the cracked skin on his hands and his frozen toes. He listened appreciatively to Nat, eagerly learning of places, things and experiences he had never thought about or even knew existed. They averaged less than nine miles a day on the slushy, furrowed roads, made worse by freshly fallen snow, followed by the thaw and the muck that sucked at the sled's runners.

Nat had been to sea since age ten. His father was a Captain and ship owner out of Marblehead. He had taken his son on many of his voyages down the east coast to the Caribbean. Nat had acquired his knowledge of cannons on board his father's armed sloop. At age eighteen, Nat had joined the Marblehead Mariners. His Regiment, he proudly told Will, now served as the personal Headquarters Guard for General Washington in Cambridge.

When Colonel Knox asked for volunteers with experience in the hoisting of cannons and their transport, Nathaniel had stepped forward. He had left Cambridge in late November on a quick overland journey by horse, carrying only what he needed and ample block and tackle for the work to be done.

At Fort Ticonderoga, Nat related that after the Colonel had sorted out the usable cannons, the soldiers and hired civilians had loaded the fifty-nine guns, carriages, side boxes and flints on pettiangers and bateaus and brought them down the lake to Fort George.

"What is it you mean by pettiangers and bateaus? " Will asked, mangling their pronunciation.

"Why, they are two-masted, light-bottom shallow craft," Nat replied, in surprise. "Have you never been on a boat?" he asked, looking at Will incredulously.

Will shook his head and then brightened, anxious to please his companion. "There is a ferry near our farm, made of planked logs and big enough to carry a team of horses and a wagon across the river."

Nat laughed. "It consumed eight full days, working into the cold after nightfall on many of them, to load our little fleet. And seven more for me with my crew of inexperienced soldiers, unaccustomed to the vigorous labor of rowing, to make it to Fort George. For a distance of only thirty three miles," he said incredulously.

Will did not understand whether seven days was too long or exceptionally short, but he nodded as if he knew, and tugged the brim of his hat lower on his brow against the wet snow that had begun to fall.

"At last, with a fair wind I sailed down to Fort George without any need for those inept soldiers to row at all. When I beached the pettianger they were mostly drunk and unable to help with the unloading."

They traveled in silence for a while before Will, overcame his fear of being ridiculed for knowing so little about the world Nat had seen.

"My older brother, Johan, is apprenticed to a merchant in Boston," Will said. "He writes infrequently and then tis only an accounting of his earnings for my father. Pray, tell me about Boston? "

Boston, according to Nathaniel was the most civilized city in the colonies. Its people were God-fearing first, rigorously and righteously observing the Lord's Day. They were the most educated, tolerant, and intelligent, kept informed by The Boston Gazette, broadsheets, books, magazines and even newspapers from London; its businesses were the most prosperous and well run, the streets were paved and illuminated at night by street lamps, the red brick buildings well kept and properly furnished; its mechanics were the most skilled and industrious, all of which had been ruined by the British Army of Occupation.

"They are Sabbath breakers," Nathaniel said vehemently. "They march on Sunday and disrupt our places of worship and meetings. They violate God's laws by flogging their soldiers and shooting deserters. On the Boston Common," he added, as if that were sacred space. He paused and resumed with more spirit.

"Only in February of this year, more than 200 of them landed at Marblehead Neck, on the Sabbath mind you," raising his eyebrows to emphasize what he had said before. "They marched to Salem to seize cannon and powder of the militia there. Well, we trapped them at the Salem Bridge, my Marblehead Regiment behind them and the militias from Salem and the surrounding towns of Essex County to their front. All of our people, be they Presbyterians, Baptists, Congregationalists or even Quakers, poured out of their meeting houses that day to oppose the breach of the Sabbath. I tell you Will, it was a grand triumph for us, marching alongside those Redcoats, mocking their martial airs as they beat a hasty retreat down the road they had taken from Marblehead."

They stopped at a clearing close to the road in the early evening winter darkness where the leading sleds had made camp. Will started a fire, using walnut bark he had stripped with his hatchet. "Tis as good as pitch pine," he explained to Nathaniel, before leaving to rub down and feed his team and carry sacks to the other wagoners. He was late coming back because his father demanded he feed the team of eight, while George went off in search of a friendly teamster with rum to spare or barter.

Nat was perched on a sack of oats in front of a cooking fire. There were some potatoes roasting in the coals, a pot of water steaming and two salted cod laid out on a freshly cut evergreen branch. "It is more tasty than the mealy biscuits they gave us at Fort Ti," he said. Will tentatively tried a bit of the salted cooked fish, nodded in agreement and tore into the hot flesh, crunching some of the bones in his teeth. He shared his dried cold venison, and after their meal, he stoked the fire and the two of them moved closer for warmth.

"What happened after the British retreated from Salem?" Will asked.

"There was a triumphant feeling of defiance among the people, townsmen and farmers alike," Nathaniel said. "One man bared his chest despite the harsh wintry day and dared the Regulars to use their gleaming bayonets. A woman shouted from the second story window of her home for the soldiers to return to Boston and tell General Gage he had broken the Sabbath." Will could not tell whether Nathaniel' blue eyes glowed from the fire or the recollection of these exhilarating moments several months ago.

"Was anyone killed," Will asked, a bit too eagerly, as if the story would be better for him if blood had been shed.

"No, Will. There were at least one thousand of us, armed and ready. It would have been a massacre. The British Colonel was on a fool's errand but he was no fool."

He leaned closer to Will. "You should know there is a religious agenda for all these British machinations." Nat lowered his voice. "They are secret Papists. This General Gage has brought Catholic troops to Boston. Irish they are and they celebrate Christmas by getting drunk and engaging in lewd dancing. North of here, across the border, there are the French, who the British let keep their vile religion. They will come down on all of us as the heathen Saracens on Jerusalem. They intend to convert us all and murder or exile those who refuse to kiss the Papal ring." [3]

Will did not understand the part about the Saracens. And what did French Catholics have to do with Jerusalem where, he knew, Jesus had been crucified? He accepted it without understanding because Nathaniel had said it.

There were many other questions he wanted to ask Nat. Were all the British soldiers Catholic? If not, why were the Protestant ones breaking God's commandments? If the Catholics took over, what would happen to the British Protestant soldiers? He kept quiet, afraid of appearing ignorant to Nathaniel who seemed so experienced and well informed. Instead, Will thought of Nathaniel and his brother, Johan, meeting in Boston by accident in some prosperous merchant's brick warehouse or on a wharf where some valuable cargo was being unloaded. In his imagination, Johan and Nathaniel became friends and took him everywhere with them.

"After the Red Jackets were frustrated at Salem, they remained in Boston and took their wrath out on the city." Nathaniel continued. "They ransacked stores, looting and taking what they wanted and destroying everything else. Why Colonel Knox's own bookstore has been turned into rubble, the windows smashed and books scattered or used for fuel. Boston is a sad shadow of its old self, I tell you. Surrounded by the British navy, no food for its citizens, homes shuttered and abandoned or plundered or simply requisitioned to house their officers. These cannons we are bringing to General Washington will drive the cowardly lobstah coats out."

Will hesitated, confused. "What is it you mean by 'lobster coats'?" he asked.

Nathaniel smiled. "That is what we sometimes call the British soldiers. Lobstah because of their red uniforms."

"And what is a lobstah," Will asked again, attempting to imitate Nathaniel's pronunciation.

"Ah, so there is the problem. You have never seen a lobstah. Of course, how could you, so far from the ocean. The fault is mine for not explaining things in a better fashion," he apologized, putting his arm around Will's shoulder. "Permit me to clarify. A lobstah is a shellfish from the sea. All along the Massachusetts coast, we boil and eat them. Their flesh is good, sweet with a salty taste from the ocean."

Will pictured a river trout with a turtle shell around it. They must look peculiar, he concluded with both legs and fins.

"When they are boiled," Nathaniel continued, "they turn bright red, like the color of the British soldiers' woolen coats."

Will stared at the flames wondering whether these lobsters tasted like the turtle meat he had once eaten- fatty and greasy with not much flavor.

"Tell me, Nat about the big battle in April. It was not until the summer when the Albany papers arrived in Schoharie. Were you at Lexington or Concord? Did you kill any British soldiers?" Will asked excitedly.

Nat smiled ruefully and shook his head. "I was at sea. Cod fishing at the time. Unfortunately," Nat continued, "General Gage did not include me in his secret plans to seize the cannon and powder at Concord. Therefore, as was true of most of the men in the Marblehead Mariners, we were rowing our dories in the Atlantic. Otherwise, we would have been on land to do our part to protect our homes and rights as Englishmen."

Nat noticed the disappointment on Will's face. "I know people who were there, Will," he said quickly. "With the militia on the Lexington Green and along the road down which the Redcoats retreated from Concord. As our train of artillery progresses into Massachusetts and closer to Boston you will hear firsthand from those who were there. Why there are even some at General Washington's camp in Cambridge."

"My father has signed us on only to the Massachusetts border," Will replied. "Not for beyond. I will be back at our farm by the time you reach Cambridge." He got up and walked over to Big Red, burying his face in the horse's neck to conceal his tears of frustration and rage. When he returned to the fire, Nat was silent for a time.

"Sometimes, Providence intervenes on one's behalf for unknown reasons. I feel it in my marrow that you and I together will see the British driven out from Boston." Will shook his head, unconvinced.

"Now," he said cheerily, "what are we going to do for warmth on this bitter cold night?" He moved closer to the fire and wrapped his cloak tighter around him. "There is nothing for it but the bags on the sled. Shall we curl up together amongst the sacks?" Will didn't answer.

"No need to worry. I am not going to bung you. I am a Presbyterian," he said indignantly.

Will had no idea what bunging meant and didn't want to offend Nat. Besides, he reasoned, Nat did not do it, whatever it was. That night, with the sacks of oats in front of him, Nat's shorter frame warming his back and Nat's heavy woolen cloak covering both of them, Will dreamt of he, Nat and Johan, standing on a cliff as the British fleet sailed off toward the horizon, the Union Jack drooping limply from their stern flagstaffs.

On the first day of the new year of 1776, the train was just south of Stillwater, the wagoners suffering from their heavy drinking the night before. Nevertheless they made good time that day and the next, and early on January 3rd they reached Lansing's Ferry at Half Moon on the Mohawk River. There they discovered the rest of the wagons and sleds. The drivers had been ordered by Colonel Knox to wait for the entire train and to travel together to Albany. The Colonel had concluded, given the poor conditions of the roads and the heavy snowfalls they had encountered, it was better to have "all hands on deck," as Nat explained, with every teamster able to help the others in case of difficulties.

William Knox, the Colonel's brother, was at the Ferry to direct the crossing over the icy river. Nat went to confer with him. Will, who had avoided his father as much as possible on the journey, now found himself feeding his father's team of eight, as well as Big Red and the mare, while George Stoner partook of the cheap rum and fireside warmth at the Ferry's low roofed, stone tavern.

Colonel Knox had hurried sleds of hay from Albany north to Lansing's Ferry, and Will was kept busy distributing the bales among the wagoners' teams. The hay, together with plenty of water, would aid their digestion. Will had worried that Big Red and the grey would bind up from their steady diet of oats. The horses needed roughage and there had not been any available since Great Falls. By mid-day, Will was in the covered shed behind the tavern rubbing Big Red and the grey down, when Nat rushed in.

"We are moving the heavier cannons across first," he said excitedly, brushing snow from his dark blue cape. "The ice appears thick enough. You and I will go together on your sled with my block and tackle, assess the condition of the ice and survey the far shore. Then, return for the eighteen and twenty-four pounders."

Will hesitated, unsure whether to enter the tavern and tell his father he was leaving. He feared he would either say no or be angry for being disturbed in his drinking, or both. Besides, he concluded he was following orders, though he realized that might not be a defense later against his father's harsh words or blows.

Will urged Big Red and the grey down to the shoreline. The heavy wooden blocks and thick braided ropes on the sled were already covered with a light dusting of snow. The horses stepped gingerly on to the ice and plodded forward at a slow deliberate pace. The Mohawk was no more than 200 feet wide at the point Nathaniel had chosen. The granulated snow crunched under the horses' hooves. Will pulled the blanket closer around his throat and shifted his body so his left shoulder bore the brunt of the strong wind coming down river. He wore the red scarf around his head under his slouch hat to protect his ears. On the far shore, the horses' hooves broke the thin ice at the rivers edge. Nat chose a flat place just below the tree line. Together they cleared it of snow and left the block and tackle there.

When they returned to the near side, Nathaniel jumped off Will's sled and went to talk to a teamster standing beside the large wooden sled with four horses in tandem and the one-ton eighteen pounder securely lashed down. He motioned Will over.

"Master Lemuel Hutchinson, this is Master Will Stoner," Nat said, introducing them. Will recognized the wagoner who had made the coffee at the campfire near Bloody Pond. Hutchinson was short, with black unkempt hair sticking out from under a dirty brown, small-brimmed hat and a dark stubble visible on his face. He had narrow eyes, almost closed in a squint even though the day was cloudy and grey. He was older than Nathaniel, but listened intently to his instructions for the crossing.

"This ship's rope is good cordage from Boston. The best," he added although Lemuel had said nothing to doubt it. "I will fasten it to the wooden bar below the rear traces of the last team," he explained to the teamster. "The other end will be tied to the tongue of the sled. You will lead your team of four across and the rope will play out. I will walk with you. Will here will be alongside this lovely cannon."

Nathaniel put his arm around William's shoulder. "You are to have your hatchet ready. If the sled cracks the ice, chop the rope to save the horses. It is thick. It will take strength to cut through. Do it quickly. You understand." Will nodded, proud to be given this responsibility by Nathaniel. "And jump clear of the sled if it goes down," Nat cautioned.

"Do not lose my horses, lad," Lemuel growled. "And what if the cannon falls through the ice?" he asked Nat.

"If the water is not too deep, we can raise it with block and tackle," Nathaniel replied confidently. "If Providence is with us, we will get the heaviest cannons across today."

Will waited by the sled as Nat and Lemuel started out. They were about thirty feet ahead when the slack of the rope played out. Will stationed himself on the front left side of the sled. He could see the four horses plodding on, the ropes taut over the frozen river like straight brown lines pointing back toward him and the cannon.

It had begun to sleet, a bad sign, Will thought. He hoped the warmer air temperatures had not thawed the ice beneath his feet. He held his hatchet tightly in his right hand, walking alongside listening for any cracking sound. If the ice cracked, it would happen next to him. The eighteen pounder, like all of the guns, was lashed down with the muzzle pointing backwards, the touch hole as well as the trunnions on the underside. The greatest weight, where the cannon was the thickest at the breech, was at the front of the sled, near the tongue where Nathaniel had tied the rope.

They were more than halfway across now. The branches of the evergreens bent over with the earlier snow beckoned as welcoming shelter from the sleet. Lemuel's team was closer to the shoreline than the length of the rope behind them when Will heard a sharp crack. He had expected a warning, a groaning of the ice before the break. The rope sprang taut, the little slack there had been abruptly taken out by the 2,000 pounds of the cannon. The ice broke behind the tongue of the sled. A jagged hole opened and the sled began to slide forward into the dark water. Will jumped over the edge of the hole and chopped vigorously at the rope, surprised at how thick it was. He ignored the cracks spreading toward his feet and hacked at the rope several times, getting halfway through before the weight of the cannon finished his work by tearing the weakened rope apart.

Will was too close to the gaping hole. He felt the ice breaking beneath him. He threw himself forward on his stomach, spreading his weight. The ice was cold and wet through his coat. He crawled forward, around the ever widening jagged hole and the dark water flowing below the frozen surface. He grabbed the frayed end of the rope attached to Lemuel's team. Then he stood up and waved, Lemuel urged his horses forward and Will exuberantly ice-skied on the soles of his worn shoes to the shore, grasping the rope around his forearm and holding on to his hat with his other hand, the sleet stinging his face.

"Well done, Will," Nathaniel said, putting his arm around him. "Now we must raise the cannon." He pointed to a stand of spruce on the hill sloping down to the shore near his block and tackle. "Start cutting those trees down," he said. "We will need poles at least eight feet tall to hold the block and tackle. I am going back across and will return with a work party."

Will, alone in the soft snowy quiet on the far side of the Mohawk, climbed the gentle slope and selected a slender straight tree. He shook it vigorously to get the snow off, trimmed the lower branches and piled them away from the spruce. He had trimmed four trees with his hatchet by the time Nathaniel returned with Lemuel and a dozen teamsters with axes. Close to shore, Will saw a wooden barrel bobbing in the icy water, marking where the eighteen pounder had gone down.

Under Nathaniel's direction the men worked quickly, taking down the trees and lashing them together into two towers, each with a double block and gun tackle suspended from the middle. Will had traded his hatchet for an axe. After stomping down the snow around the base of a tree to make for surer footing, he swung in a steady warming rhythm to the intermittent strokes of the wagoner on the tree's other side.

By the time enough trees had been felled and trimmed, Nathaniel had managed to fasten ropes around the front runners on both sides of the sunken sled. When he was satisfied they were secure, he divided the men into two groups, one at each of the makeshift towers.

"Hurry, men," Nathaniel said to the tired teamsters. "We need to raise the cannon before dark."

On Nathaniel's command they began hoisting on the ropes. Will strained, his hands wrapped in his scarf to give him a better grip. Nathaniel shouted encouragement as the front of the sled rose out of the water and stuck on the lip of the broken ice.

"Hold your position, men" Nat cried. "Do not give any slack. Will, come with me." The man next to him tightened his hold and nodded as Will let go and ran forward with Nat, who was carrying two stripped limbs.

"Get on the other side and see if you can lever the sled over this ice," Nat cried, giving Will one of the poles. Will forced the limb under the runner and leaned down on it. The green supple wood bent under his weight. He hoped the ice wouldn't crack again.

"Pull," Nat shouted as the men at each tower groaned in unison. Slowly, the sled edged up onto the jagged rim of the ice. "Back now and help," Nat yelled, and he and Will raced to the towers to join the teamsters at the ropes. The sled, with its cannon, emerged reluctantly from the water like a sea creature unaccustomed to land. The ice held as the men laboriously tugged the sled toward shore, each foot gained ensuring the cannon would be safely reclaimed. When the sled reached the shore, the men retreated to the warmth of the fire in the shelter of the slope. Will wrapped his scarf around his neck to keep the sleet from falling behind his collar. Several of the teamsters passed a crock of 'flip' around, getting progressively boisterous as the cheap rum took effect.

"Ensign Holmes," came a bellow from the river. Will looked through the wind blown sleet. Colonel Knox, on a big-boned, massive New England white saddle horse, was crossing the Mohawk accompanied by his brother William.

"We better get the block and tackle out again," one of the teamsters said, standing up by the fire. "The Colonel and his horse weigh more than this cannon we hoisted out of the ice."

"The Colonel himself weighs more than the cannon," another added to an appreciative roar of laughter.

"Well, he will lose weight here on our rations," someone else said.

Nathaniel ignored their comments and walked down toward the shore. Will followed him.

Knox maneuvered his surefooted mount over the rocky shore and dismounted nimbly for a man of his bulk. He was almost six and a half feet tall, Will guessed, gauging his size against the withers of the tall white horse, and weighed at least 250 pounds. He had a prominent, almost bulbous nose, full ruddy cheeks, and a thick lower lip that made his chin appear smaller. A shock of thick black curly hair on the back of his neck showed between the high collar of his cape and the bottom of his tri-corn. His fleshy face was stern, his grey eyes under thick full brows fixed on Nathaniel as he strode toward him.

"What is this I hear you have drowned my prize cannon, Ensign Holmes?" Knox yelled as he came up. "You should have been more careful." His deep booming voice echoed along the shore.

"It was drowned but has been retrieved, Sir," Nathaniel replied, pointing to the sled with the eighteen pounder beyond the fire. Knox walked to the sled, examined the cannon and tested the ice-shrouded ropes that held it down. He approached the fire, stamped the snow off of his black riding boots and removed his gloves to warm his hands.

"I thank you men for turning out to help. It is the unusual mildness of the weather that delays our progress in getting the artillery to General Washington. If we all return to the Ferry Tavern, I will see to it that you are rewarded with. . ." He paused, noticing the crock for the first time. "more drink and hopefully at least a hot meal. Brother Billy, would you see to these men's needs at the ferry. Ensign Holmes, attend to me for a minute."

They walked off a way from the fire, Knox with his arm over Nathaniel's shoulder, pulling the small Ensign toward him. "Leave the eighteen pounder on this side of the Mohawk. Send a team across in the morning. Tomorrow at first light we will find another place to cross, and this sled can meet us there." Will heard every word, even though the Colonel dropped his voice somewhat, for he was incapable of whispering.

As the two men returned to the fire, Nathaniel realized Will was still there.

"Colonel, this is Master William Stoner," Nathaniel said. He explained Will's role in the crossing and rescue of the eighteen pounder, while Will stood there self-consciously staring at the silver clasp of Knox's cloak that covered his ample stomach.

"Well done, lad. Well done indeed. It seems the others have left in their haste for rum and warmth," he said, laughing and looking across the river. "Brother, halooo," he roared, and on the far shore William Knox turned his horse, waved and rode back.

"Holmes, ride up behind me, and it will be William and William on the other horse," Knox said, motioning to Nathaniel. William Knox flashed a smile of recognition as Will grabbed the offered hand and swung up behind the Colonel's brother. The ride across the river was short. As he slid off the horse, Will heard the shouts of the teamsters in the Ferry Tavern, eager for the promised free food and drink.

"Let me take your horse to the shed," Will said, gesturing toward the low building attached to the Tavern. "I can rub him down and feed him, if you want."

"It would relieve me of the burden," Knox's brother replied. "My brother's horse needs attention too. We have had a long hard ride through the snow from General Schuyler's home in Albany. Come inside for a hot meal when you are done."

Will took the reins of the two horses and led them into the barn. The smell and warmth of the horses was familiar and comforting. His shirt was damp from both his sweat and the sleet that had soaked through his blanket and coat. He moved a solitary roan from a stall into one occupied by another horse, tied the Colonel's horse to the back of the now empty stall and brought Billy's in. The two horses seemed comfortable together. He was uncinching the saddle when he heard his father's voice.

"So, Wilhelm. There you are, at last, you worthless boy." George Stoner stood unsteadily in the doorway to the shed. His eyes were red and his words were slurred from drinking rum all afternoon. "I heard you ran off and lost the Colonel's cannon. And what about your duties back here, eh? Am I supposed to do your work. Feeding our teams and," his voice trailed off as he saw a whip hanging from a post. He took it in his hand, grinning maliciously, and cracked it once for practice. "I will teach you to leave without my permission."

Will looked around, gauging the distance to the barn door. His father moved more to the middle. "You are so slow witted, a sow could read your thoughts before you are finished," Stoner said, advancing toward Will, who retreated further into the barn. He looked around and saw a long handled wooden hayfork leaning against an upright. Will grabbed it, held the three tynes pointed in front of him and stood his ground. His father paused, his thoughts blurred by the rum, taking in this new development, the whip handle gripped in his hand, the whip lying like a black snake on the hard dirt floor.

"Stand down, sir," William Knox shouted as he entered the barn. He put his arm around George Stoner, firmly holding the wrist that grasped the whip. "No need to discipline your boy," he said quietly. "You have done well to haul the fortification gun this far and he has done us good service today." He released his hold and walked into the barn, getting between Will and his father. Will leaned the hayfork against the stall post.

"I need our saddle bags," he said, to explain his presence. Will unbuckled them from the two horses.

"Come, sir," he said to George Stoner. "Carry one with me back to the warmth of the tavern. Ensign Holmes can tell you in detail how helpful your son was today." Reluctantly, Stoner let himself be led from the shed, casting one malevolent look of anger at Will.

After they had left, Will leaned against the Colonel's horse, rubbing it down with a blanket, calming himself with the familiar routine. He would have fought back. He knew it for certain. He was safe as far as Great Barrington. Once they began the return trip from the Massachusetts border, he would pay for his act of rebellion and William Knox's interference.

He rode alone on the sled the next day. Nathaniel had gone off somewhere with the Colonel. Will was no longer in the van of the large convoy. No need as they approached Albany. The roads were better, although still icy, and the locals were eager to provide hay for the teams and food and drink for the teamsters. The train of artillery was a phenomenon they would tell their grandchildren about.

When the train had passed through Glen Falls, the townsfolk had turned out, lining the road to watch as the wagons lumbered by. Some had never seen cannons before and the more experienced had never seen so many. They cheered, hooted and whistled when the big howitzers and fortification guns passed. Their reaction was nothing to the greeting the train received in Albany.

The good burghers, their wives and children, dressed in their Sunday finest, drove out of Albany in their carriages to line the road as the artillery train approached. It was a cold, clear crisp winter day. Colonel Knox had ridden ahead to hire men to pour river water over the ice of the Hudson to thicken it for the imminent crossing. He too came out from Albany to lead the train into the city, waving his tricorn in acknowledgement of the cheers. At one point where the crowd was the most dense, he stopped and gave a little speech, thanking the good people for their hospitality and explaining how General Washington, with this "noble train of artillery," would drive the British from Boston. Will stood up on the sled to catch the Colonel's words, but more to look at the young girls, their cheeks red with the cold, their faces brightened by smiles and flashing eyes. He had never seen so many pretty young girls in one place. He couldn't stop from staring at their colorful bonnets, like so many flower heads bobbing in a spring meadow, and their lithe shapes, bending in the same direction like sunflowers to the sun.

At the boat dock the Colonel had one of the eighteen pounders unloaded and set upon its gun carriage. Will, like most of the people of Albany, had never seen a cannon fired before. He watched the gun crew, their uniforms reasonably clean for the occasion, go through the drill of worming and swabbing the barrel, placing the powder charge, pretending to ram down a ball, prime and finally fire. The Colonel had decided to dry fire the piece and not risk the loss of a precious cannonball. Knox, who had commanded a militia artillery unit in Boston, explained each step in his booming voice to the good citizens, their wives and children, almost all of whom seemed to have turned out for the demonstration. The cannon fired, and as the explosion echoed from the hills across the Hudson, there were shrieks from the girls and women, followed by huzzahs and cheers from the men. The Colonel resisted calls for another firing but implored the citizens to be generous in providing food and shelter to the men of his train. Will noticed that he hadn't mentioned drink, but the wagoners had already begun a brisk trade, offering a ride across the Hudson on a sled or wagon carrying a cannon in exchange for money, rum, brandy or hard cider.

For the first time since leaving their farm in Schoharie, Will slept inside a building, the servant's quarters of a wealthy merchant, ate at a table and warmed himself in front of the kitchen's fireplace. He was not the only one from the train given hospitality. The Captain of the troops from the Fort stayed in the merchant's home, and some of the soldiers were quartered in the barn.

For two days Will rose before dawn, fed and watered Big Red and the grey and walked a half mile down to the Henry Hudson Tavern, an old stone building on the river, where the rougher of the men stayed to be closer to the rum and hard liquor. He fed and rubbed down his father's team in the tavern's barn and was thankful to leave without seeing him. George Stoner would not rise early after staying up late drinking.

Will eagerly returned to the merchant's brick home, to enjoy a hot breakfast of porridge and freshly baked bread slavered with butter and bacon. The cook was a matronly woman named Agnes, with a hearty laugh and ample bosoms. On his first day, when he returned from the tavern barn, she had refused to give him breakfast. Instead, she had sent him to draw water from the well and ordered him to wash "the filth of the road," as she called it, from his head and body. She had given him an old but clean shirt to wear, and washed the one he had worn since leaving home. While busy preparing the morning meal for the merchant and his family, she and the other servants peppered him with questions as he sat in the warm kitchen. They bustled around him doing their chores and asked about the cannons and the trek down from Fort Ticonderoga. He felt self-conscious in the presence of so many women, although Agnes and the serving maids were all older than his stepmother.

The second morning, more at ease in their company, he was in the middle of describing how they had raised the cannon from the

Mohawk when Elisabeth, the merchant's blonde teenage daughter, wandered into the kitchen. Will, in his borrowed shirt with the sleeves too short for his long arms, became tongue-tied in her presence and lost the thread of his story. She had come for a scone for her mother, she said, but stayed to hear him stumble through the rest of his tale, laughing at his embarrassment and leaving him red-faced and flustered.

Will took any opportunity to walk around Albany. He had never been to a real city with so many brick and stone buildings. The homes of the wealthier citizens were built on the hills overlooking the Hudson. The streets were paved and elegant pleasure boats were pulled up on the shore for the winter. After the servants had finished serving the family's meal around three, Will sat at the long wooden table in the kitchen and took his dinner with them. He wolfed down beef and roasted potatoes, and wiped the gravy in his wooden bowl clean with freshly baked bread. Agnes laughed and said he was growing before her eyes. She filled his bowl a second time, and watched him devour the food again.

On Sunday, January 7th, when he arose in the morning, the weather was noticeably colder. The Captain of the Continentals strode into the barn and saddled up his horse while Will was feeding Big Red and the mare. He left, saying he had a conference with the Colonel at General Schuyler's home. It was still quiet at the tavern when Will arrived. By the time he had fed and watered his father's horses, the teamsters had been aroused from their stupor by soldiers with orders from the Colonel. They were crossing the Hudson today. Nathaniel found him as he left the tavern's barn.

"Will, we need your sled to carry a six pounder. Hitch up your team and meet me at the dock." When Will arrived, Nat was standing by a sled with one shattered runner. Coming down the icy hill toward the shore, the driver had lost control and rammed into one of the fine craft beached for the winter. It had crushed the bow of the yacht's hull but worse from Nat's viewpoint, had wrecked the sled carrying the six pounder. The sacks of oats on Will's sled, would be left on shore and brought over later. It was more important to ferry the cannons across while the cold weather held. The owner of the boat had been found and had been less than satisfied with a promise from the Colonel that the

Congress would authorize payment for the damage.

"That is all the Continentals get, the promise of pay by Congress, although many of them have gone without for months," Nat said, glancing up at the grey sky. "I hope the accursed thaw is gone for good," he said, blowing on his hands after he, Will and two soldiers had hoisted the six pounder onto Will's sled and lashed it to Nat's satisfaction, together with its gun carriage, wheels, artillery bucket, ram and sponge.

Will drove his team back to the shore point designated for the crossing. There were 80 or more wagons and sleds assembled, crossing at a quarter-mile width of the Hudson, where the ice had been strengthened by the poured river water. The air was bitter cold and the shore was lined with people, eager for a ride across the river on a sled or wagon with cannons bound for Boston to bombard the Redcoats. The crowd surged forward as each wagon or sled maneuvered into position for the crossing. People looked for the wagoners who had promised them rides for a shilling or a crock of rum. Colonel Knox and Nathaniel stood on the low wooden pier solidly anchored in the ice almost up to the planks of the platform.

Will was tenth in line, behind a long sled with a twenty-four pounder and several burghers and their wives who were crammed onto the teamster's seat or standing precariously on the back, clinging to the rough boards of siding, hastily added to accommodate them. He was apprehensive about having people on his sled, not because of the extra weight but because he was nervous about what to talk to them about and worried that his father would be angry if he didn't charge them enough.

"May we ride with you?" a female voice asked. Will looked down from his seat to see Agnes, the cook, and the merchant's daughter, Elisabeth, both bundled up against the cold. Agnes seemed almost twice as wide as she had been in the kitchen. Elisabeth looked glorious to him, with her blond hair escaping in golden wisps from under her bonnet, tied down against the wind with a dark blue woolen scarf. Without waiting for his answer, Agnes helped Elisabeth first and hoisted herself up, the three of them squeezed onto the narrow seat.

"So, these are your horses," Elisabeth said, pressing gently against him. "The red one is gorgeous. He looks very strong. You must be very good with horses to be able to handle him." Will blushed and mumbled something about how well behaved Big Red was and how anyone could handle him.

"Well, if that is the case, will you give me the reins when we are out on the river?" she asked coyly.

"I will, if you let me hold them with you," Will replied, surprised at his own boldness.

"Agreed," Elisabeth responded quickly. "Now we must talk about the price of passage." She nodded to Agnes, holding a wooden basket on her ample lap.

"We have brought you some brown bread and roast meat for tonight's meal," Agnes said, "as well as cured ham, bacon, a slab of lard, and some coffee beans. Also more bread and some potatoes," she said. "And three fresh apples kept on the marble shelf in the master's apple cellar," she added as an afterthought. Will saw the image of his mother, faceless, fanning her apron in their storage house behind their farm, the best apples hanging from the beams by their stems. "Is that enough for our passage?" Agnes asked, taking his silence for disapproval. Before Will could reply, he heard Nat's voice.

"Master Will Stoner," Nathaniel called to him from the pier. "Take to the left and stay wide of the twenty-four pounder," he called out. "If the ice starts to crack, move yourself to safety first, and then help the other sled as best you can."

Will waved to Nat in acknowledgement.

"Oh dear," Agnes said. "I did not think there would be any risk. Your father will have my hide if anything happens," she said to Elisabeth.

"We will be secure," Will said reassuringly. "Our load is light compared to the other sled. The driver overloaded it with people and is carrying a much heavier cannon than we. Besides, everyone else has made the crossing without a mishap." He flicked the reins and Big Red and the mare moved down the gentle slope and onto the ice. The hardwood runners made a crunching sound on the irregular ice, bouncing the sled up and down and throwing Elisabeth against his shoulder. She hooked her arm in his to steady herself. Will blushed, enjoying the feeling of her gloved hand on his forearm.

One third of the way out, the wind picked up. Loose ice flakes, chopped up by the sleds that had preceded them, whipped their faces, and the cold wind chilled his bare hands. Elisabeth moved closer to him and he could smell the sweet scent of lavender soap.

"We are almost halfway there," she said. "May I have the reins now?" Not accustomed to being refused, Elisabeth did not wait for his answer, but reached across his arm to take the reins. Will transferred the reins to her gloved hands and put his right arm around her waist, pulling her towards him so that he could continue to keep his hands on the reins as well. She nestled comfortably into his chest, and Will felt an uncontrollable joy as he held her.

"I wish the river were twice as wide," he blurted out.

"I do also," Elisabeth replied. Agnes coughed more loudly than necessary to break the spell.

On the far shore, Will took the reins back from Elisabeth and guided the team onto the road heading south. A crowd of citizens streamed back to the river, some to walk across and others to ride in empty sleds driven by their servants. Will jumped down from his seat, offered his hand first to Agnes to help her down, and then to Elisabeth. Agnes gave him a big maternal hug and wished him well on the rest of the journey. She held the basket as Will removed the food and stuffed it into his haversack, acutely aware of Elisabeth standing next to him.

Elisabeth faced him, her hands tugging at the knot of her scarf.

"I have read poems of the days of chivalry in England when ladies gave their knights a token to be remembered by. I am giving you this." She untied the blue scarf and handed it to him, one hand now raised to hold her bonnet from blowing away. "Think of me on the rest of your trek and bring the cannons to General Washington to drive the vile British out of Boston." As she gave him the scarf, Will felt her squeeze his hand.

"I will. I will think of you always," he stammered, and watched her slender back disappear with Agnes into the crowd on the shore.

Late in the afternoon, an eighteen pounder broke through the ice and sank into the river. Colonel Knox was furious, because the crossing had almost been successfully completed and it was getting dark. The raising of the cannon was postponed until the next morning.[1] Shortly after dawn Colonel Knox himself directed the construction of pulleys over the now-frozen fourteen-foot-wide hole beneath which the precious cannon lay. Luckily, it was close to land and in fairly shallow water. Will wandered down to the shore to watch. Many of Albany's menfolk had crossed the Hudson to help with the effort. The teamsters gladly let the self-righteous overweight burghers and the young dandies do the heavy lifting. By mid-afternoon the cannon was on shore.

Will scanned the growing crowd of people for a glimpse of Elisabeth, but she was not among the women who had arrived on the far shore to watch the activity. His disappointment turned to self-pity and the realization that he was not deserving of even her scarf, let alone her affection. He would be turning back at the Massachusetts border, returning to his father's farm. The adventure of her chivalrous knight would be over.

The Colonel, never one to miss a moment for an inspiring speech, christened the resurrected eighteen pounder "The Albany" and promised the good citizens it would boom out their response to the British when it arrived in Boston. The remainder of the train crossed that afternoon. By midday Monday, under an ominous grey winter sky, the wagons and sleds were five miles south of Albany on the Post Road to Kinderhook. They traveled together, as they had done since Half Moon Landing, the Colonel in the vanguard followed by fourteen sleds, the Continental Captain in the middle section of about thirty sleds pulling the heaviest cannon, approximately half a mile behind the lead, with William Knox bringing up the rear. Most of the soldiers from Fort Ticonderoga had been left behind in Albany to join General Schuyler's troops. The more fit of them, about twenty, trudged alongside the train, their bodies bent into the brutally cold wind that blew almost due north.

Nat, having spent the previous night and much of the morning with the Colonel, was with Will in the first group, on the sled now carrying a six pounder. The much-prayed-for hard frost had arrived with a vengeance. It was bitter cold and the solid grey sky promised nothing but more snow later in the day. Will wore his mother's red scarf under his hat around his forehead to keep his head warm. Elisabeth's dark blue one protected his throat and neck. He had tucked the end sentimentally over his heart.

"I see you have a lady friend," Nat said poking Will in the ribs. "She is fair-looking, that is for sure. And the name of your lady love?" he asked, grinning and nudging Will again with his elbow.

Will blushed. "Elisabeth. I only know her first name," he blurted out.

"Ahh, Will. Then I know more about her family than you. For it was I who arranged for you to be billeted at the house of Mr. Luykas Van Hooten. He is, as you can judge from the substance of his house, a man of property, a merchant and land owner. He has his own riverboats, which carry goods back and forth on the Hudson to the city of New York. And you seem to have won the heart of his youngest daughter."

Will remained silent, which Nat interpreted as pining for his lady love. Instead, Will was depressed, knowing that this adventure would soon end and it was highly unlikely that he would ever return to Albany and see Elisabeth again.

They spent the night in the sheds, barns and homes of the citizens of Kinderhook, a small inland farming community. Will was thankful for another warm meal and a dry place to sleep. Snow fell that night and continued into the next morning. The snow began as light fine flakes that the strong wind blew into drifts on the Post Road. By mid morning it had become a heavy snow, blanketing the sleds, wagons, cannons, gun carriages, boxes and baggage until all looked alike. Will assumed they had remained in Kinderhook because of the weather. Nat disabused him of this when he found Will in a shed, feeding Big Red and the mare.

"The Colonel has ridden ahead with his brother the nine miles to Claverack to arrange for more teamsters to travel with us to Massachusetts. We are to wait here for his return. I would have thought we would move down the road and meet him there, rather than his riding back." Nat shrugged.

Nat was about to leave when Will's father entered the shed, brushing the snow from his shoulders. He shook his hat to clear the brim.

"Well, Wilhelm. How many shillings do you have for me from the crossing? Or were you too tongue-tied to even ask for payment?"

"I asked for and received some food, which I thought would be of use for the rest of the journey," he said sullenly. He decided not to mention Elisabeth's blue scarf. It belonged to him, not his father.

His father snorted derisively. "You can see we are not in want of food. The Post Road is well populated and the taverns are stocked. It is not that far from Claverack to the Massachusetts border before we turn for home. You think we need provisions for that journey?" He shook his head in disgust. "Another opportunity to make money lost. I should have known. I am cursed by your stupid Dutch breeding."

"I do not wish for it," Nat interrupted, "but if Providence should continue to send us heavy snows, the slog from Claverack to Massachusetts may take us longer than you think."

George Stoner looked at Nat shrewdly. "Perhaps, Ensign Holmes," he said with some deference. "And then perhaps this caravan will not make it to Massachusetts if the winter weather is so bad." He put his hat back on, paused at the shed entrance and turned back to Will.

"Go down to the barn adjacent to the tavern and see to my horses," he ordered. "Clean the hooves of the big bay. He has a stone in one."

"Not a very optimistic man, your father," Nat said when George Stoner had left. "I put my confidence in the Colonel's judgment and his horsemanship in returning through this heavy snow from Claverack." He walked over to Will and put his arm around his shoulder. "I'm surprised at how wealthy Luykas Van Hooten is, given his Dutch heritage," Nat said, squeezing Will's arm and winking. Will smiled, appreciating the joke at the expense of his father, who would never be a quarter as rich as Van Hooten. "Besides," Nat said, "better than precious gems is having a jewel of a daughter. Right, Will?" Will nodded, admiring how well his friend spoke. His thoughts returned to Elisabeth sitting next to him on the sled, his arm around her and her shoulder against his. That memory, and her scarf, were his and his alone.

Colonel Knox arrived after dark and went straight to the tavern. Those teamsters who were not already there drinking soon arrived, having heard the Colonel had returned. The tavern, a two-story stone building, its cedar shingled roof now covered by three feet of snow, was adequate for the normal post road traffic. The main room, with its low, thick-beamed ceiling, was filled with the smell of unwashed men, crowded against the walls with their mugs in hand. Those who were not already boisterous from the rum were surly and cantankerous.

They pretended not to be curious as the Colonel sat down at the rough wood table adjacent to the fireplace. William Knox and Nathaniel were on either side of him. William, to the right, rested his hands on the familiar closed leather roster book, with a quill pen and inkwell before him.

"Now then, men," Knox's voice boomed out over the noise. "I have been to Claverack and returned in one day." He paused, waiting for their attention. "The road is good but the way east to Massachusetts from there is not. We need not go further south to turn east. I plan, instead, to leave from here for the Massachusetts border." There were grumbles of general dissent from the teamsters. Some of the men, emboldened both by the rum they had already imbibed as well as by their numbers, which seemed greater in the small tavern, muttered angrily. There were cries of "No! No!"

Knox, pushed back his chair, stood and held his hands up for silence. "You have just reason to complain," he acknowledged. "Many of you have signed up only so far as Claverack. If you wish to terminate your service in this noble train of artillery here, in Kinderhook, I will adjust your amounts for not traveling the nine miles to Claverack, and Brother Billy will pay you off forthwith. Additional teamsters with their sturdy sleds will arrive here the morrow."

There was more general murmuring and calculation of just how many wagoners would be in Kinderhook tomorrow, something the Colonel had not mentioned. The teamsters waited for his offer, knowing that the roster in front of his brother contained their names and the pay due them.

"If you come with me as far as the town of Great Barrington, on the border of the Bay Colony of Massachusetts, I will increase the rate from seven pounds per ton to seven and a half," he said, folding his arms across his chest. Will noticed his father standing on the right side of the room.

"That is very well, Colonel," George Stoner said loudly. "But what about the daily rate per span of horses. Many of us have multiple teams and are paid by the day for the use of our animals, not by the ton." He had stepped forward out of the shadows. Although he had addressed his remarks to Colonel Knox, he looked directly at the Colonel's brother.

"Yes, yes," other teamsters echoed the question, shouting out the number of horses or oxen pulling the sleds and wagons. "And tell us Colonel, how far is it from here to Great Barrington?" another shouted.

"Gentlemen," the Colonel called, again raising his arms for silence. Will noticed Knox had a handkerchief wrapped around his left hand. He wondered if the Colonel suffered from frostbite. It seemed unlikely since he wore gloves.

"You are entitled to all necessary information and you shall have it," he paused, smiling at the men as if they were his partners instead of mercenary laborers. "If we adhered to the original route, it will be twenty miles or so to Great Barrington. By turning east from here, the angle saves us a few miles, and I am willing to share the monetary savings with you. I offer to increase the daily rate from twelve shillings per span to fourteen, and leave to you to calculate how many days it will take us to reach Great Barrington, giving Providence its due for the weather," he said, glancing upward at the smoke blackened beams. He sat down, filling the chair behind the desk with his large bulk, and waited for their reaction. Will watched Nathaniel whisper something to Knox. The Colonel shook his head in the negative.

Some of the teamsters, weaker in arithmetic than others, consulted with their better-educated brethren. There was much loud talk about the depth of the snow and how it would impede their progress, to their financial benefit. Will was not surprised it had been his father who had asked for an increase in the daily rate. With five teams in the train, he stood to earn an extra ten shillings per day, based on the Colonel's initial offer. George Stoner, Will thought, usually managed to benefit, while letting others take the risks of confronting those in authority. He had seen it before. This time, motivated by a desire to get even with William Knox, his father had stood up and provoked the others.

"Well, Colonel," one teamster said. He was short man with thick hairy arms protruding from his dirty grey linen shirt. "You have generously offered to pass along your savings by leaving from here and not Claverack, as was part of the original bargain. As I see it, we're entitled to that money anyway." There were shouts of "Hear! Hear!" and "You tell him, Josiah."

Will saw his father smirk as the controversy he had stoked heated up.

"I say," Josiah continued, "you add the half you offered to the seven and half for the tonnage rate and two more shillings to the fourteen daily rate, so we get eight pounds sterling tonnage or sixteen shillings per span per day." He paused. "And you pay in advance," he said pointing his finger at the Colonel. The men roared approval for his proposal.

Knox rose from his chair to respond. Will leaned against a rough-hewn upright beam, idly rubbing his fingers along the marks left long ago by the carpenter's broad axe. The Colonel and the teamsters went back and forth. It took almost another hour. Knox knew how to deal with men without offending them. He defused their hostility and turned the discussion into good natured bargaining. In the end, the Colonel graciously conceded to pay eight pounds per ton or fifteen shillings for each span of horses, per day, but nothing in advance.

With agreement reached, each teamster willing to proceed to Great Barrington stepped up and signed the roster with the new rate written next to his name by William Knox. Although Will was listed, it was his father who signed for both of them. He swaggered up to the table, confident he was cleverer by far than the next man, and certain he had outsmarted both the Colonel and his brother.

The Colonel, to the acclamation of all, paid for one round of rum for everyone in the room, including the nine teamsters who were terminating their service at Kinderhook. Someone called for three hearty cheers for the Colonel. Will joined in the cheering with the others but refrained from drinking the free rum. He didn't like the way his head buzzed afterwards, and tonight his thoughts were of Elisabeth.

Early the next morning seven teamsters arrived from Claverack. It took until noon before the cannons were transferred from the sleds and wagons of those who were leaving to the newcomers. Nat was in charge of this. He had combined some of the lighter cannons, the brass mortars and the three pounders to make up for the loss of two teamsters and sleds - as more had left than had joined them. Will had finished lashing down a brass Coehoorn mortar and the six pounder when he heard his father call him.

"Make sure it is done right, Wilhelm. You must not make any mistakes today," he said, standing with his arms crossed next to the sled. He saw Nat walking down the line on the road.

"Hello, Ensign Holmes. Over here, if you please."

Nat scraped the snow off his boots on one of the runners. Will looked enviously at his friend's boots and imagined having dry feet all day, every day.

"You usually ride with my son," George Stoner said. "I would like your company myself, to learn more about events in Massachusetts. It never harms a man of business to know of things that may affect his economic well-being."

"Wilhelm," he commanded. "Today, you drive my sled with the fortification gun. Mind the four-span team now. Keep them in their traces and not too fast on the downhill slopes. It has weight to it." He turned to Nat. "Now Ensign, whenever you're ready, we can move out on this sled," he said as he jumped up on the seat and untied the reins. "Here's your bag," he said to Will tossing the leather haversack on the ground.

Will trudged back along the line of waiting wagons and sleds, the snow slick underfoot from being trod upon by men and horses during the loading process. He checked the four teams, their tack, harnesses and traces, then the lashings of the thick ropes holding the two-ton artillery piece. He ran his bare hands along the cold metal and the worn wood of the gun carriage. It was an ugly piece of metal, not graceful and lithe like the six pounders. He hoisted himself on to the seat, buried his chin in Elisabeth's scarf and wondered what his father was up to. He would butter up Nat to get to the Colonel, but for what purpose, Will could not figure out. Nat would be smart enough to see through him, though.

The next morning Nat walked down the line and stopped briefly at Will's wagon.

"Nothing much to report," he said conspiratorially. "Your father seems most interested in how the blockade will interrupt trade from the coast to Albany and concerned with the well-being of your brother in Boston."

Will frowned. "He is angling for something. He always looks for the advantage and definitely has no concern for either my brother or me. Be on your guard, Nat," Will cautioned, surprising himself with his audacity. Nat smiled good naturedly.

"Do not worry yourself, Will. Think of your fair lady, instead."

Will did think of Elisabeth that day, but his thoughts were not pleasant. Instead, he was gloomy at the prospect to returning to his father's farm from the Commonwealth border and never traveling anywhere again.

It took the caravan almost three days, heading east through bitter cold weather under clear skies, through light forests and over frozen streams, to reach Great Barrington on the Housatannack River. Will found himself quartered in the Court House, together with other teamsters who had the misfortune of not being lodged at the tavern, although they were there drinking now. Every room, shed and barn were filled by the wagoners from the train or the teamsters from Massachusetts, recruited in advance and now ready to begin the trek from Great Barrington to Cambridge.

Will unharnessed the first two spans and led the four horses into the stable adjacent to the Court House. He turned up his nose at the distinctive, pungent cattle smell of oxen, stolid, stupid-looking, short-horned beasts, tethered in every stall. He remembered Nat's comment when they had ridden together. It was more pleasant to ride behind horses than oxen. Unfortunately for Nat, the Massachusetts wagoners who would replace Will and his father and the others from New York favored oxen.

Will stepped over a pile of steaming manure and maneuvered two of the oxen into a stall with only one. He led his father's first span and then the second into the now-empty stall, the four horses crammed together and showing their evident distaste for the overpowering cattle smell by flaring their nostrils and pawing the sparse straw bedding. He tethered the other four horses in the narrow lane between the stalls. Satisfied it was the best he could do for them, Will walked the short distance to the Court House.

Inside, he wandered through the high-ceiling courtroom, which was almost as cold as the outside. He explored the building, looking for a place for his blanket, and found a series of small rooms at the back. A glow of light shone through a partially opened door.

"Come in, whoever you are," a gravelly voice invited him into the room. A small candle, set low in a pewter holder on the mantle, cast light on an elderly man with scraggly gray hair, wrapped in a blanket in front of a fireplace. The heat from the small fire was barely enough to warm the room.

Will kept Elisabeth's scarf around his neck and approached the fire to warm his hands.

"Who be you, lad?" the old man asked, coughing into his sleeve and clearing his throat. "One of the teamsters from New York?" Will nodded.

"Well, come on, share the fire," he said, patting a place on the bench next to him. "My name is Potts. Samuel Potts. The Town Council made me custodian of the building after we seized this Court House from the King's men. You know about that? Of course not, you're from New York," he said gruffly, answering his own question. He cocked his head, like a quizzical rooster, examining Will through his rheumy eyes.

"No more sessions of the King's Court in Great Barrington. No sir. We put a stop to that a year ago this past August, it was." [1] He shifted on the bench to turn toward Will, apprehensive he would leave. "Are you interested in hearing this," he snapped, "or do you want to go with the others to drink rum and put a hand up the skirts of the serving women?"

Will flushed. "No, sir. I mean yes," he stammered. "I want to stay and listen."

"Good" Potts said. "Everyone here in Great Barrington knows the story. I only get to tell it to those who are passing on this road for the first time. Your fellow teamsters from New York were too eager to get rum at the tavern to listen." He looked Will up and down again as if determining whether or not he was worthy of telling the story to, decided Will would do, and cleared his throat of phlegm.

"General Gage's appointed Loyalist Judges, riding circuit, pranced into town on their fancy horses in August of '74. It was the 15th, if I remember correctly." He paused, as if visualizing the Judges coming down the street to the Court House. "They had their wigs, robes and other accoutrements of their station. What they did not have was lawful authority." He slapped his open palm on Will's knee. "The Intolerable Acts which infringed the God-given rights of free Englishmen were not lawful," he said vehemently, digging his bony fingers into Will's thigh. "General Gage occupying Boston and closing the port. Banning town meetings. Nominating his own Council to govern the people of our Commonwealth and appointing these magistrates who came to town." He shook his head as if still dismayed by Gage's conduct. "All of it as unlawful as," his voice trailed off as he searched for a proper example. "As the Boston Massacre," he said, pleased with his conclusion.

"What did you do?" Will asked, mistakenly thinking Potts needed some prompting to regain the thread of his story.

"The word went out the night these pretender Judges arrived in town and were lodged in the tavern. By morning, I tell you there was a mass of men in the street. We blocked the Court House. We turned out and stood in front of the door and would not let these Loyalist toadies enter the building. Without firing a shot, we prevented the King's Court from holding session." He snickered. "You should have seen their faces. As red as a British soldier's coat. But there were no Regulars to enforce their writ. So their writ stopped, right outside this building," he said, removing his hand from Will's knee and pointing a skinny knobbed finger toward the street. "They went back to the tavern, changed into travel clothes, and rode down the road as fast as they could, heading back to Boston. They were lucky we did not do them any physical harm. We did enough harm to their pride and pricked their pomposity," he chuckled, remembering the scene.

"Did General Gage send Judges out again with troops as an escort?"

"No," Potts said. "We have not seen a Judge since. I suppose General Gage had his hands full with the good patriots of Boston and the coast. He was sent home and now there is General Howe to deal with. I hope your cannons make him abandon the occupation of the city and lift the blockade. Maybe then the King will come to his senses and treat us like the free Englishmen we are. Now, lad, that you've heard the story, do you have a morsel of food to share from that pouch of yours?"

Will cut a chunk of the slab of cured ham Agnes had given him when they crossed the Hudson at Albany and offered it to Potts. The old man took it, went to a cupboard and brought back some bread and a small tub of butter. "Now, we can share a meal and you can educate me about those cannons. The last time I saw so many artillery pieces was in '56 in the French and Indian War." He borrowed Will's knife, sparingly spread some butter on the bread, studied the ham for a moment and cut off a large chunk.

But before Will could tell about loading the cannons at Fort Ticonderoga, Potts, talking while he chewed, was off about his service in the Massachusetts Bay Colony Provincials sent to guard the New York frontier in the summer of '56. His account of his skirmishes with the Iroquois was interrupted by a shout from the courtroom.

"Will. Will Stoner? Are you in here?"

Will recognized Nat's voice. "Yes. Back here," he answered.

Nat entered the room, stamping the snow off his feet but keeping his cloak on. He nodded at Potts.

"The Colonel has sent me to find you. He is meeting with your father now. I have looked all over for you. Come quickly. We must not keep the Colonel waiting."

Will grabbed his slouch hat and stuffed his unbuttered bread in his haversack. As they hurried through the darkened streets toward the welcoming warm lights of the tavern, Nat explained that George Stoner had requested a meeting with the Colonel. Will's father had shrewdly counted the number of Massachusetts teamsters available to take over the carriage of the cannons to Cambridge and noted that more New Yorkers were leaving than there were replacements. He was bargaining with the Colonel for an improved price to continue on and had offered the four span of horses and the sled pulling the fortification cannon as well as Will as a driver, as far as Boston.

"I vouched for you," Nat said. "However, the Colonel prefers to talk with you directly." He smiled and dug an elbow into Will's ribcage. "I told you Providence would let you see Boston." Will grinned as Nat's news sunk in. He would continue on to Boston, meet Johan, and be away from his father. He would be free and who knows what would happen in Boston.

Maybe Elisabeth's father would come there on business and she would come with him.

Nat led the way through the main room, crowded with drunken teamsters from both New York and Massachusetts carousing in front of the massive fireplace, to the second floor of the tavern. He knocked before pushing the door open. The Colonel sat in front of a desk that was far too small for his massive girth, his jacket draped behind him. George Stoner sat before him in the role of a petitioner, although his confident posture indicated he thought he had the upper hand.

"Ahh. Master William Stoner. Yes, I remember you from Half Moon Landing. Ensign Holmes tells me you are a most able and willing hand." The Colonel's booming voice filled the small room, which was hot from the warm air rising from below.

"Wilhelm," his father said, turning in his chair to address his son who was standing next to the door. "I told the Colonel you are capable of driving four span of horses, as you have done the past few days with that massive cannon. If you keep your mind on your task, you can pull that piece all the way to Boston without mishap." Will bristled at the implied reprimand but remained silent.

Stoner turned back to the Colonel. "We have agreed on the price and the terms. You are to pay me in advance. You can see that my son is trustworthy although a bit slow. He will not abandon his duty," his father said reassuringly, "or he will pay dearly for such disloyalty."

I never would do such a thing, Will thought. He held his tongue. Tomorrow he would continue on as part of this great adventure, and his father's face would be turned back toward Scholarie.

"After the cannons are delivered in Cambridge, my horses together with the sleds and my son are to be sent home as soon as possible, weather permitting, of course," George Stoner continued. He waved his hand toward Knox, as if he were making a concession. "For our purposes," Stoner said, "it is agreed there are 115 miles to Cambridge, more or less, and that huge cannon is an even two tons. As you said at Fort Ti, a load of that weight needs four span of horses." The Colonel nodded and motioned for Nat to open the roster and write down the terms. George Stoner read the entry and signed his name.

"I would like Will to sign too," Knox said. "He is on his own as part of our noble train of artillery." Will came forward, a bit too excitedly. He read the entry. His father was being paid twelve and one half pounds sterling, in advance. It was a generous price, equal to half the sales price of their entire crop of hay in a year, but it bought Will's freedom to travel on to Boston. He bent down, eagerly picked up the quill and signed his name under his father's.

"You drive a hard bargain, Mr. Stoner," Knox said, rising with a grunt from the confines of his narrow chair and walking him toward the door. "Still, I am guaranteed four span of horses and a sled to carry this magnificent cannon to Cambridge, and I wager, a hard worker as well. A word with your lad, alone if you do not mind sir," Knox said, using his impressive bulk to herd Stoner out of the room.

"Now, Will," the Colonel said, gesturing with his right hand for Will to sit in the chair his father had been in. Ensign Holmes has informed me you read and write. Is Will or Wilhelm your preference?" His question boomed out in the low-ceilinged room.

"Will, sir," thinking it better not to correct the Colonel and tell him his real name was Willem. "It was my grandmother, my maternal one," he added for emphasis, "who taught me how to read and write and some mathematics."

"Good. That's very good. You know I was a bookseller in Boston before General Gage occupied our city. Do you know Tom Jones?

Will was puzzled. "I am sorry sir but I am not acquainted with everyone in the train yet. Is he a new fellow from Massachusetts?"

Knox frowned, his clear gray eyes assessing Will, trying to discern if Will was slyly making fun of him. He broke out in a roar of laughter, his huge frame shaking so hard that the fragile chair on which he sat seemed in danger of shattering. He wiped his eyes with the handkerchief wrapped around the end of his left hand and reached behind him to open a wooden chest.

"Books are important, Will. They are the key to understanding the world. I learned artillery from books. First from John Muller's great treatise on artillery, the standard British text, and then from drilling, drilling and drilling. On the Boston Common. I learned French the same way. Although it was a different kind of drilling," he said chuckling, remembering something he found amusing. He pulled a book from the chest. It was leather bound with gold lettering on the binding.

"Will Stoner. Meet Tom Jones," he said, laughing heartily again. "Return it to me when you have finished and I will lend you another."

"Thank you, sir," Will said, taking the volume carefully. He read the gold lettering: The History of Tom Jones by Henry Fielding. Gingerly, he opened the binding and flipped through the pages, admiring the few engraved drawings. "Thank you again, sir. I will not disappoint."

"I know that," the Colonel replied. "Otherwise, I would not have agreed to your father's rather exorbitant demands. He thinks he has gotten the better of me but I believe, before this journey is over, the bargain will be mine."

Will left the room, clutching the book in his hand. He would follow Colonel Knox to the ends of the earth. He was free to be part of this great adventure on his own. If only he could talk to Elisabeth now and tell her of his good fortune. As he came down stairs into the sweltering, boisterous tavern, his euphoria was deflated by the sight of his father beckoning to him. He hid the book in his pouch, his hand brushing the hatchet handle, and reluctantly walked to where his father was standing.

"I have special instructions for you, Wilhelm. Listen carefully now. I will repeat them to you tomorrow morning so they sink into that thick Dutch skull of yours." He rapped Will's head with his knuckles, none to gently. Will smelled the rum on his father's breath, as he leaned closer to Will's face.

"When you get to Cambridge, make contact with your brother. Tell Johan to write me what his business prospects are in Boston, either under the British or if they are driven out, with General Washington." His father paused as if to allow time for Will to absorb what he had said. "He is to give you a letter detailing his prospects and you are to carry it back with you. It is my intention, if Boston remains closed as a port, or blockaded by the British, to bring Johan to Albany and apprentice him to a merchant there. You understand my instructions?" As he raised his arm to knock on his son's head again for emphasis, Will caught his father's wrist in mid air and held it tightly.

"I understand," he said looking his father in the eye, before pulling Stoner's arm down and releasing his grip. As he walked through the snow, in his mind, it was he, not Johan, who was apprenticed to the merchant Luykas Van Hooten, spending time with Elisabeth in her father's library reading books together.

The uphill slope leading east from Great Barrington was deceptively easy. Will's sled was in the middle of the vanguard of twenty or so, spread out on the snow-covered road as the train assembled behind them. He stood up on the seat, oblivious to the strong, cold wind blowing the wet snow off the tall hemlock and spruce. The branches, finally free from the weight, sprang back, pointing upward again. Will stretched, raising his arms to the clear blue sky.

He looked past the train waiting in position, lined up on the road behind him. A plume of grayish white smoke curled from the chimney of the tavern and blew quickly toward the grist mill by the frozen Housatannack. Beyond, curving away from the river and partially hidden by trees, the road extended west, back the way they had come, toward Albany and Schoharie.

He felt amazingly free and unburdened. His view of Great Barrington, as seen from this height was like looking at himself through a window into his past. Ahead, he was beyond the control of his father, free from the incessant and boring work of the farm, of his menial existence as nothing more than an indentured laborer with no hope and no future. True, he thought, he was his own man only so far as Boston and back. But he would be with his brother. Either Johan or Nat would think of something when the time came. Ahead was the adventure of the road, and liberating the great city of Boston from the British.

And then, who knew what Divine Providence had in store. Hadn't Providence, as Nat had predicted, freed him to continue on?

Will let out a long yell of pure joy and exuberance, scaring a flock of junkos and chickadees foraging among the oxen's manure for undigested seeds. They took to the air. Concluding there was no imminent danger, the birds returned to the business of searching for breakfast. A gruff teamster on the sled immediately behind, wrapped in his blanket against the morning cold, bellowed for Will to sit down, be quiet and mind his four-span. Will waved in a friendly manner and settled himself on the bench, smiling. It was a wonderful morning to travel. The lead sleds were on the move. He flicked the long whip and called to Big Red to pull.

That morning, without asking his father's permission, he had brashly switched Big Red and the grey with the first span of his father's team. He depended upon Big Red and could not leave him behind. When George Stoner had seen him off, repeating his instructions of the night before, the teams were already hitched and the sled in line in the train. His father had accepted the change with a frown and a dismissive comment that it didn't matter to him which horses his son took. "They will all be back in a month's time," he had said.

The Colonel and Nat were in the lead, scouting the road, followed by the light cannon and then Will's sled with its massive fortification gun. The other double fortification cannons and the eighteen and twenty-four pounders were immediately behind, trailed by the few remaining light guns and small mortars and the sleds carrying flint boxes and shot. At the very rear were the sleds and wagons with the supplies for the entire artillery train. The Colonel's plan of march, as he explained in the early dawn before they left Great Barrington, was to keep the heavier-loaded sleds and wagons close to the middle. If the horses and oxen could not pull the big guns uphill, or hold them from running out of control on the down side, other teamsters and soldiers, forward and rear, could be called upon for help.

Once they were up the first slope, the land appeared to level off, although, across the snow-covered pastures and fields, Will observed the gradual incline of the tree line of evergreen pitch, white pine, spruce and hemlock and the bare-branched birch, ash and maple.

The strong winds created drifts, three to four feet deep in places, and obscured the outlines of what was a poor road to begin with. The train covered almost six miles that first day and camped in the middle of a thick pine forest. The lower boughs were bent almost to the ground with the heavy snow. Higher up the trees, where the wind had blown the snow away, the green branches merged into twinkling river of stars coursing through the night sky. The local Massachusetts teamsters called it Greenwoods.

That night, after Will had unhitched the eight horses, hobbled six together and tethered Big Red and the grey to a tree, he wandered over to share the warmth of a roaring fire and listen to the talk of the Massachusetts men. They were mostly farmers who had been recruited by the Colonel's brother on his way through in November to Fort Ticonderoga. Will found their manner of speech strange but not as broad as Nat's, to which he was now accustomed.

"They say Knox is not a genuine Colonel," one of the men closer to the fire said. "He was promised a commission, by whom no one says or seems to know, but the Congress in Philadelphia has not yet approved it."

"It makes not a whit of difference to me," another replied, "what the Congress does. Knox has the money to pay and a letter from General Washington. That is all I need to keep my part of the bargain."

"You will wish your hardest you had bargained for more once we get into the mountains," the first man said. "That brother of his never told us the weight of some of these cannons. Besides, it will not matter even if the cannons do get to Boston. I heard tell Admiral Howe has four men-o-war in the harbor with a total of two hundred guns. More than enough to blast General Washington back to Virginia." He put one finger to his nose, blew snot out of the unblocked nostril, repeated the process and rubbed his thumb knuckle vigorously against a raw cold sore at the right corner of his lips.

"Ahh, stop your complaining, Lazarus Palmer," a stout older teamster snapped. "'Tis found money. No one ever paid me to stay at home waiting for the spring thaw. What would you be earning on your farm in the dead of winter? Sitting at home carving neck yokes for your oxen or a washing stick for your wife?"

Will listened to more of their idle talk before walking away from the fire to relieve himself. The deep snow soaked his stockings and fell into his shoes. He took his hatchet from his leather bag, shook the snow from a few low-hanging pine branches and lopped them off. He dragged them back to his sled, swept some of the snow from the ground and leaned the broader limbs against the wagon to form a shelter. He restoked his fire with some bark he had peeled from a nearby pitch pine and lay down on the remaining cut branches that did little to shield him from the frozen ground. Wrapping Elisabeth's scarf over his head, with his blanket pulled over him, he drifted off to sleep.

He awoke in the early dawn, to the promise of a frigid but clear sunny day. The hair on the back of his head was covered with frost and his feet were numb and frozen. He rose, moving his legs to get the circulation going. Using the still red embers he rebuilt the fire, warming his hands over the newly blossoming flames. He melted a little of the lard over the fire and coated his split fingers and raw knuckles with it, thinking they would be bloody again by mid-morning. Cold as he was, his spirits were high, rekindled by the certainty he indeed was on his own, free from his father's control, with limitless possibilities stretching into the snowy wilderness leading him to Boston and a reunion with Johan.

Nat found him hitching the horses to the sled. Will smiled to see him. "The snow is so deep off the road, it is coming in over the top of my boots," Nat said stamping his feet. He noticed the cracked thin leather and torn seams of his friend's low shoes. "Will," he exclaimed. "We must get you some proper boots. These will be rotted through before we get to Cambridge."

"I pay it no mind," Will said, not wanting to admit to Nat his toes were already frozen. A pair of high leather boots would keep his calves dry and warm, he thought. "I have straw inside them and besides, I am out of the snow on the wagon seat," he replied.

"Not today. The road ahead, if you can call it a road, is much more forbidding. There are many steep slopes up and down. The Colonel and I turned back when the snow reached up to our horses' bellies." He pulled his round hat tighter on his head as the early morning wind picked up.

"The Colonel's plan is to have the lighter loads smooth the way. Your sled is the first of the one and two tonners. We will stop often and cut trees to slow the wagons and sleds from sliding backwards on the up slopes." He did not have to add that, on the downside, a runaway two-ton load would crush the teamster and his horses.

"My intention," he continued, "is when necessity demands, to use drag chains, ropes and block and tackle affixed to trees. I need you, when we stop for an ascent or descent, to work an axe with vigor. We must keep all hands employed to move the heavier loads along." Will nodded, not sure what was expected of him, except to work hard.

The descent before the first incline was moderate. The road smoothed out by the sleds bearing the three and six pounders had flattened the surface, making it icy and treacherous in places. Will kept his team in check and halted his sled at the dip before the rise. He dismounted, walked along the length of his team, clicking his tongue and patting them as he passed. He surveyed the rising slope. Even with the studded metal runners, it would be difficult for the horses to prevent the sled from sliding backwards. He stopped at Big Red and scratched the horse's chin and jaw.

"We can do this," he said to the horse although it was more for his own reassurance.

"Will. We need you," Nat shouted.

Nat had organized the Continentals and some of the teamsters from the following wagons and sleds into work crews. They set off through the snow banks toward the nearest trees. Will's contingent was divided by the Sergeant in charge into pairs. The soldier opposite Will began swinging his axe in short, quick strokes, hacking small chips from the trunk. Will gauged the heft of his axe to satisfy himself the head outweighed the bit. It had a good feel and balance. He placed his hands on the long straight handle and began to swing the blade methodically in an accurate arc, quickly cutting a deep notch. When he was more than half way, mindful of the direction of the fall, he motioned for the soldier to step to the side.

After trimming the larger branches, the crews dragged the fallen trees back through the snow to the road. Will's upper body was clammy with sweat from the exertion while his feet, from soles to calves, were numb from the cold. He headed back to the road through the deep, heavy snow, lifting his legs high and ploughing ahead. The other crews let him lead, following in the narrow path made by his dragging a tree behind him. No matter, he thought. Someone has to do it and if this meant the cannons would reach General Washington sooner, he was ready to do his share and more.

Back on the road, when a dozen trees had been stacked and further trimmed, Nat took Will aside. Even with his thick blue cloak, Holmes was shivering. "It is worse when one stands still in this bitter wind," he said, as Will moved his arms around, trying not to stiffen up.

"You are first to haul a heavy gun up this hill," Nat instructed. "We will be along side and place the logs behind the rear runners. I hope we shall not need ropes or block and tackle to pull this cannon to the top. It would delay us significantly." He looked up at Will. "If by your example, you do it, others will know it is possible with their lighter loads."

"I will do my best."

Will mounted the sled, stood up and called to Big Red and the mare to move, flicking the whip across the haunches of the nearest two spans. The heavily loaded sled creaked as the eight horses hauled it out of the deeper snow and onto the road. Will felt the deep, biting chill of the wind freezing his damp linen shirt to his body. He wrapped the blanket tighter around his shoulders and thought quickly but longingly of Elisabeth. He wished she were sitting next to him, warm, cuddly and smelling of lavender. He urged the horses forward.

It was a slow ponderous uphill haul. Midway up, thirty yards from the top, the sled perceptibly slowed, the horses straining in their traces against the weight.

"Nat," Will shouted. "Hurry or we will slide backwards." He stood up in the sled and flicked the whip over the last four horses. He knew Big Red and the mare would pull on their own, causing the two behind them to do so as well. Nat with some of the Continentals alongside, threw the logs behind the runners. Slowly, they gained another few feet with the horses struggling for traction. Anxious to maintain any forward momentum, Nat still on the left side, yelled for those behind the sled to use some of the trees as lever poles.

"Put your shoulders into it, men," he shouted. The sled inched up the icy slope. Will glanced at the decreasing distance to the summit and pressed the eight horses on.

"Pull, Big Red," he shouted into the wind. "Pull hard." The horses put their heads down, their chest muscles straining against the leather traces, their hooves biting into the frozen ground beneath them. Will glanced at the distance to the summit, calculating it was almost time to hold the horses back from charging down the other side. He tugged the reins in his left hand as they crested and the team headed into a drift. The sled came to rest, just off the road. Will's arms ached from the strain and the cold wind at the summit knotted his stretched muscles. He dismounted and walked forward to Big Red and the mare. He stood between them, staring ahead at the hill sloping steeply down before him.

Nat shouted halloo and signaled to the driver on the sled ahead of them at the top of the next hill. The man waved back. Three Continentals, the red trim of their blue jackets clearly visible from the distance, unloaded chains, ropes, block and tackle from the sled and carried them to the bottom of the hill, leaving them in a tangled pile.

Nat walked down the steep incline with the Sergeant and some of the teamsters. He unraveled the ropes, left the ends lying part way up the far side and trudged back toward Will's sled laying the lines out as he came back up the slope. The others followed carrying the chains and block and tackle.

Nat muttered to Will, his words lost in the strong wind blowing across the summit. "Never coiled a rope or wound a chain in their entire sorry lives," he said more loudly as he assessed the nearby trees. "Now with the ropes laid out from here to beyond the dip we have the proper length measured to restrain the sled."

Nat sent the men to retrieve the ends of the ropes lying past the bottom of the descent. He selected a thick evergreen several feet below the summit and wound one rope low, several times around trunk. He did the same thing with the second rope on the other side of the road. Carrying both ends, Nat knelt down, cleared the snow from the rear of Will's sled with his bare hands, found the thick rear oak crossbar and attached each rope to it.

Will squatted on his haunches, leaning on the runner, and watched over Nat's shoulder.

"A fisherman's bend hitch for the bar," Nat explained, nodding toward the knot he had dexterously finished. 'It will not slip," he said, grunting as he tested it.

But the ropes can snap, Will thought.

Nat seemed to read his mind. "Do not worry, Will. The ropes will hold. I can vouchsafe for that. Once wound around those stout trees, the men will have enough purchase to hold you back," he said with confidence.

Will watched Nat attach the chains to the same crossbar. "Sergeant," Nat called. "I need your men to chain those logs into bundles, six or seven of the shorter ones together and stack them behind this sled."

"What for," the Sergeant replied, without moving.

Nat ignored his surly tone. "We need them to serve as a drag, as a ship's anchor, slowing the descent of this two tonner," he said matter-of-factly. He watched the men carefully as they struggled to get the logs lined up and fastened with chains at each end. Will looked dubiously at the chained together logs and shook his head.

"Nat. The logs will roll down on to the back of the sled. I do not see how they can be of help."

The untrimmed stubs of the branches will catch and accumulate the snow, slowing the sled's forward momentum," Nat explained. "And there will be iron spikes in the links. You will see."

Nat tested each bundle. He ran the six-foot long chains from the sled's crossbar to the first two bundled logs so they lay horizontally behind the sled. The other two bundles were chained to the first pair another six feet behind them. He hammered thick metal spikes randomly into the links of the chains connecting the two pairs and from the foremost pair of logs to the sled. "These will serve better than the studs on the runners," he said, standing up and brushing the snow from his knees.

"You men carry the remaining poles alongside and, upon my command, be quick to throw them under the front curve of the runners," Nat ordered. "Sergeant, when we reach the bottom and I wave my hat, untie the ropes and walk them down."

Nat waited until the men, with their poles were in position.
"Ready Will?"

Will nodded and swallowed hard. He called out to Big Red and the mare and flicked the reins on the hind quarters of the two closest horses. The sled began a slow descent of the snow covered hill. He knew the horses would not go straight down the middle of the road. Instinctively, they would slant first to one side and then the other, weaving their way down the slope. He had to prevent them from going too far either way and running the cannon off the road. Crossing back over the icy flattened middle of the track was the treacherous part. The sled could hit a frozen patch and by its sheer weight slide out of control either straight down on the horses or slip in a different direction, pulling Will and the team of eight over. Will tightened his grip on the reins and carefully watched the road for ice.

He couldn't look back to see how the chained logs were working but tensed to hear any noise of them breaking loose and crashing into the back of the sled. If that happened or the ropes broke, he would urge the horses ahead as fast as they could go. Hopefully, he would be able to keep them on the road and the far upward slope would eventually slow the two-ton load behind him. If that failed, he would have to leap off the sled far enough to the side to avoid being crushed. He felt the presence of the huge cannon behind him, an ominous black iron beast with its fat rounded breech eager to crush his spine.

A third of the way down the steep slope, the sled began to slip sideways as it passed over an icy patch. Will shouted a warning and tightened the reins pulling the horses back. Nat jumped forward jamming the long pole against the edge of the runner as a lever. Quickly others ran to join him. Together, pushing against the runner, they managed to straighten out the sled so it was once again directly behind Will's team.

He heard a bump behind him and panicked, unable to turn around.

"One of my log anchors hit the same frozen snow," Nat called out. "They are holding, Will."

The sled was nearing the bottom of the incline. Despite the straining of the team, the men holding on to the ropes at the top and logs dragging behind, they were picking up speed because of the steepness of the slope. Will stood up, his legs spread wide for stability. The frigid wind was at his back. He braced himself and pulled on the reins as hard as he could.

"Big Red," he shouted. "Hold back, hold back."

The horse pricked up his ears at his voice. Will imagined Big Red's massive chest muscles and front legs straining against the pressure behind him, his head up, his haunches tightening to hold against the weight. They were still going too fast down the icy incline. They were less than twenty yards from the bottom. Big Red and the mare slanted toward the deeper snow on the right.

Will decided to chance it. He let up on the reins and pulled back on the left one. Big Red and the mare took the slack and turned toward the center. The sled, released from the eight horses slowing it down, raced forward the remaining yards, and plunged part way up the incline before the weight of the cannon cancelled their forward momentum and the sled came to a halt.

Will lowered himself on to the wooden seat, his forearm and upper thigh muscles burning from the exertion. Out of the corner of his eye, he saw Nat waving to the men to release the ropes at the summit. Will dismounted. His legs were wobbly. He walked up and down the length of his team, patting each horse. When he reached Big Red, the horse lowered his head and Will buried his face in the red mane and stroked his nose.

"The anchors held," Nat said, holding out his clenched fist. "Not all of the spikes did." He opened his fingers to reveal one of them sheared off a few inches below its flattened head. "Most are broken," he said. "We have more in the boxes on a wagon toward the rear. I will have them brought forward."

Will stood with the mare and Big Red, preferring to hold the team steady from the front while Nat and his crew detached the drag chains. The horses shielded Will from the wind that was now blowing harder. It would mean a colder ascent of the next slope. After what seemed to Will a very short time, he was back on the sled, the eight horses straining to pull the load, the men alternately blocking the sled from sliding back, and leveraging and pushing it from behind. The uphill was not as steep as the downside leading toward it. They made the summit without having to resort to ropes or block and tackle.

In this manner, the entire train covered barely three miles the second day and four the third, the heavier cannons slowing the entire convoy's progress. There was no other way. They needed manpower for each steep slope, in both ascent and descent, as well as for righting the wagons or sleds that slid off the road and had to be hauled back before the Colonel would let that segment of the train proceed.

After three exhausting days, with a plodding sameness, Will thought the only difference was that the nights were getting colder and the snow deeper. He deliberately avoided the New Yorkers. They reminded him of the part of the journey with his father. He preferred the company of the Massachusetts men. A few of them had been to Boston, and some evenings the talk turned to Boston and the blockade. None of them had been at Lexington or Concord. But they repeated accounts they had heard in the inns and taverns from those who swore they were there. Will was an avid but discerning listener. He knew these were embellished campfire tales. When they got to General Washington's camp, he vowed to seek out the real veterans of those battles and learn firsthand from them.

Will had overcome his earlier embarrassment with Nat and slept with the Massachusetts teamsters at night, on freshly cut evergreen boughs, the men curled spoon-like in crescent clumps to take advantage of their common body heat. When he awoke in the morning, cramped and stiff, the smell of unwashed wagoners filled his nostrils.

In the late afternoon of the fourth day, in the January winter darkness, they descended an especially precipitous slope. Part of the train was already camped on a relatively flat plain between two frozen ponds. Gaunt, bare dead trees stood like macabre sentinels, their grey trunks rising from their icy graves. That night, however, when he joined the Massachusetts teamsters around their fire, the talk was uglier and nastier. The older farmers were angry their duties included more than driving. They were exhausted from cutting and dragging trees through waist high snow, serving as work crews and walking alongside the sleds and wagons when they should be driving their own teams. They found fault with every facet of Knox's leadership.

"It is certain that he is not eating the same sparse rations we are," Lazarus Palmer said, biting into a piece of hard bread. Some crumbs stuck to his frozen beard. "My God, look at the man. Sleek and fat as the day we met him in Great Barrington," he said making a gesture with his hand to illustrate the Colonel's large belly.

"I hear he sleeps in a tent," another teamster said. "Not on the ground as we do, I'll wager."

"You know," Lazarus said, "he is married to a Tory. Yes, it is true," he added although no one had contested the point. "The daughter of Thomas Flucker himself, the Royal Secretary of the Massachusetts Bay Province. I have never seen him but I hear he is a pompous strutting cock." He waited for someone to say something and when no one did, he went on. "Now you tell me how Secretary Flucker, the King's man in our Province, is going to let his daughter marry someone who is a not a Tory at heart."

"Where is this leading," one of the teamsters asked, warily.

Lazarus picked at his cold sore, grown into a deep scabby red circle at the corner of his mouth, taking his time now that he had their attention. "It is obvious to me," he replied. "Our Colonel has taken us over the roughest terrain either to delay delivery of the cannons until it is too late to help General Washington, or to prevent them from ever reaching Cambridge. Why, for all we know, even now the British may have attacked and driven our men from the field. Or worse. The Redcoats are waiting up ahead to intercept us and take the cannons for themselves."

Will hesitated. He wanted to say something in the Colonel's defense. He was not accustomed to speaking up in groups and was unsure of how to present his argument. Besides, he anticipated the men would laugh at him.

"Nonsense," a teamster bellowed from the other side of the fire. "You mean the Colonel traveled all the way to Ft. Ti, loaded up sixty cannon, brought them this far and his object is to sabotage General Washington's effort? The cold has addled your brain, Lazarus. If he were a Loyalist, and I'm not saying he is, he never would have set foot out of Boston," he snorted, putting another log on the fire. "You think he likes the cold any better than we do? He would rather be before a warm fire in a stone house and in a warm bed with Miss Lucy Flucker than out here with a collection of nitwits like you."

"All I am saying," Lazarus replied a little heatedly, "is that I would not have my daughter marry a British soldier, so why would the Royal Secretary permit his daughter to marry a true patriot? It is most peculiar and strange, I tell you." He took a swig from his rum flask and offered it around.

"I hear that Miss Lucy is an ample woman," a voice added from the fringe of the fire. "She would keep me warm at night. That is a fact."

"My God, think of the sight," said another. "When the two of them are coupling together in bed. It must be a stout four poster to hold them." The teamster who had challenged Lazarus' logic, stood up laughing at his own joke before telling it. "Why I might even like to fluck her myself," he said. "Her name says it all for me. She is there to be flucked," he chuckled. "The whole house must shake when Knox puts it to her." The talk degenerated into more ribald comments, the men forgetting Palmer's original accusation.

Will blushed at the image in his mind of the Colonel in bed with his wife. In Schoharie, in their small farmhouse, there had been little if any privacy. He had seen and heard his father and stepmother coupling. It hadn't seemed very loving to him. Once he had entered the barn looking for a scythe and interrupted his father, having thrown his stepmother on the hay, her skirts hoisted up, her expressionless face turned away from her husband, and George Stoner fumbling with his pants. Will had backed away, confused and unseen. Perhaps it was different with the Colonel and his wife. He thought of making love to Elisabeth and rushed to shut out his thought as impure. She didn't deserve his lewd fantasies. Embarrassed, he felt himself getting hard.

"This is not the bargain I made," he heard another teamster say loudly over the jokes and laughter. "I signed on as a driver. Not to slog through deep snow chopping trees or have my arms pulled from their sockets holding on to a rope attached to a sled with a ton and a half of iron cannon at the other end," he said angrily. "My oxen are worn out and a dead team will do me no good for the spring plowing," another said. "I say we quit and go home and the cannons be damned." There were cries of agreement while others shouted for more money for the work they were doing or argued about how much of their promised pay they were entitled to for coming this far but not all the way to Springfield. Finally, they decided to demand a meeting with the Colonel in the morning, before they would even hitch up their teams.

Will moved away from the group as they settled down for the night. All that loose talk of sex made him uncomfortable. While he was not afraid of any of them, nor had they given him any cause to be, the thought of spooning with the men tonight was repulsive. He was also petrified that he himself might get hard, having already had lewd thoughts about Elisabeth. He trudged glumly back through the snow to his sled, built his own fire and comforted himself by taking out the book the Colonel had given him. He caressed the rich leather cover and read a few short chapters in the flickering light. It was such a strange world being described, Somersetshire, England and the wealthy Magistrate Allworthy. He marveled at how much there was to read of faraway places and people he knew nothing about. Somewhat despondently he realized how little he knew and how big the world was beyond his father's farm in upstate New York. He fell asleep. He dreamed of Johan escorting him around Boston with the British gone and the city thriving.

The next morning dawned grey and overcast, with the promise of snow later in the day. William Knox had already started the vanguard on their way when the Colonel was approached by the delegation of Massachusetts men, demanding a meeting. Knox arrived with a grim faced Nat beside him. The men formed a semicircle in front of their sleds and wagons, their teams unhitched as a visible sign of their intent not to proceed. Lazarus Palmer stepped forward as their spokesman, voicing their complaints. Will moved Big Red and the mare closer and stood between them, alternately brushing their shaggy winter coats and leaning into them for warmth.

The Colonel patiently heard them out. Nat wore a path in the snow, pacing up and down and glancing occasionally at the threatening sky, making it plain he thought they should be done with this useless talking and on their way.

"There is nought you can say, Colonel," Lazarus concluded, "to persuade us otherwise. It is a miracle we have gotten this far. We have our families to think of and the necessity of healthy oxen for the spring planting. We need grain to sell and store for next winter. Now," he said, his hands on his hips signifying he had made their case, "what is your offer to pay for our teamstering this far to this God-forsaken flatland between the ponds?" Or," he paused, dangling what he believed was a clever thin reed of hope for the Colonel, "what will you pay in addition for those of us who may wish to continue on to Springfield?"

Knox seemed to ponder the question, as if calculating how many more pounds sterling he could afford to offer them. He startled them by talking not about money but about Massachusetts, their homes, and his pride in Massachusetts men standing up to the tyranny of the Crown. His deep voice rumbled out over the assembled teamsters standing sullenly before him. He recalled the resistance to the Stamp Act, the boycott of all imported British goods, not just by the people of Boston but throughout the Province, the occupation of Boston under the Intolerable Acts, the fortification of Roxbury Neck and confiscation of weapons from Boston citizens, General Gage's closing the Boston Port and abrogation of their Massachusetts Charter, the banning of town meetings and Gage's refusal to declare a day of Fasting and Repentance. He spoke of the suffering of the decent people of Boston with food scarce and the water turned bad, of the Redcoats destroying churches, homes and businesses, including his own bookstore, he added, using furniture for firewood and pews for horse troughs, of Catholic troops desecrating Christmas by drinking and partying, and the constant harassment of the citizenry and limitations on their liberties.

"The occupation of our homes and lands by Regulars did not come without cost," Knox said, lowering his voice somberly. "It was five years ago this March when the brutal massacre by the King's troops of unarmed citizens in Boston occurred." He recounted the recent events of the past April when the Regulars marched out of Boston toward Lexington and Concord, the Redcoats' unprovoked attack on the men assembled at the Alarm Post on the Lexington Green, the bravery of the militia at the North Bridge in Concord, the rallying of the militias from the surrounding countryside and the thirty-three mile British march back to Cambridge.

"They plundered our homes on their retreat," Knox thundered, "stole the communion silver from our churches, bayoneted innocent travelers, set fire to buildings and incinerated women and children trapped inside. They slaughtered livestock in an orgy of savagery not seen in our land since the French and Indian War. In Menotomy, I was told innocents in Cooper's Tavern had their heads bashed open by British rifles. Their brains splattered the tables and walls where they fell. And yet, despite this savagery, and even in the face of certain death, brave Massachusetts men defended their hearths and homes, dying on their own thresholds of multiple bayonet wounds while their loved ones watched their murders in horror from the safety of nearby woods."

He opened his arms, spreading his dark blue wool cape like the wings of a giant bird to encompass the group before him, and lowered his voice. "It was your fellow teamsters in Menotomy and Lincoln who harnessed their teams of oxen to their wagons and sleds and carried our heroic dead militia, piled high and stiff, in their homespun stockings and coats dyed with the bark of the trees of the hills where they had lived, fought and fallen, more dignified in death than a British Officer in his brilliant finery. They bore them back to their towns and villages to be buried not with the full honors they deserved, but in trenches covered with boughs and limbs to hide their bodies should the savage Red Jackets return and seek revenge even upon the deceased."

The Colonel paused, wiping his forehead with his left hand as if to clear a memory. "A doctor friend of mine attended to an old soldier, a veteran of the French and Indian War who had fought alongside the King's troops against our then common foe. This past April, as the British retreated from their foul deeds at Lexington, he was compelled to defend his own home in Menotomy against them. With musket, pistols and sabre. Lame and old as he was, he killed five of the Regulars before he himself was shot and bayoneted and left for dead. The doctor counted fourteen wounds on his aged frame. But he lived, his body a testament to British brutality. At the end of this, our noble endeavor, I will take you to meet this valiant patriot and we will all hoist a glass with him to his recovery."

There was a stirring and shuffling of feet among the teamsters, pretending to move to keep warm. Their manhood had been challenged by the Colonel's recounting of the recent bloody battles. Their complaints of hard labor paled in comparison to the sacrifices made in the face of British guns. Will could sense a change in mood. He noticed Lazarus no longer stood in front of the group but had retreated to become one of them.

"Men. At Bunker Hill, made sacred now by the blood and courage of our militia, sturdy farmers like yourselves and tradesmen too, stood united in the face of charge after charge of British Regulars and the Death Head's Cavalry. They inflicted a grievous blow to King George's minions before leaving the field. The militiamen who died on that Hill gave their lives for a reason. Their belief in our collective rights. We, all of us, have our birth rights as Englishmen. Foremost among them is the right, as a free born people, to be governed by the laws of our own making. This is our public liberty, our responsibility as a free people to regulate our own affairs. The tyranny of the Crown is opposed to our exercise of this freedom to govern ourselves and our right to be treated equally before the law." Knox waved his arm toward the men in front of him. "The King's representatives in our Province regard you, all of us, as inferior human beings, a lower order of being. They are disdainful of our history of town meetings and congregational churches, of our observance of the Sabbath, of our common liberty. To them, we are fit only to be ruled, taxed and governed as they see fit to impose their will on us."

He turned his large frame and pointed past the flatlands to the snow-covered steep hills to the east. "Beyond those mountains lies Boston. When I left, General Washington was headquartered in Cambridge and had surrounded the Redcoats in the city below. Our lines are within musket shot of the British, who have heavily fortified Bunker Hill. These cannons, the very ones you have struggled to bring so far, will end the tyranny of the King and his Army in Boston and all of Massachusetts. We will retake the sacred soil of Bunker Hill," he bellowed.

"You have not come so far nor will continue to struggle because I ask you to do this," he said, lowering his voice slightly. The men strained forward to hear his words. "Nor do you do so for the pay you are promised. You are part of this noble endeavor, this noble train of artillery, for all of Massachusetts. For the citizens who live here now and in generations to come, so that those who inhabit our Province in the future will live as free men without fear of arbitrary rule by a King and Parliament across the ocean, free to speak their mind in town meeting or Church, and free to live under the laws they themselves have made." Knox stopped and scanned the front row of teamsters. He smiled at the few he recognized.

"Now men. You good Massachusetts men," he said with affection. "Let us complete the trek which together we have set out to accomplish, and with the help of Divine Providence, fulfill the mission upon which the fate of our fellow citizens depends." He waved as if in farewell, walked to a nearby tree, untied his horse and rode off without another word. [1]

Will estimated the Colonel had spoken uninterrupted for more than an hour. He had never heard a speech like it. Before this, he had only attended sermons. The Colonel's oration was awe-inspiring. Some day, he would like to be able lead men like that. To marshal thoughts and put words together in such a way as to make men want to follow him in some noble endeavor. The teamsters disbanded, with calls to quickly hitch up the horses and oxen and get moving. There were cries of "Follow the Colonel" and "On to Boston." Not a single one abandoned the caravan.

Nat approached Will. "Tis is a later start than we wanted. A good thing they are eager to push on. The Colonel's brother scouted ahead late yesterday afternoon. The next slope up to Blandford is the steepest by far. Then, from the summit is a dangerous precipitous hill, almost straight down with few open places between the trees. It will be a tough and trying slog." He patted Will on the shoulder. "The Colonel wants you to be the first of the heavy cannons to make the descent."

Will smiled back. "In case it becomes a runaway, I do not crush the others ahead of me," he said knowingly. He saw the look of concern on his friend's face. "Do not fret, Nat. The team will hold," he said confidently.

"I will be there with a crew and extra drag chains." Nat replied. "It is dangerously steep, Will. Be careful."

A fine white snow began to fall, whipped by strong gusts from the west. Will sat exposed on the sled seat. He turned his body away from the steady bone chilling wind, so that his left side and back were soon coated in white and only his right arm and shoulder were clear of the fast falling snow. When the train halted at the beginning of the incline, he was thankful to climb down from his frozen perch. He ploughed the way into the woods, sinking in deep soft drifts around the trees. He swept the snow away around the trunk with a lopped off branch so as to have a secure footing. Eagerly and with youthful energy he swung the axe rhythmically, his blade biting into the soft pine and passing through the reddish core before the Continental on the other side had reached the middle.

As they proceeded up the long slope toward the summit of Blandford, the evergreens gave way to a hardwood forest of tall red oaks and shorter twenty-foot-high bear oaks, ash and beeches. The deep snow concealed dense thickets of barberry and other thorny bushes. When they went off the road to cut more trees, the brambles impeded their progress, and their efforts at chopping were made more laborious by the harder wood. They broke out the block and tackle midway up. With the snow whipped almost horizontally by the strong wind, Nat attached the ropes to the sled's front cross bar. Men emerged from the snowy greyness to join others in hauling on the ropes. Finally, with humans and horses pulling, Will's sled with its ponderous fortification gun crawled up to the summit.

Will had expected some sort of village at the top. The place had a name, he reasoned. Instead, Blandford was a plateau, sparsely covered with snow-laden trees, stunted and buffeted by even stronger winds, and with not a barn, building or shelter to be found. Big heavy flakes fell, rapidly obscuring the path carved by the sleds and wagons that had preceded them. All Will could see before him was a long steep decline, the bottom of which was somewhere far below lost in the thick swirling flakes. Nat leaned on the sled and stared down the slope.

"Nothing for it, Will, but to do as we have done since leaving Great Barrington.

We will chop down more trees, attach them and the drag chains and make the descent."

"The snow seems wetter," Will said encouragingly. "It should pack up on the chains and logs and slow us down." Nat moved off through the falling snow with chains and block and tackle slung over his shoulders. Will took his axe from underneath his seat and trudged off toward a nearby bear oak, his head and shoulders hunched down into the wind.

The rest of the afternoon and into the early darkness of the evening was a blur of a hellish five-mile descent in a snowstorm. Will's shoulders ached from swinging the axe, his forearms burned from pulling on the reins, his thigh muscles were knotted from lifting his knees high in walking through drifts, his legs below the knees and especially his ankles and toes were so numb as to be beyond feeling. He held the icy reins in his chapped hands. The blood from his split fingers and knuckles froze in thin red streaks, like dyed strands of wool.

With his head down and Elisabeth's scarf wrapped around his throat. he recited out loud the Colonel's speech about the reasons why they were fighting. He forgot about the anchors and chains with their spikes, the men holding on to the ropes behind him, the interminable waiting in the blowing snow and bitter wind as the block and tackle were retrieved higher up and affixed to other trees lower down the slope. Alone on the sled, Will threw the Colonel's words to the teamsters defiantly out against the storm. He imagined the old farmer in Menotomy, crouched behind an overturned worn oak bench at his front door, loaded muskets at his side, firing at uniformed Redcoats as they closed in, bringing them down with each shot, discharging his pistols as they charged him, and then using his waning strength with his sabre to keep them at bay. He winced at the vision of the old man's body being pierced by the long narrow bayonets, wielded by vicious soldiers laughing savagely as they stabbed him again and again. Anger at this atrocity and the hot desire for revenge warmed Will's spirits and served to keep him going. Disoriented in his reverie and exhausted, he lost all sense of time, until he caught himself letting the reins go slack. He jerked up with a start, brushed the snow off his arms and shoulders, and focused on the back of Big Red's head, the long red mane coated with ice and snow.

It was dark when they had reached the bottom. Will barely had the strength to tether the horses and give them a meager meal of oats. He clung to Big Red to steady himself before staggering off to fall asleep under his makeshift lean-to of boughs against the sled. The pine branches kept some of the falling wet snow off him, but he was almost past caring. Numbed by the constant cold and drained of his last reserves of energy, he was asleep instantly, with no thoughts of Elisabeth, Tom Jones, or Johan.

He awoke in the morning and felt Nat's cloak over his shoulder and Nat's body spooned around him for mutual warmth. He rose, careful not to wake his friend, aware of the stiffness of his body and the gnawing hunger in his stomach. Daylight revealed the forward two sections of the caravan stretched along a flat road. Here and there a few of the teamsters were up, the blue smoke of their cooking fires spiraling up into the cold air. Will looked back up toward the Blandford Summit. The sky was clear save for a few wispy white strands of clouds. Near the top, some of the sleds and wagons of the next segment of the train were beginning to negotiate the steep descent in the crisp early morning.

"It had to be the hand of Providence that guided us down through yesterday's storm," Nat said, standing beside him, looking upward at the sharp precipitous decline. He offered Will a piece of hard bread and Will shared with him the last of his cured ham. They ate standing up, occasionally bending down to warm their hands on the small fire between them. Ahead, to the east, the terrain was flat. They were in a river valley. Farther to the east, on the far side of the frozen Westfield River, snow-covered bluffs rose with grey granite slabs piercing the white like an occasional dark feather on a snow goose. Will shaded his eyes against the glare of the rising sun on the icy river and the snowy fields and hills beyond.

"One of the locals says it is six miles to Westfield, which is this side of the river. The weather is good," Nat added, scanning the sky, "the road is flat ahead and with luck we shall be snug inside the Westfield Inn, before a warm fire and sleeping in a dry place by nightfall." He glanced back toward the summit. "They will have an easier time descending than we did yesterday, but even so, they will not be in Westfield until tomorrow."

As Nat predicted, the train made good time over the packed snow on the road. Until the Blandford descent, they had not met a solitary person since leaving Great Barrington, and nor seen even an isolated home or barn. Now, on the road to Westfield, there were tradespeople, farmers, peddlers, men traveling between the farms and homes that dotted the river valley. Many had never seen a cannon at all. They stopped and gawked as the vanguard of the caravan passed by.

Nat, sitting on the sled next to Will, waved cheerfully at a bearded farmer standing by the side of the road, next to a sled loaded with trimmed logs. "There are still more behind us, coming down from the Blandford Summit," he shouted.

"Where you coming from?" the farmer asked, apparently puzzled by Nat's Boston accent.

"Great Barrington. Before that Albany, and before that, Fort Ticonderoga," Nat answered exuberantly, now that the most tedious part of the journey was over. "Two days ago, we were in the frozen marsh between two ponds below the summit," he added to emphasize how difficult it had been to get to the Westfield Road.

"If you were at Spectacle Ponds, there is no road from there to the summit," the farmer replied. "Never has been. What passes for a road from here to Great Barrington is more to the north." He shook his head in wonderment. "I would not try it with my load of logs. It is a wonder your sled with that monstrous cannon made it over."

The rest of the trip to Westfield was similar, the citizens inquisitive and eager to talk, their normally taciturn nature overcome by the length of the train and the size of the cannons. When they reached Westfield, the people lined the road. Dogs darted and snapped at the heels of the oxen, and barked from a more respectful distance at the horses. Small boys ran between the wagons and sleds, daring each other to time their dashes closer and closer to the oncoming team. As each driver stopped near the Westfield Inn, the citizens rushed up to touch the cannons, caressing the massive iron and brass, and putting their hands down the muzzles. They tried to lift the cannon balls and shouted out their guesses at the cannons' weight and circumference.

Will had no trouble finding a barn for the horses. The populace were eager to help. He was offered hot mulled cider, which he eagerly accepted, feeling the heat through the pewter warm his frozen fingers. He tarried to talk to townspeople who invited him inside the cozy warmth of their houses on the way to the inn. After seven days in the wilderness without having spoken to a soul outside of the caravan, Will was gratified by the friendliness of strangers and their willingness to provide free food and drink.

The Westfield Inn was at the junction of two roads. One continued east to Springfield and beyond to Cambridge and Boston. The road north led to Northampton and Vermont and still farther to New Hampshire. The Inn was a three- story brick building with three gables and two huge chimneys at either end rising higher than the roof line. A barn with a wood rail-fenced pasture stood on one side and a small salt box home on the other. Candlelight streamed from the long windows on the first floor, like flickering yellow tongues of flame around a campfire.

Colonel Knox was holding court in front of the huge fireplace in the main room of the inn. The room was warm, almost stifling, from the number of people present. Will squeezed himself in among the townspeople and teamsters at a corner table. The noise, the warmth and the smells of roasting meats all assaulted his senses, attuned to the vast silence and freezing cold of the woods. Seeing and smelling cooked food aroused a tremendous hunger in the pit of Will's stomach. He eagerly seized a plate of boiling hot stew, reached for a hunk of warm bread and went to work with his spoon satisfying his most basic immediate need. Two plates and a loaf and a half of bread later, he leaned back on the bench against the brick wall, licked his fingers and surveyed the room.

The Colonel was sitting at a linen-covered table, eating a large slab of beef with a knife and fork. He was surrounded by several men of the town, dressed in Continental or militia uniforms, their coats brushed, their boots shining, their white vests and breeches without a spot of dirt to soil their splendid appearance. One particularly fine looking officer, resplendent in a dark blue coat with polished brass buttons, a gleaming sword at his side, and the finest and highest pair of black boots Will had ever seen, presented himself to the Colonel and bowed from the waist.

Knox politely finished chewing and wiped his mouth with his handkerchief. "Another Officer," Knox's voice boomed out over the crowded room. " Well, Captain. It is a pity that our soldiers are not as numerous as our officers." He laughed heartily and clapped the embarrassed Captain on the shoulder. The Colonel was in a jovial mood. The most arduous part of the journey was over. The teamsters were relieved, having made it through the Berkshires. The townspeople were in a celebratory and generous mood, buying food and drink for the weary wagoners and pestering them incessantly for details of the journey, the size of the cannons, their purpose, and how soon the British would be driven from Boston. Will, after satisfying his neighbors with what he believed was an accurate and unembellished account of their trip to Westfield, took out the book the Colonel had lent him and eagerly read in the ample candlelight. He read for about an hour, oblivious to the noise and activity around him, lost in the world of Tom Jones and his courtship of the beautiful Sophie, who in Will's imagination, despite the author's description, assumed the visage and figure of Elisabeth.

"So, there you are," Nat said, jostling to squeeze in next to Will in the corner and pulling him back from the world of Tom Jones into the boisterous inn.

"The Colonel has determined we all shall enjoy the town's hospitality for another day. The men have worked hard and drunk enough to make tomorrow a day no single teamster will want to be on the road. Let alone be able to hitch their teams and proceed."

Will smiled and put the book carefully in his pouch.

"How can you read in such a place?" Nat asked, surveying several drunken teamsters at the nearest table. "For myself, I need a quiet dock or my room in the attic."

Will shrugged. "I get lost in the words of the pages and do not hear anything around me. Nat, did you ever feel the need to hurry through books so you can get on to the next one? To want to read everything that was ever written?"

Nat looked surprised. "I cannot say that I have. My tastes run more to the Bible and the religious side. I have a copy of Dodd's Sermons to Young Men I can lend you when we reach Cambridge." Will didn't know who Dodd was but knew he certainly wasn't going to waste any time reading sermons. He acknowledged Nat's offer but determined to let the Colonel guide him with his future selections.

They slept in a real bed, sharing it with the Continental Captain and a Lieutenant, in a room of the house on the other side of the Inn. Nat had procured the quarters after the innkeeper had seen him in the company of the Colonel. Will awoke early and discovered their room was on the same side as the inn's kitchen. The cooks were already preparing breakfast for the guests. He was given bread and hot porridge, by the inn owner's wife, who was supervising the preparations. He devoured breakfast in the kitchen and went to see to the horses. It was frigid but clear. The snow around the barn quickly soaked into his shoes and froze his stockings. After feeding and watering his team, he found some clean straw and stuffed it around his feet before reluctantly putting his wet shoes back on and going outside. When he returned to the inn's main room, Nat waved him over.

"I thought you would be tending to your horses. You must be starved. Get your bowl out. They are about to serve breakfast."

Will sat down, ignoring the knowing and mischievous smile of the serving girl who had seen him in the kitchen less than an hour before. He ate as if he hadn't seen food since last night, glad for the warmth of the room and the extra porridge and bread. The tea in his mug was made of sassafras, the drink of patriots who boycotted the real tea and other goods from Britain.

"The Colonel is upstairs taking breakfast in his room," Will heard Billy Knox say to Nat. "He would like to see you, and Master Will. Your presence in a 'meeting' will keep some of the local dandies away. At least for awhile." He pointed to a group of well-dressed young men, many in their resplendent uniforms of the night before, in a side room off the entrance door.

The Colonel had indeed finished breakfast and was affixing a wax seal to a letter. "For General Washington. I have told him of our arduous progress to date, apologized for the delay and alerted him we are likely to reach Cambridge by the 20th of this month. If Divine Providence continues to favor us," he added hastily. "It will go off by courier this morning, together with a letter to my beloved Lucy." Will was embarrassed by the affectionate reference, recalling the bawdy remarks of the teamsters around the fire and the imagined coupling of Knox and his wife. Knox handed the two letters to his brother. Will heard him clomping down the steps calling for the rider. Will saw himself dashing up to General Washington's camp on Big Red, waving the pouch and calling out, "An Important Letter for the General from Colonel Knox. The cannons are coming," to the cheers and huzzahs of the soldiers. The Colonel drew him out of his reverie.

"Do you write, Master Will? Of course you do, you told me yourself. But you said you can write. Not that you do."

"I have not had occasion to write letters, sir. And I do not have thoughts others would want to read like you and General Washington." He looked down at the floor. There were bits of dirty straw was sticking out of the torn seam of his left shoe.

"Nonsense, Will. Every man has important thoughts. When we get to Cambridge, I will give you some paper and writing implements. Surely, there must be someone you want to tell your thoughts to." Will thought he saw the Colonel wink. He glanced quickly at Nat who was innocently staring over Knox's shoulder at something out the window.

The Colonel heaved himself out of the wooden armchair, which creaked in relief. "I have a more practical gift for you now, Will. The good people of Westfield are beside themselves to help. I praise the Almighty for their generosity." He looked up at the ceiling. "Last night when they pressed me for what they might do to assist our noble train, I told them a few of my men and the Continentals needed boots. Come, Will, and pick first from the fruits of their liberality." He dramatically opened the twin doors of a large armoire revealing several pairs of boots in a pile on the floor.

Will knelt down and felt their soft leather. They were used, some were scuffed and more worn than others. He put his hand inside, feeling for nails or rough leather that would cause blisters. He turned them over, checking the thickness of their soles. There was a pair of high black boots, smartly polished, and several with decorative buckles.

He rejected them as too fancy. He settled for a well-worn brown pair with a broad square toe and no internal defects. They were almost mid calf and would keep all but the deepest snow out. When they were on his feet, he rocked back and forth and strode around the room, trying them out.

"Good choice, Master Will. Chosen like a true cordwainer. Well selected indeed."

"Thank you, sir," he stammered, "I mean not for the choice but for giving them to me." He bent down, embarrassed, and quickly scooped up his worn shoes and tucked them under his arm.

"You deserve them, Will. I know from what Nat has told me, I indeed bested your father in the bargain. He received only money. I, in turn, a teamster who, by his hard work and example, helped bring a train of artillery through a New England blizzard." Will blushed, accustomed only to harsh words and blows from his father. He wanted to express his appreciation for the Colonel's praise, but the words would not come.

"Now, gentlemen. We must satisfy the enthusiasm and curiosity of the good people of Westfield. Today is a day of celebration. We will reciprocate and give them a show in return for their generosity. Tomorrow, we leave for Springfield and on to Cambridge."

Will practically flew down the tavern's stairs and out into the fresh air. He smiled broadly, recalling the Colonel's complimentary words. He, Will Stoner, had helped Colonel Knox bring the cannons over the mountains. The appreciation by the Colonel was, for him, worth more than all the pounds sterling paid to his father.

It took until early afternoon for a crew to remove "The Old Sow," a twenty-four pounder so named because of its ungainly shape, from its sled. It now rested on its gun carriage beyond the crossroads, pointing toward Springfield, as if it could shoot a cannonball that far and beyond. The townspeople had gathered and waited with a mix of curiosity and excitement, watching the preparations and shouting questions to the gun crew, who ignored them. The good people were crowded together, behind the cannon but at a respectful distance, many of them unsure of what would happen when the piece was fired.

Colonel Knox rode the brief distance from the tavern to the site, dismounted from his horse and led the populace in a brief prayer of thanks for their safe journey to date and a speedy delivery of the cannons to General Washington. Raising his voice, he made a speech in favor of their cause. Will thought it was not as inspiring as the one the Colonel had given to the Massachusetts teamsters before the ascent at Blandford, but it elicited three cheers from the crowd for General Washington.

The gun crew manned their stations, ceremoniously and unnecessarily worming and swabbing the cannon, which had not been fired in years. Even Will knew there was no likelihood of any remnants of a previously fired shot being lodged in the barrel. He surveyed the crowd and to his satisfaction, found not a single young girl who was half as pretty or as well dressed as Elisabeth.

The gun commander crisply called out his orders. There was a collective intake of people's breath in anticipation. The women covered their ears and their men folk protectively put an arm around them as the command to fire was given. The blast was like a clap of thunder. They were enveloped by the sound, as if they were standing in the center of a storm. The echo off the nearby hills was almost as loud, as the noise dissipated into the distance. The smoke from the powder remained an acrid white blanket over the road, as if a cloud had suddenly dropped from the sky and shrouded the people of Westfield at ground level.

Some women were still screaming. Men grinned as if they had showed great courage and survived in the face of danger. Will observed that the Colonel's horse had snorted and lowered his head but otherwise remained still. He would like to train Big Red to be that calm under fire.

The gun crew cleaned the piece and made ready to hoist the gun back onto the sled. Colonel Knox resisted the crowd's calls for another firing, explaining the powder was needed to drive the British from the Boston harbor. The teamsters began a brisk trade in betting games on the weight and size of the cannons, taking money or drinks in return. They let the male citizens straddle the barrels and the women sit demurely on them as if they were riding a horse side saddle. Some men were affecting more knowledge than others and opined the handles were too small to lift such heavy cannons. Others, using their own measurements and liberally interspersing their speech with references to diameter, circumference and trajectory, explained to those who were listening, the distance the cannons could propel a ball, and the damage it would do, though they had never seen a cannon fired until this morning. The drivers, liberally imbued with free hard cider, whisky and rum, were fully into the spirit of the day. They regaled the crowds with tall tales of the cannons' origins, the service they had performed during the French and Indian War and fictitious first-hand accounts of how the Green Mountain Boys had captured Fort Ticonderoga from the British in 1775.

Will soon tired of watching the townspeople make fools of themselves. Uninterested in the merrymaking, he spent the rest of the afternoon striding around in his new boots, more for the joy of walking in them than having any place to go. He dried his old shoes in the sun outside the barn and placed them in his rucksack, thinking he might use them for leather scraps or patches in the future.

He found a quiet place in the loft, took off his boots, admired them and read Tom Jones for a while. He couldn't concentrate. He was confused. First, he thought of the Colonel's promise to give him paper and a quill. What would he write to Elisabeth? How would he even begin such a letter? "Elisabeth. Dear Elisabeth. My dearest Elisabeth. My dearest." It sounded awkward, almost childish. He wanted to write to her as a man would, not a tongue-tied boy. Maybe he could find the right language in Tom Jones. He read a few more short chapters before his mind wandered again. He wondered why he had thought about training Big Red to stand still during cannon fire. He was not going off to war. He was delivering a cannon to Cambridge and returning to Schoharie and the farm. That would be the end of his adventure. But he did have hopes to do more, to be part of something grander. It was too much to think about for now. Besides, it was time to care for the horses and he was hungry again. Or still. It didn't matter as long as he ate.

The next morning, under cloudy skies with a light warming wind from the east, the train began the relatively easy journey to Springfield. Will was in high spirits. Stuffed in his haversack were a loaf of freshly baked bread, a wedge of hard cheese and pieces of roasted chicken left over from the evening's dinner. His feet were snug in his new boots. Yesterday he had decided, while grooming the horses, to wait and see what would happen when they reached Cambridge. Something Nat had said to him last night gave him hope.

"Merely showing up with the guns will not frighten the British to abandon Boston," Nat observed. He was certain General Washington and the Colonel had plans for building forts and deploying the cannons in strategic positions to threaten the British army.

Surely, Will thought, the Colonel would be able to use him. And with his brother, Johan, trapped within the city until the British were driven out, he could not contact him and fulfill his father's instructions. So, he concluded logically, he would be compelled to stay in Cambridge for a while. His adventure would not end immediately.

The road to Springfield was wide and relatively level. As the temperatures hovered above freezing during the day, the ice and snow drifts turned to slush and mud under the weight of the sleds. Those sleds in the vanguard, hauling the lighter cannons, had easier going than the heavier cannons in the middle section. It was worst for those at the end of the train. By the time they reached West Springfield, the road had been churned into a dirty brown ribbon of thick mud, weaving its way through pristine white snowy fields like a streak of filth from an overflowing latrine.

Will's team struggled to pull the two-ton fortification gun through the sticky clay-like ooze. At one point, when the tops of the runners had sunk beneath the muck and he was holding up the train, they had to resort to levering the runners out of the mud's grasp. The soldiers used the trees they had cut before the Blandford Summit and strapped to the already overloaded sleds. It was fortuitous, Will thought, they hadn't discarded them along the road. He was thankful his boots, now caked with mud, didn't leak.

The drivers were exhausted and mud splattered when the last of the train slogged into Springfield. They were in no frame of mind to accommodate the enthusiastic curiosity of the townspeople. They did accept the free cider and rum, but there was none of the celebratory mood or gaiety of their stay in Westfield.

Nat, who had ridden with the Colonel for most of the day and arrived in Springfield a good few hours before Will, reported that the New York teamsters were leaving that night. The Colonel didn't even try to persuade them to stay. He knew they were tired and far from home and there was no promise that the roads would freeze to make the journey to Cambridge that much easier.

"There are plenty of other sleds and oxen for hire in Springfield," he said confidently, as Will sat next to him behind The Black Horse Inn, scraping the caked mud off his boots with a stick he had carved in the shape of a flat spoon. "Closer to Cambridge, we can leave the heavier cannons behind and come back for them with more men and soldiers from the camp. And fresh oxen too," he said, assessing the practical aspects of the situation.

"My team will pull the cannon all the way," Will said confidently, examining the seam where the boot met the sole and thinking he should rub lard in and seal it better. "I am not the one to let the Colonel down," he said vehemently, recalling the Colonel's words of praise at the Westfield tavern.

"I did not think you would," Nat replied quickly. "We should make Worcester in two days if the roads remain muddy. Perhaps only one day, if the ground freezes again. After that, the Colonel intends to ride quickly with the light cannon into Framingham and then on to Cambridge. It is possible General Washington will ride out from Cambridge to meet him."

In his imagination, Will saw the Colonel tipping his tri-corn to the General and pointing behind him to the unending train of artillery winding through the snowy countryside, with Will's four-span team and the large iron fortification gun glinting in the sun, clearly visible. In his mind, he was standing on the seat waving his own hat to the Colonel and shouting exuberantly at the top of his lungs. Silly daydream, he thought to himself. Only an inexperienced youth would drop the reins of eight horses to show off.

"Are you thinking of Elisabeth? Again?" Nat said to Will, seeing him smile.

Will blushed, shook his head and put his boots back on. "No. It was something else."

"You must write to the young lady," Nat said. "I myself am courting Miss Anna Gibbs, a servant in the home of Benjamin Edes, a Boston printer. She assists Martha, his wife, who is kindly toward her. He is a good patriot, a Mason and Presbyterian," he added quickly, as if her employer's membership and religion would matter to Will. "The young lady favors me. Her father, a farmer near Salem, is not as certain of his suit. He worries that I will not be able to protect and provide for his daughter. I am either away at sea or as he puts it 'engaging in these foolish rebel activities,'." He shrugged. "I hope I will be able to persuade him. I do not know what I will do if Anna's father does not consent."

Will looked at his friend in a new light. He hadn't thought of Nat as struggling with love.

"Have you written to her?" he asked.

"Every day in my mind and occasionally on paper," Nat replied, with more emotion than Will had heard him express before. It gave meaning to the phrase he had read in Tom Jones, "pining away," which he hadn't really understood until now.

"What do you say? How do you begin? How to do you address her?" Will asked, eager for his friend's advice.

Nat paused before answering. "I address her simply as Dear Anna and I write her of where I have been and what I have been doing. I end each letter telling her when I estimate I will return and repeating my hope I will be able to call on her."

"That is all?" Will asked, thinking of some of the more romantic passages of courting he had read in Tom Jones. Nat's letters seemed so devoid of love and passion.

"I am not good with words," he said defensively.

"You certainly are," Will immediately replied. "You tell stories well. Of great interest. You talk easily with men, many of them older than you. The teamsters of this train respect and follow your orders. I have seen them do so."

"Thank you, Will, for saying this. However, commanding men and earning their respect is far different from courting."

Inexperienced as he was, Will knew that was true. Nat's description of his letters to Anna revealed nothing of his feelings or affection for her. If he were writing to Elisabeth he would tell her how much he missed hearing her voice and laughter, seeing her smile, how every day there was an emptiness in his life, in his very existence by not being with her. He would tell her of his adventures but only to write that they were nothing compared to a day spent in her company. He hoped he would remember these thoughts when he arrived in Cambridge and could write to her. No. He knew he would recall them word for word because they were heartfelt, something deep within him. He would have to begin his letters with more than "Dear Elisabeth."

It took an entire day to pay the New York teamsters, unload their sleds and wagons and reload the cannons on those of the newly hired Springfield drivers. Will helped the soldiers and drivers hoist and lower the cannons, lashing them down using the knots Nat had taught him.

The Colonel rode by frequently, urging the men to work faster, his impatience obvious. The weather turned colder by mid-afternoon, auguring well for the resumption of the journey tomorrow. Perhaps energized by the prospect of the end of the thaw, or simply a return to his own good nature, the Colonel assembled all of the teamsters, the New Yorkers and the new Massachusetts men, gave a short speech thanking all for participating in this "noble endeavor," offered up a prayer for the safe journey of all concerned and generously stood a round of drinks at The Black Horse, for one and all.

They made good time, passing through Spencer and Worcester, heading north from Shrewsbury to Marlborough and then south to Framingham, which they reached two hours after dark, the evening of January 24th. It had been a monotonous, bumpy, bone-jarring ride over deeply rutted roads, the mud having frozen again as hard as iron. Will had dismounted once to check the wooden stays and traces after a particularly nasty stretch of road. The Colonel rode up and down the train, urging them on with words of encouragement. Clearly, with the worst of the journey over and the end within a few days reach, the Colonel wanted no further delays. /1

Will's arms ached from pulling on the reins all day and he was hungry as always. The bread and chicken saved from his dinner in Springfield had long since gone and the small towns they passed through barely had enough food for the occasional winter traveler. They could not adequately provide enough for all the drivers and soldiers of the train and would not sell their victuals. As for spirits, the locals sold them dearly.

He saw to the horses, spending extra time with Big Red, rubbing him down and checking his hooves and ankles for stones and bruises from the rock-hard mud. He sat on a bale of straw and scraped horse manure from the soles of his boots before walking the short distance to the Framingham Inn. He found Nat in the large room at a wooden table listening to the talk of the newly recruited Massachusetts teamsters, who were drinking heavily.

"I hear the Lobstah Backs in Boston are running out of food. Nothing but rotting vegetables and little meat for them," one of the Springfield teamsters said.

"And how do you know that?" another asked, with contempt in his voice. He had a narrow weasel face, marred by the telltale scars of smallpox. His thinning grey hair was matted and hung down in unkempt wisps over his ears. "Been to Boston, have you?" weasel face sneered. "No. I thought not. Well, I myself made several trips from Watertown to Cambridge, carrying supplies, wood and provisions for General Washington's army." He blew snot into a dirty handkerchief, examined it and tucked the cloth into his shirt. "Some army. It is a rag-tag collection, I can tell you. They look like scarecrows, underfed and diseased, and they drill like the untrained farmers they are. And then, I took my wagon over for a look of the harbor." He paused, waiting for their attention. "There were dozens of British ships in the water, all bright and clean and sparkly in the sun, going through their gun drills and the like. General Washington is going to get beat and beat bad. I see that coming, for sure." He took a draught from his mug and leaned back, as if he had the last word on the subject.

"You always see nothing good in anything anyone says or does, Israel Hosner" the first man rejoined. "I received a letter from my nephew in Boston and he wrote that the British troops are underfed and poorly disciplined. Their officers spend most of the time flogging the malcontents and trying to prevent more desertions. I tell you the Redcoats are sorry now they ever occupied the city."

He turned to Nat. "What do you say, Ensign? You are from Marblehead, you said."

Nat leaned back and folded his arms across his chest. "When I left General Washington's headquarters, more than a month ago, he was working to bring the different forces together. Militias were streaming in, not only from Massachusetts but the other colonies as well. It takes time to make them into an army. I have confidence General Washington will accomplish it." He looked Hosner in the eye, and the man dropped his gaze. "And with these cannons, those fine British ships will be driven out of the harbor. If there are no British ships, the garrison must surrender. Boston will soon be liberated. I guarantee that, gentlemen." There was a general murmuring of agreement, except from weasel-face.

"There are more cannons on those British ships, and trained gunners, than in Washington's entire army, and the powder to use them," he replied. "The Redcoats drill and fire. Washington's troops just parade around without firing a rifle or cannon. I know what I have seen and heard," he said, gesturing to his eyes and ears.

Nat sat listening to more of the back-and-forth among the men. After a while he stood up, and Will followed him outside. It felt good to breathe the clear night air.

"He is right. We do suffer from a shortage of powder and shot. The Colonel is worried about that," Nat admitted. "Tonight he is dining with John Adams and Eldridge Gerry. They rode out from Cambridge." He saw Will's blank stare of non-recognition. "They are two members of the Massachusetts delegation to the Congress in Philadelphia," he explained. "They have seen the artillery train and were excited. I was there when the Colonel showed them the cannons. I am certain the Colonel will educate them on the need to obtain ample powder and shot and persuade them to find the necessary funds to do so."

"Nat," Will asked. "Will there be a battle when we get to Cambridge?"

"I believe not immediately. It depends on General Washington of course," he added quickly. "My sense is that we will need to get the guns in place and test the Redcoats' reaction." He shrugged. "It may take a week or more. But once these cannons are in place, we will drive the British out of Boston."

"And you will get to see Anna?" Will asked, grinning.

"That will be one happy result of liberating the city," Nat admitted. "Unless she has already left and is with her father in Salem," he said, brightening at the thought.

He looked up at the night sky filled with stars. "Will," he said, reaching up to put his arm around his friend's shoulder. "Divine Providence has not permitted us to deliver the cannons to Cambridge so we should fail. Of that I am sure." He squeezed Will's upper arm and grabbed his hand.

"Tomorrow we part. The Colonel has asked me to ride with him to Cambridge. We will take many of the three and six pounders with us. Billy Knox will be in charge of seeing to the rest of the train. When you arrive in Cambridge, probably in two or three days' time, come with him to General Washington's headquarters." He held his friend by the forearm. "The Colonel will give you paper and quills and you shall write to your Elisabeth."

"While you court Anna in person," Will responded.

"Until we meet again in Cambridge, Master Stoner" Nat said, firmly grasping his friend's hand.

"Until then, Ensign Holmes," Will replied.

Chapter 6 - In the Employ of Colonel Knox

Will arrived in Cambridge on January 28th together with the eighteen and twenty- four pounders and mortars, and the sleds carrying the flint and shot. He and the teamsters in his segment, with their fortification guns and some of the eighteen and twenty-four pounders were directed to continue beyond Cambridge to Lechmere Point. The remaining heavy cannons and mortars were sent to the entrenchments below Roxbury.

They passed along the American lines on the road heading east out of Cambridge. Will had never seen so many men in one place. The militias were encamped on both sides. There was a constant movement of people and a cacophony of sounds. Soldiers marched and drilled, wagon drivers delivered supplies, horses were being exercised, sheep and cattle grazed nearby, dogs ran across the road. There was hammering and sawing, shovels striking the frozen earth, shouting of orders and just general yelling, the beat of many drums and the piping of fifes, and the smoke of cooking fires too numerous to count. Will was caught up in the excitement of being in the midst of this large army.

There were neat orderly rows of tents in some fields and rough makeshift shelters, made of boards, stone, turf or brush in no particular order, in others. Will noticed that the fields around the camp were stripped of fences. Lines of freshly cut stumps stood like tombstones in the snow, marking where fruit orchards had been before the trees were chopped down for firewood. Some soldiers, with nothing to do, wandered up to the road to view the cannons and cheer. Others ignored them and went about their business of cooking, cleaning their muskets or sharpening daggers, knives and bayonets. Here and there clusters of men crouched in tight circles, intently occupied in some game of chance. Away from the road he could see more groups engaged in drills, marching back and forth in the snow, some precise, some in ragged lines, their officers shouting at them to straighten up their lines. It seemed everyone on their separate muddy makeshift parade grounds were either learning to move and turn as a unit, or to load, mock-fire and reload.

Will had no idea what an army should look like. It seemed that every unit was distinct with its own flag flying in front of a larger tent or from a wooden pole on a drill field. The soldiers were dressed differently from each other. One militia on parade wore brilliant scarlet coats trimmed with buff facings and gauntlets and yellow metal jacket buttons, black tri-corn hats with gold trim, knee-length pants and tall black half-boots topped by white stockings. These, Will discovered from their name emblazoned on their flag, were the Baltimore Independent Cadets. Their tents were pristine white, standing out against the muddy snow. From the vantage point of his seat on the sled, he could see rows of cots and blankets inside, with haversacks and wooden canteens neatly stacked beside the open tent flaps.

The next unit was as different as a moth to a butterfly. The men of the Pennsylvania Associators, who were rigorously drilling on a field in the center of their encampment, wore plain brown coats over white buttoned vests, round hats, and tapered pants without leggings that were tucked into simple low shoes with buckles. Will thought their shoes were better suited for strolling through town than for marching. The trek from Great Barrington to Westfield had taught him the need of proper footwear. He noticed some of the Associators were limping, their stockings stained and frozen from the slush. He moved his feet up and down, taking pleasure in the feel and sound of his boots on the sled's wood.

There were units from Connecticut, also in red coats over red vests with two rows of gold buttons, buff breeches, stockings and buckled shoes. He drove the sled past a group of soldiers marching on the road, heading toward Cambridge. The pennant at the head of their column declared them to be a regiment of the Pennsylvania Battalion. Their uniforms were brown with green facing. At least, Will thought, they were properly equipped with their buff-colored half-gaiters to protect their feet from the mud and slush.

The bulk of the troops were from Massachusetts, militias composed of farmers, tradesmen and mechanics. They were dressed in an odd mix of hunting shirts and cloaks, long black frock coats, thigh-length hunting shirts, broad-brimmed hats cocked and worn in every possible way, or tri-corns, some adorned with feathers, others with red or white cockades.

As the train slowly moved through the Army's encampment, Will noticed a group of lean-tos and shelters made of branches abutting one of the few remaining stands of trees on the opposite side of the road. It was the only unit there. Smoke curled from their cooking fires, and the smell of roasting meat wafted toward him, reminding Will of the deep gnawing in his stomach. He couldn't see any flag or pennant. Several of the men loped from the tree line toward the road to watch the procession of artillery. They moved with a fluid grace coming down the paths already worn in the snow, their bodies naturally bent to present a smaller target with their rifles held in one hand. Their powder horns, yellowed from use and age, were strapped close to their hips on broad dark brown leather belts. They came on like wolves running down an elk, not like men curious to see the cannon train. They were generally tall and lean. Some were bearded, with their hair long over the ears. They wore dyed nut-brown hunting shirts, and a few had fur or buckskin hats, some with white deer tails attached to the side. Many carried large hunting knives in leather sheaths strapped to their waists. A few wore tomahawks or hatchets. They had long rifles almost as tall as their bodies, much longer than the muskets and fowling pieces he had seen the men of the other militias carrying. Will stared at them as they assessed the fortification cannon on his sled.

"That piece able to shoot that big ball?" one of them asked.

"Yes, sir," Will replied. "Colonel Knox says once the cannons are in place, they will send a cannon ball far enough to drive the British out of Boston," he added enthusiastically.

"Well I can hit a man in the throat at 250 yards," the soldier replied, patting his rifle. "You be sure and leave some of the Redcoats for me." He grinned. [1]

"What militia are you?"

"We are from western Pennsylvania. Go by the name of our Captain, Samuel MacDowell. We're MacDowell's Rifles." He waved his arm to encompass the others and their camp in the woods behind. [2] "We'll come by and see a demonstration of that big cannon of yours. You come visit us and I will show you what this rifle can do."

Will put his hand to his hat in acknowledgment, proud the man had considered the cannon his. "I will do that, sir," he said, flicking the reins and making a clicking sound to urge the team forward, as they passed through the American lines.

From Lechmere Point, Will saw the city, the harbor and the British fleet for the first time. He stopped counting the British men-of-war at 46. The ships were spread out beyond the harbor, off the land he knew from Nat's description as Dorchester Heights. Several ships were heading out to sea. He could make out the small black dots of sailors in the rigging, as the ships turned and cut a narrow white line of spray with their bows. The wind filled their sails. He thought it was a fine sight with their canvas billowing out in taut white squares.

Will stood up on the sled's bench and marveled as the ships maneuvered in the harbor. He had never seen ships this big before. They had crossed the ocean, he thought. They were under full sail now. The scene unfolding before him was so beautiful. He imagined being out on such a ship with Nat in command, sailing full speed with the wind behind them. His reverie was broken by the booming sound of cannons. The first ship leaving the harbor had tacked into the wind and fired a broadside out to sea. He watched it come around and fire another from the other side. The second and third ships performed the same maneuver, firing broadsides one after another, practicing for a sea battle against enemy ships. American ships, he thought. Do we have a navy, he thought. And how could it fight against so many British ships?

From the vantage of Lechmere Point, Will could see the buildings and streets of Boston: the steeples of several churches and the many wharves on the southeast side, one long pier stretching out like a finger into the harbor, with British ships tied up alongside. In the distance, was the slender strip that connected the city to the mainland. There was a massive fort and gate at the narrow neck, leading to Roxbury. It was protected by smaller forts with blockhouses on either side. Masses of red-coated troops marched up and down the Common, located on the side of Boston closest to the American lines. Immediately he recognized the contrast between the American militias he had seen and the perfectly even ranks of the British troops. Every soldier was dressed identically. Orderly red squares of men, the winter sun glinting off their bayonets and the metal plates on their dark caps, wheeled and turned, knelt and fired in perfect unison, at commands he imagined, though from that distance he could not hear them.

William Knox rode up and down the line of sleds, instructing the teamsters where to halt and place the cannons. He greeted Will enthusiastically.

"We made it from Fort Ticonderoga to Cambridge in forty days. My brother says he knew there was something biblical about our journey," he shouted before riding off. Will was going to respond that it had taken the entire train almost fifty days, but Billy Knox was already gone. Will maneuvered the sled into place and unhitched and hobbled six horses of the team together. He left Big Red and the grey loosely tethered to a tree.

Several militia men, supervised by the Massachusetts Regiment of Artillery, a gun crew of the Colonel's own unit, hoisted the fortification piece off the sled with well worn gun tackle and expertly lowered it onto its gun carriage. Will had nothing to do. He stood unexpectedly idle, stomping his feet in the brown, dirty snow. Two men from the gun crew gathered up the worm pole, the swab, the powder box and bucket from his sled. He joined them in carrying the cannon balls. They accepted his help but it was clear they didn't need him. He wandered away, staring across a narrow body of water toward the charred ruins of Charlestown and the British fortifications on Bunker Hill. The sight of redcoats drilling in the distance, on what Colonel Knox had called sacred soil, increased his gloomy mood.

He returned to the gun emplacements and looked down toward the Common and the streets beyond, and then along the line of the

American artillery. Several of the fortification guns and mortars were already in place. He counted fifteen pieces, including his fortification cannon. The trek was now truly over. There was nothing more for him to do. He was uncertain as to what was next for him. The gun crews were busy and he was shy about asking them where to find Colonel Knox.

Will re-hitched his team and followed the other drivers back through the lines and along the road to Cambridge. They bedded down at farms on the outskirts of the town. That night Will sat around the fire with the few New Yorkers who had remained with the train and some drivers from the Springfield region. They talked eagerly about returning home, something Will dreaded and desired to postpone as long as possible. He ate the last of his hard cheese and bread from Framingham and fell asleep in the loft of a barn, partially protected by the bales of straw he erected as a barrier to the bitter cold wind that whistled through the boards.

He awoke hungry and stiff from the frigid winter temperature. After seeing to his horses, he rode to Cambridge on a sled of one of the Springfield teamsters. The drivers were in a boisterous mood, anticipating being paid and leaving for their homes. As he hoped, he found the Colonel's brother at the aptly named Golden Goose Tavern with a ledger, a pay clerk and a leather saddle bag filled with coins. A table had been set up on one side of the large room, away from the fireplace, and the wagoners lined up against the far wall. Will waited for a long time while each of the teamsters received his pay and signed his name in the ledger. Will was conscious of the hot food being served at the nearby tables. The aromas and scents of bacon and bread, the bowls of hot porridge, and the sight of others eating tortured him. He wiped saliva from the corner of his mouth and pulled his gut muscles tight to stop the noise of his stomach, which growled in rebellion at not being fed.

After the last driver had left, Will approached the table. He had taken off his blanket in the warmth of the Inn. It was rolled between the straps of his haversack, which hung from his right shoulder. The pay clerk, having closed the ledger and re-buckled the saddle bag, looked annoyed, assuming Will was another teamster arriving late to be paid. Billy greeted him warmly.

"Master Stoner, come join me for breakfast. These teamsters were in such a hurry to get their pay and be off, I haven't yet eaten," he said putting his arm around Will's shoulder and walking with him back into the main room. Billy was several years younger than the Colonel and while a tall man, he had none of his brother's large girth. Will eagerly accepted his invitation and was so busy devouring the porridge, slices of bacon and buttered bread, and drinking from his mug of weak hot coffee, followed by second helpings of each, that he barely said a word.

"It seems that you have not eaten since Springfield," Billy remarked, smiling, as Will wiped his bowl clean with another piece of bread.

"In truth, I have not eaten much for the past two days, sir," Will replied, thinking that his haversack was now empty and he didn't know when or where his next meal was coming from. He knew to eat as if each meal would be his last. "Thank you, sir," Will added somewhat ashamedly, knowing his manners suffered while he wolfed down food.

"Well, my brother did not bring you all the way from Great Barrington to starve you to death," he said. "He is riding along somewhere, overseeing the installation of the cannons and the preparation of fortifications. He has been given a house in Cambridge as headquarters for his Regiment. I must return there before attending to other business and you shall come with me."

They walked from the Inn through the frozen slush. The buildings were shabby, run-down structures, low wooden houses with paint peeling off the siding and crumbled mortar between the slats that let in the cold January air. The homes became noticeably more substantial as they moved further away from the Charles River. Here they were made of brick, with tendrils of smoke wafting out of their chimneys, many with wide double wooden entry doors and matching painted shutters. The cobblestones were icy under foot, which made their walking treacherous.

Will listened to Billy describe the gracious welcome General Washington had given his brother, meeting him west of Cambridge and praising his prodigious effort for the cause. The soldiers had enthusiastically cheered the cannons' arrival, as if that alone would pry the British out of Boston. The cannons had been a boost to their flagging morale, he said. The men grumbled about the constant drilling. They were cold and hungry much of the time, and sorely in need of firewood. Each day many more of them succumbed to the bloody flux and outbreaks of the pox. There were more than fourteen thousand soldiers encircling Boston, although he had to admit most of them were untested in battle and many were ill and unfit for service. Almost six thousand troops, he said, their enlistments up at the end of December, had simply decamped and gone home.

"General Washington calls them 'chimney corner soldiers,'" Billy said, as they hurried along. "The new companies, raised from the other colonies, are eager enough, it seems. The General says they need discipline and training and he is worried there will not be enough time."

"Will the army attack Boston?" Will asked.

"I have heard rumors General Washington is considering it. Nothing is known for the moment." Billy replied. "I have been busy helping my brother. Henry's commission as Colonel was approved by the Congress in Philadelphia while he was bringing the artillery to Cambridge," he said proudly. "Now, he is in charge of all the artillery."

"What about Ensign Holmes? Do you know where I can find him," Will asked.

"He should be with the Mariners at the General's Headquarters. It is half a mile from Cambridge center." As they walked, Billy explained that General Washington had taken over the home of a wealthy Royalist who had fled in fear of his life when threatened by the patriotic Safety Committee of Cambridge.

"The locals still refer to it as the John Vassall house," he said, adding with satisfaction the former owner now lived in meaner dwellings on tighter rations, dependent upon the protection and hospitality of General Howe in Boston. "That will change," he predicted. "When we force the British out of Boston, the place where General Howe now sleeps will be General Washington's Headquarters."

They came to a handsome brick building. "This is my brother's temporary residence until we take Boston," he said. He directed Will to continue up this street until he came to a broad road called Brattle Street and to proceed down it. There would be fewer houses and more open fields. The largest of the homes, the one guarded by troops, he said, was General Washington's headquarters.

"Be certain to return here later. I will tell my brother we have met and you are ready to be of service."

"Yes, sir." Will replied. He would do anything the Colonel asked of him but he had no idea how he could help now that Knox was Commander of Artillery.

Will had no trouble finding General Washington's headquarters. It was a substantial two-story wooden building, light brown in color with black shutters framing the eight large windows, four on each side of the central entrance, as well as the two peaked gables on the roof. Two tall brick chimneys rose at both ends, promising large fireplaces and warmth within. White columns, which supported the triangle over the entrance, made the door seem small in comparison. The imposing structure was enhanced by decorative additional columns on the four corners of the building, placed there as if needed for support of a non-existent marble structure.

Even from a distance, as Will approached, his boots crunching on the snow crusted street, he thought it was the grandest building he had ever seen. A three-foot-high grey stone wall, now partially covered with snow, surrounded the property. It was level across the top around the entire perimeter, indicating it had been constructed by masons and was not some simple farmer's effort to mark off his pastures with stones unearthed by his oxen pulling a plow.

Four sentries barred the long carriage road, lined with tall evergreens, that led up to the Headquarters building. He recognized the familiar navy blue jackets with the broad red cuffs at the wrist and the white canvas breeches of the Marblehead Mariners.

"Pardon, sir" he asked one of the men. "I am looking for Ensign Holmes."

"That will be Lieutenant Holmes you would be seeking," he replied, lowering his musket from the ready position. Even though he held his musket loosely, Will could see he had the powerful shoulders of a man accustomed to rowing for a living. His black hair was pulled back and tied neatly in a queue with a dark blue ribbon.

"Colonel Knox spoke to our Colonel Glover, who recommended

him for promotion. We men voted our approval," he added, "although 'tis a bit hard to swallow—a Mariner promoted for deeds he performed on land." He laughed at the concept. Will liked the easy lilt of his voice.

"He may be down with our Colonel at his house, the big square one over there," he replied, gesturing to the left of the headquarters building, past the leafless trees of an apple orchard. "He just rode hard in, his horse all a lather. And who are you?" he asked, eyeing Will up and down. Will was conscious of his mud-stained breeches and dirty brown jacket. He shifted his haversack to his side, pulled the blanket tighter between the straps, and stood up taller.

"Lieutenant Holmes and I are friends. I was part of the artillery train from Fort Ticonderoga," he said by way of explanation, unsure whether he should add more to persuade the sentry to let him pass.

"Ahh. So you were part of the great trek. 'Twas truly important work you and the Lieutenant did, bringing those guns here. Most of the militiamen in camp have never even seen a cannon." He snorted derisively. "I heard there were high mountains you went over," shaking his head in disbelief and not waiting for Will to respond. "Give me the sweet smell of ocean spray anytime." He was going to launch into a paen to the virtues of the sea but was interrupted by a call from the other sentry. A heavily laden wagon, it's contents covered by a canvas tarpaulin was approaching the entrance. "Well, 'tis back to my duty," he said. "Go on. Pass through," he motioned with a wave of his hand.

Will was halfway up the slushy path when Nat dashed down the steps of the Mariner's headquarters building. When he saw Will, he let out a shout of recognition. They ran forward and embraced, clasping, pounding each other on the back.

"I am so pleased to see you. No. I mean I'm glad you're here but there is important work to be done and you are just the one for it."

Nat had just ridden in from Salem, a distance of slightly more than 17 miles. A privateer had captured the British brigantine *Nancy* three days before and brought her into Salem. She was loaded with six and twelve pound balls too numerous to count, racks of muskets, barrels of powder and tons of musket shot and flint. "We need sleds, wagons and teams to bring this fortuitous gift of arms to Cambridge."

In no time, Will had Big Red and the mare and two of his father's eight other horses in their traces and was through the lines heading to the Mystic River. Behind him, was a hastily assembled small procession of sleds and wagons. Nat, riding a fresh mount, caught up with Will after their little train had crossed the causeway and was already on the road to Marblehead and Salem. His horse trotted alongside for a while but the strong wind made talking difficult. At Nat's suggestion, Will stopped, Nat tied his horse behind the empty sled and joined Will on the seat.

"It is like when we sat together before Glen Falls," Nat said, "though I miss a sack of oats for a cushion."

"I gather you are now a Lieutenant," Will said, beaming at his friend.

"I care not a whit for the rank," he replied. "It is enough my fellow Mariners approved and voted for my promotion," he said with pride. "However, it does have its advantages. I am slightly more acceptable in Anna's father's eyes."

"Where is Anna? Have you seen her?" Will asked grinning.

"She slipped out of Boston less than a month ago and returned to her father's farm. Mr. Edes her employer, together with his wife, are in Watertown, with no need for her services in their temporary quarters. I am relieved because in the letters I found waiting for me, she described the conditions in Boston, especially for a single young girl, as especially perilous."

"So? Did you see her?" Will persisted.

"Of course. I was in Salem on Colonel Glover's orders, outfitting another schooner as a privateer, when I learned she was there. I called on her to see her and to formally ask her father for her hand in marriage."

"And,. . . Go on." Will asked, imagining his friend importuning Anna and she blushing and swooning as when Tom Jones had kissed Sophia's hand.

"Well," Nat continued. "It was," he sighed, "difficult to speak. Her mother and sisters were in the room. The time was short. Mr. Gibbs came in and upon hearing I had been promoted to Lieutenant made clear while it was a mark in my favor, said I probably would be away more rather than less, having a higher rank and greater responsibilities." He shook his head. "I could see that he was impressed but not enough.

I lost courage and did not ask for his consent." He saw Will's look of surprise and disbelief. "It was not the right moment," he explained lamely.

Will quickly changed the subject to cover his friend's embarrassment. He told Nat about the remainder of the trek from Framingham to Cambridge and the installation of the fortification guns on Lechmere Point.

"I am pleased to be of service now but soon I have to find my brother and decide what to do."

"That will have to wait until we liberate Boston. It is too dangerous for you to enter the city. You can write your father and tell him so and also," Nat paused and nudged Will with his elbow, "Elisabeth to whom you have not sent a word since leaving her in Albany."

The entire round trip between Cambridge and Salem took two and a half days. There were many willing and able hands in Salem to load the wagons and sleds. The crew of the American privateer, pleased the *Nancy's* cargo would help the cause of the Revolution and more pleased with their anticipated shares of the prize money, eagerly told their story of the quick chase off the coast of Cape Ann and the short exchange of cannon fire which had made the *Nancy* theirs.

"They were lucky," Nat observed, seated beside Will on the sled, as they rode back to Cambridge. "If Admiral Howe had anticipated we would outfit privateers, he would have sent escort vessels from the fleet lying in Boston harbor. We would have been hopelessly outgunned."

"What happens if our men are captured?" Will asked.

"They will be hung as pirates or imprisoned, which may be worse," Nat replied.

"Would you go privateering? You said the prize money is good."

"It is tempting. I would be Captain and receive the major portion of any prize money, after the backers and outfitters had been paid properly, of course." He pulled his cloak higher over his neck against the northerly wind at their backs. "But now I am betrothed to Anna. I will continue to serve in the Mariners and not put to sea as a privateer." He grinned at Will's surprise.

"When did you ask her father for her hand?" Will said.

"The morning after you and I arrived in Salem."

Nat described in detail how Colonel Glover had ridden with him to Anna's father's farm both in their dress uniforms. The Colonel, a gentleman very well respected in Salem, had vouched for Nat's character and seriousness of purpose, and had not left until Mr. Gibbs had given his consent. Colonel Glover and Anna's father had sealed their understanding with a bottle of brandy, brought by the Colonel and generously left behind as a token of his appreciation for Mr. Gibbs' acceptance of Nat's formal request.

"And now I'm to be wed and Colonel Glover has assigned me to Salem for the outfitting of two more schooners as privateers. Even working at our fastest, which we most assuredly will do, I will be there until mid March. I cannot tell you Will, how happy I am to know I will be with my Anna."

The teamsters delivered the *Nancy's* captured treasure of cannonballs and musket shot to the Cambridge Powderhouse, a tall stone tower capped by a conical roof, where the powder for the artillery and guns was stored. The muskets and flint were unloaded at the main armory. The drivers, as if by pre-arranged signal, drove their now empty sleds and wagons to Cambridge's outskirts and assembled in the cold, outside a paymaster's tent of the Massachusetts Militia. Will was about to follow Nat.

"Where do we go now?" he inquired, turning to watch his friend untie his horse from the rear of the sled.

"Are you so wealthy you will forego your pay?" he asked Will.

"I thought I was helping the Colonel, Colonel Knox, I mean," he said confused.

"You are. The Colonel paid your father for your services to bring the cannons to Cambridge. It is now your turn to be paid for your own services in bringing the *Nancy's* cargo from Salem. Come to the Mariner's Headquarters, and wait for me there if I am gone." He put his hand to his tri-corn and rode off.

An hour later, with ten shillings, the first money he had ever earned for himself, tied securely in a small leather pouch inside his haversack, Will left the militia encampment and drove his sled down the road back toward Cambridge. A crowd of off-duty soldiers dressed in a variety of uniforms were standing behind a line of riflemen leaning nonchalantly, almost carelessly, against a few stacked hay bales. Will stopped his sled and stood up on the seat. He recognized the frontiersmen as MacDowell's Rifles. He watched as one of the rifleman paced off a distance and drove a rectangular board on a wooden peg into the ground with his tomahawk. He affixed a square piece of white paper in the center. The man loped effortlessly back through the light powdered snow.

"That is two hundred yards," he announced to the onlookers, barely short of breath. "Each of us will fire once from here, behind these bales. Then we'll run forward a bit, fall to the ground and shoot. There are ten of us, firing twice. There should be twenty holes in that paper out there."

Will stamped his feet to keep warm and hugged his arms to his chest, tucking his hands under his armpits. The bitter cold did not seem to bother the riflemen, who stood quietly waiting their turn. He watched as the first man knelt in the snow, rested his rifle on the hay bale, fired and stepped back to reload. Will couldn't see whether his shot had hit the paper, but when the tenth man had fired, there was a large black ragged mark in the paper. The riflemen ran toward the target for about twenty or thirty yards, flung themselves on the ground and fired rapidly at the paper. When the last one had finished, one ran the remaining distance, pulled the board and stake out of the ground and brought it back to the watching soldiers. A cheer went up as the board was passed from hand to hand.

"That one on the edge of the paper is mine," one of the riflemen confessed, his voice tinged with disappointment. "I hit my elbow when I fell down to fire and my arm was a tad numb," he said by way of apology.

The soldiers clamored for more demonstrations as others from MacDowell's rifles wandered down from their encampment in the tree line. Will wanted to stay but knew he should not keep Nat waiting. He stopped at a barn to retrieve the other four horses and hitched them to the empty sled.

He made fast time with the eight-horse team on the road to Cambridge and was waved through by the sentries at General Washington's headquarters. Following their directions, he pulled his team into a barn in the far corner of the stone-fenced property. He placed them two to a stall. Big Red and the grey shared one enclosure together. Will knew the food for his eight horses would not be given free. He would have to arrange to pay for it, maybe by labor as a stable hand in exchange, he thought.

He scraped the mud and frozen slush off his boots on a low iron bar outside the door to the Mariner's Headquarters. Inside there were many men, most in uniform, seated on long wooden benches, chatting or waiting their turn to be admitted upstairs to see Colonel Glover. An orderly in charge of the process looked at him quizzically.

"I am here to meet Lieutenant Holmes," Will said in a firm voice, trying to overcome his shabby appearance. "My name is Will Stoner." He took off his battered hat, thinking it would make him seem more respectful.

The orderly smiled in recognition. "Ah, the Lieutenant mentioned you would be by. He said you were to be made comfortable and extended every courtesy as his friend. You can wait for him in that room over there with the fireplace." He pointed to his left.

Will walked into the warm room, removed his haversack and blanket and sat down on a bench in a bay window. He was embarrassed his boots had left tracks from the entrance into the room. Several men, some tradespeople, some officers, overflowing from the crowded entrance hall were seated in armchairs closer to the fire. They ignored him. The civilians were carpenters, sail makers or riggers with proposals for modifying sloops into privateers. The others were merchants anxious to sell provisions for the voyages.

The officers talked more of when and where General Washington would order an attack on Boston, and what role the Mariners would play in ferrying the troops across from either Charlestown or the marshy ground below Cambridge.

"It will have to be a night assault, when the tides are ebbing," one said. "He will order landings at Barton's and Hudson's points, on either side of Mill Pond, and attack the center of the city from two sides."

"Nonsense," another responded. "There will be no need for us and our boats. The General will wait for the ice to freeze on the bays below Cambridge and Roxbury and move the troops across the Pond with a simultaneous straight frontal attack at Boston Neck. [3] It is the only way to neutralize the British Navy's firepower."

"And why is that?" asked the first man.

"Because if our troops at the Neck give close pursuit to the Redcoats, their ships will be unable to fire for fear of hitting their own men."

"They will simply blow our troops to bits as they march down from Roxbury to the Neck," another said. "And it will not just be broadsides from His Majesty's warships. Those forts on the Neck have twelve and twenty-four pounders. It has to be a surprise attack by water. The problem is how to amass the bateaus without the British being alerted."

Will listened to their back-and-forth military talk, envisioning the city as he had seen it from Lechmere Point. A battle was certainly coming. He wanted to be part of it.

Nat stuck his head in the room and beckoned to Will. He nodded at the other officers as Will jumped up from the bench and grabbed his hat and haversack. It was dark outside as they went, almost at a run, past the sentries and down Brattle Street toward Colonel Knox's house. The Colonel had been in Roxbury and Nat had met him, purely by chance, as he crossed the Charles River. Nat had mentioned bringing the shot from Salem and Will's role, and the Colonel had asked to see him. An orderly from the Massachusetts Regiment of Artillery, resplendent in his clean white breeches and dark blue coat, directed them to the Colonel's quarters upstairs.

They knocked and found Colonel Knox immersed up to his shoulders in a large deep wooden tub, washing himself. William Knox was seated at a desk, quill in hand. He smiled, waved at them and continued writing. Nat took the vision of the naked Colonel in stride. Will felt his face flushing and couldn't help but stare at the rolls of white fat around the Colonel's middle. A clean uniform was laid out on the bed.

"Ah, Will," Knox said. "Forgive me for not getting up." He laughed at his own joke. "I have been at Roxbury for two days and nights, mucking around in the mud of the fortifications, and now am wanted at a staff meeting by General Washington. I thought it appropriate to be presentable." He eyed Will's appearance. "You, Master Stoner, are in need of a bath as well. And perhaps some clean clothes. Billy can you see to that?" He turned his head to his brother, who nodded. "The clothes I mean," he said chuckling to his brother. Billy laughed heartily.

"Now, Will. I am in need of your able assistance," the Colonel said, rinsing his shoulders with a sponge. "My Regiment is constantly moving supplies across our entire lines. Balls, shot, powder, flint, victuals and firewood for the men, and hay and oats for the horses. These goods, which are in great demand by every militia unit, have a way of either disappearing or coming up short weight when they arrive." He stood up dripping and wrapped a tan blanket the size of a small tent, around himself, rubbing his body vigorously. Will noticed the last two fingers of his left hand were mere stubs.

Knox caught Will staring. "This is my secret," he said quickly covering the disfigured hand with a corner of the blanket. "A duck-hunting accident in Boston Harbor in July of '73. The musket exploded and blew away parts of my fingers. It is no matter any more but I keep my hand hidden in public. It makes me uncomfortable when people stare."

Will looked away and stammered an apology.

"No need, Will. No need. Now, where were we? Ah, yes," he said, "the supplies. I need trustworthy men to deliver these goods to my Regiment. You will be hired as one of the teamsters. Billy will make the arrangements. And if you happen to see or learn anything untoward, report to me, or Billy if I am unavailable."

"I will certainly do that, sir." Will replied, feeling more at ease now that Colonel Knox had put on his white breeches and was buttoning his shirt.

"How many of your father's horses did you bring?"

"Four span."

"Well, eight are too many for the weight of our supplies. Are you willing to rent the extra horses out?" he asked. Will nodded, intending to keep Big Red and the grey mare for the sled.

"Good. Billy will find haulers or others in need of horses and conduct that business on your behalf. I should think two shillings per week per horse would be fair." Will nodded. He had no price in mind for the horses, having no idea whether they were scarce or plentiful in the area. "And you of course," the Colonel continued, "will be paid the going rate for teamsters for your hauling, plus five shillings a month for being my eyes and ears."

Will recalled the Colonel's speech to the Massachusetts teamsters before the ascent to the Blandford Summit and the campfire talk in Salem among the local wagoners that the Colonel had paid for the trek from Ft. Ticonderoga to Cambridge out of his own pocket, more than 500 pounds. He felt he had to speak, to contribute to the cause, to acknowledge the Colonel's generous spirit and patriotism.

"Sir. If you think it is fair, pay me for what I do as a teamster. But I would do that and more without pay to help you. As for the five shillings, I . . ." He was uncomfortable accepting money from the Colonel for what he regarded as his duty to report anyway, but was too unsure of how to express himself further.

"Nonsense," Knox said, silencing him with a wave of his hand. He sat down on the bed, which sagged under his weight and grunted as he pulled on one of his high black boots. "You are performing a service for me and my Regiment, and deserve to be paid for it. It is less than half the monthly wages of a Continental and you," he pointed at Will, "unlike them, have to pay for your own food and housing. Where are you quartered, Will?"

"He is staying with the Mariners on the grounds of the General's Headquarters," Nat interrupted before Will could answer. "There is room. Our ten companies are not up to full strength in Cambridge," he explained. "Some of our men are away outfitting schooners as armed naval vessels."

Colonel Knox put on his blue coat. It was tailored with tight sleeves faced with red and interspersed with gilt buttons. The two broad slits in the back favored his corpulent figure. He looked so commanding in his resplendent dress uniform that Will almost saluted him on the spot. He completed his outfit by tucking a white handkerchief into the left cuff and wrapping it around the stubs of his fingers.

"So, Master Stoner. It is settled then. You have employment until we free Boston and good warm quarters with Lieutenant Holmes' regiment. Is there something else, perhaps I have forgotten?" he asked, his eyes dancing with mirth.

Will hesitated but inspired by the thought of Elisabeth, spoke up.

"Sir, in Westfield you mentioned that I might have paper and a quill for writing."

"So I recall," Knox said smiling. "You must also write to your father, briefly if you wish, to tell him you are in Cambridge waiting for our Army to enter Boston so you may be reunited with your brother." He walked toward the door, his boots resounding on the scuffed wood floorboards. "I believe there may be a courier with a pouch of letters leaving for General Schuyler and Albany later this week. If you have other correspondence, perhaps to someone in Albany," he said opening the door and winking at Will, "bring it to my headquarters by tomorrow evening and I shall see it is included."

When they were out in the street, Will was overwhelmed by his good fortune. He clutched the precious sheets of paper the Colonel's brother had given him under his coat to protect them against the wind and blowing snow.

"There are three buildings assigned to us as barracks. Sixty men per building. We have allotted ten men to a room and each man has his own cot," Nat said as they walked quickly in the dark back to Brattle Street. It was past seven. There were few civilians on the streets, but crowds of drunken militia staggered about, impervious to the icy winds. "I know the room next to mine has three empty beds. I will see you placed there first and then I have other business to attend to."

Will didn't reply. Already he was composing his letter to Elisabeth in his mind. It would have to be perfect before he wrote it. He would not want there to be cross-outs and he couldn't afford the luxury of throwing away the paper and starting over on a clean sheet.

"All I need for the moment, Nat," he said, "is a quill and ink, and a place to write."

When they reached the Mariners' barracks, Nat established Will in the Officers' room and left him, hunched over, at a small writing desk in front of a single candle. Will ignored the hunger in his stomach and wrote his father first. The words came easily. It was a businesslike letter. He knew his father was not interested in his well-being. Will wrote he could not pass through the American and British lines to make contact with Johan. He added that he was earning money while waiting for the battle of Boston. He had decided he would keep only the money from his own labor and give his father the shillings paid for renting out the horses. After all, they were his.

He folded the paper, sealed it with a drop of wax from the candle, turned it over and wrote his father's name and Schoharie, New York. The farm where he had been born and worked were part of a life he had willingly left behind. He thought of his stepmother, half-brothers and sisters as distant relatives one rarely saw. As for his father, he realized until tonight, he had not thought of him at all. Nat and Colonel Knox were the people he cared about.

His thoughts next turned to Elisabeth and he began to compose his letter to her. This was more difficult. He pondered how to strike the proper balance between describing the dangers of runaway cannons on icy descents and the bitter cold of winter blizzards, and bragging about his ability to overcome these hardships. After a while he settled on a perfunctory muted tone to tell of the trek through the Berkshires and on into Cambridge and a more descriptive, personal and lively tone for his observations of the townspeople in Westfield and Springfield and the army in Cambridge. The intimate portion, his expression of how he missed her and thought of her constantly, was the part he reworked in his mind and mouthed out loud in the empty room. He was not yet ready to commit his thoughts to paper.

Note: Phips Farm was also known as Lechmere Point.

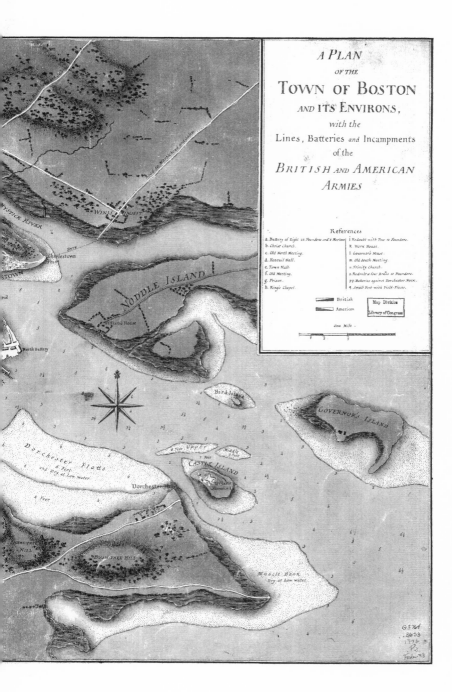

A PLAN

OF THE

TOWN OF BOSTON

AND ITS ENVIRONS,

with the

Lines, Batteries and Incampments

of the

BRITISH AND AMERICAN

ARMIES

References

a. Battery of Eight 24 Pounders and 2 Mortars.
b. Christ Church.
c. Old North Meeting.
d. Faneuil Hall.
e. Town Hall.
f. Old Meeting.
g. Prison.
h. King's Chapel.

i. Redoubt with Two 12 Pounders.
k. Work House.
l. Governor's House.
m. Old South Meeting.
n. Trinity Church.
o. Redoubt a four Brass 12 Pounders.
p.p. Batteries against Dorchester Neck.
q. Small Fort with Field-Pieces.

British
American

Map Division
Library of Congress

One Mile

G3764
.B6S3
1776
.P5

For the next several days, Will drove his sled, pulled by Big Red and the grey, from Roxbury, on the far right of the American lines, to Cambridge, from Cambridge to the fort at Prospect Hill and further on beyond to Cobble Hill where the emplacements faced Charlestown. The Colonel's Artillery Regiment and the guns of other artillery units were positioned in a giant arc on the mainland surrounding Boston and the British fleet riding in its harbor.

Cambridge, because it was at the center of the arc, was the main hub for the stores of supplies. Merchants scoured the countryside for food and sold it at a profit as suppliers to the Army. Munitions were also stored in Cambridge for easy dispersal to the different units. Will hauled cannonballs and kegs of powder, stacks of muskets and boxes of flints, barrels of apples, flour and salted fish, sacks of potatoes and turnips, slabs of salted pork, bags of beans and rice, freshly cut trees or billets of wood and bales of hay and sacks of grain for the horses.

Billy had provided him with a long, nut-colored hunting shirt, a dark brown woolen coat with a high collar, and two pairs of wool stockings. Will wore the hunting shirt over his own linen one, with Elisabeth's blue scarf tied around his neck under the coat, and his mother's red one covering his ears against the bitter cold. With Big Red and the mare pulling the sled, he outpaced the slower teams of oxen used by the local teamsters. He usually arrived at a camp ahead of the others. After unloading the sled and seeing to his team, he was free to walk around, observe the gun crews practicing and listen to the soldiers' talk.

One day, in the early afternoon following his delivery of powder for the artillery emplacements in front of Roxbury, he lingered outside the tall powder tower. It was surrounded by low hills and was placed well back from the cannons. Several men from one of Knox's companies were inside the cold, circular stone building, carefully measuring the precious black powder with a brass scale before pouring it into rectangular canvas bags.

"If you are going to stay and watch," one man said, as Will peered inside, "do not make any sudden moves to alarm us." His linen overalls were smudged grey from the powder.

"I would not do that, sir."

"Better not," another said. "Or we may drop the scale, it will strike a spark on a stone and we will all be blown to kingdom come."

Will noticed there was a thick canvas cloth under the wooden table where the scale was, for just such an eventuality. He realized the men were making fun of him.

"Why do you put the powder in the bags?" he asked one of the men sitting on a bench, sewing the canvas shut with a large curved steel needle.

"So we can charge a cannon with powder and fire quickly," he replied. "Surely you do not think we have the time to pour the powder down the barrel in the heat of battle? Do you?" He laughed at the thought and looked to his companions for approval of his comment.

"Now, Walcott, not everyone can be as smart as you first time out," said the one who was working the scale. "The lad is only curious and that is a good thing in a person." He looked up quickly from his work and nodded at Will. "The amount of powder we put in determines how far the ball will carry. These are light loads for dry firing later today. The Lieutenant said we are to have gun exercises this afternoon. Then it will be the Redcoats' turn to be on the receiving end of our shot."

"That will happen pretty soon," Walcott added. "The Colonel is as eager to begin bombarding Boston as a terrier is to catch a wharf rat."

"The trouble is," the man at scale replied, "the Redcoats, unlike wharf rats, may not wait to be caught. They can row across to the lowlands as they did earlier this month, and come after us before we are ready."

"Well," the man named Walcott retorted, "we extended the line and built redoubts below Roxbury and on either side of the Upper Neck for the very event. With the cannons we have, we will give the Regulars a warm reception they do not expect."

Will listened to more of their talk, thankful to be out of the biting wind. He delayed his return to Cambridge, even though he had not slept there a single night since accepting the Colonel's assignment. There was no load for him to transport there anyway. He left the powder tower and drove his sled over the crusty dirty ice to the gun emplacements. He walked freely among the tents of the men of the Massachusetts Artillery and beyond them, down the well-trod, slushy pathways toward the cannons. They were a mix of ugly iron howitzers and mortars, mounted on heavy wooden blocks without wheels, several twelve and twenty four-pounders and the more lithe, mobile three, six and nine pounders, with their large oversized wheels. He thought he recognized some of the guns from the trek, particularly the Coehorn mortars, because they were stubby and ungainly. The only one he was sure of was the Old Sow which he had seen close up. He heard a shouted command behind him and saw the gun crews emerge from their tents and line up. They marched forward, each crew taking their position on both sides of their piece, and waited. Will moved away from the emplacements and walked back to where his horses were tethered.

"You there," he heard a voice call to him. "We need to move powder to the cannons. Do you know where the powder tower is?"

"Yes sir," Will replied. As he hitched his team to the sled, Will heard the Lieutenant reprimand his Sergeant. The powder was supposed to have been in place before the drill began. Will helped the soldiers load the canvas bags on the sled. He drove the sled down the line of artillery and remained in his seat as the gun crews at each position removed the bags and stacked them in the wooden powder boxes. At the end of the emplacements, he turned the sled back toward the tree line and tethered the horses. Then, on impulse, he untied Big Red and led him to a place about thirty feet behind the nearest cannon. It was one of the

Coehorns. The gun commander shouted orders from his position at the left side of the mortar near the touchhole. The mortar was wormed and sponged. The commander reprimanded the sponger for not using enough water. The charge was rammed home, the quill placed in the touchhole, and the gun commander shouted his warning of "Primed."

Will moved his hands up the reins and held them close to Big Red's huge jaw. "Easy, easy," he said, tightening his grip at the command of "Give Fire." The flame sputtered down the powder in the quill. At the loud boom, the horse jerked his head up, wrenching Will's arms, and hurriedly backed up, wide-eyed with fear.

"Easy, easy. It's all right," Will repeated, moving Big Red forward a few steps to where he had been standing. He calmed him down by stroking his neck and offering him a handful of oats from his coat pocket. The horse snuffled the oats, his rough upper lip brushing against Will's hand.

Will walked Big Red through the snow to the next emplacement. Another mortar. He kept the same distance and braced himself for the horse to pull back, holding him firmly in place.

He continued the process, walking down the line to the first cannon. It was the Old Sow. He knew from the firing at Westfield it would be louder than the mortars. He held on tightly to the reins, but to his pleasure, at the shout of "Give Fire," Big Red reacted no differently than he had at the firing of the two mortars, only jerking his head up and backing up a few paces.

By the time the two of them had reached the end of the line, Big Red responded to the lighter booms of the six and nine pounders by standing tensely in place, lifting his head up before lowering it for his reward of oats. Will's hand was raw from the horse's saliva freezing on his skin. Satisfied with Big Red's performance, he determined to take him to at least one firing of artillery and muskets a day if he could, moving closer each time. He intended to train the horse to stand still behind a cannon when it was fired. He would also remember to wrap a rag around his hand before offering the treats.

It was dark when Will arrived at the Mariners' barracks in Cambridge. [1] He watered and fed the horses, rubbed them both down and left them content together in one stall. He scraped his boots at the entrance to his barracks building and pushed open the door to the room where Nat had said he could stay. By the candlelight he saw three men, two of whom appeared to have just come off sentry duty. One was taking off his short navy blue wool jacket, the other had removed his hat and was retying his queue with a scarlet ribbon that matched the color of the facing on his jacket. The third was sitting on his cot in a long shirt, bare legged, sewing a seam in his canvas pants. He was black. Will examined him in the candlelight. He had never been this close to a Negro before. The man had small ears beneath tightly curled hair and a broad nose between high cheekbones. His legs were thick and muscular and, Will noticed, without much hair. At first, Will assumed he was the servant to the other men. He thought otherwise as soon as the man spoke.

"And who be you?" the black man said, pointing at Will with his long needle. Will noticed the heavily muscled forearms and broad shoulders, typical of the other Mariners. He was confused.

"I am Will Stoner, a friend of Lieutenant Holmes," he stammered. "He said I could stay in the barracks and showed me this room." He glanced around at the empty beds. "Nat, I mean Lieutenant Holmes, said some of the men are away and there are cots available."

"Well, if the Lieutenant approves of you, who are we to gainsay nay," the black man replied. He looked at the other two. "Right, what say you." Will thought he saw the black man wink at them.

"I am not certain," the taller of the two said, laying his jacket on the bed and scratching his armpit. "That would mean four of us in the room together. There are ten beds but it was nicer with just the three of us."

"It will be acceptable to me if Will adheres to the barracks rules, like the rest of us have to do," the other replied.

"Oh, I will definitely do so," Will replied too eagerly. "Tell me what they are and I will comply."

"Well," the tall man said, "first, no women in the barracks." He paused, pulling off one of his boots to reveal a big toe sticking through a hole in his right stocking, then added "after the shift change at two a.m."

"The men coming in off duty need their sleep," the black man added by way of explanation.

"Next," the tall man continued, "no rum, brandy or hard liquor allowed ever, unless it is shared with all. Next, no chamber pots under the beds- - - you go outside for that and use the latrine at all times; and finally, one bath a week is required, no matter how cold the weather or water."

"Or whether you need it or not," the black man added, drawing his needle through the canvas and examining the seam, without looking at Will.

"I am willing to abide by the barracks' rules," Will replied with a tremor of anger in his voice, "but have the courtesy to tell me the true rules and not mock me." He looked from one to the other. They broke into smiles, having had their good-natured fun with a newcomer.

The black man stood up. In his bare feet he was shorter than Will but, like Nat, very solid and brawny. "The rules about the chamber pots, latrine and bathing are the true ones. We do not allow drinking or wenching in the barracks at any time. We are, after all, God-fearing seamen." He put out his hand. "My name is Adam Cooper." The tall man introduced himself as Solomon Vining. His unusually long arms and large big-knuckled hands belonged more to a farmer than a fisherman. The other, Jeremiah Fisk, had deep-set sad eyes capped by thick bushy eyebrows, which gave him a melancholy look. His crooked smile revealed two pointed upper teeth closely grown together on the right side, which pushed his lip outward, seemingly in a snarl. Will shook hands with each one, feeling their thick callused palms.

"You should not have misled the lad as to barracks rules, Solomon. There is enough whoring and drunkenness among the militias in their camps," Jeremiah said. "And with your joking, you forgot the rule that all able-bodied men must attend Sunday sermon before the drill."

"You can have any of those three beds," Solomon said, ignoring Jeremiah's comments and gesturing to the cots without any sea chests beneath them. "Best to choose toward the center to be away from the end walls. It is colder there."

"We lack much opportunity to spend time with strangers," Jeremiah said after Will had picked out a cot, taken off his coat and haversack and hung his two scarves on a peg over the bed. "Since we are sharing our barracks room with you, we need to know who you are, where you come from and how you know the Lieutenant." Adam and Solomon nodded in agreement. Adam stopped his sewing and all three stared at him, waiting for him to begin.

Will was apprehensive at first, stuttering nervously through a few details about his father's farm in Schoharie. But he warmed to the story, starting with the loading of the cannons at Fort Ticonderoga. He told them of the crossing of the frozen Hudson at Albany, almost losing the thread of his tale, thinking of his arm around Elisabeth and the smell of her hair brushing against his face. He described the Massachusetts teamsters' refusal to proceed and Colonel Knox's speech, surprising himself at how much he remembered of the Colonel's words, although he might have had some of it in different order. He detailed the bitter cold and the harsh, slow struggle through the Berkshires until they reached the Westfield River Valley. "After that, we slogged through the mud to Cambridge," he said, omitting the departure of the teamsters from New York, the freezing cold nights and his ever present daily hunger.

Emboldened by their pleased reaction to his recounting the trek, and their favorable comments about the way he described Nat, who they obviously held in high regard, Will questioned them about the Marblehead Mariners. It was only fair, he said, that they tell him about themselves as well. It was Adam's story he wanted to hear. He had never been in the company of a black man before. Solomon went first followed by Jeremiah. Both men came from fishing families. Their fathers, and their grandfathers before them, had taken to the seas, catching cod, halibut and mackerel, selling them to fishmongers in Boston, or to merchants to be dried, salted and packed in barrels for "the Popish Catholics and their hocus-pocus meatless Lent practices," as Jeremiah put it, using his shirt sleeve to wipe away the saliva that escaped where his defective teeth pushed his lip out.

"And you, Adam?" Will asked, barely able to contain his curiosity.

"Jeremiah mentioned barrels, and indeed it is fitting because it is where my story begins." Will had avoided staring at him but now since he was speaking he was free to look directly at him. Adam's teeth were a dazzling white in comparison to the stained yellow and brown color of Solomon's and Jeremiah's. The skin inside his lips seemed pinker. Will thought it might just be the contrast to his skin color which was lighter than charcoal but darker than the old oak table at his father's farm. Adam's voice was deep but as he spoke Will could detect no difference between his accent and those of Solomon and Jeremiah. All spoke with that broad enunciation he had grown accustomed to, listening to Nat for the past month and a half.

"My father," Adam said, drawing out the a sound and dropping the r at the end, "was born into slavery. He bought his freedom in the year '54 for twenty-seven pounds, from his master in New York City. There he remained to work, and in another year he had earned enough money to purchase my mother's freedom as well. She was a house slave for my father's former master's wife," he added by way of explanation. "When I was born in 1756, my parents were already living in Boston where my father worked as a cooper. He also did some metal working, making rims for wagon wheels, runners for sleds and such. It followed naturally from doing the hoops for the barrels." He looked at Solomon and Jeremiah. "You two, whom I have known for five or six years, have never heard this part."

The four of them were on two beds facing each other, the candle closer to Adam, casting a flickering shadow of his silhouette on the far wall. Will observed all their shadows were black in the candle light, Adam's being no darker than his. That made sense, he thought. A white candle and a black table cast the same shadows.

"My father decided there would be no slave name for me. Not his last name, Gooding, which had been his master's family name. And not a slave first name, the masters used to give, taken from Roman history, such as Cato or Caesar." /[2]

"We have a few named like that in the Mariners," Solomon interrupted. "There's Quintus Gill and Titus Fuller."

"And Fortunatus Fleming and Caesar Winship," Jeremiah added.

"You mean, you are not the only black in the Mariners," Will blurted out.

"Solomon and Jeremiah just named four others," he replied quickly with an edge to his tone, pointing out the obvious. "And there are several mixed bloods from the Azores as well." Adam saw Will's puzzlement. "Those are islands off the coast of Portugal in the Atlantic Ocean," he added by way of clarification. "You need to learn some geography," he said, pointing his finger at Will.

"Get back to your naming," Solomon reminded him, stretching his long frame on his cot.

Adam nodded. "My father decided since I was the first in our family not born a slave he would call me Adam. After the first man. And then, because he was a barrel maker, he took the name Cooper as our family name. So that is how I am named as I am," he concluded and stood up. He pulled his white canvas breeches on and then his boots.

"Enough of this talking. There may be food for us in the kitchen, behind the General's headquarters. Otherwise, we need to repair to the common room and see what remains available. You are welcome to join us," he said to Will, motioning for him to follow.

Over the next few days, when Will was not on the icy roads hauling provisions to the artillery companies, or training Big Red during the dry fire drills, he joined the men in the common room of their barracks building for the late-afternoon meal, and listened to their speculation about the battle to come. Most expected General Washington to order an attack by water, launching south of Charlestown and landing just north of the Mill Pond, accompanied by a simultaneous direct assault at The Neck.

It was Adam who urged Will to recount Colonel's Knox's speech before the ascent of the Blandford Summit to the Mariners crammed in the common room. There were about thirty men at the time. Some continued their conversations, but as Will recited from memory the Colonel's description of the impact of the Coercive Acts and the suffering of the people of Boston from the occupation of their homes and the denial of their rights, they ceased talking. There were nods of agreement as they listened intently to Knox's praise of the innocent citizens who died at the Boston Massacre, the bravery of the militias at Lexington and Concord, the savagery and pillaging of the Regulars on their retreat and the lonely, courageous stand of the old soldier at Menotomy. "They left him for dead and the doctor counted fourteen bayonet wounds on his body," Will said, repeating the Colonel's account, adding that he himself would like to visit the old man to pay his respects. He concluded with the Colonel's exhortation to the Massachusetts teamsters to continue as part of the noble train of artillery so future generations in Massachusetts would live as free men without fear of arbitrary rule by King or Parliament, free to speak their own minds and live under laws they themselves had made.

The room was silent for a moment, the men mesmerized by the Colonel's words. Then the Mariners broke into prolonged cheers. Will knew they were not cheering for him but blushed anyway. His recitation of the Colonel's speech gained him some notoriety. He was invited to the other barracks to perform, and in return to eat in their mess. He improved his delivery with each telling as he became more confident and recalled more of what the Colonel had said and how he had said it. He even picked up some of Knox's intonation and rhythm, although he never tried to imitate his accent.

He was accepted by the Mariners, whether for his oration or for the squash, potatoes, turnips, pickled onions, beets, dry corn and peas, and occasional pears or apples Will contributed to the common meals. He readily purchased food from farmers willing to part with something stored in their stone-walled, dirt-floored root cellars, or in the simpler charcoal-lined pits, mounded and covered by corn stalks. Most of the Mariners were only five or six years older than Will. He regarded himself as simply in the company of many older brothers, and settled gratefully and comfortably into the routine of barracks life.

On Saturday, Will returned to the barracks early, after a short run to deliver a light load of tent canvas, poles and cooking pots from a warehouse in Cambridge to one of Knox's artillery companies, posted temporarily along the road to Roxbury. During the day he had been composing another letter to Elisabeth in his mind. He had decided he would not wait for her reply to his first letter. Instead, he would inform her of his life with the Mariners guarding General Washington and his constant thoughts of her. He would ask the Colonel's brother when another courier might be leaving for Albany.

He arrived at his barracks building just as Adam and others were marshalling in the main room for their shift as sentries. Will watched the two uniformed columns of ten men each march out smartly down the road to the main entrance and disperse evenly along both sides of the stone wall. There were two other black men among the twenty sentries. The fresh snow powder, which had fallen before dawn and had turned into slush under the late morning sun, had frozen back into dirty, treacherous ankle turning ice as temperatures dropped by mid-afternoon. He sat down at a table, first making sure there was no food grease to stain the paper. Carefully, he removed his remaining sheet which he kept protected behind the inside cover of The History of Tom Jones. He was almost finished reading it. He would have to ask the Colonel for another book soon. Taking the inkwell and quill from the mantle, he loosened Elisabeth's scarf from around his neck and began to write.

Two shots rang out followed by loud cries of "Marblehead Mariners to me." He heard the pounding of boots on the wooden floors as the Mariners erupted from their barracks. Will jumped up and dashed out, sprinting toward the sentries at the gate, a distance of more than fifty yards. He was aware other Mariners were pouring out of their buildings in response to the alarm. Ahead, Will saw a group of militia men, clad in brown hunting shirts and leggings the color of dead leaves, pushing the Mariner sentries back from the entrance road. Others clambered over the stone wall and attacked the remaining sentries, some of whom were already on the ground buried under a mass of brown-shirted men.

Will was slightly ahead of the Mariners from his barrack. He launched himself at a man who sat astride one of the sentries banging his head against the hard frozen ground. Will's impact knocked the man off and Will drove his elbow hard into his throat and punched him in the face for good measure. He rolled over and grabbed at the legging of another running by, felt the bony ankle beneath the fabric, and yanked hard with both hands. The man fell on his stomach and Will was on him instantly, kneeing him in the small of his back and jerking his head up by the hair before slamming his face into the icy slush.

He fought with a berserk rage, lashing out with his fists and feet at any brown-clad soldier, sometimes standing, sometimes rolling on the ground, snarling, gouging, biting, barely aware it was his own voice that was screaming in anger. The cold air caught in his lungs. The sprint from the barracks made his breath come in gasps. Still he fought on. He was aware of being grabbed, his arm almost wrenched from its socket, but he spun away and jumped on the back of a militiaman who was intent on punching a downed Mariner.

All around him, men were fighting, singly or in groups, slipping on the frozen ice, cursing, yelling and shouting at they went at each other. It seemed as if the entire field was filled with swarms of the nut-brown-clothed militia attacking the outnumbered blue jacketed Mariners.

Will heard someone shout, "Get the negrahs. Over there, over there," and turned just as he was punched on the back of his head by a blow meant for his nose. He staggered forward, fell rolling to his right to avoid a kick, grabbed at the foot, lost his grip on the man and was left holding a worn leather moccasin. He saw a tall, wiry man jumping at him. He managed to get his knee up in time to land an effective blow to the groin before the man's weight knocked Will's head against the hard ice. His vision blurred. Instinctively, he grabbed the man by the ears and twisted his head hard, rolling his assailant off him.

Groggy, down on his hands and knees, panting to regain his breath, Will wondering why his hand hurt so much. He noticed his thumb was at a strange angle. He was vaguely aware of shouts of "the General, the General," and cries of "Stop fighting, Stand down, all of you. Stand Down." The ice was cold on his knees and the palms of his hands. He forced himself to get up. All around him Mariners and the militia were standing, recovering from the shock of the fighting, bruised, bleeding, with clothing torn, holding broken wrists or arms, or hobbling on injured feet, bashed knees or twisted legs.

"Marblehead Mariners. Line up by Companies," Colonel Glover commanded. "Lieutenants. Get your men in order. Immediately." The Colonel, his hat in his hand, his fiery red hair loose and blowing, strode among his men as they shuffled into place. The anger in his voice was controlled. His cold blue eyes stared through the Mariners, while he waited for them to form up.

In the gathering darkness, the militia men limped off the field, through the entrance and down Brattle Street toward the town. Will turned back toward Headquarters and saw General Washington dismount from his white horse. His manservant walked their two horses around the side to the barn. The General did not look back as he strode into Vassall House. Will, not belonging to any company just stood where he was, next to a column of Mariners.

"You there," Colonel Glover ordered pointing at Will with his crop. Will looked down at his boots. "Be gone with your fellows or I will have you arrested and thrown in the brig."

"He is one of us, Sir," Solomon said stepping forward and out of his line. Solomon was bleeding from his nose and mouth. There was an ugly red welt on his throat. "A friend of Lieutenant Holmes, Sir. He is staying with us in the barracks."

"Is that so, Lieutenant?" Glover asked angrily, turning toward Nathaniel.

"Yes, Colonel." Nat said, limping toward Glover from his place in front of his Company, favoring one leg. "This is Master Stoner, Sir. The young man I told you about on our return from Salem." Nat held a handkerchief to a bleeding scrape on his forehead.

"Well, Master Stoner," Colonel Glover said, eyeing Will up and down, noting his torn sleeve and breeches and the bruises, lumps and cuts on his face that Will felt but couldn't see. "I hope you gave better than you received."

"That I did, Sir," Will replied, drawing himself erect and involuntarily wincing from a sudden stabbing pain in his ribcage.

"The good Book tells us it is better to give than to receive," the Colonel said loudly for the Mariners to hear, the anger in his blue eyes diminishing. "I am proud you Mariners fulfilled your religious obligations today." He turned to Lieutenant Holmes. "Organize an able-bodied complement of sentries for the evening. All others are to return to barracks. There will be doctors and surgeons making the rounds to address your wounds. Now march the men off smartly. I have to report to General Washington along with Captain Morgan."

When Will returned to the barracks, two steaming iron pots of boiling water hung from long sturdy hooks in the fireplace. Several cots had been moved into the common room. The more seriously injured, those with broken bones and dislocated limbs, lay on them, closer to the warmth of the fire, waiting for the surgeons. The others washed their own cuts and bruises and recounted the fighting. Will hobbled up to the fireplace, took a hot wet cloth and wiped his face, wincing when he raised his right arm and again when he tried to use his left hand. He put the cloth to his mouth and gently pressed it against his split and swollen lower lip. He loosened Elisabeth's scarf around his neck and absent-mindedly began cleaning the dirt from it. Some of the stains did not come off. He realized her scarf now was dyed with some of his blood. The thought appealed to him as if he somehow was more closely bonded to her than before.

"You have received your baptism of fire but only on land, Will. Nothing is meaningful until you have been to sea." Will turned and saw Adam sitting on a cot, his jacket hanging off one shoulder, the arm at the socket of the other out of the joint. The skin of his face was a mass of darker bruises, one ear was swollen and Will thought a chunk was missing from the lower lobe.

"I do not feel like going to sea right now and you do not look ready to row me," Will replied.

"Oh come spring, after we retake Boston, I will row you out of the harbor and we will catch fish, Will. That is a promise. You need to experience the rhythm of the sea." He smiled at Will through swollen lips. "You are one of us now. The Colonel himself approved it."

Will remembered seeing Adam swing his rifle as a club, before going down in a mass of brown-clad militia. The exhilaration and thrill of the fight drained out of him. Will's body now sent urgent signals to his brain he was in pain. He found space and sank down against the wall near the doorway, aching and exhausted and vaguely aware of the conversations around him. He looked at his crooked thumb. The sharp stab in his ribs was present every time he shifted his weight or took a deep breath. He didn't recall being kicked. Maybe it happened when he had fallen on the frozen ground. A dull throbbing from the top to the back of his head caused him to gingerly feel the large knot under his thick hair, which was matted and sticky. There was congealed blood on his fingers. He wiped the blood off on his pants. They were torn at one knee. He held the now-warm cloth to the back of his head and pressed it against the wound.

Will surveyed the room, attempting to see how badly his friends were injured. On the floor near one cot he saw his precious piece of paper, muddy and unsalvageable. It had been tread upon countless times as the men returned from the melee. He noticed thankfully that the inkwell and quill had been returned to their usual place on the mantle. He would have to ask the Colonel for more paper. There was something else he was wanted from the Colonel. He couldn't remember it now. Through his pain and grogginess he heard his stomach rumble and felt hunger pangs. He stifled a laugh so that it came out as more of a snort. He didn't want the others to think he was being giddy.

"What I want to know is, how did it start?" a loud voice demanded. "One moment we are on normal sentry duty, the next, these foul-smelling backwoods militia are charging the gate and climbing over the walls."

"Did they not know this is General Washington's headquarters? At first I was afraid they were after the General."

"No, they were after us," another Mariner said.

"I saw the General," Jeremiah said. Everyone was quiet. He dabbed at his bleeding mouth. His lips were swollen and cracked from the blows he had taken. One side of his face was a solid bruise from forehead to lower jaw, as if he had been kicked in the head or stomped on. Someone gave him a mug of warm water, he took a sip, swished the liquid around inside his mouth and spat out bloody liquid into a bowl. His two teeth which had grown together and earned him the nickname "Snaggletooth" were broken off. They were now jagged stubs protruding from his swollen bloody gum.

"I was to the right of the entrance about thirty feet back when I saw General Washington on his big white horse come sailing over the stone wall at full gallop." Jeremiah paused to run his tongue over the rough edge of his broken teeth. "His manservant, Lee, jumped the wall right behind him." Jeremiah rinsed his mouth again. "It would be nice to have something to drink," he said wistfully.

"Go on with the story, Jeremiah," someone said. "Tell us what you saw," another yelled impatiently.

"Well," Jeremiah continued, smiling at the attention. "The General leaped off his horse even before it had stopped. He grabbed two of the militiamen from behind by the neck and shook them like geese readied for the chopping block. I was in front and saw their faces. Their eyes were bulging out from the tightness of the General's grip. All the time he was shouting 'Stop fighting. Cease this immediately.'" [3]

"So that is how it ended," someone said and there was a murmur of men recounting where they were and what they were doing or having done to them at the time the General intervened.

The conversations died down as the exhaustion, cold and shock set in. The Regiment's surgeon, Dr. Timothy Thaxter, arrived, accompanied by an assistant. The doctor was a plump man with ruddy cheeks and frizzy powdered hair, which fluffed out on the sides of his head like uncombed cotton. He removed his cloak that hung over his shoulders, held it behind him, without looking, for his assistant to grab, and scanned the room.

"Well, it does not appear as bad as the other barracks I came from. No one unconscious or gouged-out eyes in here, it seems."

The doctor cut a comical figure with his yellow waistcoat buttoned tightly across his broad stomach. However, Will sensed from their polite greetings that the Mariners knew and respected him. He handled the more serious cases of the men on the cots himself, while his assistant made the rounds of the room, feeling for broken bones and dressing cuts and bruises. Will watched as Dr. Thaxter felt Adam's dislocated joint with his long fingers. He couldn't hear what he said to Adam. Adam nodded, folded a cloth into a square and bit down on it. The doctor stood up, his ample rear blocking Will's view, and manipulated Adam's arm. It was accomplished quickly. When the doctor sat down next to Adam, his friend's arm was back in its socket and Adam was wiping the sweat off his brow with the cloth. Will thought his face looked more grey than black. That must be how blacks turn pale, he thought.

When the assistant put down his bag and knelt next to Will, he first examined the knot on the back of his head. He cleaned the blood from Will's hair, using a cloth he dipped in a basin of warm water. Will heard a snipping sound, but the assistant held his head firmly so he couldn't move.

"Do not worry. A young man like you. It will grow back in a

week's time." He let go of Will's head and dropped his shorn brown hair on the floor.

The assistant knelt facing him and pulled Will's eyelids up, looked in each eye and told him to follow his finger with first one eye and then the next. Will did as he was told, watching the assistant's finger move from left to right and back and forward.

"Good. You will be shipshape in no time," he said reaching forward and taking Will's bad hand. Before he could object, the assistant pulled Will's dislocated thumb forward and twisted it toward his palm. Will yelped in pain.

"The thumb will be sore for a few days. Try not to strain it. And there is no need to thank me," he said, with a smile, moving on to examine the Mariner next to Will. Will looked down at this hand and cautiously wiggled his thumb.

"Not too hard now," the assistant said, looking up from cleaning a nasty-looking abrasion near a Mariner's eye. "You do not want it to fall off. You will need it to hold a fork or spoon when the Colonel sends over food."

True to the assistant's prediction, cooks soon brought in loaves of bread and pots of stew, with thick chunks of beef lurking in the dark brown gravy, amidst peas, onions and beans. The men shared the food, taking small portions at first to ensure all received an equal amount. Those with swollen or split lips, missing teeth and bruised jaws ate more slowly than the others. By common, unspoken consensus, it was only after the Mariners with mouth wounds had finished their first portions that the men who had eaten more quickly took second helpings.

Some of the men had wandered off to their rooms before Lieutenant Holmes returned to the barracks. The bruise on his forehead had turned an ugly purple color. He limped to the fire, warming his hands, and then turned toward those of his men who remained. They were slumped against the walls or seated on the few chairs and on the cots of the more seriously injured. Will estimated there were almost forty men still in the common room, all attentively waiting for the Lieutenant to speak.

"I have just come from the Colonel," Nat announced. "He and Captain Morgan met with General Washington, who is satisfied the

Mariners did not provoke the attack and properly defended themselves and his Headquarters. The General however, is greatly displeased with soldiers in his army fighting among themselves and the lack of discipline among the militias. He will soon be issuing general orders to be read to all troops. Anyone, militia or Continental levy, engaging in such unmilitary conduct in the future will be severely dealt with."

"Who is this Captain Morgan and his militia?" someone asked. There were cries of "Why did they attack the Headquarters? Where do they come from? Was any Mariner badly hurt?" Nat held up both hands for silence.

"They are Morgan's Rifles," Nat responded, "named after the man who recruited them, Daniel Morgan. There are two hundred and fifty-five of them, and most are from the western part of Virginia. Colonel Glover told me Captain Morgan claims his men marched 600 miles in twenty-one days to help General Washington end the occupation of Boston."

"So they can march. So what," one Mariner called out. "Do not these ignorant backwoodsmen know they are supposed to fight the British and not us?"

There were murmurs of assent and Will caught words like "illiterate deer hunters," and "buckskin idiots," before Nat again signaled for silence.

"General Washington demanded an explanation. Colonel Glover said Captain Morgan claims that when his men arrived last week, a delegation approached Vassell House to pay their respects to the General. They were turned away in a rude manner by armed Negroes in uniform."

"Not true," some cried. "They are illiterates and liars," others called out. "Look to the sentry rosters," another yelled.

"I am only recounting what our Colonel said Captain Morgan represented to General Washington," Nat reminded them. "Captain Morgan also told the General it was objectionable, disagreeable and degrading for his men to serve in the same army as Negroes dressed as soldiers. He told the General that he, as a Virginian, should understand." [4]

"And what did the General respond," Solomon asked, glancing at Adam first.

"General Washington told Captain Morgan he was Commander of the Continental Army and not a militia officer from Virginia. The Colonel said he had never seen the General so angry. He reminded Captain Morgan that he decided who would be his Headquarters Guard and that the Mariners are and will be his Guard for as long as the General is in Massachusetts."

The room erupted into hooting and clapping and cries of "Long Live General Washington," and "Three Cheers for the General."

Nat waited until they had finished the lusty last huzzah. "Several of our men have been seriously injured," he said grimly. "Titus Fuller had one eye gouged out. Caesar Winship is still unconscious. Dr. Thaxter is hopeful he will improve." The room was quiet. "It seems the men of Morgan's Militia singled out the black freedmen of our Regiment for special attention." His words hung over the room before he added, "I am pleased Adam emerged relatively unscathed." Adam made a fist and raised his good arm in defiance, to loud cheering. "Colonel Glover said there were about 200 of them involved in the fight, to 123 of us," Nat added. "Tomorrow, all those who are able should assemble for roster. We want the General to know we are able to continue to serve."

Sunday morning dawned dull and grey with a low ominous sky promising more snow. A bitter northerly wind added to the men's discomfort as they lined up before breakfast in ranks, their bodies stiff and aching. Will, with the approval of the men in his barracks, lined up with Lt. Holmes' company, filling in a gap made by several Mariners too badly injured to report for active duty. He held no rifle and stood in place with his hands alternately held awkwardly at his sides or tucked inside his coat for warmth, looking decidedly unmilitary in his torn breeches and brown coat.

Colonel Glover sat astride his horse at the front of the columns of Mariners. He opened the Bible resting on his saddle horn, read a prayer and added a special plea for the Mariners who were in need of God's healing powers, and led them in singing a Psalm. Will was aware he was one of the few who did not know the words. The Colonel read a brief chapter from the Bible, cognizant that the cold made his men's pain and stiffness worse.

"General Washington has asked me to convey his appreciation for your devotion to duty. He has expressed his continued confidence in you, and I have given him my assurance that you will fully satisfy his expectations. This means you will set aside any feelings for revenge or any ill will you may harbor within your hearts. So long as we serve as the General's Headquarters Guard, each and every one of you must do your duty properly, acting with polite firmness and rectitude to all who approach Vassell House. The honor of the Regiment demands nothing less from you. I know you will act appropriately."

He looked over his men and smiled for the first time that morning. "Dr. Thaxter has advised me that nothing would help you to heal better than healthy food in ample supply. You will not be disappointed at today's meal. General Washington has ordered cured Virginia hams from his own larder, and fresh beef and mutton to be provided to the men of the Marblehead Mariners in recognition of your stalwart duty as his Guard."

The men greeted this news with three rousing cheers for General Washington and waited to be dismissed.

"Lieutenants. Have your Ensigns read out the day's orders to your companies."

Nat saluted, pivoted and shouted a command to the Ensigns at the head of each file of men. The orders read by the Ensigns were short."The rosters for today's sentries are posted. Those not on duty are to clean and repair your uniforms. The necessities will be provided. Uniforms must be ready for inspection by day's end. There will be no drills today. Forward march in file to barracks."

Will stayed with the ranks until they were dismissed and sought out Nat, who was standing outside the red brick barracks building.

"How are you," he asked, looking at Nat's purple bruised temple.

"It is a good thing for me that Colonel Glover obtained Anna's father's commitment to our marriage. My God, it is less than a week from today, and I will be limping into Church looking like a common tavern brawler. And you? No lasting damage?" he asked, as they walked slowly away from the barracks and the men.

Will showed Nat that his thumb was in its right place and removed his slouch hat to reveal the scab on the shaved spot on his head. "My head aches less this morning. I can tolerate the pain in my ribs. How are Titus and Caesar?"

Nat looked glum. "Dr. Thaxter will sew Titus' eye lid shut today or tomorrow. Caesar is still unconscious. The Doctor is of the opinion he may never recover and has warned the Colonel. If he dies, the Colonel does not want the men to go into Cambridge seeking revenge." He held Will by the elbow and drew him closer.

"Privately, the Colonel has asked General Washington for permission to file charges against Captain Morgan if the General will convene a courts martial."

"Why does Colonel Glover need permission to do that?"

"He does not. Will understand, the Colonel does not want to embarrass General Washington. If the charges are made public and the General does not convene the court, it will create the impression the General favors his fellow Virginians over Massachusetts men. This could reverberate at the Congress in Philadelphia and give comfort to those who are disappointed with the General for failing to drive the British from Boston."

"So, what is to be done?"

"Colonel Glover hopes to persuade the General. If he cannot, he does not want the Mariners to make matters worse by exacting an eye for an eye, so to speak." Nat lowered his voice. "I tell you if the Colonel had his way, Captain Morgan would be hanging from a gibbet like the pirate spawn he is."

"Nat. I barely grasp the politics you talk about. Now I do not even understand your words. What is pihrot spaahn?" he said with exasperation, imitating his friend's accent.

"The Colonel says that Captain Morgan is somehow related to Henry Morgan, the infamous pirate who pillaged and burned his way up and down the coast. As a seafaring man and himself from a shipping merchant's family, Colonel Glover has a special aversion to pirates. Besides, he said that Captain Morgan is a poorly educated gambler, with a reputation of a fondness for hard liquor and insubordination during the French and Indian War. He has no respect for such a man." He sighed. "Well, we have circumnavigated the barrack," Nat said as they approached the front steps.

"Navigation. That is it, Nat," Will said excitedly, suddenly remembering. "I need a book of maps. Adam mentioned some islands the other day and I had no idea what he was talking about. Do you think Colonel Knox has books of maps?" he asked eagerly.

"That I do not know. More importantly, remember what I have told you is to be held in confidence. Take advantage of the soap and bleach and clean your clothes," he said, motioning for Will precede him.

"I am more looking forward to the meal than the washing of my clothes," Will responded honestly.

"There is time enough for both," Nat replied as they went up the steps.

Inside the barracks, the common room was warm from a roaring fire, cauldrons of hot water and the body heat of the waiting men. They took turns washing the mud stains and blood from their clothes, and restoring their canvas britches to match the pristine white of the snow that had begun falling in thick swirling flakes. By mid-morning the field in front of the Headquarters was covered in a snowy blanket and the grey stone wall perimeter was barely visible from the barracks. The Mariners recounted their part in yesterday's fight, oblivious to how ridiculous they looked, re-enacting their roles, wearing long shirts with no pants, or walking around in spare pants borrowed from others, either too large, too short or too tight. Their mood was enhanced by the arrival of hot oat cakes, warm bread and kettles of weak coffee, made more from bark than from beans, but still with a coffee taste to it.

"If I could find the fellow who did me the favor of breaking my crooked teeth, I would give him a hug, no matter how badly he smelled," Jeremiah announced, eating a piece of oat cake from the other side of his mouth. "If Doctor Thaxter will not remove the stubs, I will find a Boston silversmith to do it," he stated with conviction. "It will not be long now before we drive the Redcoats out."

"We should all thank the fellow for making you easier to look at," Solomon said, standing near the fire, unaware of his own appearance. He was temporarily clothed in a pair of old linen long pants with holes in some places and patches of different-colored cloth in others, and a borrowed shirt, once white but now faded to a dirty yellow color, too short for his lanky frame. His long bony arms protruded from the sleeves just below the elbow like branches from a tree trunk. A brown blanket, thin enough to show the color of the shirt on his back, was draped over one shoulder as if it were a magnificent cloak of the finest fabric.

"If you, Solomon, appeared before Morgan's militia dressed as you are now, you would scare them back to Virginia," one of the Mariners said, provoking general laughter.

"Yes," another yelled. "And they would make their 600 miles in faster time than it took them to get here."

The morning continued in much the same manner. Will volunteered to bring in more firewood before he washed his clothes. When he returned, his coat and hat covered with snow, he was welcomed with shouts from the Mariners to hurry in and close the door, and with mock cries of horror about how they were freezing in their various states of dress. The men took turns drying their clothes by the fire, and most were back in their uniforms by early afternoon, when the cooks and orderlies brought over food from the Headquarters' kitchens. In addition to the cured hams promised by the General, there were chicken stews, roasted beef and mutton chops, salted fish, loaves of bread, potatoes, even butter and hard cheese. Will, his hunting shirt and pants still slightly damp but clean of stains and dirt, sat on the floor sandwiched between Jeremiah and Adam, his wooden bowl balanced on his lap, eating voraciously.

"Is your shoulder feeling sore today," he asked Adam, between spoonfuls of hot chicken stew.

"Dr. Thaxter said we Mariners have so much muscle supporting our joints we are easier to fix and heal faster than others," Adam replied, studying the fish skeleton he had picked clean for any missed morsels of flesh. "The thick muscles hold the displaced joint better once it is back in socket," he added by way of explanation. "Still, I must keep it close to my ribs until it fully heals. When we go fishing, I will teach you how to row and handle the nets. We will make a Mariner out of you yet."

"He is better now at giving speeches, not his own but Colonel

Knox's, than any of us," Jeremiah said, leaning across Will to make his point to Adam. "And, you fought well yesterday," Jeremiah added. "You ran faster than most of us to join the fray."

Will acknowledged Jeremiah's praise with a nod. He looked around the room and felt a sense of well-being and belonging. The barracks were his home and the Mariners his family. He hoped he could explain this to his brother. Will had no plan other than to find Johan and give him their father's message. Without knowing how, he wished Johan would find a way for both of them to stay in Boston.

Will hurried alongside Nat through the dark streets of Cambridge. He was terrified, more terrified than he had ever been in his life.

"Why did you have to invite me?" he asked plaintively, jumping over a pool of slush to avoid dirtying his recently polished boots.

"Because you are my friend and Colonel Knox permitted me to invite whom I wanted," Nat responded, limping ahead of him. "The Colonel is giving a dinner for me before my marriage to Anna. You will not be at the Church in Salem so I asked for your attendance at this dinner," Nat explained with some exasperation in his voice.

"Tell me who will be there again," Will asked, seeking some reassurance.

"Colonel and Mrs. Knox, the Colonel's brother, William, Colonel Glover without his wife Hannah, who is ill in Salem, and you and me." He stopped and grabbed Will by the shoulders. "It is only six people. You know everyone except Mrs. Knox. Your nervousness is inexplicable to me." He clapped his friend on both shoulders. "You are going to dinner. Not your execution. Come on. We must not be late."

Will muttered something in response and Nat stopped and turned. "Now what, Will?"

"Nat, I have never been to a dinner before. I don't have your manners or experience. I always eat in a kitchen, or in a barn, or around a campfire. From a wooden bowl. What if I do the wrong thing? What if I spill some food or gravy on the table? Or break something? Or forget and eat with my knife? And this shirt you gave me to wear is too fancy. I feel funny in it, with these cuffs and frills. This is all wrong," Will said, shaking his head. He quickly reached behind to make sure his queue was secure. Nat had lent him a black ribbon and showed him how to tie it. He stood stock still, as if his boots were frozen to the snow covered cobblestones.

"Will," Nat said sharply to get his attention. "Calm yourself. I promise you will enjoy this evening. Here is the thing to remember. Just do as I do," he said more gently, ignoring several drunken militiamen who staggered past them, supporting each other. "When I use a fork, use a fork. If I cut meat with a knife, you do the same. Watch and follow. We will all be doing the same thing. Colonel Knox and Colonel Glover. It will be easy. Now come on. I am not going to be late for a dinner in my own honor." He grabbed Will's wrist and pulled him along until they reached a solid square brick house, two stories high. The first-floor rooms were all warmly aglow with candlelight.

"We are here. Wipe your boots on the scraper," Nat ordered, pointing to an iron blade mounted on a low worn wooden frame to the left. Nat lifted the lion's head brass knocker and let it fall twice.

Will took a deep breath. "I can do this," he repeated to himself. "All I have to do is to follow Nat's lead." I must not embarrass myself for Nat's sake, he thought, as an orderly of the Massachusetts Artillery, resplendent in his dark blue uniform, opened the door.

"Ah. Our guest of honor, the bridegroom to be," Colonel Knox boomed out, emerging into the entry hall. The candles in the overhead chandelier flickered from the cold wind and steadied as the door closed behind them. "And Will. It is good to see you, my boy. Come into the front parlor near the fire. You must meet my Lucy."

Will glanced to his left into the dining room and felt his stomach knot up. The table was set with silverware and real dishes. He counted three different-sized glasses beside each plate. He gaped at the elaborately carved dark wood spiral posts supporting the banister of the stairs leading up to the second floor. Hesitantly, he followed the Colonel and Nat into the parlor. Colonel Glover stood in front of a marble fireplace, one arm resting on the mantel, the other tucked behind the back of his long navy blue dress coat. His bright red hair was tied back with a black velvet ribbon and his cheeks seemed more ruddy in the glow from the fire. Will felt self-conscious in his white ruffled shirt and coarse brown pants.

"My dear, our other guests have arrived."

Mrs. Knox was sitting in a high backed chair facing the fire. She rose and turned to greet Nat and Will. She was a tall woman with a long round face and thin lips. Her eyes were deep brown and exuberant. Her chestnut brown hair was gathered in a bun in the back, held by a thick pink ribbon that matched the color of her dress. The dress was modestly cut to reveal some, but not too much, of the pale white skin of her neck and bosom. The sleeves ended in a kind of bloused bunch of fabric at the elbow with a sheer handkerchief fabric extending midway down her forearms. Her eyebrows were long and curved in a charming way to accentuate her deep brown eyes. She was taller than Nat and shorter than Will. And she was obviously very pregnant.

Will did his best not to stare at her swollen belly. Mrs. Knox held out her hand, first to Nat, who affected a slight bow, and then to Will, who awkwardly imitated his friend, scraping his boots on the floor in the process.

"It is good to see you again, Lieutenant Holmes. And looking so handsome in preparation for your wedding." Nat's hand involuntarily went to the bruise on his forehead that had progressed in color from purple and yellow to a darker blue. It would not be gone by the day of the ceremony, although it would not be as obvious as it was tonight in the brightly lit room.

Mrs. Knox turned her attention to Will. "So, you are the young man who has been reading Tom Jones," she said, holding on to his hand. Her voice was light and mirthful with a distinct English accent. "I very much enjoyed Mr. Fielding exposing the hypocrisy of British nobility and their class distinctions, although I found his attitude condescending toward women." She cocked her head to one side and looked up at him. "What do you think, Will? May I call you that?"

"Yes ma'm," he replied.

"Oh, please. Call me Lucy," she said waving her hand at him. "Ma'm sounds too formal and too old. Do not you agree? I despised all the titles and formalities everyone had to use in my father's home."

Will tried to recall what he had heard about her father, whether he was the Royal Secretary of the Province or Secretary to the Royal Governor. He forgot which. "I read the book as a love story between Tom and his beloved Sophia," he answered. "Their love endures through everything that happens to them," Will said with passion. He ran on, not knowing where to stop, aware Colonel Glover, standing with both arms clasped behind his back, was staring at him. "Tom is falsely accused, involved in fights, almost caught by an impress gang; Sophia is misled and lied to by people she trusts, given false information to damage Tom in her eyes. She's betrayed by her benefactress who has plotted a violent seduction against her," he said blushing, briefly lowering his eyes and wondering if it was proper to say such things to the Colonel's wife. "And yet, their love is true throughout." He took a breath. "I'm afraid I missed the points you mentioned." He almost said ma'm. He couldn't yet bring himself to say Lucy, so he let the sentence hang.

"Well," Lucy said, laughing. "That is spoken by someone who clearly is in love himself." Will blushed, not knowing what to reply. Colonel Knox rescued Will from his awkwardness.

"Come, my dear. We should not delay dinner and you must not stand for too long periods of time." He offered her his arm, she leaned her head against his shoulder and they led the way across the entrance hall into the dining room. The Colonel escorted his wife to the end of the table, held out the chair for her, and when she was comfortably seated, bent down and kissed her lightly on her hair, and took his place at the head of the table. Colonel Glover sat to Knox's right, brother William next to him, Nat to Knox's left and then Will, who to his panic found himself across from Billy Knox and next to Lucy, and unable to readily watch Nat's example of table manners.

"A toast," Colonel Knox's voice boomed out, after the wine had been poured. "To Lieutenant Nathaniel Holmes and his bride, Anna. May they be happy and long-lived, healthy and blessed with a large family." He raised his glass, Nat acknowledged the toast by nodding to the company, thanked the Colonel and his wife for hosting the dinner, and took a sip. Will followed suit, tasting the warm pleasant bitterness of the red wine, careful not to spill a drop on his borrowed shirt or the white tablecloth. He followed the example of the others and placed the cloth napkin on his lap. Fearful of knocking something over, he sat on his hands.

"Well, Will," Lucy said. "If you read Tom Jones as a love story, which I do agree it is in a large part, you must be in love yourself. Tell me about her." Will turned red and admitted he had written a young lady he was fond of in Albany but had yet to receive a reply.

"You must keep writing to her," she said encouragingly, waiting for the uniformed orderly to finish ladling the soup into her bowl. "My Harry and I exchanged letters frequently when he was courting me." It took Will a moment to realize her reference to Harry was to Colonel Knox.

"My dearest, those were most difficult days for me," Knox said, interrupting his conversation with Colonel Glover. "I was anxious for news of whether you had spoken to your father."

"Oh, Harry, there was no need to worry," she said waving off her husband's comments. "My father," Lucy said vehemently, turning to Will and Nat, "flatly forbade me to marry 'that tradesman' or 'bookseller' as he sometimes called him. It was only my threat of elopement that caused him to relent." [1]

Colonel Knox raised his glass toward his wife. "My dearest. It was your perseverance and determination that carried the day. And now I am the happiest man in Massachusetts, and your father calls me much worse than before, I am sure."

Will caught the look of distress in Lucy's eyes as she returned her husband's gaze. "Perhaps," she said quietly, "the birth of a grandchild will soften his heart. I have not seen my mother, brother or sisters since Harry and I escaped from Boston."

"Brother William," Knox said. "I charge you not to let my darling Lucy become melancholy. You too, Will. Keep up your end of the conversation." He waved his hand in encouragement.

Lucy smiled at both of them. "I cannot be downhearted when I am in the company of my dear Harry. And of course you two gentlemen," she added graciously. "Now, Will," she commanded, "tell us about your love. What is her name and how did you meet?" she asked, bringing a spoonful of soup to her lips.

With some trepidation, Will found himself telling her about Elisabeth, the crossing of the Hudson, her gift of the scarf, his first letter to her and the loss of the precious piece of paper before he could draft a second one. To his surprise, by the time he had concluded the account, he had finished his fish chowder, without exhibiting crude table manners, overloading his spoon with chunks of potato, or even spilling a drop.

The rest of the meal passed the same way. Will conversed with Lucy, Billy and occasionally Nat, while he dutifully devoured the slabs of roast beef, slices of chicken and turkey, and fish placed before him, always careful to use the same utensil Lucy did and to cut his food before placing it in his mouth. She had a small mouth with thin lips, and when she laughed, which was frequently, he noticed she had good teeth. He found himself following her lead instead of glancing at Nat to his right, justifying his looking at her as necessary to know what to do for which course. He was mindful to drink only small amounts of wine and larger quantities of water although he already felt his head was less clear than normal.

"Good gracious, Will. My husband tells me you are in the Mariners' barracks at General Washington's headquarters. Do they not feed you there?" Lucy asked teasingly, as Will eagerly took another piece of venison from the serving platter. "You eat almost as much as my husband," she said, which caused Nat to stifle a laugh and the Colonel's brother to chuckle.

"No one can do that my dear sister," Billy said. "Besides, Will here is a growing boy whereas my brother is in his prime."

"He is indeed," Lucy said fondly, gazing at Colonel Knox, as if there were no other people in the room. Will noticed that other than himself, the Colonel was the only person still eating. Will hurriedly cut the meat and wolfed it down, so as not to be the last. He glanced at the Colonel to be certain there was still food on his plate and saw Knox recoil from something Colonel Glover had whispered to him.

"He has refused?" Colonel Knox said, incapable of speaking quietly.

Glover nodded. "After I informed him one of my men has died at their hands."

"You refer to Caesar?" Nat asked, knowing the answer.

Colonel Glover nodded. "You and I have the solemn task tomorrow of bringing his body home to Salem for burial. I am sorry the somber occasion impinges on the joy of your matrimony."

Nat put down his glass and looked at the two Colonels. "It is not fair to treat freemen differently because of their skin. Caesar Winship went to sea with us. He was one of the first among all of the fishermen to volunteer for our Regiment," he said hotly. "He was a constant attender at our church, present at every Sabbath, an observant man. He was willing to die in battle with the British, not be beaten to death by illiterate backwoods militia."

"The General must have his reasons for not convening a court martial." Knox said. "He is trying to bring together militias from the different colonies and meld them into a single army. His goal is to forge a force capable of defeating the British. That is his paramount concern. I, for one, must defer to his judgment." He looked from the Colonel to Nat. "Even though I do not agree."

Colonel Glover put down his wine glass. "General Thomas, himself, has complained about these southern riflemen, characterizing them as exceedingly vicious and repugnant to all kinds of duty." He paused, shook his head and said more softly, "I would have preferred General Washington had ordered a court martial be convened. Nevertheless, we all will defer to General Washington's judgment. And he has done right by commending my Regiment and retaining the Mariners as his Headquarters Guard. But Henry," he said, turning to address Colonel Knox, "if, as you say, we are going to be one army, fighting the British instead of amongst ourselves, what is to prevent this from happening another time?"

Colonel Knox simply shrugged and shook his head in response, uncharacteristically at a loss for words.

"It is true the men in my company revere the General and cheered him after the riot," Nat said. Will saw his jaw muscles tense as he controlled himself. "They respect him and will follow any orders they are given. I for one can submerge my heartfelt desire for revenge. I am not certain that, if the opportunity arose, one of the Mariners would not seize upon it."

"We must prevent such an incident from happening," Colonel Glover said firmly. "Officers lead their men, both by example and by instruction. I will not let the honor of our Regiment be tarnished by an individual act of vengeful spite. Nor will you Lieutenant." It was clear to Will that the Colonel intended to hold Nat responsible if any of his men sought revenge for Caesar's death.

"Gentlemen," Lucy called out, smiling graciously. "Enough of this talk. I have a different charge to Lieutenant Holmes." Nat turned toward her and managed a slight smile. "After your time in Salem together, you are to bring your wife Anna to wherever my Harry and I shall be abiding so I may become acquainted with her."

"With pleasure," Nat said, inclining his head to Mrs. Knox and smiling broadly. "This is something I can most willingly comply with and, on her behalf, I thank you in advance for your most gracious invitation."

The conversation continued through dessert, two large apple pies, one topped with strips of cheese, the other with ground cinnamon. Another wine like drink was served. Lucy explained to Will it was a simply a 'sherry.' By the end of the meal, Lucy had promised to lend Will two novels she had read, one being The Vicar of Wakefield, and the other a title Will had forgotten.

Will, more confident now that he had survived the dinner party without mishap, was surprised how much he had enjoyed the company. He had drunk sparingly of the wine and sherry but due to their effect, he no longer felt shy and reticent in the company of the two Colonels and Mrs. Knox.

"Colonel, Knox, sir. If it is not too much to ask, one of the Mariners has pointed out that I am sorely deficient in geography and suggested I study maps. Perhaps I could borrow such a book from you?"

"Ah ha," Knox said, finishing his sherry and dabbing his mouth with a napkin. "That will have to await our army's advance into Boston. There, if the British have not destroyed them, I know several gentlemen with fine libraries containing books of the geography of the known world." He leaned back in the large wooden armchair that comfortably accommodated his large bulk, and saw Will's look of disappointment.

"You will not have to wait long, Will. I can assure you of that. General Washington intends to move against the Redcoats by the first week of March. He has asked all regiments to assign every available driver, wagon and sled for the preparations. You will be part of that important effort. Come here tomorrow before eight to collect the books my Lucy has promised. Billy will give you instructions then."

He raised his glass. "Let us end the evening with a final toast to Lieutenant Holmes and his bride, to the success of General Washington and our army, and may we all dine together again, and soon, in our beloved Boston."

"Keep writing to your Elisabeth," were Lucy's encouraging words to Will as he and Nat stood in the entrance hall preparing to leave. The two Colonels and William had military matters to discuss. "May God bless you and your wife-to-be," she said, smiling at Nat. "My Harry does not want me to stand here when the door is opened, so as to avoid the chill. I will say my goodbyes now." Nat bowed from the waist. Will did the same, which brought his eyes level with Mrs. Knox's protruding belly.

On Friday, the first day of March, Will was northeast of the Charles River and Cambridge near some pond. He had been up since the pre-dawn darkness, and for the third time that morning, he was helping soldiers load his sled with saplings, eight to ten feet in length, of pine, spruce, maple, ash, hickory and birch, and the occasional ironwood, the butt ends loaded in first, the tops dragging on the frozen ground past the sled's runners. Will preferred to be in the woods with the militia chopping down the young trees. That would have kept him warm. Instead, he had to stand by the sled in the freezing cold until it was fully loaded and drive his laden sled to the assembly point in the hills behind Roxbury. And then return again. The roads were crowded with wagons and sleds, some like his filled with saplings, others piled high with barrels or hay bales and, closer to Cambridge, still others with stones of all sizes. It was clear the Army was preparing for battle, but he had no idea what the saplings, barrels and stones were for. The hay was food for the horses, but it seemed to him there were too many bales for so few animals.

All day Friday, when he knew Caesar Winship was to be buried in Salem, Will made the same journey, carrying the same loads, on the busy, frozen rutted road to Roxbury. It was boring, cold, numbing work and despite the anticipation of the upcoming battle, he found himself occasionally nodding once or twice and letting the reins slacken. He focused on composing a letter to Elisabeth. He hoped he would have time to write before the attack on the city. He was not clear whether he would be with the Mariners or the Colonel's artillery, but he knew he wanted to be part of it and, if possible, in the forefront.

By mid-afternoon the fields behind Roxbury were filled with work teams of soldiers. Some were busy hammering together large rectangular wooden frames of planks or logs. Others were manning bellows at makeshift forges, as skilled blacksmiths welded ten to twelve-foot-long iron chains to barrels and added extra hoops. Militiamen at the site where he deposited the saplings were binding them tightly with leather strips into ten foot long rolls. Will estimated they had a uniform circumference of two to three feet, but he could not see what use they would be, unless the intention was to set them on fire and roll them down on advancing British troops. Roll them down from where, he wondered. And didn't someone know the green wood would not burn?

On Saturday, the second of March, in the dark cold of the pre-dawn, the Colonel's brother gave Will a pouch with coins and sent him toward Watertown, together with three other teamsters, to load their sleds with wheelbarrows and return quickly to Cambridge. Local farmers had already provided barrows, but Billy said there were more to be had. Will was to use his judgment in buying as many as possible.

"Why do we need wheelbarrows?" Will asked. "We have good sleds and wagons for hauling."

"For the wounded, Will," he said grimly. "Sleds and wagons will not be on the battlefield. General Washington himself ordered them for the care of the wounded," Billy added as Will mounted his sled. "As we speak, the barracks are being cleared and prepared for the surgeons. I fear there will be much bloody work to be done." [2]

It was close to nine p.m. when Will returned to Cambridge, aching from bouncing over the rutted roads, wishing he had thought to bring a sack or blanket to cushion the hard wooden seat. He was cold and hungry. The sled was piled high with the last of the needed long-handled wheelbarrows, a few with a metal rim covering the wooden wheel, all stacked inverted in tall pyramids behind him.

At Cambridge, after crossing the river, he was directed to continue on toward the Lower Fort. The road was crowded with troops marching in the same direction, moving from Cambridge toward the American lines nearer to Charlestown. This must mean an amphibious assault was imminent, he thought, the ice in the harbor having broken up in the past few days. He wondered if Nat was back from Salem and with the Mariners.

If the troops saw the wheelbarrows on his sled and knew what they were intended for, none acknowledged it. Instead, as they marched briskly in the cold night air, eager to be on the attack after the incessant drilling and boredom of camp life, they joked as Will's sled passed.

"That must be for us to carry General Howe's silver dinner plate home," one yelled out.

"Or for all the fine clothes the Officers' ladies will have to leave behind."

"I would rather carry off one of the fine ladies and her behind in a barrow," came the cry, answered by laughter, followed by the command, "Silence in the ranks."

It was too dark for Will to recognize the Regiment. It was clear to him, from their accent and ribald joking, it was a Continental unit from New England. He was relieved they were not Morgan's Rifles.

Will deposited the wheelbarrows in an open field filled with pitched tents. The glow from the soldiers' cooking fires revealed shadows of the men crouched around the flames for warmth. The aroma of roasting meat reminded Will he hadn't eaten since dawn. There were some coins remaining in the pouch Billy had given him. Will had thought to buy food at a tavern but deemed it to be a betrayal of the trust placed in him. The money was to purchase wheelbarrows for the wounded, not to spend on himself. He pulled the collar of his brown coat higher and knotted the blue scarf tightly around his throat against the wind.

Suddenly the relative peacefulness of the night camp was shattered with the roar of cannons. He recognized the deeper booming of howitzers from the redoubts on the slopes of Cobble Hill. Eager to see the bombardment close up, Will drove his sled toward Lechmere Point, tied the mare to a tree and walked forward leading Big Red. He recognized a battery of the Massachusetts Artillery and saw the corpulent figure of Colonel Knox riding up and down the line. The American bombardment of Boston had begun. Below them, among the snow capped rooftops and the white on the Common, Will saw lights in buildings of the city and the campfires of the British troops. He noticed a few flashes from the British lines first, followed by the whistle of howitzer shells and the noise of shells bursting harmlessly in the night sky. They fell short of the American artillery. More British cannons joined in and the counter-fire became heavier.

Will could see there were far more guns in the British artillery emplacements than the American army possessed. Their guns blazed in an almost continuous arc beginning at the forts at The Neck, opposite the salt marshes below Roxbury to his far right, and from their floating batteries in Roxbury Bay. In front of him the British cannons on the Commons and along the shoreline to the mount below Beacon Hill revealed their positions with bright yellow flashes of light, before being hidden again in the darkness. Far off to his left, the Continental's artillery dueled with the British emplacements above Charlestown.

Will stood quietly with Big Red, pleased that the horse neither shied nor pulled away from the booming of the cannons twenty paces away, or from the incoming retaliatory fire of the British. He felt the thrill of being under fire, however ineffective it was. Out of habit, he stroked the horse's neck, calming himself as well in the process. A few buildings in Boston were on fire. The flames illuminated the smoke pluming upward into the moonlit sky. He thought he could hear human voices, some high-pitched screaming and others deeper, barking orders, although he could not make out any words. The entire British line was now marked by an almost continuous series of bright orange-yellow flashes of flame as their cannons returned fire, followed by the whooshing sound of cannonballs in the air and the whistle of howitzer shells before they exploded overhead.

Will moved down the line following the Colonel's large caped figure. The moon's light revealed the artillery men were no longer Knox's regiment. They wore scarlet coats and pointed dark caps. As they went through the drill of worming, sponging and ramming home the charge, their accents confirmed to him that they were not Massachusetts men. Colonel Knox sat on his horse, talking to their officer and occasionally shouting out encouragement in his deep booming voice. Big Red whinnied, attracted by their horses. The officer turned, pointed at Will and said something to Knox.

"Is that you, Master Stoner?" the Colonel called, just before the vent tender's shouted of "Primed," quickly followed by the Gun Commander's order, "Give Fire." There was a brief pause as the powder in the quill caught fire, igniting the packed charge, and the carriage of the twenty-four pounder rolled back in recoil.

"Yes, Sir," Will answered. The Colonel and the other officer watched for the impact. One of the gun crew was already worming the cannon as Will, obeying the Colonel's wave, walked forward.

"I thought I recognized your horse in the darkness. What are you doing here?" Knox asked.

"I am accustoming Big Red to cannon fire," Will answered.

"I can see that he is taking to it," Knox said approvingly. "He will make a fine artillery horse. You may ride with me down the line if you wish," he said, inviting Will forward. Will walked Big Red over to a cannon and, using a powder box as a step, swung up on the bare back of the tall horse. He bunched the traces in his hands, his feet hanging loose without stirrups, feeling the warmth of the horse beneath him. "This is Captain Crane of the Rhode Island Train of Artillery. His men are excellent gunners but we will have to do something about their scarlet coats. When the British advance to attack us, as they must, there can be no confusion as to who are the enemy."

"The good people of Rhode Island raised the funds to equip our Regiment," Captain Crane replied. He brushed a gloved hand over his gilded epaulet. "I can see that blue is the color favored by General Washington. In due course we will change. For now, our black leather caps will have to suffice as a distinguishing mark between friend and foe."

"Your men will be safe enough in fixed artillery emplacements" Knox said, as they arrived at another battery. "Once we drive the

British out of Boston and take to the field, your red coats may prove to be a distinct disadvantage." He shouted encouragement to the gun crew loading another ball into the twenty-four pounder.

"Make this shot count, men. Let those Regulars feel the heat."

From the vantage point of being mounted astride Big Red, Will surveyed Boston under bombardment. Artillery to the south near Roxbury and beyond were bombarding the forts at the Neck and guns near the Commons with a steady fire. He watched the howitzer shells arc high in the sky, sometimes falling short of the British cannon emplacements and showering the city's buildings with fiery debris. The roofs of some were already on fire, the flames a constant deep red glow against the darkened city.

Will could tell when a mortar was fired. Its trajectory was lower and the first shots were ranging ones, falling short and moving progressively closer to the chosen target as the gunners added more powder to the charge. In the moonlight he saw a church steeple crumple under the impact of a cannonball, the triangular top blown off, leaving a truncated jagged wooden stub, like a broken tooth, poking up above the stone gum of the main building.

The massive bombardment and counter-shelling by the British continued for several hours. They had completed riding the line, and Will had followed the Colonel back to the Massachusetts Artillery batteries on the northerly end of Lechmere Point. The Colonel pointed to a cannon in its emplacement being loaded with a ball. A fog of blue smoke and the smell of gunpowder hung in the air around the battery. Beyond them, further up the line, were the howitzer emplacements.

"Remember that one, Will? It is The Albany. I wish the good people of that friendly city could be here now to see her in action."

Will thought there was only one person from Albany who he wanted by his side at this moment. He watched as one of the crew lit the gunpowder in the quill. He spoke softly to Big Red and waited for the explosion of the charge. The horse barely twitched at the roar.

Then, as if by predetermined signal, the American guns fell silent. The British continued their fire for a few more minutes and it was over. Will looked around, aware in the night's silence of shouts and cries for help. Smoke spiraled up from a howitzer emplacement where the gun had been. Pieces of smoldering wood from the carriage lay on the ground. Large chunks of the iron firing tube were scattered at a distance.

"The piece simply exploded," the Lieutenant said. He was standing next to the charred site as Colonel Knox dismounted. "It just happened. We lost three of the crew, " he said, pointing in the darkness toward a wooded area behind the emplacement. "The howitzer had been firing all night. There must have been a weakness in the metal."

Will peered in the direction the Lieutenant had indicated. He didn't see any bodies but smelled an odor of seared flesh. It was familiar, reminiscent of when his father castrated their cattle and cauterized the wound. He shuddered.

"Will, where is your sled?" Colonel Knox asked.

"It is behind the second battery, sir, along with the mare."

"Be a good lad and fetch it and harness up your team," he said soberly. "I need you to perform a grim service for me tonight."

Will walked Big Red back, put him in traces and slowly returned with the sled. Reluctantly, he approached the small group of soldiers who were placing the bodies of the three dead men on blankets. Will had seen dead people before. They had been in their beds where they had died, laid out in their clothes, their eyes closed, as if in a deep sleep. They had always been whole as if they were still alive, except for their pale color. The bodies of the gun crew were in pieces. One was missing half his head, the top of his skull blown off from below the cheek and across to his nose. His one remaining eye was open, staring at the evergreen branches heavy with snow, bending down to embrace him like angels' wings. His brains had spilled out onto his shoulder, as if he were wearing a grey cloth on one side, over his blue coat. Another had been almost cut in two by the flying metal. Will stared at the reservoir of blood in the man's stomach cavity. The pale coils of his intestines protruded from a sea of red. The soldiers had already covered the third man.

Will felt his belly contract and hurried off to the side of a thick tree. He dry heaved, vomiting up nothing because he had not eaten since the morning. He tasted the bitter acid in his mouth, reached up for a handful of crusted snow from an overhanging branch, and washed his mouth. By the time he returned, the soldiers had placed the three bodies head first on the sled and covered them with blankets. The dead men's boots were the only part of them exposed to the cold.

"Will. Follow Lieutenant Hadley back to our barracks. He will tell you what to do," Colonel Knox said. Will nodded and climbed up on the seat, turning the sled onto the narrow road leading from the battery. The Lieutenant rode ahead, two of the soldiers riding silently on the sled, until they reached the Regiment's camp. Will brought the sled to a halt in front of a one-story brick building, which had been set up as a hospital for the surgeons. He shivered in the dark night, made colder for him by the three bodies on the sled behind. He wondered if the men were still bleeding or whether the frigid air coming in contact with their open wounds had frozen their blood. He started to imagine the wounds of the third man, envisioning body parts missing and internal organs exposed. He forced himself to think of anything else. In his mind, he saw Elisabeth next to him on the sled seat. Agnes was not with them. He and Elisabeth were on the sled, hauling the bodies of the three men to a cemetery.

"No need for you to take them any further," Lieutenant Hadley called out from the barracks steps. "We have wheelbarrows for that."

Will watched the soldiers transfer the blanketed bodies into a wooden wheeled barrow, piling the dead men on top of each other. Each one grabbed a handle. They grunted as they struggled through the snow to the rear of the temporary hospital. In the moonlight, Will could make out the irregular dark stains of the congealed blood on the wood planks of his sled.

"Colonel Knox instructed me to find you lodging and food. He wants you here tomorrow with the Regiment instead of at Cambridge," the Lieutenant called to him from the doorway. "The next building down is a barn for the Regiment" he said pointing. The Lieutenant's horse, tied to a post in front of the barracks, pawed the snow with its front leg and turned to watch Big Red and the mare move down the compacted snow toward the shelter of the long low wooden shed.

"Return here when you are finished," the Lieutenant called out before closing the door.

Will left the sled alongside the shed, unhitched the horses, led them into a single stall and gave them hay and water. There were a few other horses inside. Not a bad place to sleep if he had to, he thought, realizing how tired he was. He estimated it was close to midnight. For no particular reason, he put a few handfuls of oats in his pocket and trudged across the frozen ground to the barracks. Before going in, he fed some oats to the Lieutenant's horse, feeling the warm snuffling breath on his palm.

The barracks were empty, except for rows of cots up and down each wall. Piles of neatly folded linen for bandages were stacked at the foot of the beds. Long wooden tables, used for eating when the barracks had been full of men, lined the center of the room. This is where the surgeons would operate. Will hesitated in the doorway, visualizing the broken bloody bodies on the tables. He imagined the surgeons sawing through mangled limbs, the pulpy stumps of arms and legs pulsating spurts of blood onto piles of severed limbs around the tables.

"Shut the door," the Lieutenant shouted from the back of the room. "There are sick men in here. The cold will do them no good."

Will saw a half-dozen cots grouped around the large stone fireplace at the rear. The Lieutenant was standing before the hearth warming his hands. He had unbuttoned the red facing of his blue coat. His white breeches were stained with soot and gunpowder. His black tri-corn rested precariously on the mantle's corner.

Will's boots echoed on the wood floor as he walked the length of the room. "The only food I can offer is the leftover soup in the pot. And what is your name?"

"Will Stoner, Sir," he said facing the Lieutenant with his back to the fire. He let the warmth seep through his wool coat and creep up from his lower back to the ache in his shoulders. He turned and looked into the iron pot hanging from a hook over the fire. The contents were barely bubbling.

"I am Lieutenant Hadley. Samuel Hadley." They shook hands. He followed Will's gaze. "It may be a little thin," he said. "The company cook will be by in the morning with breakfast for these men. I will inform him to supplement the rations to include you."

As tired as he was, Will squatted down and put two small logs on the fire. He peered into the pot and thought he saw a beef bone, bare of any meat, through the thin gruel. He reached into his pocket and threw the remaining oats into the broth. As he stood up, he studied the men lying under blankets on their cots, arranged so they shared the warmth of the flames. Most of them were feverish, their damp hair matted on their brows, their tongues occasionally licking their dry lips. The faces of the two nearest to him were covered with pustules, small rounded bumps as if there was bird shot buried under their skin. The bumps continued down their necks until hidden by their shirts. He looked at the others who were similarly afflicted.

"They have small pox," the Lieutenant explained. "The Colonel ordered our entire Regiment to be inoculated. Some of the men do better than others. Thank God, none have yet died from this dread disease."

Will nodded. Nat had told him Dr. Thaxter had inoculated the Mariners in the fall of '75. It was a condition of serving as General Washington's Headquarters Guard. Will was uncertain what inoculation entailed and he was too tired to ask for an explanation.

Will studied the Lieutenant in the firelight. He was tall, with exuberant brown curly hair that peaked in the middle of his forehead. It covered his ears on the sides and was tied loosely behind his head. His eyebrows were equally thick, arching over deep brown penetrating eyes. His face, unshaven for a few days, showed a thick dark stubble which gave him a more manly, physically fit appearance.

The barracks door opened and shut quickly with a bang. A short and portly soldier limped down the room toward them, the wood of his cane thumping in a regular rhythm on the floor boards.

"Ah, there you are, Sergeant. This young man, Will Stoner, is a guest of the Regiment for the night. Colonel's orders," he added by way of explanation.

The Sergeant limped to the fire, sat down with a groan on an empty cot, stretched out his right leg and extended a hand to Will.

"Thomas Merriam," he said by way of introduction.

"How is the foot healing?" Hadley asked.

"Better every day sir. It has been five days since the ball rolled into my ankle. I will be ready when the time comes."

"That will be soon, Sergeant. Very soon, indeed," the Lieutenant said, adjusting his tri-corn and buttoning his coat. "I must be getting back to camp," he said.

"Good night, sir," the Sergeant said. Will nodded and took his wooden bowl and pewter spoon from his haversack. Careful not to touch the iron pot, he ladled out the soup and oats, now soft from boiling, and sat down on the cot next to the Sergeant.

Merriam massaged his calf and flexed his foot. "Carelessness occurs when you least expect it. One of my crew did not stack the balls correctly. One rolled off as I was near, and I could not get out of the way because of the ice. The ball hit me hard. I went down as if it had been fired from a cannon." He leaned forward, easing off his boot. The ankle, through Merriam's thin white stocking, was an ugly bluish purple and swollen to at least twice its normal size. The Sergeant gingerly rubbed his ankle down toward the arch.

"Because of this, I stay with these men at night, nurse them and get relief in the morning. There was none today though because of the bombardment," the Sergeant said as Will eagerly slurped the soup until the bowl was empty. "Only the doctor came by around midday. At night I could hear our artillery pounding away at the Regulars. I pray to God their aim was accurate. Many of us still have family down there."

Will took another bowl and told the Sergeant about what he had seen and the explosion at the first howitzer battery.

Merriam became more somber. "That crew was Bixby, Jarvis and Phineas Stowe. There were only three men for that howitzer and Sergeant Otis as the gun commander. All good men," he muttered. He clasped his hands together and closed his eyes. Will took the opportunity to study him. Merriam had a high broad forehead with barely any hair for eyebrows or eyelashes. His cheeks were ruddy and jowly. His lips seemed too thin in comparison to his strong square chin. Except for an odd long hair on his neck, no one would notice if he didn't shave for a week. He moved his lips silently. When he opened his eyes, Will saw there were tears in them.

"I prayed for all four," he said by way of explanation to Will. "Tomorrow, I will know which one God has permitted to be still of this earth," he added, running his hands through the tufts of ill-kempt black hair sticking out of the side of his head.

One of the sick men groaned and Will motioned for Merriam to stay seated. He took a basin of water to the bedside, removed the dry folded cloth from the man's forehead and dipped it in the water. At the sound, the man's eyes opened. Startled, he looked around, attempted to sit up, recognized where he was, and collapsed back on the linen sheet, wet with his own sweat. Hoarsely he whispered, "Water. Please some water."

Will took the cloth from the basin, wrung most of the liquid out, and brushed it against the man's lips. The man opened his mouth in anticipation and Will squeezed the cloth, letting a steady stream of drops fall on his tongue. The man nodded, his eyes pleading for more. Will found the soldier's pewter cup under his bed, filled it a third with water, and lifted it to his lips. The man swallowed slowly, snorting through his nose in appreciation. The pustules around his eyes were oozing and Will wiped the yellowish thick liquid away. After a few minutes, the man, with a small satisfied smile on his face, lapsed back into his feverish sleep.

"If you could take a watch of two hours, it would give me a brief respite," Merriam said, looking at his cot longingly. "As you can see, there are plenty of empty beds for you to choose from."

"I can well do that," Will said. He was physically tired but not in need of sleep. "Perhaps for longer, if need be."

"Thank you, lad" Merriam replied, lying down and covering himself with his coat. "If they wake, give them water and keep them covered," he said. "Those two over there," he pointed at the two cots to his left. "They have trouble keeping down the little food they ingest. It happens with the pox at this stage. You may have to help them up to clean themselves. You can use some of the linens," he said helpfully. He shifted to favor his ankle, sighed and fell into an exhausted sleep.

Will found a three-legged stool, roughly carved and well worn, and moved it closer to the fire. He opened his haversack, caressed the precious paper Mrs. Knox had given him along with one of the books she had promised, and began, in his mind, to compose a letter to Elisabeth. Perhaps tomorrow he would find a quill and ink. There still was no word from her, but Mrs. Knox had urged him to continue writing. He resolved he would because he couldn't bear the alternative of not doing so.

By the time he had satisfied himself, going over the words of his final draft in is mind, he was alert and wide awake. Two of the soldiers were moaning and tossing with fever. He quickly went outside and under a cold, clear starry night scooped snow into the basin and applied it with cloth compresses to their foreheads. It seemed strange to him to be cooling them off and keeping them warm at the same time. He threw a few more logs on the fire, heating his cold wet hands in front of the crackling flames. He opened the pages of The Vicar of Wakefield and looked at the illustrations before setting it aside.

He untied a packet of newssheets, expecting to find another novel protected by the papers inside. Instead, they were prior issues of The Boston Gazette & County Journal from the month of February. The masthead proclaimed, almost defiantly, that it was printed in Watertown due to the illegal British occupation of Boston. He read a broadside of The Salem Gazette, looking closely at the drawings of forty black coffins above the headline in large type proclaiming "Bloody Butchery by the British, or the Runaway Fight of the Regulars." He absorbed the account of the particulars of the battle of Concord, "twenty miles from Boston," the previous April. There were other papers and journals, and copies of the Royal American Magazine, which he at first thought was pro-British. From the cartoons Will quickly understood it was making fun of the King and various Lords and Earls for trampling on the rights of the Colonialists.

There was an issue of The Essex Journal, which supported what Nat had told him when they first met, that a British General was a secret Catholic and intended to make the Colonialists swear obedience to the Pope. He found a pamphlet entitled "A Sermon Preached at Lexington, by Jonas Clark, Pastor of a Church in Lexington." Will read the bold letters explaining that the sermon was to commemorate the "MURDER, BLOODSHED, and Commencement of the Hostilities between Great Britain and America." [3]

He skimmed over many of the newssheets, magazines and journals, intending to return to them. The sermon captured his interest and he read it first. The Pastor described how the British troops had set fire to buildings with people inside. Women in child-bed were either "cruelly murdered in their beds, burnt in their habitations, or turned into the streets to perish with cold." Will read on about the ravaging and plundering of homes along the road as the troops retreated from Concord to Lexington and on to Cambridge, of the bayoneting of the "unarmed, the aged and infirm, who were unable to flee and were inhumanly stabbed and murdered in their habitations." The Pastor confirmed what Colonel Knox had told the teamsters in the Berkshires. If anything the Pastor's account was more accurate, Will reasoned. This man had been in Lexington and had digested what he had seen and been told by his neighbors and parishioners. He felt a cold hatred inside of him of the troops who could commit such atrocities and the Officers who ordered them to do so. The Americans had no choice but to defend themselves against such savage and inhuman barbarism.

The novel, lying on the cot in its leather binding, no longer interested him. Will read page after page of the newssheets, leaning close to the fire to make out the smaller type of the articles. He read about the hardships caused by the British occupation and blockade of Boston, the unprovoked attack almost six years ago by British troops on the unarmed people, called "the Boston Massacre," the burning of small towns along the coast, and the forays of the Regulars into the countryside, even on the Sabbath. He devoured the tracts on the illegality of the Crown's actions under the abominable Coercive Acts, banning all representative government in Massachusetts, and the blockade of the port of Boston.

He was in the middle of the tract explaining the right of the Colonists, as free Englishmen, to govern themselves and elect their representatives, when one of the soldiers cried out. Will helped him sit up and offered him water from the man's cup. The soldier waved him off, signaled for something else that Will didn't understand, and then rolled to his side and vomited on the floor. Will waited until the man had stopped and lain back flat. He unfolded a linen sheet from nearest pile, wiped up the floor with it and threw the soiled fabric in a corner.

"Would you like me to get you some broth," Will asked. "There is some in the pot."

The man shook his head. "It will not do me any good if I cannot keep it down," he said. He tossed his head from side to side, the pustules blossoming through his unshaven skin. "This ache in my head never leaves me. I am so weak," he whispered. Will had to lean closer to hear. "I will not be able to lift the rammer." He mumbled something else that Will couldn't make out. The soldier, sapped of the little energy he had by the strain of awakening and throwing up, closed his eyes. Will put a fresh cloth on his forehead. The man mouthed the words "bless you" but no sound emerged from his lips. Will put his hand on the man's arm and sat on the edge of the cot until he was satisfied the soldier was asleep.

He returned to his stool by the fire and opened another newssheet. It set forth the argument, the logic of which was plain to Will, that if the Crown could impose the Coercive Acts and punish Massachusetts, it could do so against any of the Colonies. If the Colonies did not remain united in their opposition to the Crown, the author argued, the King and his army would devour them one by one. And finally, Will reread Pastor Clark's Sermon and The Salem coffin broadsheet. He ran his fingers over the two rows of twenty coffins and noted the names of the men they represented, killed by the Redcoats at Concord.

If he could be part of the battle for Boston, Will thought, these words and the memory of the British atrocities would strengthen him in his resolve to fight. He stepped outside to relieve himself and saw that it was near dawn. He carefully packed the novel and papers in his haversack and woke Sergeant Merriam. As Will lay down, he realized The Vicar novel had come from Mrs. Knox. The rest had been given him by the Colonel. He smiled at the realization the Colonel thought enough of Will to provide broadsheets and gazettes about the nature of their cause. He fell asleep immediately.

Will was on the verge of awaking. Subconsciously, he knew it was daylight. He was jarred into consciousness by a deep voice shouting near his cot.

"Sergeant. Who authorized this man to be here?"

Will sat upright and recognized Dr. Thaxter, his round, dignified figure drawn up in righteous indignation, his hand extended toward Will, his face red with anger turned toward Merriam.

"Has this man been inoculated? Do you understand the risk he has been exposed to if he has not?"

"Doctor," Merriam said hastily, nervously smoothing his thinning hair back on his forehead and limping forward on his cane. "All I know is the Lieutenant brought him here last night, after midnight it was, and said it was the Colonel's orders to give him lodging and food."

"Lodging, to any intelligent person, would mean" the Doctor replied, staring sternly at the Sergeant, "anywhere but in a smallpox ward. Well, the lad is awake and we shall soon find out. Have you been inoculated?" Dr. Thaxter peered at him, waiting for his response.

"No sir. I am not sure precisely what it is but I am reasonably certain it has not been done to me. I have had the pox though," Will added almost as an afterthought.

"Have you now. When and where may I ask?" Doctor Thaxter cocked his head and studied Will.

"Johan, my brother who is older, had it first. His face bears more marks than mine. My grandmother kept me in the same room as him so I would get it also." He pushed the hair away from his temples. "I have some marks there and a few on my neck," Will said, holding his chin up.

"So you do," Dr. Thaxter conceded, coming closer and examining Will's head and neck. "So you do. And one or two on this side of your nose, if I am not mistaken," he said examining Will's face closely. He held Will's chin in his hand and turned Will's face toward the daylight.

He walked over to the cots, still grouped around a now-roaring fire. "Let me examine these men first. Then I will decide what to do with you. I cannot have you spreading the pox, ravaging the Army and decimating its ranks," he said gruffly.

Sergeant Merriam stirred a large container of porridge over the fire. A tall pot of what smelled like coffee sat on one of the logs. The small side table was laden with loaves of bread and wedges of cheese.

"There is more than enough for you, Will," Merriam said. "These men will not eat much.

Take what you want and you can help me feed them afterwards."

"Who was the third man of the gun crew," Will asked, lowering his voice. "Did you ask the doctor?"

The Sergeant nodded, taking a bite of bread. "It was Bixby, Jarvis and Stowe who died. Sergeant Otis was unharmed. Those iron howitzers are untrustworthy beasts. Give me a solid brass twenty-four pounder any day."

Dr. Thaxter grunted as he raised himself up from the last cot. "You will all live," he concluded, addressing the sick soldiers. "The fever and pox must run its course. Each day is better though. One day closer to recovery." He turned and rolled down the cuffs of his overcoat. "Now let me take a look at you again, young man." He motioned Will over toward the window and examined his face again. "Your grandmother was a very wise woman."

Will nodded in agreement. "Yes sir. She said it was the way it was done in Holland in her parents' time. To put well children in with their sick siblings, I mean."

Dr. Thaxter absorbed this information and studied Will's face. "You do seem to have had a very mild case. I do not know if that is enough to protect you. How long ago was it?"

"I believe I was four at the time." The doctor waited, until Will realized he was not about to guess his age. "I turned sixteen in February, Sir."

"Well," Dr. Thaxter said, rinsing his hands in cold water and drying them on a linen sheet. "What we do know is that if we inoculate soon after exposure, the patient is either protected or the pox is of less severity. I will inoculate you now. With Providence's help, you will not even develop the pox. Now, take off your coat, roll up your sleeve and sit at that table by the window."

Will did as he was told, shivering in his shirt in the cold drafty room. Dr. Thaxter removed a glass vial from his brown leather bag and placed it on the table. He took out a scalpel, went to the fireplace and heated it over the flames. Will watched him with apprehension as he returned.

"Are you able to hold your arm steady or do I need the Sergeant to help?" the doctor asked.

"I can, sir, if I may rest it on the table," he replied with more courage than he felt. The doctor nodded his assent and plopped down on a chair opposite Will, after first fanning out the tails of his coat so as not to sit on them.

"You will not even feel this," he said, as he drew the scalpel across the inside of Will's forearm, making a shallow cut three to five inches long. Will looked at the thin line of blood that marked the incision. Dr. Thaxter removed the cork top from the vial. With a tweezers he pulled out a thread covered with a thick yellow pus. It looked like half melted lard. He grasped the free end with another tweezers and carefully lining up the thread in the cut, pulled it back and forth, leaving some of the pus in the wound.

"Hold this cloth tightly on it until I say you may remove it," the doctor directed, as he reinserted the infected thread into the vial and put his equipment back into his bag.

"I was with the Mariners when you came to their barracks," Will said, pressing the cloth on his arm. "Your assistant treated me. How is Titus Fuller?" Will asked.

Dr. Thaxter studied Will before answering. "So, you were a participant in the fight with Morgan's Rifles." Will nodded.

"A colossal waste of good men," he said bitterly. "And a disgrace to the Army," he added. Will was not sure whether he was referring to the Mariners and was about to rise to their defense, when the doctor added, "What can one expect from illiterate backwoods people." He shook his head. "Titus is recuperating nicely. His right eye is gone but otherwise he is physically fit and ready for duty. If Colonel Glover will have him, the man desires to stay with the Mariners." He noticed Will was still pressing the cloth to his forearm. "You may remove it. No trying to rub it off now. Leave it alone and let it heal by itself. You understand." Will nodded. "I will trust my instincts you are not infectious. You have my permission to leave the barracks."

Will had not realized he might have been confined. "Why did you inoculate me then?" he asked, trying not to rub his arm.

"As a precaution," Thaxter answered, putting on his coat.

After the doctor had left, Will helped Sergeant Merriam wash and feed the six occupants of the ward. He brought in more firewood, stacked it by the hearth and went to feed and water the horses. When he returned, Lieutenant Hadley's horse was tied to the post outside the barracks. Inside, the Lieutenant was giving the sick men an account of the bombardment. He had on clean white breeches. His blue coat still bore the marks of powder and cinders from the night before, although he had made an attempt to brush and scour it. His brown curls were combed and neatly tied up in a queue. The skin of his face was freshly shaven and red from the winter wind.

"It is all in preparation for the attack on Boston. Tonight we will make the Regulars shake in their barracks again. It will not be long now," he said enthusiastically. "Ah, there you are, Will. Colonel Knox wants you to help us gather cannonballs today. They lie like pumpkins in a field in October. What they have fired at us last night, we will return with pleasure this evening." He twirled his tri-corn on his hand.

"Hitch up your sled, Will. A few more minutes of conversing with my men and we go to collect the gifts our gracious King has seen fit to send us."

"Yes sir," Will said, grabbing a wedge of cheese and half a loaf of bread and stuffing them in his haversack before heading out the door. As he harnessed the horses to the sled, he shuddered, seeing the dark stain of the dead soldiers' blood on the wooden slats.

In front of the lines down to Lechmere Point and closer to the salt marshes, soldiers of a Connecticut Regiment had gathered cannonballs that had fallen short of the trenches and batteries. Will drove his team along a frozen road sitting on the sled, his coat drawn close against the strong wind and his collar held against his neck by Elisabeth's scarf, as the men loaded the balls. Lieutenant Hadley had exaggerated the use of the British balls for the bombardment that night. Most had been damaged upon impact and were no longer spherical. The main smelter was at Cambridge, where they would be recast using existing moulds. After leaving the welcome warmth of the smelter, he was sent on toward Roxbury to collect those cannonballs the Regulars had fired from their forts on the Neck and the adjacent floating batteries at the American redoubts.

It was long after dark when Will returned to the Massachusetts Artillery camp above Lechmere Point. The bombardment renewed shortly thereafter. Will again stationed himself with Big Red at the batteries. Warily, he stayed closer to the cannons and consciously avoided the remaining howitzers and mortars. If anything, the cannonading was heavier than the previous one. It lasted intermittently until after midnight. He imagined the cannonballs smashing into the barracks of the officers and soldiers who had committed the atrocities he had read of the night before. Serves them right he thought, as he rode Big Red slowly back to the temporary hospital.

Perhaps tomorrow, after leaving the retrieved cannonballs at the foundry, he could go toward Charlestown. That is where the attack across the water would begin. He would look for Nat and the other Mariners and see if he could be of some service.

Early Monday morning, March 4th, Lieutenant Hadley sent Will to the Cambridge powder tower. Preparations for battle were underway. No more carrying of wheelbarrows, saplings and hay bales. Will's sled, and the sleds of the other teamsters working for the Regiment, were loaded with crates of powder charges in their canvas bags, marked by colored cloth tags for the different-sized guns: white for the twelve pounders, red for the eighteen pounders, blue for the twenty four pounders, and black for the howitzers and mortars. They delivered their explosive cargo to the Roxbury powder tower. Will didn't see the purpose in that, since there seemed to be plenty of powder already for the night's bombardment, but there was no one he could ask. He had learned, from his time with the Mariners and his shorter service with the Artillery, simply to do as he was told and only ask questions of those likely and friendly enough to answer.

It was late afternoon when he returned to the Regiment's camp in a field adjacent to the hospital. There were many more horses tethered to the few remaining fences outside the barn. Will recognized the Colonel's large white mare and that of his brother. In the gathering winter darkness, he glimpsed Lieutenant Hadley striding toward the Colonel's tent in the company of a few other officers. Will wandered among the men, smelling the beef roasting over their fires, but unwilling to beg to share their meal.

"Will? Is that you?" A voice called out. "You will need to eat tonight to keep up your strength. Come join with us." He recognized Sergeant Merriam's short pudgy figure, leaning on his cane by a cooking fire. Will eagerly went over. One of the men remained squatting, slowly turning a large leg of mutton on a spit over the fire. Fat from the meat dripped onto the fire, making the flames hiss and sputter, before flaring up.

"This is the lad who was at the barracks the other night, assisting me in taking care of our own, suffering from the pox," Merriam said by way of introduction. Will shook hands all around. He immediately forgot the men's names, his mind focusing on the roasting meat. He inhaled the delicious aroma in a long lingering breath.

"When the Lieutenant told me the plans for tonight, I could not stay away," Merriam said by way of explanation of his presence. "He will be out shortly with our final orders," he said, motioning toward the Colonel's tent. "What we know for sure is that we are taking Dorchester Heights tonight and the Regulars will try to dislodge us tomorrow. I can ride a supply wagon up and hobble around on my cane at the battery," Merriam said excitedly. "This is the battle we have been waiting for. Finally, with Providence's blessing, we will defeat the Redcoats and reclaim our beloved city."

One of the soldiers probed the mutton with his knife and pronounced it done.

"Good thing too," Merriam said. "This lad has been trying to get by on the smell alone." He smiled at Will.

Will took his wooden bowl from his haversack and held it out. It was quickly filled with meat and beans cooked in molasses from a pot hanging over a second fire, which he had not noticed, concentrating on the spit with the mutton. Will offered his remaining bread and cheese, but Merriam told him to keep it.

"You will need it for tomorrow. We have bread here freshly baked today," and he produced two loaves for the eight soldiers.

As he ate, Merriam told him he had spent the day with his crew, binding straw and cloth around the gun carriage wheels with leather strips, stuffing straw into everything that could rattle and greasing the axles with lard.

"Everything must be as silent as possible. Our watchword is

surprise. At dawn, when the Regulars awake, they will be looking up at our cannons on the Heights," Merriam said confidently.

"Will not the bombardment cover our movement?" one of the men asked.

"We are not that far from the Neck and the Redcoat sentries. They will hear us if we make noise. Look, here comes the Lieutenant. The conference must be over." A crowd of officers emerged, illuminated by the lanterns from the large tent. The Lieutenants ran briskly to their companies. The Captains and higher ranks remained clustered around the large figure of Colonel Knox.

Lieutenant Hadley went from cooking fire to cooking fire, stopping briefly to talk to the gun crews.

"Sergeant Merriam. Sorry to disturb your delicious repast and repose," he said mirthfully, as if the soldiers were seated around a dining room table under a chandelier. "You and your men will move out on orders once the bombardment begins. That will be in another hour, around 8 pm. Have the horses hitched to the gun carriages before then." He noticed Will standing off to the side.

"Ah, Will. The Colonel knew you would be here." Will wondered how but refrained from asking. "He has special instructions for you. He would like you to pull The Albany up to the Heights."

He knew the eighteen pounder weighed close to 2000 pounds. It had taken a team of four horses to haul it by sled through the Berkshires. That had been almost a dead pull uphill. With the cannon rolling on wheels, Big Red and the mare could do it. Will wished he had a saddle. He would have to ride Big Red bareback. "My team is ready," Will replied.

"Good," Hadley said. "The Albany is part of my battery. I will see you there."

"He is a good officer," Merriam said to Will, as Lieutenant Hadley left to talk to the next group of men. "I have served with him since the beginning." Will was on the verge of asking when that was, but the Sergeant was limping away from the fire toward the dark shapes of the cannons.

Will rode Big Red from the barn to the battery at Lechmere Point, feeling the heat of the horse's body between his legs. He would have been more secure with stirrups and a saddle, but there was something more exhilarating about riding without. The mare, in her traces next to them, trotted placidly alongside. He tied his team to a tree and walked behind the battery. The cannons that were going up the Heights were easily distinguished by their oversized wheels, wrapped in cloth stuffed with straw. The wheels of the ones remaining behind had bare studded metal rims. The Albany, one other eighteen pounder and three twelve pounders were ready to move. Each carriage had two side boxes loaded with cannon balls and powder. They would add to the total weight, Will thought. Still he was confident Big Red and the mare could pull The Albany.

Although there was no need for silence at Lechmere Point, the gun crews spoke softly among themselves. At a hand signal from the gun commanders, the teamsters moved forward and hitched their teams to the cannons. The bombardment was about to commence. Will stood in the darkness next to the mare. He thought she needed him to calm her more than Big Red. Although he anticipated the sound of an explosion after hearing the command "Give Fire," tonight Will jumped at the roar of the nearest howitzer. The mare tried to rear but he restrained her, holding tightly onto the reins. Big Red stood still, preventing her from moving sideways or forwards. Will heard the distant boom of the British counter-fire followed by the high whistle of the howitzer and mortar shots and the deeper noise of their heavier cannon. He imagined the scene of the night before, the flash of flames in the darkness forming an arc from the Neck to the side of Boston closest to Charlestown and beyond.

Lieutenant Hadley rode slowly down the line of waiting teamsters.

"All right, men. Saddle up and follow the lead cannon. Remember, no shouting to your teams, use the whip as little as possible, and silence. At all times silence. Our lives may depend upon it."

Will was second in line. The well-traveled road to Cambridge was reasonably smooth. Even with the wheels covered in cloth, they rattled over the icy paved stone streets of Cambridge. At the Charles, Will saw that there were more teams pulling cannons ahead of them. These, he reasoned, must be from the batteries below Cambridge. They rumbled across the Charles River Bridge and on to the familiar road to Roxbury he had traveled so many times in the past week. Once through the town they turned left, the muffled sound of the many cannon wheels on the frozen ground drowned out by the thunderous cannonade from the American batteries below Roxbury.

They were parallel to the road from Roxbury to the Boston Neck. The British had heavily fortified the Neck. There were cannons in two redoubts outside the main fort across the road. On either side were floating batteries as well, large, flat-bottomed wooden platforms, with several guns and powder casks protected by planks and sandbags. The noise from their far more numerous cannons, concentrated at the very point where they were closest to the British lines at the Neck, helped to mask any sounds the gun carriages made. The real danger, Will realized, was if they were discovered at this point on the low Dorchester causeway before ascending the Heights. They were within easy cannon range of the British guns and less then a mile from the British sentries beyond the Neck. The caravan passed behind a screen of hay bales stuffed into the wooden frames. Will had seen them being constructed at the Roxbury assembly point. They had been dragged by teams of oxen and positioned before the cannons and the silently marching soldiers began their ascent.

A damp mist-like fog swept in from the flat ground beyond the salt marshes and enshrouded the beginning of the climb on the rock-hard frozen dirt road to the top of the Heights, one hundred feet above. Will shivered in the clammy mist, although he was thankful for the poor visibility. As they climbed slowly higher, on the side of the road closest to the British lines, Will saw more of the wooden frames from the Roxbury assembly point. Higher up, the rolls of saplings lashed together, at least eight feet high, blocked them from the view of the British sentries below and also offered protection for the troops. Midway to the summit they passed hundreds of soldiers, toiling with pickaxes and shovels to construct a strong redoubt that jutted out from the road, anchoring the left flank of the lines. Will marveled at the silence. Hardly a man spoke. There were no shouted orders or cries of encouragement, just the constant booming of cannons and the closer noise of steady rhythmic digging and men's feet marching toward the summit, all behind the pre-constructed screen of hay and saplings.

Will hoped that if the British sentries below looked up at all during the thunderous cannonade, the wall would appear through the mist as simply the impenetrable darkness of a forest or rock outcropping.

At the top of Dorchester Heights, Will's horses emerged from the thinning fog into bright moonlight. It seemed as if there were thousands of soldiers working feverishly to throw up fortifications on the two hills, secure the gun emplacements and establish defensive lines. Lieutenant Hadley pointed and Will maneuvered The Albany into position. Its brass muzzle overlooked the harbor which he couldn't see in the darkness but knew was below.

Once he had tethered the horses, Will set to work with the gun crews and soldiers. They collected the pairs of wooden barrels, joined by the iron chains and filled them with the stones they had uncovered in preparing the parapets. When they ran out of stones, Will shoveled in frozen earth. The barrels were positioned in front of the parapets. When the British Regulars began their assault up the slope, the barrels would roll down on their tightly grouped disciplined ranks, maiming and killing many of them. Will helped build temporary shelters for the powder charges, moving large rocks to form a low wall, unloaded cannon balls from supply wagons and stacked them behind each gun emplacement.

Working steadily, Will lost all track of time. He was aware the bombardment from the guns at Roxbury, Lechmere Point and Cobble Hill had diminished, as had the British counter-fire. Outside of the occasional drunken shout from the town below, or the whinnying of a horse, there was complete silence. There were now twenty cannon in place on the Heights, with Boston and the British ships in the bay within range. The sky faintly began to lighten to the east beyond the harbor.

Will gathered with the gun crews at the edge of the Heights and watched dawn come to Boston. The day promised to be clear and reasonably mild. A few seagulls swooped low over the harbor, squawking raucously. He sniffed the tang of the salt air, borne by a light breeze from the east.

All along the Heights, soldiers weary from laboring through the night stared down at the occupied city. In the growing daylight, Will could make out rows of American troops to his left, standing behind low earthen works, fortifications of bundles of saplings, and hastily erected stonewalls. The eleven heavy guns of the Massachusetts Artillery were in the center of the line, all brass eighteen and twenty-four pounders. To his right, the temporary fortifications extended to the round knoll at the end of the Heights. Will guessed there were several regiments in line, perhaps as many as 2,000 men. Below them, in the flats leading up to the Heights, where the British troops would have to land to make their assault, Will could make out the movement of men in brown hiding behind trees and brush. They were riflemen, an advance line of skirmishers to harass the Regulars from a distance when they landed, or pick off their officers. He wondered whether they were Morgan's or MacDowell's men. Where were the Marblehead Mariners? He was fairly certain the Mariners were not on the Heights.

A loud cheer went up from the men at the far right of the line. Will turned and saw a group of four officers on horseback, a Regiment lined up in parade before them. Even at that distance, he recognized General Washington on his white horse, two men in dark blue uniforms and the large, bulky figure of Colonel Knox. He heard another round of cheers and saw tri-corns thrown in the air before the band of officers rode on to the next closest Regiment. As they progressed closer down the line, Will could hear the regimental officers' calls for three cheers for General Washington and the soldiers' lusty response.

Sooner than he expected, the command troop was at the artillery batteries. Lieutenant Hadley ordered his men to parade rest. They lined up with the entire Massachusetts Regiment, their backs to Boston. Before them, General Washington sat on his horse, the two others, whom he guessed were Generals, flanking him slightly behind, and Colonel Knox further back, accompanied by the Regiment's two Lieutenant Colonels. Will moved closer, standing off to the side of the soldiers lined up in ranks. Some hastily straightened their blue coats and white crossbelts. Others adjusted their tri-corns trying improve their appearance for their Commander.

"Men of the Massachusetts Artillery." Washington paused, although he had every soldier's attention. "Today is Tuesday, March fifth. It is the sixth anniversary of the Boston Massacre." The General's voice was deep but it didn't carry. The men strained forward to listen. Washington's words were more rounded and softer in accent than Will had become accustomed to hearing since arriving in Cambridge. "It is a fitting day to show the British how Massachusetts men avenge the murder of innocent unarmed civilians by regular troops. Your patience and fortitude during the long siege are now about to be rewarded. Our position is strong and becomes stronger every hour." There was a rustling as the men closest to the Commander turned and repeated his words to the men behind, who in turn passed the message down the ranks.

The General sat easily on his horse, his gloved hands resting on the pommel, the dark blue of his cape contrasting sharply with his clean buff colored waistcoat and breeches. The black saddle and his riding boots were highly polished. Probably, Will thought, by his man Lee who he had seen riding with the General the day of the fight between the Mariners and Morgan's Rifles. "We will draw the British out and they will dash their hopes of victory on the ascent to these Heights. Avenge your brethren whose innocent blood was shed this fifth of March in the streets of Boston." He pointed dramatically toward the edge of the Heights, where Boston lay below, as if it were necessary to remind Massachusetts men that the atrocity had been committed within cannon shot of where they stood. "I expect every man to not only do his duty, but to fight like avenging angels of Providence on this historic day." He touched his hand to his tri-corn, signaling the end of his speech. [1]

It was not so much his words that were inspiring. The General's sentences were short. His cadence was clipped, and his mouth, even as he spoke, remained a tight thin line as if he were frugal with his words and conserving energy. It was his whole bearing, his complete calmness in the face of the imminent assault, his reassuring faith in the capabilities of his troops, the ease with which he sat on his horse, the way he looked at, instead of over, the men, which earned their respect.

Colonel Knox, in a much louder voice, boomed out the command, "Three cheers for General Washington." The men of the Regiment responded immediately with three loud huzzahs, the General smiled and the four officers continued their slow ride along the lines to the troops entrenched on the left.

"Well, they know we are here now," Sergeant Merriam called to his crew, motioning for Will to step up on the parapet. The sun was well above the horizon, bathing the city in early-morning light. The Sergeant leaned on his cane and pointed down below. Red-coated figures were visible on the rooftops of buildings and on the ends of some wharves. Dark figures with telescopes stood in the crow's nests of the closest men-of-war. Will restrained the urge to wave to them. Instead he assumed a serious—and he hoped determined—look, in case one of the telescopes was trained on him. He knew the British would focus on the cannons. There seemed to be a flurry of activity, with officers hurrying through the streets to headquarters and a hastily convened council of war. He imagined their surprise and consternation that the "provincials," as the British called them, had occupied the Heights. Next would follow the plans and orders to dislodge them. And then the battle.

The Americans didn't have to wait long. The first reaction was a cannonading from the westerly floating battery and artillery from the forts at The Neck and on Winchmill Point. The light wind blew the smoke toward the salt marshes below them. The cannonballs struck harmlessly midway up the Heights, well below the Massachusetts batteries and above the unseen riflemen hiding in the woods.

"That is the best they can do," Sergeant Merriam said confidently. "They cannot elevate their guns to reach the summit. It is a good lesson for them to learn." Will looked at him quizzically. "The British will not be able to bombard our positions before their infantry assault. Every cannon in the batteries will be intact. We can depress our guns and fire down the slopes. Every Regular will know it and the fear in their hearts will help break their discipline and resolve."

Will watched the gun flashes as another round of cannonballs struck he guessed fifty feet below the summit. The sound of a yell began to the left of the Massachusetts artillery position and flowed past them along the entire line of American troops. It was not so much a cheer as a taunting cry of defiance. It came from the throats of New England men, who, together with their families, communities and congregations, had endured the British occupation for too long. Will joined in, shouting both to belong and to quell his own fear of being under fire.

"Lieutenant Hadley," Colonel Knox shouted, riding up quickly. He dismounted rather easily despite his weight, as the Lieutenant ran up. Will followed and took the horse's reins.

"We are to save our ball and powder for the British assault. However, General Washington has given permission for one round to be fired. To illustrate to General Howe the difficulty of his position and perhaps, to prod him into a decision to attack." He addressed the men of Hadley's battery. "The honor has fallen to us. I would like The Albany to send our message to General Howe."

"Sergeant Merriam. Ready your gun crew," Lieutenant Hadley ordered. Colonel Knox and the Lieutenant walked to the edge of the parapet. The Colonel, never one to whisper, had his arm around the Lieutenant's shoulder.

"The floating battery off The Neck will do nicely as a target," Knox said. Sergeant Merriam hobbled forward, removed his hat, took the Lieutenant's telescope and studied the flat-bottomed wooden platform. There were two British eighteen pounders in the front facing toward Roxbury, and several lighter field cannons mounted on the side covering the road leading to The Neck.

"It is a difficult task without firing a ranging ball first," he said, taking off his tri-corn and scratching his balding head. "It is our opening shot on March fifth," he said grimly to Hadley. "We will do our best."

Will watched the four men wrestle the bright brass eighteen-pounder into position. Sergeant Merriam limped up to the cannon with his gunner's quadrant. He placed the long end of the L into the bore and let the plumb bob swing free. He motioned for one of the men to lever the cannon at the breech. Merriam stuck a wooden wedge under it, elevating the cannon even more. He stuck the quadrant down the bore again, noted the mark on the quadrant and seemed satisfied. One of the crew brought him a canvas powder charge. The Sergeant held it in both hands and shook his head. "Too light for that distance."

The man took a smaller bag from the side box and Merriam weighed both. "That will do. Reload both charges into one bag," he commanded. This took a while because the seam had to be undone and re-sewn with the extra powder added. Satisfied with the weight of new charge, Merriam checked the angle and elevation one more time and nodded. The four-man crew stepped forward and removed the side boxes from the carriage and carried them to the rear of the emplacement. They returned, two men on each side of The Albany. By now the other gun crews were crowded off to the sides on the parapet to see where the shot would land. Will thought if cannon exploded like the howitzer, it would kill a good portion of the active artillerists on the Heights.

"Sponge and ram," Merriam ordered. One of the crew stepped forward, dipped the sheepskin-covered sponge at the end of a pole in a bucket of water and swabbed down the barrel while another of the crew blocked the vent with his thumb. The canvas charge was rammed home, followed by an eighteen pound ball. Will heard it rolling down the angled barrel until it hit the powder bag. He watched as the soldier leaned his weight on the pole, forcing the ball snug against the powder charge.

Merriam stepped up to the vent and inserted a wire to prick the canvas. He pulled a quill filled with powder from his pouch and slid it into the touchhole. "Primed," he shouted. He placed a slow match to the quill. "Give Fire," he yelled. The gun crew stepped a pace away from the cannon. Will glanced at the Colonel, standing to the left of the gun with a telescope to his eye, his mouth formed in an easy smile of anticipation.

The Albany roared, the extra powder producing a deafening noise. The smoke rolled back on their position. Will inhaled the intoxicating acrid odor of gunpowder. He heard the cheering and ran forward. The cannonball had struck the closest edge of the floating battery, tearing a hole along the railing and wooden deck. The battery listed and immediately began taking on water.

"Well done, Sergeant. Well done indeed," Colonel Knox said, clapping the smaller man on the back. "An excellent shot across their bows, so to speak," he said to the gun crew, who were all standing on the parapet examining their handiwork.

"I was hoping to hit it dead on, sir, and perhaps ignite her powder,"

Merriam said, grinning sheepishly. "The explosion would have been more spectacular."

"Sinking a floating battery with one shot is spectacular enough," Knox replied exuberantly. "When we capture Boston, those cannons will be useful to us. More so than if you had succeeded and blown them into the harbor."

With nothing to do now except wait for the British attack, Will watched additional troops marching on the road behind the batteries. The fresh troops coming to fill in the lines brought entrenching tools and hacked at the frozen ground, deepening the trenches and adding height to the parapets. Light cannon of the Massachusetts and Rhode Island Artillery Regiments, three, six and nine pounders, passed by and were dispersed along the forward edge of the lines to the right. Will noted that each field piece was pulled by one horse, ridden by a nattily uniformed soldier. He imagined himself on Big Red, wearing such a blue coat, wheeling the gun into battle, with Sergeant Merriam and his crew at the ready to fire it into the lines of advancing Redcoats.

By mid-morning, after the euphoria of the successful cannonball shot had worn off and the weariness from lack of sleep had set in, Will joined the gun crews looking silently down on the city.

"There is General Howe's answer to our occupying the Heights," Sergeant Merriam said soberly, gesturing below with his cane. Several units were parading in neat red squares on the Common. Some were visible marching down a broad street before disappearing from view behind the dark brick buildings. In the harbor, men of war were leaving the wharves under sail, moving out toward open water, while others maneuvered in toward the piers.

"Those ships tying up at Long Wharf," Merriam said. Will nodded. "They are troop transports. See, they have no gun ports."

Columns of Redcoats emerged from King Street leading down to Long Wharf. The late-morning sun glinted off their bayonets. They marched, in perfect unison, down the pier and onto the waiting transports. They were followed by a unit of dragoons. The sound of the horses' hooves drumming on the wooden planks carried up to the Americans on the Heights. Will watched the cavalry men dismount and lead their horses up two broad ramps to a ship.

"Those will be the Light Dragoons," Merriam said. "They were at Bunker Hill. The Death Heads will find the slopes up these Heights much tougher going."

"Death Heads?" Will asked.

"They have a skull emblazoned on the front of their black caps," Merriam explained.

"We have riflemen this time," one of the gun crew said, "and we did not at Bunker Hill. They will aim two inches below that skull and blow the Dragoons out of their saddles." Will thought of the ease with which General Washington had leaped the wall outside his headquarters. He saw the Dragoons coming over the parapets with sabers drawn. He realized he had no weapons other than his knife and hatchet. He had hunted on the farm with a musket before and knew how to use one. Maybe he could get one. The gun crews were armed, some with muskets affixed with long bayonets, others with lances or pikes. Lieutenant Hadley carried both sword and pistol.

"The longer they take to embark and land, the hotter their reception will be," Lieutenant Hadley said, pointing to a militia unit marching past them on the road behind their battery. He rubbed his unshaven cheeks and chin as if they itched. "As General Washington said, we get stronger with each passing hour. When they attack, we will carry the day. Of that I am certain."

"Sir. Do you know where the Marblehead Mariners are stationed?" Will asked.

Lieutenant Hadley looked at him. He took off his tri-corn and wiped his brow. There was little wind. It was getting warmer as the sun was directly overhead. "They are below Cambridge, manning our flatboats. As General Howe draws his troops out of Boston to attack the Heights, General Washington has ordered General Putnam to attack the city, landing at the west end of Mill Pond. They only await a signal from us that the Redcoats are fully committed in their attack here at Dorchester Heights."

Will nodded and imagined his friends, Adam, Solomon and Jeremiah, and especially Nat, ready to row the troops across. He wasn't sure of the positions of the British batteries but hoped there were none nearby. He wondered how quickly the Mariners could row a flat-bottomed boat, heavy with standing soldiers, across the inner harbor. Somewhat guiltily, he realized he had thought of himself as one of the artillery men a few moments ago, instead of being with the Mariners.

"It will be a few hours before they land," Sergeant Merriam said. "At least enough time to eat and drink. It will be another long day."

Will remained at the parapet, studying the activity below. He watched a unit of Grenadiers, easily identifiable by their high black bearskin caps, emerge from the city streets onto a pier adjacent to Long Wharf. The sound of their drums drifted up as they marched in cadence to the beat, down the long pier and up the ramps onto a waiting transport. The noonday sun flashed off the long bayonets fixed to the end of their muskets. More troops emerged from the city streets and flowed in steady red lines, boarding the ships tied up at the stubby finger-like piers.

Will tore a piece of bread from the loaf in his haversack and cut a piece of cheese off the wedge he had brought with him. Johan was down there, somewhere in Boston. He hoped he was safe.

Sergeant Merriam, having discarded his cane, limped up and stood next to him. "Those Grenadiers are going to be hot in their bearskin caps in the hold of that ship," he observed. "Ah. I wondered when they would load artillery." He pointed to several light cannon being wheeled down a wharf closer to them. "That's Oliver's Wharf, near their south battery. Those are three and six pounders. Good for firing across open fields at massed troops. I doubt if they will be of any effect on our positions."

Will looked at the defensive lines stretching out on both sides of the batteries. Some soldiers were still endeavoring to improve the works. To the left, earthen battlements had been thrown up. In front of them, the bundles of saplings had been dismantled and intertwined to form an interlocking barrier, shaped like a long arrowhead pointing downward. In the center, the stone- and earth-filled barrels stood upright as protection, ready to be turned sideways and rolled down the icy slope, which had thawed and turned to mud in some places. He could picture the barrels smashing and breaking the legs of the advancing Grenadiers, the chains cutting them in half and throwing them back down the hill.

Will heard cries from below, and one by one, six transports pushed away from the wharf. With sails unfurled, they moved slowly out of the harbor on a northeasterly course, avoiding the American guns on the Heights before turning south. Will watched them parallel Dorchester Heights and disappear around the point.

Sergeant Merriam offered Will his canteen.

"They are heading for Castle Island, around Dorchester Point," he said. "The shoals there are dry at low water. They will have to watch their tides."

Will took a long drink. It tasted like watered hard cider. He drank thirstily as he watched several empty transports maneuver into position and dock at Long Wharf. More troops marched down the pier and boarded.

"They had better be quick about it," Merriam said, scanning the sky to the south. "There is weather moving in." Will turned around, away from Boston. Close to land the sky was a light grey. In the distance, out to sea, scalloped clouds preceded ominous long strips of deep grey until, near the horizon, the sky was a threatening solid mass of darkness. The light breeze, that had come from the harbor early in the day was now blowing from behind them, a harbinger of the weather to come.

Throughout the early afternoon the wind continued to strengthen and the skies became blacker. By four o'clock the British transports leaving the wharves were encountering a strong southwesterly wind, making it difficult for them to cross the harbor and reach Castle Island. A few of the last to depart turned around and quickly skittered back to the wharf, aided by the stiff wind at their backs. Will felt the temperature dropping and wrapped his coat tightly around his body. The surface of the ground, which had begun to thaw in the mild midday temperatures, once again became hard and treacherous underfoot.

In anticipation of the foul weather, Lieutenant Hadley ordered the gun crews to protect the powder and keep it dry. Canvas tents and cooking pots had been brought up during the day. Will helped one of the crews spread the canvas on the ground, anchor it with the cooking pots and carry the side boxes onto it. They covered the boxes with more canvas, tucking the ends under each one and securing the remaining canvas to two tent poles. The end result was a lean-to structure with the powder boxes wedged at the low southeast end, and the tent opening to the northwest, away from the direction the wind was blowing. The wind was now much stronger. There was no question of erecting tents on the exposed heights for shelter. Instead, each crew tied one end of their tent to the trunnions of the cannon and formed a low triangle of the remaining canvas, holding it down with large rocks or the remaining but useless cooking pots.

There was nothing to be done for the horses. Will did not want to leave the Heights and ride to Roxbury in search of a shed. Instead, he led Big Red and the mare down a slope away from the crest, found a reasonably sheltered hollow, and tethered both horses to a tree. As he returned to the summit, the rain swept in from the southeast, pelting down in enormous cold sheets. He ran up the back of the slope and crawled, wet and shivering, into the lean-to shelter around The Albany. There were five men, including Sergeant Merriam, already crowded together. It was clear to Will that although he was welcome to stay, his presence was a burden. Without a word he dashed out into the storm and crept into the shelter erected to protect the gunpowder. The tent poles holding up the canvas flap as an opening swayed in the now gale-like winds. Will pulled down one of the poles, piled stones around the base of the remaining pole to give it more support and retreated to the low end, away from the opening. He leaned up against the powder boxes. Through the narrow slit he watched the rain change first to sleet and then to hailstones. The sound of the icy pellets bounced off the cannons with a high pitched metal noise. The hail on the canvas roof over his head was more like drumming. He swung his haversack around to his chest to make sure it would stay dry, pulled his knees up to his chest, and waited. After a while, the noise of the hail abated, replaced by the softer whisper of sleet whipping against his flimsy canvas shelter as the wind continued to howl.

Lieutenant Hadley pulled back the flap and duck-walked in, taking his blue tri-corn off and shaking it at the narrow entrance. His curly brown hair was coated with granulated snow, as was his cloak. He moved to the back of the small shelter and leaned up against a side box next to Will.

"Sergeant Merriam thought you might be here," he said, wiping the melting snow from his dripping hair with the back of his hand. "My horse split his front left hoof and is lame. We need to ride to Roxbury and bring food and drink back for the men. Where are your horses?"

They ran down the back of the slope together, the Lieutenant leading his lame horse. He tied it up, un-cinched his saddle and placed it on the mare. Will looked for a tree stump and finding none was about to hoist himself on to Big Red as best he could. Hadley grabbed him by the shoulder to get his attention in the roaring wind. He made a stirrup with his two gloved hands, and Will vaulted onto Big Red's back. He followed the Lieutenant down the road leading off of the Heights, riding with the wind at their backs. Will was conscious of the snow on Big Red's back melting from Will's own warmth and the friction of riding. It soaked his legs and buttocks. They turned off the low Dorchester causeway toward Roxbury and rode straight into the storm. The Lieutenant's cape blew behind him in the wind like a large, dark blue sail. Pellets of sleet struck Will's face. His bare fingers, clutching the reins, were frozen in their grip. The wind clawed at his hat and found ways to drive sleet through gaps in his scarf, where it melted on his skin and dripped down his neck. The granules stuck to his coat and the icy wetness permeated his inner layers of clothing that were quickly almost as wet as his outer garment.

They rode past the junction of the Dorchester and Boston Neck Roads and clattered through the rutted streets of Roxbury until they reached the Old Oak Tavern. Will slid off Big Red, cold, wet and stiff. The Lieutenant pointed at the barn and shouted something to him. His words were lost in the storm. Will led the two horses in, grateful to be under cover. Outside, the wind continued to howl and the sleet hammered on the cedar shingled roof. All of the stalls were filled. Several carriages were crowded into the shelter. Will tied Big Red and the mare up temporarily to an iron ring, and pulled one of the carriages outside to make more room. He found a relatively warm place well back from the door and tethered the horses there. Without giving it a thought, he removed a blanket from another horse in a stall and rubbed Big Red down. He un-cinched the Lieutenant's saddle from the grey, hung it on a wooden peg and rubbed her down as well. Then, he prowled around the shed until he found oats and a bale of hay fit for his horses. Only after he had fed them did he wrap Elisabeth's scarf tightly around his neck over his mother's red one and, holding his hat on his head against the strong gusts, run the short distance to the tavern. The candles on the tables flickered as the wind and sleet followed him in, until he slammed the thick wooden door shut behind him.

Will looked around the crowded room, mostly filled with

townspeople, merchants and tradesmen, with a few farmers scattered here and there. He sniffed in the mucus running from his nose and inhaled the overwhelming aroma of roasting meats mixed with the smell of wet wool. Lieutenant Hadley had commandeered a snug table near the large roaring fire in the chimney corner. His cloak and hat hung from a hook near the fireplace, dripping water onto the floor beneath them. He was the only man in uniform in the large room. Two prosperously dressed middle-aged men, their vests buttoned and their jackets well tailored, shared the table with the Lieutenant. Their clothes were dry and they seemed to have eaten well, Will thought, judging by the bones of some fish and fowl that littered the plates in front of them.

"Master Stoner. Over here," Hadley shouted over the noise of the packed room. Will gratefully took off his soggy coat, hung it next to the Lieutenant's cloak and warmed the wet seat of his pants against the fire. His linen shirt under his short coat was soaked. His fingers tingled as he thawing them out, turning his hands in front of the blaze as if he were cooking them on both sides. He was aware, as he stood close to the endirons, water was leaked out from the seams of his boots. If he could have taken off his boots and dried his stockings by the fire, he would have. Instead, still dripping, he sat down shivering on the oak bench next to Hadley.

"These two fine gentlemen were explaining to me how Divine Providence has intervened by this storm to save General Howe and the Redcoats from certain disaster."

"That is definitely the fact. Do you not agree, Sir?" the pudgy man nearest to Will said. He moved slightly away from Will as if repulsed by either his smell or his wetness. "We were on the hills behind the Heights and had a grand view of our lines. Impregnable, I must say."

"Yes," the other added. "From our vantage point, although we would not have been able to see the devastation as the Regulars charged up the slopes, it was clear to me they would have been slaughtered," he said with complete conviction.

"Will," Lieutenant Hadley said, encompassing the room with a sweep of his arm, "these two gentlemen, and most of the others here came out this fine morning to view the battle and our great victory. From a safe distance and afar, it must be noted. No disrespect is intended, gentlemen," Hadley added politely, noting they had scowled when he had pointed out their distance from the American lines. "You are not soldiers and are not be expected to be in harm's way." The two gentlemen nodded their agreement, pleased the Lieutenant understood their position and was not questioning their courage.

"Then the storm came up suddenly and they have been trapped, and I use the word deliberately, confined to this fine tavern, until it abates. This dreadful winter storm deprives them, snug and comfortable as they are here, from loved ones, their homes and the warm hearths that undoubtedly await them."

A serving girl brought three pewter mugs of hot mulled cider and smiled at the Lieutenant. She curtseyed slightly and put them down in front of Hadley and the two gentlemen. The Lieutenant took one of the mugs from the nearest gentlemen and gave it to Will. He stood up, with his drink in one hand and his right leg nonchalantly resting on the bench."

"Gentlemen," he cried in a loud voice. "A toast to the success of our Commander in Chief, General Washington." Conversation stopped, there were cries of "Hear! Hear!" as the men in the room raised their mugs. "And to Generals Ward and Thomas, who are in command of these Heights." More cheers of "Hear! Hear!" and "Well done!" echoed around the room.

Hadley took a sip and smacked his lips in pleasure. He stood tall and erect, surveying the room. Even though his uniform was stained with mud and wet in places, he exuded a commanding presence among the civilians in the tavern.

"Gentlemen, I pray your indulgence again. A toast," he cried, raising his mug in the air. "To the brave men of Massachusetts, of my own Regiment, who man the battlements at this very moment, and stand ready to repel the contemptible Red Coats if they should even dare to attack." His call was answered by more cheers. Will took a long swallow, savoring the warmth of the hot cider and the heat of the mug in his hands.

"And now, on behalf of my gallant men, I ask for your support. They struggled up the slopes and labored long and hard throughout the night, not ceasing until the dawn broke over Boston. They have stood watch throughout this long day, the sixth anniversary of the most heinous crime ever committed by British troops against innocent civilians." He paused, scanning the eager faces in the room, attentively watching him. "And now they brave the dangers of this gale to man our batteries and prepare for the battle on the morrow. They are cold and wet and hungry. Their morale is high but it will be improved by hot meats, cider, rum and ale."

Hadley unbuttoned his buff colored vest and removed a piece of paper from his shirt beneath. He held it high and waved it to the crowded room. "I have an order from General Washington, authorizing me to requisition victuals and supplies for my Regiment. To effectuate this order, the proprietor of the Old Oak Tavern, a good patriot I am certain, will surely comply." Will saw a stout bald man come out from behind the long table where he had been pouring ale, an alarmed look on his face, nervously wiping his hands on a cloth. Will surmised he was the owner. "He will be paid in due course," Hadley continued. "However, the immediate financial burden will fall solely on his patriotic head. Or should I say, his pocketbook." There was nervous laughter, as the merchants and tradesmen cautiously waited to see where the Lieutenant was heading.

"Gentlemen. I propose each of you reach into your own purses and purchase the necessary victuals and drink for the gallant and brave men of my Regiment. Who will be the first to do so?" Hadley looked at the two townsmen seated at his table. Under his direct gaze, they both reddened and hurriedly reached into their coats and pulled out some coins. The Lieutenant inclined his head imperceptibly toward Will, who took the coins and stacked them in front of him.

"Well done and most generous, I must say," Hadley cried out in praise of his two tablemates. "Who is next? Please place your coins on the table for Master Stoner to tally." There was a general shuffling as men came forward and deposited shillings and pence, mindful of the amounts others were giving. The stacks of coins multiplied as Hadley shouted encouragement and thanks to those giving, however reluctantly. Will divided the shillings, half shillings and pence into stacks until there was a veritable wall of coins, like miniatures of the barrels standing protectively on the parapets in front of the batteries.

The Lieutenant called for the proprietor to step forward. The pudgy man approached the table, unsure of what would happen next, his eyes darting nervously from the Lieutenant to the rows of coins.

"Here is the money generously donated to buy food and drink for my men," Hadley said towering over the owner and putting his arm around the fat man's shoulder in a comradely fashion. "Give your fellow patriots a fair price for their contributions and perhaps you can err on the side of more rather than less if the occasion should present itself," the Lieutenant said, his tone more of a suggestion than an order.

"I certainly will. It will be my honor to be of service," the owner said pleased he was being paid in coin for provisions which he had earlier feared would be requisitioned. He began sweeping the coins into a pouch he had removed from under his apron.

"Good man" the Lieutenant said clapping him on the back. "I can see you are a fine fellow. Please be so kind as to lend us a wagon to bring these supplies back to my brave men on the Heights. Master Stoner is an experienced teamster. He will return your wagon tomorrow. Unless, of course, General Howe sees fit to inconvenience us by assaulting our positions." The pudgy man frowned, obviously thinking he might never see his wagon again. He smiled sheepishly at his customers who were anxious to avoid giving up their carriages, as they called out for him to acquiesce.

"Permit me, Lieutenant, to provide you and this young man here with food and drink, at my own expense," he added quickly, still uncertain if the Lieutenant had finished making demands on him. "Stay in the warmth of my tavern's fire while the supplies are being prepared and loaded on my wagon," he said more loudly so the men in the room could hear his offer, emphasizing it was his wagon which would be at risk on the Heights.

Hadley grinned broadly, accepted the invitation and shook the owner's hand vigorously. "You are a true patriot," he said earnestly. "A true patriot indeed."

In a few minutes, the serving girl brought out two steaming bowls of hearty fish chowder, followed by a platter of roast beef, bread and hard cheese. She returned with mugs of spiced cider.

"Please, sir," she said shyly to Hadley. "I would like to contribute also to purchase food for your men." She reached out and placed a few small coins in the Lieutenant's hand.

Will looked at her, comparing her unconsciously to Elisabeth. He guessed she was about the same age. She was much more homely he thought. Her long brown hair was wispy and somewhat unkempt, her figure seemed to him a little on the plump side, and her face was more harried and careworn than welcoming.

Lieutenant Hadley sprang to his feet as if he were greeting Martha Washington herself. He snapped his heels together, bowed low from the waist and kissed the serving girl's hand.

"I am deeply touched, young lady, by your gesture," he replied, continuing to hold her hand, while staring into her eyes. She blushed and looked down. "If my duty did not interfere, I would be courting you day and night because you have reached my heart." He said it with such tender emotion and conviction, Will could see the Lieutenant riding up on his horse and calling on the girl at the tavern. "However, as a gentleman and an officer, I cannot accept your coins. I pray you keep me in your prayers for safe passage through the coming battle. And I will be stronger in knowing you are thinking of me." With a gesture of great reluctance, he folded her fingers around the coins and released her hand.

Will held the reins in his hands. The Lieutenant sat next to him on the tavern owner's wagon as they retraced their way through Roxbury, across the causeway and up the slope to the batteries. Behind them, beneath two stout canvas sheets tied down with strong ropes, were kegs of rum and hard cider and wooden crates containing roast beef, venison, chickens still warm from the spits, bread and cheese.

It was close to nine o'clock and the storm had not abated. Sleet and ice pellets drove down at them in the dark. In a matter of minutes Will was soaked through and chilled again. The wind that had been in their faces on the road to Roxbury, was now at their backs, but as soon as they began the ascent, it lashed at them with renewed vigor. The batteries loomed in the dark, a sorry soggy, muddy encampment of drooping canvas and puddles of wind-whipped water. The Lieutenant jumped off and ran from one makeshift shelter to the next. As the men rushed out, Will stood in the back of the wagon, bracing himself against the wind, handing the kegs and boxes into their eager hands.

When the wagon was empty, he drove it down to the same hollow and unhitched the horses. He left Big Red and the mare exposed to the storm, feeling sorry for them as he ran back through the slush and water that flowed downhill in rivulets and small streams. He scuttled into his lean-to, shivering and wet. Hadley was leaning against the side boxes. Will collapsed, exhausted, next to the Lieutenant. The floor canvas was stained from the mud of their boots and the moisture seeping up from underneath. The memory of the brief respite of warmth and food at the tavern was not much comfort to him as he tried to stop his shaking under his waterlogged coat.

Hadley offered Will a piece of ham he had sliced, along with soggy bread. Will took the ham, nibbled on the meat and balled the wet bread in his fist. The dough stuck to his palm as he squeezed it.

"Too bad we could not have brought the men fish chowder," he said.

Will nodded, thinking of how good it had tasted. A few months ago he had never even eaten it before. Now, he knew a good chowder had more fish than potatoes, with salt pork and onions for flavor.

"General Washington plans for every eventuality," Will said, trying out a thought. After tonight's shared experience, he no longer felt shy of Hadley.

"What do you mean?" the Lieutenant asked, chewing thoughtfully on another piece of ham.

"Well, midmorning, we had pots and provisions for the Regiment, and enough food to cook and eat before the transports left the harbor. The General must have foreseen the weather would interfere with their cooking and issued an order to requisition food prepared somewhere else" he paused, "say for example, a tavern." Will looked slyly at him.

Hadley laughed. He reached inside his coat and handed Will the piece of paper. There was no light for Will to read it. "It's an order, signed by Colonel Knox directing the Regiment to move from Lechmere Point to Dorchester Heights," Hadley explained, taking the paper back.

"I cannot abide these pompous civilians who neither join their local militias nor enlist in a Continental regiment and yet have views on every aspect of military strategy although they have never been on a battlefield. Even worse," Hadley continued, "they dare to observe the assault from a safe distance as if it were a theater performance, a show put on for their benefit, when real men will be maimed and killed. It matters not, whether the casualties be Redcoats or Continentals. War is not a event performed for audiences of non-combatants," he concluded vehemently.

"So you made them pay a price," Will said after awhile.

"I gave them the opportunity to do their patriotic duty and feed my men," the Lieutenant acknowledged. "If I could, I would have stuck them for more."

Will moved his back against the boxes, trying not to think of the numbing cold from the soggy ground, his chilled body and his frozen, raw hands.

"Are you from Boston, Sir," Will asked. "I was hoping for advice on where to look for my older brother, Johan. He is an apprentice to a merchant."

"I was born there. I have not been in the city since the end of April of '75." The Lieutenant was in a talkative mood. There was nothing else to do in the darkness, except listen to the storm or try to sleep. "My mother and sister escaped and I escorted them to Worcester, where they now live with my mother's relatives, my uncle and his family. I hope to return them to Boston and our home once the British have been driven out."

It was awkward carrying on a conversation in the dark without seeing if the other was about to speak or not. Will didn't know if the Lieutenant had paused or finished. He waited until Hadley asked, "Do you know the name of the merchant?"

Will shook his head. "No. My father omitted telling me when we parted." The Lieutenant pondered the problem for a moment. "Perhaps the best place would be to start at the wharves. Most of the merchants maintain their offices in their warehouses. Of course, with the British blockade, I doubt if many of them have remained in business. There is no trade to speak of. Unless one is a Tory."

"I thought it would be easy. But when Nat, that is Lieutenant Holmes, described Boston to me, I realized how many people live there. It seems larger than even Albany, which is the biggest town I have ever been to."

Hadley chuckled. It was a warm, comforting laugh. "It is definitely more populated than Albany. I can assure you of that although I have never been to northern New York myself. Who is this Lieutenant Holmes? I do not believe I know of him."

Will described how Nat befriended him at the beginning of the great trek and the journey itself, how he was quartered with the Mariners, the riot with Morgan's Rifles and Nat's courtship of Anna with Colonel Glover's aid. "He was to be married, in Salem, before we scaled Dorchester Heights. I suspect he is now with the Mariners, as you told me, waiting to row the troops across."

"He is a lucky man to have married his true love," the Lieutenant said wistfully. Will shifted his weight, easing the stiffness setting into his legs.

"Why did you leave Boston?" he asked.

"Because I was suspected of activities against the Crown and I was a member of the Massachusetts Artillery Regiment. I secreted myself in a hay wagon and slipped past the British sentries, making my way to Cambridge to rejoin the Colonel."

"Were you at Bunker Hill?" Will asked excitedly, forgetting for a moment the clinging wet fabric of his pants pressed against his skin.

"No," the Lieutenant said in the dark next to him. There was a definite tone of regret in his voice. "I was with Colonel Knox at Roxbury, preparing fortifications. The two redoubts we passed on this side of the town before beginning our ascent," he said. "The morrow's battle will be my first."

"And where is your father?" Will asked. He feared his question may have been too personal. In the murky dark of the lean-to he could not see the Lieutenant's face to judge his reaction.

"Ah, therein lies a tale of happy coincidence, although my father is no longer alive to see the fruits of his generosity. He died four years ago this past January, in the winter of '72." Will waited in the darkness for Hadley to continue.

"My father was a teacher, a poorly paid yet highly respected profession. He taught at the Boston Latin School and young Henry

Knox was one of his students. When the Colonel's father died, Henry was compelled to leave and support his widowed mother." He coughed lightly. Will heard him untop his canteen, drink and felt a tap on his arm as Hadley offered him a drink. Will put the canteen to his lips and felt the rum warm his throat. He handed it back to the Lieutenant, wiping his mouth with his wet sleeve.

"Henry was apprenticed to the booksellers Wharton and Bowes, known to my father because they supplied books to Boston Latin. He prevailed upon Mr. Bowes to make available for Henry's education certain books in the store, destined for the school, for him to read." Hadley sneezed three times in quick succession.

"Every Sabbath, after services at the Church of the Presbyterian Strangers, which Mrs. Knox and her two boys attended, as did my family, my father would bring Henry to our home and question him about his readings. He would also have him practice declamations, which Henry could not do before the other boys because he was no longer a student."

"I heard the Colonel give a speech to some teamsters from Massachusetts during the great trek," Will said. "It was truly inspiring." He remained silent, hoping Hadley would not ask him to recite it, certain his efforts at declamation would be deemed insufficient by a man as educated as the Lieutenant.

"The Colonel has a way with words," Hadley continued, "due in part to my father's attachment to him. And he to my father, I should add. When my father died, I was around your age. The Colonel offered me a position in his militia. At the time it was called the Boston Grenadier Corps. And so here I am, my father's kindness repaid by the Colonel's, for which I am both grateful and resolved to do my utmost to uphold the Colonel's trust in me."

"If you permit me to say so Sir, the way you acted at the tavern, cajoling the townspeople and graciously speaking to the serving girl show you too have the power to move people by speech."

Hadley laughed. "I will take that as a compliment, Master Stoner. I always treat every member of the fairer sex as if she were a queen," Hadley replied. "Besides, the young girl possessed more integrity in her dainty little fingers than all of the men in the tavern." In the ensuing silence, Will was unsure whether the Lieutenant was musing about the events in the tavern, the serving girl or another matter.

"Well," the Lieutenant finally said, "it will begin again tomorrow. And we must be rested and ready to greet the King's men."

At the mention of sleep, Will felt overcome by exhaustion. He thought about making his bed on top of the boxes but the canvas was too low. There was nothing for it except to lie down and endure the water.

"So, Will, what are we to do about our palatial quarters?" Hadley asked cheerfully. "My suggestion," he said quickly, answering his own question, "is that you put your coat down on top of the floor canvas and I use my cloak to cover us both. And I hope you told Dr. Thaxter the truth when you said you had smallpox as a child. It would be unpleasant if you developed a case from his inoculation." Will sensed the humor in his voice. "I would not be able to shelter some young maiden under my cloak unless I first asked her if she has had the pox. And such a question could lead to embarrassing complications." He chuckled to himself as Will took off his wet coat. He didn't understand what the Lieutenant meant, but by now he was too tired to ask. They both lay down, the Lieutenant's back against the wooden side boxes and Will next to him, facing the makeshift entrance to their shelter. Will pulled a corner of Hadley's cloak over his shoulder. He fell asleep wondering whether to tell the Lieutenant about Elisabeth.

The next day, Wednesday March sixth, the only improvement in the weather was an increase in the temperature, changing the sleet to rain. The wind continued unabated from the southeast. At midday Lieutenant Hadley borrowed the mare and rode off to an Officers' meeting at General Thomas' headquarters at the parsonage in Roxbury. Will hitched Big Red to the wagon and drove it to the Old Oak Tavern. It was a cold wet trip. He comforted himself with the thought that he would be inside and sheltered, however briefly, which is more than the rest of the Regiment would enjoy that day. He tarried in the barn, now mostly empty. It appeared the tavern's patrons had finally gone home. He led Big Red into a stall and gave him oats and hay, waiting until he finished before rubbing him down with a blanket he took from another wagon.

Inside the tavern, Will told the owner he had returned his wagon and offered to pay for his horse's feed. The man waved him off with shake of his plump hands, motioning Will to take a place at a table near the fire. He brought him a tankard of mulled cider. Will's offer to pay for a steaming bowl of fish chowder and warm bread was likewise refused. Maybe, he mused, the owner never expected to see his wagon again.

Will ate his meal hastily and with a tinge of guilt, thinking of Sergeant Merriam and the others at the battery. He assuaged his feelings by reasoning he had helped bring food back last night and the men had been appreciative. He left without seeing the serving girl, which was for the best, as he only wanted to study her closely for the purpose of comparing her unfavorably to Elisabeth. "What a mean thought," he muttered to himself as he mounted Big Red, using an anvil as a step to get up on the horse's back. He rode back to the Heights, chastising himself for not taking more to heart the Lieutenant's words about how to treat women.

The rest of the day passed uneventfully, the men alternately huddling in their low canvas shelters or, when driven by boredom or necessity, braving the incessant rain and emerging to stare down the slopes toward Boston Harbor below, or to dash off into the sparse woods to relieve themselves.

In the late afternoon Will crawled into the canvas shelter attached to The Albany. Sergeant Merriam, his back against the gun carriage wheel, was biting off a piece of meat speared on the point of his knife. His tri-corn rested on the gun carriage's hub. Will greeted Merriam and the two others of the crew and squatted in the center of their small space.

"On behalf of this crew, we thank you for your efforts last night. Warm meat never tasted so good as it did then," Merriam said. In the dimness of the lean-to, he seemed thinner in the face and less cherubic-looking than the night Will had first seen him at the barracks. There were bags under his eyes. His jowly cheeks moved slowly up and down, as he methodically chewed the meat.

"Tomorrow we need to bring dry powder up from Roxbury. I have been to your shelter and opened the side boxes. The canvas charges are wet. We cannot trust any of the powder we have here to fire." Will nodded. "There are wagons and sleds in Roxbury at the Powder Tower. Do you still have your horses?"

"I have Big Red. Lieutenant Hadley took the mare when his horse split a hoof. Big Red can pull any load of powder you need," Will said confidently.

"Well, we will wait orders from the Lieutenant but I believe that will be the first one on the morrow. Unless this storm continues," he added. "Then, I do not know what we will do."

"But the Regulars' powder will also be wet," Will said. "They will be unable to fire."

"Their plan is to storm our lines with bayonets at the ready," one of the gunners said. "As they did at Bunker Hill," the other added. "Without powder for our cannons or muskets, we cannot blast them before they reach the Heights."

"And the barrels we intend to roll down on them are not enough?" a gunner asked, anticipating Will's question.

"You men are forgetting the Death Head Dragoons," Merriam said. The lean-to was silent as each of them contemplated the British cavalry charging over the low walls and slashing about with their sabers. "Without dry powder, our soldiers on foot will be no match for them."

There was a shout from outside. Will quickly stood up, brushing his head against the canvas. A steady drip of water seeped through where his head had met the ceiling. "Sorry," he said sheepishly, backing out of the opening, careful not to bump the waterlogged canvas again.

Several of the gun crew were standing near the edge, shoulders hunched, their tri-corns pulled down against the steady rain.

"There is a ship coming from Castle Island to the harbor," one explained, pointing to the white sails of a small transport running before the rain-driven wind. It tied up at Long Wharf. A red-cloaked figure ran down the gangplank and jumped into a waiting carriage. Will watched the carriage disappear down the wharf through the mist before retreating to his lean-to. He sat there alone. Unwilling to risk getting the broadsheets and journals wet, he left his haversack unopened. With nothing to read, he resorted to composing another letter in his mind to Elisabeth. He did not think he would be killed in the coming battle but felt he must write her before something happened to him. In his solitary shelter he recited the letter out loud.

That night Will slept alone with the side boxes. It was colder and less cheery without the Lieutenant's company, body warmth and cloak. Sometime in the early hours of the morning Will was aware, through the fog of his deep sleep, the rain had stopped and the wind had abated. He was awakened by Lieutenant Hadley shaking his shoulder.

"Will wake up. Wake up. Now."

He sat up quickly, frozen in body and panic stricken that the Redcoats were attacking. He could see Hadley's face in front of him. It must be dawn or close to it, he guessed.

"Saddle up and get to the powder tower in Roxbury." Will, still half asleep, thought, "What a silly thing for the Lieutenant to say." He knew Will had no saddle. Will peered at Hadley's face. It was clean shaven. Somewhere he had found a razor and warm water, he thought. "There should be wagons and sleds there. Load up quickly and return here. I want some dry powder immediately."

Will, now wide awake, needed no further urging. He clambered down the muddy slope to where Big Red was tethered. The sky, just beginning to lighten in the predawn, was clear, the air fresh and crisp. The road from the Heights down to Roxbury was empty except for an occasional courier and a few militia men, from what unit he could not tell, who had strayed into Roxbury for the night.

He was challenged at the powder tower by a sentry. Will explained his mission. The sentry was adamant. Without written orders, the sentry would not permit him to remove any charges. Will, motivated by Lieutenant Hadley's sense of urgency, thought to ride the sentry down . Before he could act impulsively another sentry, a soldier from the Massachusetts Artillery, recognized Will and vouched for him. "He took care of us when we had the pox," he explained to the others. "Make way and let the lad through."

Will hitched Big Red up to a wagon and, with the help of the sentry who had spoken up for him, loaded the precious canvas bags onto the flat wooden floor. The sun was rising over Boston when he returned to the Heights. The lean-tos and shelters were gone, taken down and laid out to dry. The gun crews had emptied the side boxes of the doubtful powder and placed them in rows, lying on the canvas facing east to catch the morning sun, but well back from the batteries. While the men unloaded the fresh gunpowder, Will explained to Lieutenant Hadley the difficulty he had encountered trying to get powder without written orders.

"I have not my kit with me and no ink and quill to write with. I cannot spare anyone from the gun crew. The British may attack in the early morning." He reached inside his coat and gave Will, Colonel Knox's order to move the Regiment to the Heights. "Wave it in their faces if our man is not there. Otherwise, ride to General Thomas' headquarters in Roxbury. Perhaps Colonel Knox will be there. Now hurry. Bring back a heavier load. If you hear cannon fire, come back with whatever charges are already on the wagon."

Will nodded, turned Big Red around and clattered down the road toward the causeway. The road was crowded with all manner of wagons and sleds heading up the slopes. He was slowed by wagons drawn by docile, plodding oxen laden with all sorts of supplies that Will could see were not essential to the imminent battle. There were wagons with bales of hay, tents, bedding, pots and boxes filled with whatever. "Someone should have sorted all this out," he muttered to himself, looking down the road for a wider place to pass. He waited impatiently behind a train of empty wagons heading down to Roxbury, or maybe Cambridge. At the junction with the low causeway he swerved around an ox cart and managed to move briskly along the familiar road to Roxbury. He listened for the sound of cannon fire, which would signal that he was too late.

This time there was no problem at the powder tower. The sentries on duty recognized him and worked willingly. The soldier from the Massachusetts Artillery had found several side boxes, which were already filled with canvas bags when Will arrived. It took six of them to lift each box. These soldiers, too weak from their illnesses to serve on the line, had not yet fully recovered their strength. To Will, it seemed interminably long before all the side boxes were laboriously loaded on the wagon.

Will headed up the slope, the metal studded wheels skidding in the deep ruts of frozen mud and slush. He hoped he would not hear the sound of firing. He followed a slow moving oxen drawn wagon laden with bales of hay, one of which was precariously balanced at the edge. Will dismounted and led Big Red at a walk. His horse had not eaten since yesterday. He dropped Big Red's reins and clicked for the horse to keep following him. Will strode ahead and grabbed the loose bale from the wagon. He slowed his walk, waiting for Big Red to come alongside him and quickly hoisted the bale over the wagon's edge, dropping it on top of two of the side boxes. Quickly, he mounted the wooden seat, took the reins in his hands again and resumed the slow ride to the top, still nervously listening for sounds the battle had begun. The agonizingly slow pace, behind a long train of plodding oxen, was maddening, but impatient as he was, Will realized there was no way past them. He hoped he had already delivered enough powder for the batteries.

When he reached the cannons, there were several ox-drawn carts in front of him. The gun crews were unloading their cargo. From the way the men strained, Will knew the wooden crates were heavy. He jumped down, pulled a few sheaves of hay from the bale and put them in front of Big Red. Leaving the horse to eat, he ran forward to help the gun crews.

"Over here, Will," Sergeant Merriam called, as he struggled with two other soldiers to drag a long wooden box toward the cannons. Will grabbed a corner and staggered. Even with the four of them, it was difficult.

"What is in here?" he asked, as he strained to keep his end up.

"Grape shot," one of the gunners grunted. "To cut the legs off of the Grenadiers and the horses from under the Death Heads." He grinned devilishly, revealing a mouth of brown stained teeth with significant gaps in his lower jaw. "We can bowl them over with the cannon balls or cut them in half with the canister." Merriam said. "Mind your fingers now," he cautioned as they lowered the box to the ground. The Sergeant grunted as he straightened his back.

"And you have brought us some more powder, I hope."

"Yes Sir. Several side boxes worth."

After the oxcarts had been unloaded, Merriam directed Will to drive his wagon behind the batteries. The side boxes were quickly taken off and opened, and the bags of powder placed next to the old side boxes that were drying in the mid-morning sun.

"We are ready for them now," Merriam declared, satisfied with the preparations around The Albany. "I heard from one of the drivers that dry powder has been brought for the infantry too. If that is so, then we are as fit for battle as we were before the storm."

"What do we do now?" Will asked.

"We wait," one of the gun crew said. "And dream of the lovely young ladies waiting for us in Boston," another added.

"None of that, men," Merriam said sharply. "First we must deal with the British. You unmarried men, keep your minds clear and out of the brothels of the harbor. Avenge the innocents killed by the Redcoats before you wallow in your sinful thoughts."

Will walked away from The Albany. Some of the men began mocking their Sergeant for his puritan attitudes. "And the married men, Sergeant. They are not to think about the beds waiting for them, warmed by the bodies of their wives who have been without for months?" Will heard one shout.

"The married men of this Regiment have been tormented to the core every day of the Redcoats' occupation, by thoughts of the perversities and dangers their wives, mine included, are exposed to. Not to mention the stray cannonballs from our own bombardments," Merriam shouted, losing his temper and turning toward the gunner. He stared around him at the men. Some, embarrassed for having mocked their Sergeant and provoked his outburst, looked down at their worn muddy shoes.

"Everyone do their duty today," Merriam muttered, stalking off to be by himself.

The shelter where Will had slept for two stormy nights had been dismantled. He couldn't tell which sheets of canvas drying on the ground had been his, but it didn't matter. He moved Big Red down to the familiar hollow that now seemed more hospitable in the crisp air and bright sunlight. He walked back to the batteries, joined the men at their makeshift cooking fires and listened to their chatter. Sometime after noon, Will took off his boots and tried to dry his stockings over the flames. When he walked, the wet leather rubbed against his bare feet, and before long he gave up and pulled his wet stockings on again. It would be good, he thought, to be inside a brick barracks in front of a fine blazing fire, warming his toes and hands. Restless, he walked to the edge and looked down at Boston.

"They will not come if you look for them," one of the gun crew called out, noting Will's frequent trips to the parapet. A few of the men laughed. He moved away from the edge. The men's readiness for action in the early morning had worn off. Will, like the others, was bored, tired, cold and hungry. Most of all, he was keen for something to happen. He wanted a release from the pent-up eagerness, of getting on with the fighting, of testing whether he would do his duty under fire. As he thought about it, he wasn't sure what his duty was. He would try and help where needed. Maybe he could be more useful with the Mariners. He quickly rejected the thought. He didn't know how to row, and the Mariners were taking General Putnam's troops into battle, not hangers-on from their camp. Unofficially, he was a hanger on with the Artillery as well. True, it was Colonel Knox's unit but the Colonel didn't need him. Will was jarred from his sense of uselessness by a cry, "Ships sailing from the Island."

He ran with the others to the parapets. First one vessel appeared around Dorchester Point, followed by the rest of the transports, their sails billowing and full in the afternoon breezes. Like a line of white swans on a lake, they glided across the calm waters of the harbor and docked. The gun crews silently watched the troops, Dragoons and artillery disembark on to the wharves.

"What does it mean, Sergeant?" one of the men asked.

"I am not sure," Merriam replied. "We will have to await word from the Colonel."

"It means no good," another said grimly. "I would say they are planning a night attack."

"Yes," another agreed. "Straight across The Neck. They did not spy us when we came up the slope to the Heights. We will not see them when they come across The Neck."

"Have you no head on your shoulders or eyes to see with?" Merriam said, waving his hand in disgust. "Once they cross The Neck, they either have to follow the causeway and come up the narrow road, or go into the salt marshes below the slope and charge straight up." He shook his head angrily. "No good will come of your guessing at military strategy." Having said that, he turned his back on them and limped toward The Albany. Will followed and sat next him at the campfire behind the cannons.

"The addle-pated fools," Merriam muttered, more to himself. "If it is not brothels then their thoughts run to the impossible. This is what comes of idle minds," he said looking directly at Will. "We need more attention paid to the Bible with regular readings for the troops." He stretched out his leg and leaned forward with a grunt, reaching over his paunch to rub his bad ankle.

"Is it better?" Will asked solicitously.

"It is good enough," Merriam responded. He sat silently, his lips moving. Will respectfully remained quiet.

"I have prayed for the Lord to give me strength to help these men to see His ways, to guide me so I refrain from lashing out at them in anger, and to be an example for them to follow."

"Am I included in your prayers, Sergeant?" Lieutenant Hadley asked mirthfully. His voice was hoarse. "No need to answer. I know you to be a God-fearing man who seek to help all of his fellow men. Call the men to parade, Sergeant. The entire battery is meeting at the center."

Will stood up, uncertain what to do. Hadley's eyes were watering and his nose was red from constant blowing. A soggy handkerchief protruded from the cuff of his sleeve.

"I have developed a cold and fever," Hadley said to him. "And you, Will. No sign of the pox yet?"

"No, sir," Will replied, feeling sorry for the Lieutenant.

"Good for you. I am sure Dr. Thaxter will be relieved."

Will unconsciously scratched the mark on his forearm.

"Do you have news, sir?" Will asked, eagerly.

"I do indeed." He coughed from deep in his throat and spit the phlegm out on the ground. "Come along and hear of our great victory, won without firing a shot," he said, his voice tinged with regret.

"Or more correctly, only one shot, The Albany's cannonball."

The gun crews quickly assembled, ninety men lined up in ranks on a relatively flat area behind the batteries. Lieutenant Hadley stood in a row in front together with the other Lieutenants, facing Colonel Knox.

The Colonel sat on his large white New England saddle horse, his cape loosely around his shoulders. The Regiment's two Lieutenant Colonels and Majors were mounted and slightly behind him. Knox was grinning broadly.

"Men," he cried in his booming voice, loud enough for the troops on either side of the batteries to hear. "I have just come from General Thomas's headquarters in Roxbury. A delegation of Selectmen from Boston have passed through the British lines with a written message. General Howe will not destroy the city if we do not impede his troops departure. Boston is ours." With that, he raised his tri-corn in the air and waved it as the gunners shouted loudly. Will joined in the general celebration. [1]

Knox let the men continue before raising a gloved hand for silence. Down the line, on both sides of the batteries, there were sporadic cheers as the word spread, followed in some cases by the irregular discharge of muskets.

The Colonel frowned at the sound of gunfire. "General Washington has accepted the Selectmen's message. We will let the Redcoats depart unmolested. However, we must remain vigilant. Some of you will return to barracks. Some will remain here, manning our cannons, the very guns which have forced General Howe's decision." He looked down at the gunners with pride. "With Providence's blessing, soon many of us will be returning to our homes in our dear city. I personally look forward with fervent anticipation to that glorious day."

Will walked back to the guns with Sergeant Merriam and the crew of The Albany. They were part of the Regiment assigned to remain on the Heights. He was thankful there would be no assault on the Heights and the British were leaving. But he was confused. Can we have won without beating their army in a battle? If he was honest with himself, wasn't he more relieved from not being tested under fire than that the siege was over?

"At the Officers' meeting this morning, the Colonel reported that General Washington suspects a ruse," Lieutenant Hadley said to

Merriam. He motioned for them to follow him to the parapet and pointed to a rocky hill about fifty feet below. It sat, like the knuckle of an index finger, facing The Neck and the eastern edge of Boston.

"From Nook's Hill, nine and twelve-pounders could easily reach the British forts at The Neck, their batteries on this side of the harbor and even the wharves. Do you agree, Sergeant?"

Merriam nodded. Will looked at Hadley. His face was flushed, his eyes bright either from fever or enthusiasm.

"To get there, we would have to make our own road below the Heights and go up the back of Nook's Hill," Merriam said thoughtfully. "How many guns would we be moving, Sir?"

"No more than eight. The ground is still frozen. It would not be rutted and churned by the caravan of wagons and sleds on the slope road up to the Heights." Hadley surveyed the ground between the Heights and Nook's Hill with his telescope, grunted, and handed it to Merriam.

"It definitely can be done, Sir," Merriam agreed, as he held the scope to his eye.

"Yes it can, Sergeant. Yes it can. And we will do it," he said with conviction. "Colonel Knox has approved. We will use our three nine-pounders. The Colonel will make arrangements to draw some guns off the line and perhaps bring others up from Roxbury. Care to look, Will?"

Will took the telescope and focused on Nook's Hill and beyond to the forts on The Neck. It seemed as if from the Hill, the gun crews could throw snowballs down on the British positions.

"Are you game to pull a cannon or two for us?" Hadley asked.

"Certainly, Sir" Will replied without hesitation, ignoring the stomach cramp of fear which returned as he spoke.

By midmorning the next day, extra rations and rum had arrived and been distributed. The rum was quickly consumed by the men of the Regiment who were going to occupy Nook's Hill. Around noon, the eight cannons, supply wagons and men moved off the Heights. Big Red easily pulled a nine pounder over the rough frozen terrain between the Heights road and the base of Nook's Hill. Lieutenant Hadley, still riding the grey mare, pointed ahead up the hill. There was a trace of a narrow cow trail snaking the fifty feet up to the summit. The Lieutenant led the way, followed by the cannons. The metal studs of the large gun carriage wheels spun, striking sparks before gaining traction on the frozen mud and stones. Reaching the top, Will looked back. The artillerymen had left the wagons they were riding and were pushing the gun carriages from behind as the oxen plodded up the narrow twisting path.

At the Lieutenant's direction, the eight guns were positioned in a loose half circle facing the harbor. The ox drivers quickly left the exposed hill, anxious to return to safety. They took Big Red and the mare with them back to the Heights.

The gun crews grabbed shovels and pickaxes and began hacking at the frozen rocky turf. Will took an axe and chopped down several trees. He worked alone, concentrating on the rhythmic swinging, the blade biting into the soft pitch pine and releasing easily. It was clean work. After all the sitting and waiting on the Heights, wet and shivering, he felt invigorated, energized by the stretching of his muscles. He trimmed the branches with his hatchet, the smell of the freshly cut evergreen boughs filling his nostrils. He dragged the trunks, bottom first, to the gun emplacements, where the crews would decide how to use them, and returned to fell more trees.

They finished the fortifications in the late afternoon, just as it was turning dark. They had constructed a protective wall of stone, earth and pine trees on the forward edge of Nook's Hill around the guns and powder. On the far side of the hill facing the Heights, they had erected their tents in a relatively flat rocky area, away from the British gunners line of sight. Will squatted near the cooking fire of Sergeant Merriam's crew, warming his hands and anticipating a dinner of roasted meat.

He heard the boom of a cannon and flinched. One of the gun crew looked up from stirring a large cooking pot. "They will not be able to elevate their guns," he said returning his attention to his soup. Will tried to assume an attitude of studied indifference to the booming of the increased cannon fire.

"Mortars," Merriam yelled suddenly, throwing himself sideways onto the ground and covering his head with his arms. Will was aware of the rest of the gun crew doing likewise as the whistling sound overhead grew louder. He heard, rather than saw, an explosion in the sky over the gun emplacements. A shower of fiery metal fell on their little battery. They scurried up the hill, grabbed the side boxes with the gunpowder and carried them down to the relative safety of the slope where they were camped. The whistling of the mortar and howitzer shells was constant now. The British gunners had the range and the shells burst consistently over the nine and twelve-pounders. A few cannon balls struck below the summit, but close enough to send stone fragments against the protective parapets.

Lieutenant Hadley scrambled down from the gun emplacements on the hill and crouched with them behind a low stonewall they had hastily erected. "We have certainly twisted the British lion's tail," he shouted between bursts. He was grinning with excitement. "Take those extra buckets from the gun carriages. Fill them with snow, slush, water, anything. We will need it to throw on the side boxes if any of this fiery metal falls on them."

Will ran out and grabbed a wooden bucket, scooped up snow with his bare hands and left it near one of the side boxes. He raced back to the meager protection of the stones and crouched there as the shells continued to burst overhead. The noise was continuous and deafening. From this vantage point of relative safety, the shells were bursting in front of them, right on target if the gun crews had been manning the cannons.

"They are firing at us from other batteries," Merriam shouted. "It is too thunderous to be only their guns below Nook's Hill."

"The safest place for us is back with the Regiment on Dorchester Heights, where these mortars cannot reach us," Hadley replied wryly. "We must hold our position without counterfiring. Colonel Knox specifically forbade us to fire back from Nook's Hill. General Washington's orders," he said, with disappointment in his voice.

Will was thankful the Lieutenant could not return fire. Their little eight-gun battery was enduring a hailstorm of flaming metal from the sky. The mortar and howitzer bursts were so intense, it seemed like fiery sheets were hanging from a fixed imaginary rod in the starry sky over Nook's Hill.

The cannonade continued unabated in sound, volume or fury. In a brief respite between incoming rounds, Merriam laconically observed that the British seemed to have plenty of powder, shot and shell. Will and the gun crews hunkered down, behind the stones, and waited.

Will had stopped flinching at each blast and had almost lulled himself into a numbed state for protection. He concentrated on the pattern of lichen on the grey oblong piece of granite in front of him. He jerked up when a shell, overshooting the battery, burst directly above them.

"Unexploded shell near the side boxes," he heard someone shout in a panicky voice. A mortar shell, thirteen inches in diameter, had hit higher up the Hill, bounced and come to rest between two of the boxes, nearest to the men. The fuse hissed and sparked, the orange flame a scant few inches from the dark iron casing and the shell's gunpowder within.

Will dashed from the stone wall toward the shell and tripped on an icy rock. He lost his balance and fell forward on his chest toward the shell. Grabbing the red hot fuse with his outstretched right hand, he tossed it farther down the hill. Then he lay on the frozen ground panting, his face inches from the iron of the mortar shell and the dark rim of the fuse hole. He held his breath and prayed no spark remained alive inside that ugly black cavity or smoldered among the grains of gunpowder within. The frightening whistle of an incoming howitzer round jarred him to move.

Will ran back to the stone wall in a crouch and hugged against it, aware the artillery barrage was continuing and the palm of his hand had been burned by the fuse. Gingerly, he put some dirty snow in his palm and closed his fingers. He lay there and closed his eyes, willing the pain of his blistering skin to subside.

"You men. Get those side boxes further down the hill," Hadley ordered, placing a restraining hand on Will's shoulder.

Suddenly, it ended. Will stood up and curled his fingers gently back on his burned palm. They moved but when he straightened them out, the pain from his seared skin was intense. He followed the Lieutenant and the gun crews up to the summit. The light of the early March half moon showed the ground littered with shards of metal. In places it was so thick Will could not see the frozen earth. The brass of the nine and twelve-pounders was scratched and nicked here and there, but otherwise, the cannons were unharmed.

"It is fortunate that in the barrage, none of the wood of the gun carriages caught fire," Hadley observed. "And none of our men were killed or wounded."

"We should give thanks to Providence for that," Merriam said, removing his tri-corn and bowing his head.

"Will. Come here," the Lieutenant commanded. "Let me take a look at your hand."

Hadley peered at Will's right palm and the ugly narrow red diagonal line seared into his flesh. "It looks like it will keep until tomorrow. You will come back to Cambridge with me in the morning."

Hadley put his arm around Will's shoulder and they walked down the slope to the tents. "The normal practice of artillery men is to kick a smoldering fuse away from an unexploded shell. You are the first I know to have attacked a British mortar shell barehanded."

"I think I did intend to kick at it," Will replied, "but I slipped before I reached it. There was nothing else to do."

"None of the other men moved," Hadley replied. "They owe their lives to you." He patted Will on the shoulder. "Including me."

Will did not know how to respond. He welcomed the praise from the Lieutenant and the respect he sensed from the men in the gun crews.

They had restarted the cooking fires. Will squatted on his haunches feeling drained and weak. Once the aroma of roast meat filled the air, he realized that despite the pain in his hand he was voraciously hungry.

"No soup tonight," a soldier said, looking at a pot pierced by several pieces of shrapnel. He grinned at Will.

"Better that than being blown to hell in pieces," another said soberly.

"I know," the first man said. "Come here Will. I have some pork fat in my food stores. Use it on your hand and keep it greased. It will help with the healing and make you smell more appetizing," the soldier added. They all laughed, good-naturedly teasing him. It was, Will realized, their way of welcoming him as one of them and thanking him for his actions. He fell asleep in the early morning hours, lying on the ground in a tent, his injured hand with the bent fingers cushioned by his good arm.

Three hours later, he awoke at dawn stiff and sore, covered by Lieutenant Hadley's cloak. The line on his hand from the hot fuse had puffed up into an ugly blister. He tried to stretch his fingers but they would not extend. Not much use for dropping his pants and pissing he muttered, as he relieved himself outside. Nor for writing he thought, ruefully.

He made the ride from Nook's Hill to Cambridge with Lieutenant Hadley in a daze. He could hold the reins in his cupped right hand but he had use his good left hand to control Big Red. He gripped the horse tightly with his knees, thinking he would be more secure if just this once he had a saddle. He was grateful they rode at a slow pace. At the Regiment's solid brick building, which had been converted from a hospital back to their barracks, Hadley talked to a Sergeant and Will was assigned a cot near the fireplace. He struggled awkwardly with his one good hand to pull off his muddy boots, before he collapsed exhausted on top of the blanket.

It was dark when he awoke and the room was filled with the chatter of tired soldiers, enjoying the warmth and safety of the barracks. Will closed his eyes and listened to the fragments of conversation swirl around him.

"That first night's bombardment, before we moved to the Heights? Several of our shots hit the barracks at The Neck. Took off the legs and arms of at least six Redcoats."

"Now, how would you know what went on inside the Regulars' barracks?" a gruff voice said disparagingly.

"No. It is true. There were Redcoat deserters who came through the lines the following night. They had been told we had no cannons or mortars. There was much distress and confusion in their ranks when our bombardment began."

Another voice, deeper chimed in. "I heard our batteries at Lechmere Point struck the Old South Church which the Death Head Dragoons had turned into a stable. Our cannon shot went through the roof and killed a few of them and their horses as well."

"Pity about the horses. Though it was Divine punishment being visited on the Dragoons," someone answered.

"The British desecrated every church in the city, except for the Episcopal ones of course," another voice added. "They made the Brattle and Hollis Street Churches their barracks. They used the pulpit area as their latrine. The pews are gone, ripped out and used for firewood."

"I used to attend at Hollis Street. At least they are still standing. I heard the Regulars tore down the Old North Church for the timber and for fuel."

Will listened as the soldiers' voices became angrier at the embellished stories of desecration and destruction of Boston's churches. "I am not surprised. They were Sabbath breakers from the day they occupied Boston," one said. "More the pity we have to let them depart peacefully, instead of teaching them a lesson on the Heights."

"We almost had the battle. I heard, and I cannot say from whom, General Washington was furious we occupied Nook's Hill. The entire British line erupted in cannon fire against our positions. They say our troops collected more than 500 cannonballs from below Nook's Hill alone." [1]

"I would say your source is the orderly who empties the General's chamber pot," someone said derisively, "judging by the quality of your information."

"Nonsense, men." Will recognized Lieutenant Hadley's voice. He opened his eyes and sat up. "Corporal. You are wrong on both counts, but right in the main," he said, addressing a soldier who was in the process of shaving. "It was closer to 700 cannonballs, all now waiting to be melted down and recast, courtesy of King George." He executed a low bow toward the Corporal as if greeting the royal monarch. The men smiled and chuckled at Hadley's mockery. "General Washington has taken note of our Regiment and commended Colonel Knox for his aggressiveness and initiative in seizing Nook's Hill. The General still fears a ruse and praised us for strengthened our position by moving cannon to a point overlooking the harbour." He unfastened his cape, threw it over his arm and looked around.

"Ah, Will. Well rested I see." He sat down next to him on the cot. "Still in need of a bath though," he said, wrinkling his nose. He was clean-shaven with his hair brushed and tied in a queue. The brass buttons on his blue waistcoat sparkled in the firelight. "I have brought a clean linen shirt for you to wear," he said reaching in his leather carrying bag. "And this, both compliments of the Colonel." He pulled out two envelopes. The handwriting on each was small, neat and cursive, slanting attractively from left to right. In large letters across the middle, it said "For Colonel Henry Knox." In the lower left hand corner were the words: "Personal Correspondence for Master Willem Stoner."

Will instinctively reached for the letters with his right hand. Just as quickly, he dropped his injured hand greasy with pork lard, and took the letters gently in the fingers of his left.

"I was at headquarters this morning when the Colonel gave them to me," Hadley said by way of explanation. "My intuition tells me these are from a young lady. Let me see your hand." Will held out his arm. The Lieutenant took the right wrist in his hand and peered at the palm. "I believe the pork lard has done some good." He released Will's hand. "I can see you are eager to read these letters. Perhaps it would do more honor to the young lady who wrote them, if you washed first." He grinned at Will. "After they have traveled all the way from Albany, it would be a pity to get them smudged now."

"How do you know. . .?"

The Lieutenant laughed. "It came in the pouch from General Schuyler to General Washington. Your true love must have a very influential father. Influential indeed to have such correspondence included." Will blushed, ashamed of his dirty clothes and appearance, even in the presence of Elisabeth's letters.

Later that night, Will crouched on a stool reading the two letters from Elisabeth yet another time. He had waited his turn on line, washing in the wooden tub of lukewarm water, shivering in the cold air of the barracks. Dressed in the clean linen shirt, which was too big for him, he read the letters twice before joining the gun crews at the long tables for food. For once, food didn't interest him. He ate quickly, washing down the bread, roast meat and beans with bitter hard cider. He left the soldiers to their talk, made louder by an extra ration of rum. He read the letters again and again, until he had them memorized. Each one started off "My Dearest Will," a salutation that brought a warm flush to his face and turned his thoughts to galloping immediately to Albany. She had received his first letter and decided the distance was too great and her thoughts of him so overwhelming, to wait for a response from him, before writing again. She wrote of her fear for his health and safety, the cold he must be enduring during the journey, the dangers of being with rough men, the possibility of an attack by the British to prevent the train of artillery from reaching Cambridge, and the raging of a smallpox epidemic in New York City that she had read about in an Albany paper, wondering whether there was a similar danger in Boston.

She wrote of the mundane details of her life, all of which made her more real for him- her embroidery of a floral pattern of heather and thistles as a cover for the large armchairs in the front parlor and the book of poems she had been given for her birthday. Will regretfully realized he did not even know the date of her birth. She recalled for him the sermons her family had heard in Church and news from New

York City her father passed on at the dinner table. She wrote that every word, reference and bit of news made her think of him, a thought that thrilled him to the core.

Each time he read both letters, he was elated throughout until he reached a place where his spirits sank. Elisabeth had attended a dinner dance, given by General and Mrs. Schuyler. The small orchestra played all the latest dances. She wrote she had not sat down for one moment, so great was her popularity with the young officers, one in particular having monopolized her for most of the evening. Her words cut directly into Will's heart. He did not know how to dance. He imagined himself standing outside the General's ballroom, in his scuffed boots and in his worn brown coat, covering the linen shirt that was too large. In his mind, he saw the Schuyler's ballroom as the enlarged dining room of Colonel and Mrs. Knox's house with a long row of chandeliers. Elisabeth's partner, a Captain, resplendent in a dark blue uniform, looking much like Lieutenant Hadley, moved gracefully around the room with Elisabeth in his arms, as Generals and ladies beamed at the elegant young couple.

Angrily he thought, who was he to love her. He was nothing but an ignorant farm boy without means or profession. But the ending of her letters rekindled his hope. She wrote she thought of him every spare moment and was frantic for a word from him. She worried for his safety and he must write her in great detail about his life and the great events he was part of. Will went over in his mind the last letter he had composed but had not yet put down on paper. It would not do. He lay down on the cot, closed his eyes, oblivious to the raucous sounds of gun crews celebrating their time away from the Heights and Nooks Hill, and began to write anew to Elisabeth, turning the phrases over in his mind.

Two days later, after a hearty midday meal, Will returned to Nook's Hill with Sergeant Merriam and the guns crews who had endured the British bombardment that first day. The men were well fed and cheerful, anticipating a few days of quiet duty followed by a triumphal march into Boston. The weather was cold and clear with little wind to speak of. Rumors swirled through the camp that General Washington would permit only troops who had been inoculated against smallpox to enter the city and that Colonel Knox and the Massachusetts Artillery would be in the vanguard.

On the narrow path on the back of Nook's Hill they met the gun crews coming down. The men were silent and grim. Will found their lack of high spirits and boisterousness surprising. After all, they were leaving their tents and the cold windy hill for the comforts of the Regiment's solid barracks in Cambridge.

"The Regulars and Tories are plundering the city. You can hear the cries of our innocents day and night," one of the Sergeants told Merriam as his crew marched morosely past.

"Tis worse at night, when all you hear are the screams of women and your imagination completes what must be happening below," he said loud enough for Will and the rest of the crews to hear. "Tis a terrible burden, this duty of permitting the British to commit their depravities and destruction under orders not to fire a shot" he growled, kicking angrily at a loose stone before departing. "Your Lieutenant has been with us watching it all," he said pointing toward the summit."

The gun crews scrambled up the cow path, more slippery now from constant use than when they had first occupied the Hill. They deposited their haversacks and muskets in the empty tents, located closer to the summit now that the danger of British artillery fire was gone, and gathered at the newly reinforced parapet. Will followed them. Lieutenant Hadley was studying the town with his telescope.

Below, the harbor was a scene of agitation, as if an anthill had been kicked over by a giant boot, and its inhabitants, exposed to the elements for the first time, were racing around in disorganized frenzy. Groups of people crowded the quays, which were piled high with trunks, boxes of every description, and furniture. Carts, wagons, sleds, even wheelbarrows, were lined up, waiting to disgorge their cargo of personal possessions and household items onto the motley assembly of vessels lining the wharves. Streams of people and carts emerged from the streets leading to the harbor, adding to the chaos caused by the press of people and their piles of goods ahead of them.

"It is the Tories and their families who had sought protection of the King's troops, who are leaving first," Lieutenant Hadley said, not taking his eye from the telescope."

"There are not enough ships for them and their belongings. Much is being thrown in the harbor."

Will watched as sailors on the closest wharf pitched chairs, divans, cupboards, and even a harpsichord into the water, while their owners wailed in protest and tried to protect their other possessions. People carried what they could up the ramps and disappeared below the decks, until finally the gangplanks were hauled aboard. The ship then pushed off from the wharf and moved out into the harbor, to be replaced by another. The entire harbor was dotted with vessels riding low in the water, indicating they were fully loaded with their human cargo of Tories and the personal property they had salvaged. More transports, riding high, angled toward the wharves. [2]

"Look there," Lieutenant Hadley said, handing the telescope to Sergeant Merriam. "On the east side of The Neck. The warehouses between Arbuthnot's and Child's Wharves. See the Redcoats and that group of men."

From this distance, Will could see figures in the street, some in red uniforms, others in brown and black coats. "They are loading bales of something onto wagons," Merriam announced to the others. "My tannery is on Short Street, between those wharves and Essex," he said. "I know the merchants about and the men who own and work in those warehouses."

"We all have family, relatives and friends in the town," Lieutenant Hadley replied. "They will not be safe until General Howe, his troops and their Loyalist toadies have embarked and left us in peace."

Will remained on the parapet for a while, fixing the scene in his mind. He listened to the angry talk of the gun crews, obsessing first over what they could see at the warehouses and then what they could not observe but only imagine as the troops disappeared down the narrow streets, followed by carts laden with their plunder.

Lieutenant Hadley lent Will his field desk, ink and a quill and offered his tent as well. Will spent the remainder of late afternoon, transcribing his letter to Elisabeth from memory. He wrote slowly and carefully, pleased his hand had healed enough for him to comfortably grip the quill.

It was a long letter. He mentioned the bombardment of Nook's Hill, omitting anything about his burned hand or pulling a fuse from the live shell that had landed amidst the powder boxes. He ended with a description of the harbor and the British plundering of the city, adding what the Lieutenant had told him, that Mrs. Knox's mother and siblings would be embarking with General Howe. The Colonel's wife would be without her mother or sisters with the birth of the Colonel's first child so imminent. He recalled the wistful look on Lucy Knox's face at dinner when she had spoken of her parents. He knew she would be sorrowful at being separated from her family. The sentiment he expressed about her was correct. It felt peculiar to be writing it to Elisabeth. He stared at the words. If he could have crossed them out, he would have. Elisabeth would think him foolish for mentioning it. Her Captain at the dance would not have done so. With that thought, he was overcome by a feeling of hopelessness. Writing Elisabeth was an act of futility, a message from his heart for her affection that would not and never could be returned.

"Finished writing to your true love?" Hadley said cheerfully, returning to his tent. He unclasped his cape and tossed it nonchalantly on to the cot. "I hope so. I am dining with the Colonel and Mrs. Knox tonight and can deliver your letter to him for the next dispatches to General Schuyler." He winked at Will, who suppressed his melancholy thoughts, dipped the quill in the ink and added the last line: I conclude in haste in order my letter be included in the pouch. I trust this hurriedness will not offend you and ask you continue to keep me in your thoughts and prayers. You are always in mine. He signed it Your Dearest Friend and folded it carefully in half.

Lieutenant Hadley offered him an envelope. Will shook his head.

"Please, Will. My personal gift to the continuing courtship of your lady love." His brown eyes shone in the candlelight. Will took the envelope, addressed it and handed it back to Hadley. It seemed as if he was irrevocably committing himself to a course of action he could not control, nor have much hope for a favorable outcome. Still, he had written the letter and it must be sent.

Hadley stood up from the camp chair, smoothed his coat, placed the tri-corn on his head and threw his cape over his arm. "The wind remains from the southeast. The British will not leave until it is favorable. Perhaps in another day or so. Keep your spirits up, Will." Hadley commanded. "We all are anxious to get to Boston." He ducked through the tent flap with a wave of his gloves.

There were few stars in the sky that cloudy night. Will joined Merriam and the others at the cooking fires. Their subdued conversation was interrupted by occasional musket shots from the town, sounds of glass being broken, shouting of unintelligible words, and occasionally, a woman's piercing scream. At that sound, all conversation would cease, a soldier or two would walk to the parapet and look down into the blackness of Boston, where only a few buildings were lit by candles, before returning.

"I can hear drunken men singing," one of the soldiers said.

"The sailors are getting the last chance at cheap Boston rum and Yankee whores before they leave for sea," another remarked.

"Neither will do them any good on judgment day," Merriam said. "The sins they commit in Boston will follow them to the end of their lives."

The men fell silent. Even the ones who usually had a bawdy comment or lyric were quiet. Merriam got up and walked to the overlook. Will followed him.

"You wife is down there?" he asked, knowing the answer.

Merriam nodded. His thin lips formed a tight line between his jowls. "And my two little girls. They are staying with my wife's older brother and his family. My brother-in-law," he said with some contempt, "is neither a patriot nor a Tory. He is the type of man who tries to thread the path through the thorn bushes without getting pricked." He laughed sadly. "The perfect man then to protect my wife and precious little ones during the perilous siege." Merriam gestured toward the men silhouetted behind them at the fires. "The men in our Regiment. Most are from Boston. Some have sent their families away. Many, like me, have not. Only the good Lord knows what we will find when the British leave."

"Lieutenant Hadley says they are waiting for a favorable wind."

"He is right about that. May God grant the British a favorable wind soon to leave us and our loved ones alone."

On Friday, March 15th, Will, with nothing to do but wait along with the other soldiers in the Regiment, left Nook's Hill and rode Big Red to Dorchester Point. The wind was in his face, still blowing strong off the ocean from the southeast. The sky was grey toward the south and lighter blue with wispy strands of clouds over land to the west. Below him, the narrow inlet between the point and Castle Island was filled with the motley fleet of transports, wallowing low in the water with their human cargo of fleeing Loyalists and their possessions. May the wind and waves make them miserable and seasick, he thought with malice.

On the ride back across the Heights and past the American lines, he tried to compose a new letter to Elisabeth. The words did not come to him, nor any thoughts worth conveying. He couldn't very well tell her about waiting the past seven days for the British to leave. Soon, he said to himself, he would be in Boston. Somehow, he would find Johan. He knew the wharves and warehouses from talking to Sergeant Merriam. He would start there. Johan would know what they should do, maybe even help Will find work with a Boston merchant. Anything but returning to their father's farm. He was despondent, unable to occupy his mind with a letter to Elisabeth and further depressed by the thought of life on the farm.

Back at camp, rumors were flying from mouth to mouth. General Howe had issued orders to depart. "It is nothing but camp gossip," Merriam told him sourly. "Look down below. There are no troops boarding. The wind is still from the southeast. Even you, a lad from a New York farm, can tell that," he said, clapping Will on his shoulder. "It is merely wishful thinking by men tired of waiting," he sighed, shaking his head.

At midday Saturday the weather was almost balmy, with no wind and the sun pleasant and warming. Will was sitting on the ground outside Lieutenant Hadley's tent, idly thinking of nothing, when he saw a familiar figure in white canvas breeches and a short blue jacket striding up to Nook's Hill. He jumped up and ran down the trail, meeting Nat halfway. They walked briskly up the path together, Nat's smile, and his obvious pleasure at seeing him, washing away Will's dark mood.

"Anna is in Watertown, working for Mrs. Edes again. And I have brought the latest broadsides and a special issue to celebrate the Redcoats' departure."

Lieutenant Hadley emerged from his tent and Will eagerly introduced him to Nat.

"Will seems to collect Lieutenants and Colonels," Hadley said, laughing.

"I was an Ensign when we first met on the trail," Nat pointed out.

"Then maybe a promotion is imminent for me, although I have done nothing to deserve it," Hadley replied.

They walked to the parapet. "Are the Mariners still at Cambridge?" Hadley asked.

"We are down the Charles at the water's edge. We have orders to ferry General Putnam's troops across the inner harbor on a moment's notice. Colonel Glover expects us to do so on the morrow."

"How can you be so certain?" Will asked. "All we receive here are rumors."

"The British sentries have become lax. More of the good citizens of Boston, and a few deserters are slipping through to our lines. General Howe indeed has issued the orders to depart. Much of their troops' gear is stowed. Anything deemed of use to us has been destroyed or confiscated. Here, it is all as reported in the *Boston Gazette* as of this morning." He reached into his leather pouch and produced several copies. Hadley smiled and waved the papers in the air.

"Note, gentlemen, the wind is no longer from the southeast," he shouted boisterously. "Let us celebrate this event by returning to my tent. We do not want any of these precious broadsheets to fly away."

Will ran off to bargain for some coffee, using one of the broadsides as currency, while Nat and Hadley remained in the tent. When he returned with a hot pot, his two friends were seated, Hadley on his cot, Nat on the camp stool. Hadley poured a finger of rum into their mugs of weak coffee.

"Here, Will," Nat said, handing him the broadside. "I am familiar with it. I am doubly blessed with the good fortune to have a wife who loves me dearly and who works in a printer's household."

"To your good fortune," Lieutenant Hadley replied, "in have a loving wife." He raised his mug of steaming coffee and rum. "To a long, healthy and happy life together. The printer's household is merely a dollop of thick cream on the delicious pie."

"And to our friendship," Nat added, touching mugs with Hadley and Will.

Will scanned the familiar masthead and the heading "Containing the Freshest Advices Foreign and Domestic." Eagerly, he read about General Howe's order to collect all linen and woolen goods from the inhabitants to deprive the provincials of their benefit. According to eyewitness accounts, the order was effectuated by a Tory named Crean Brush, together with other Loyalists and Redcoats. They had plundered and pillaged at will, and committed other evil deeds unspeakable in nature as they terrorized the good and peaceful citizens of the town. The article concluded that the inhabitants of Boston yearned for the imminent relief from a set of men whose unparalleled wickedness, profanity, debauchery and cruelty was unimaginable. Will was not certain whether this referred to General Howe and the Regulars, or just to Crean Brush and his minions. [3]

"Here, Sam, is the dollop of cream you refer to," Nat said, giving Hadley several sheets. "They are two favorite songs, composed for the British evacuation of the town."

Hadley grabbed them from Nat, read them quickly, nodding approvingly of the lyrics. "You must teach me the tunes. We will circulate them among the men and be ready to sing when we march into Boston."

Will left them in the tent, the sound of the Hadley's fine baritone and Nat's higher but sweeter tenor attracting some of the gun crews. He walked away from the Hill, down the path to the site where they had endured the ferocious bombardment. He tried to sort out his feelings. He was eager to enter Boston but was apprehensive of what loomed before him after he crossed that threshold. He was hopeful Johan would have a plan to rescue him from what he saw as a life of boredom and drudgery. This great adventure was coming to an end. The uncertainty frightened him.

Without thinking, he found himself walking toward Dorchester

Heights. When he reached the place where the horses were tethered for the night and made a clicking sound, Big Red raised his massive head in recognition. He brushed the horse's neck with his hands, feeling the muscles beneath and taking comfort in his company. The acrid smell of the urine of many horses confined to the small thicket filled his nostrils. He chuckled to himself, knowing he was pleased by the familiar odor.

"We will do all right," he said, reaching in his pocket for a crust of bread. "Somehow, this will be for the better." He scratched Big Red's jaw. The horse stretched out his neck in pleasure.

Will awoke in the dark, sat up and listened. Sergeant Merriam and the other four men were still asleep. One was snoring loudly. Below the Hill came the rhythmic sound of a drumbeat and the notes of a fife. Will hurriedly pulled on his boots, threw his coat over his shoulders, slipped out of the tent and ran to the parapet. He glanced at the clear sky and guessed it was less than two hours before dawn. Several of the wharves were marked with torches, as were the troop transports tied up alongside. A line of troops, led first by a torchbearer, followed by the unit's drummer and a soldier playing the fife, emerged from the dark streets on to the pier. Sergeant Merriam and many of the gun crews came out of their tents and grouped around the parapets. Silently, they watched the torches first become visible on the parade grounds outside the barracks, disappear behind buildings and reappear on the broad streets leading to the wharves.

"They are really leaving," someone whispered, as if saying it out loud would break a spell, end the dream and instantaneously dissolve the scene below. By early dawn, with the sky pink and glowing and sea gulls soaring overhead, the transports lay anchored in the harbor, waiting for the remaining troops to board.

"There must be ten thousand of them," Merriam said.

Hadley put one foot on the stone parapet and sipped from his mug of coffee. "There would have been many fewer leaving if they had stormed the Heights. Their army is intact, Sergeant and we will have to fight them elsewhere."

The last of the transports untied from the wharves and moved out into the harbor under light sail. Will estimated it was near nine o'clock.

Escorted by several armed sloops and schooners, the transports sailed a northerly course out of the range of the American guns before turning south toward Castle Island.

Cheers erupted among the gunners on Nook's Hill. Men waved their tri-corns, laughed and shouted. Will looked back toward the Heights where the troops lined the edge, firing muskets into the air, waving and cheering. Men were dancing with each other. Clapping their hands above their heads, they pirouetted about, silly with joy. And then the crews on Nook's Hill, having learned the lyrics Nat had brought yesterday, broke into song.

"Some say they sailed for Halifax,
And others for New York,
Howe let none know where he was bound
When the soldiers did embark.

Where they are bound there's none can tell,
But the Great God on High
May all our heads be covered well,
When cannon balls do fly." [4]

They repeated the last verse, and as their lusty voices died down, there was the sound of a tremendous cannonade coming from beyond Dorchester Point. They stopped singing and listened.

Lieutenant Hadley counted on his fingers. He held up both hands twice and then one finger. There was silence and the cannonade resumed. Another twenty one shots, followed by a brief silence and again the roar of the cannons.

"General Howe must have arrived on his flagship and the fleet is saluting him," Hadley said by way of explanation. "That, gentlemen, is not the sound of a defeated enemy," he added somberly.

"We must thank God for their departure and ask for His protection in what is to come," Merriam said. "After all, today is the Sabbath." Amidst some grumbling, the gun crews stood bareheaded on Nook's Hill as the Sergeant opened his Bible. The light wind blew his thinning hair around his high forehead. Will, holding his battered slouch hat in his hands, thought the Sergeant looked like a benevolent prophet as he read the Psalm aloud.

Merriam glanced around at the familiar faces. He spoke briefly about the hardships the men had endured in the siege of Boston and the even greater sufferings of the people of the town during the British occupation. "Let us pray the Lord soon reunites us with our families and we discover them safe and in good health." The men voiced a heartfelt Amen.

And let me soon be together with my brother Johan, Will muttered under his breath.

"Your brother may very well not be in the town," Merriam said. He was in a jovial mood. On Monday, the day after the British evacuation, his nephew had come from Boston to Cambridge, a long trip for a nine-year-old boy, to bring him the news that Merriam's wife and two daughters were unharmed and well and eagerly awaiting his arrival. The roads from the neighboring counties were crowded with women and children returning from their safe havens in nearby towns. Now that the hated British sentries in their guard posts ringing the city were gone, the citizens of Boston clogged the roads in the other direction, seeking out the families they had sent away. Throughout the surrounding countryside there were scenes of rejoicing and happy reunions everywhere, complicating the movement of troops into the city.

The rumor proved true. Only those troops who had been inoculated were allowed in on that momentous Sunday. General Ward had led several Massachusetts units across The Neck, past the formidable British forts. The Mariners had ferried General Putnam's troops across the Bay to enter Boston from the opposite side. Colonel Knox's Regiment had returned to their barracks in Cambridge and enjoyed the company of General Washington at the full Regiment's Sunday services. [1] They had remained in camp following services and on this bright, clear cold Monday, March 18th, were assembling to follow General Washington and his staff into the city. [2]

"Johan may have fled Boston for the comparative safety of the nearby towns and be making his way to Boston as we speak." Merriam winced as the wagon hit a rut in the road. They had passed through Roxbury and were heading directly toward The Neck. It had been the Colonel's idea to save his men the march by ferrying them from Cambridge to the Neck by wagon. Each wagon carried the gun crews and pulled a nine or twelve-pounder.

Will flicked the reins over Big Red and the mare and shook his head in bewilderment. "He does not even know I am here. I must start with the merchants' warehouses. That is the only point of certainty," he said.

Will brought the wagon to a halt on the Roxbury side of the Boston Neck road. He unhitched Big Red and waited as the gun crew pulled the brass twelve- pounder into position behind the horse. When all the cannons were in place, the men of the Massachusetts Artillery formed into ranks.

General Washington was at the front of the column on his white horse followed by his immediate staff. Several drummers and soldiers with regimental flags and banners separated the Commander from Colonel Knox and the Regiment's officers, who were mounted in columns of two. Behind them the gun crews marched four abreast. They had spent yesterday sprucing up their blue and buff uniforms and polishing their bayonets and brass buttons. Many wore their tri-corns adorned with sprigs of pine, spruce or, for those lucky to have been reunited with their wives, woven decorations of ribbons.

Will had done his best to clean his worn brown coat but was conscious of how shabby he looked. He also regretted not having a saddle for Big Red but there was nothing to be done about that. At least the brass twelve-pounder shone and he had brushed Big Red until his coat glistened.

Will heard a roar and cheers as General Washington's horse rode onto the previously impregnable Neck. People, informed of the General's entry into the city by flyers printed that morning, lined the narrow causeway. The crowds were thicker near the two forts and fortified gate. Many shouted out the names of the soldiers marching by, recognizing their neighbors and relatives in the ranks. Perhaps he would not have to search for Johan. Maybe his brother would see him. He swiveled his head from side to side, scanning the faces in the crowd. Most were men. Will noticed the lack of young girls. The only females lining the street were either middle-aged women or children restrained by their mothers. Perhaps, he thought, the residents of Boston had sent their sisters and daughters to live with relatives during the British occupation, as Lieutenant Hadley had done.

Exuberant young boys, uninhibited and unrestrained by their elders, scampered back and forth from one side to another, running between the horse drawn artillery, touching a cannon as they darted past, as if on a dare.

"Want to buy a "gaad chevo", a small street urchin called to Will, running to keep up with Big Red. "Only one shilling." He held up an iron four sided spike. Will smiled and reached down as the boy handed it up for inspection. "I saw the bloody lobster backs throw them on the streets when they left. Swept this one up myself."

Will turned it over in his hand and felt the point of the three-inch spike. This could cripple a horse and go through a soldier's boot or shoe. No wonder the Regulars had strewn them on the pavement.

"No, I do not want it" Will said, letting it drop into the boy's cupped hands.

"A half a shilling, sir," the boy responded quickly, holding it up again. "'Tis a genuine crow's foot, it is." Will shook his head and the boy, seeing he was not going to make a sale, ran back and offered it to the teamster pulling the next cannon.

The triumphal parade proceeded down the broad street toward the center of the city. Here there were more women in the crowds, dressed in dark cloaks over their coats to protect them from the cold. To his left Will could see the green of the Commons with patches of dirty snow and the remnants of the Redcoats' wooden barracks. The column stopped. There was some commotion up ahead. Will could not determine the cause, and soon they resumed their march, now more slowly, farther into the city. After months of siege, Boston did not resemble the neat, orderly, clean city Nat had described to him. The broken doors of some houses bore the marks of being smashed by axes or battered off their hinges. Cloth hung across window frames that had been shattered. Piles of fabric, chairs without legs, fragments of desks, cabinets, armoires and all like and manner of furniture, torn books and papers, boxes with their lids pried off, and other unidentifiable debris littered the streets and alleys. The roofs of some buildings were holed by cannonballs, especially as they moved closer to the center of town where the British barracks and gun emplacements had been, Our artillery did that, Will thought.

At the top of a broad street that Will knew led down to Long Wharf, the artillery regiment turned left into a large square, passed a courthouse, paraded left through sparser crowds, and headed back in the direction of The Neck. At the Commons, the Regiment lined up for the reading of the orders of the day and then disbanded. All married men or soldiers with relatives and family in Boston, which was most of the Regiment, were given three days leave. The rest were given leave for the remainder of the day, to return to barracks at night, and to report for the morning roll call on the Commons. Leave for them would be granted, depending on the availability of other troops to patrol the town.

After settling Big Red in one of the sheds that served as a barn, Will walked into one of the wooden barrack buildings and found himself alone. It was now early afternoon. The wind had turned chilly. He pulled Elisabeth's scarf more tightly around his neck and thrust his hands deeper into his pockets. He retraced their parade route to the central square and found the street leading to Long Wharf. That would be as good a place as any to start, he reasoned. People seemed to be going about their normal business. He passed women coming up the cobblestoned street from the harbor with shopping baskets, the occasional fishtail protruding from underneath a cloth. Several patrols of soldiers marched briskly by. They were from units whose uniforms he did not recognize, bayonets fixed on their muskets. As part of the orders of the day, read to the Regiment earlier, General Washington had promised the severest punishment for pillaging and looting. From the show of troops patrolling Boston, Will thought he intended to enforce them.

Will passed several taverns crowded with soldiers on leave and men of Boston celebrating, drunk and boisterous, spilling out of the taverns, leaning against brick walls, and making lewd remarks about any women passing by. Will hurried down to the wharf, astonished at the number of people and the activity. There were sloops sunk alongside the piers, with their masts cut down to thick stubs a foot above the decks. Soldiers and dock workers trod along the awash decks, lowering ropes and chains under the hulls in preparation for raising them. He walked along the pier, part of the curious crowd staring into the harbor waters. People scrambled and fought to pull out of the shallow water the goods their Loyalist neighbors had jettisoned in their haste to depart. Men's waistcoats and women's dresses and shawls floated amidst the broken wood of carts and furniture. A man emerged dripping wet and fully clothed from the cold water, hoisting a trunk above his head. He handed it to an accomplice before diving back under.

"There's hogsheads of sugar and salt down there," the man said gesturing to the dark waters. "No use to us wet, but there is treasure to be found still," the accomplice said to the small group of inquisitive bystanders. He cocked his thumb toward his wheelbarrow. It held a small wooden night table, the place where the drawer had been now gaping like a mouth without any teeth. Will saw it had been carelessly tossed on top of a clock in an intricately carved case. The man cradled a china tea pot without a lid in his hands while keeping a foot on an already tarnished silver tray. "And there are frilly ladies' things to purchase the favors of the harbor whores without spending a shilling," he said. He leered knowingly at the men around him, smirking to himself in anticipation of such encounters.

Further down the wharf, Will stopped to watch soldiers of the Rhode Island Artillery haul a brass nine-pounder from the waters alongside the pier, swivel it over the wooden planking and lower it next to three other cannons they had salvaged. Will observed that the trunnions were broken on all of them and they had been spiked. He guessed there were gunsmiths in Boston who would know how to repair them.

He was tempted to stay and observe the activity on the wharf but felt compelled to look for Johan. He scanned the faces of the men around him. He hoped that perhaps Johan, now free to move around the city, would be among the curious on this wharf. He made his way back up the pier, turned right and found himself on a narrow street lined with solid brick warehouses. Two sentries, dressed in buff britches and red scarlet coats crossed with white straps, blocked the double doors, which hung askew from their broken hinges. Will peered through the opening and saw more red-coated soldiers inside.

"What unit are you from?" he asked the sentry. The man shifted his feet. Will noticed his thin black low shoes and the stain of slush and mud on the lower part of his white wool leggings. His feet must be frozen, Will thought, thankful once again for his boots.

"We are the Essex Militia," he answered proudly, holding his musket with the bayonet affixed at the ready.

"You were on the far right on the Heights, closest to Dorchester Point, were you not?" Will asked.

The sentry smiled, pleased Will knew the Militia had been ready to repel the British assault. "Yes, we were there," he said. "We were ready for the Redcoats and would have made them sorry had they attacked our positions" the other sentry added boastfully. He readjusted his tricorn and squared his shoulders.

"What are you guarding?" Will asked.

"Chaldrons of coal. The finest of English coal the Redcoats brought over will now heat our barracks and homes," the first sentry answered, stamping his feet.

"Good thing too," the other added. "The Sabbath breakers burned everything for fuel, including our churches. And there is not a single fence or shack left standing in the town."

Will moved down the street until he found another warehouse with a street-level office. He saw two men seated, copying into large bound books that were propped up on writing desks. He knocked and entered.

"Excuse me, gentlemen. I am looking for my brother, Johan Stoner, who was employed by a merchant in Boston. Perhaps you know. . ."

"Never heard of him," the older one interrupted, eying Will's dirty coat and the worn red and blue scarves loosely tied under his collar, before resuming making entries in the ledger.

The younger clerk was more sympathetic although his information was not helpful. "When the British closed the port, many merchants lost everything. If they managed to scrape by, it was most likely without a clerk." He blew on his fingers to warm them.

Will nodded, thinking his search was an impossible task.

"Your brother, if he was let go, may have been employed by someone not on the wharves." He noticed Will's look of hopelessness. "There are more warehouses down by the Town Dock and Woodman's Wharf," he offered. "And of course there are the wharves east of Long Wharf toward The Neck." He lowered his voice. "I would exercise more caution in that part of the harbor, if you know what I mean."

Will did not understand what he meant. He intended to work this side of the harbor anyway. He spent what remained of the afternoon and early evening, knocking at the doors of warehouses and shipyards, and talking to fishermongers, all to no avail.

The next day, he resumed his quest, working his way north through Burrell's Wharf, Clark's Wharf, Gallop's Wharf and Halsey's Wharf. At each place he stopped, the answer was the same. No one had heard of Johan. Sometime after midday, while he was sitting and watching the sea gulls dive for offal thrown by a fisherman cleaning his catch at the end of the short pier, there was a tremendous explosion, followed by another. Then silence. Everyone around him began talking at once. One man yelled the British fleet was back. "The Redcoats have blown up Funnel Hall," another shouted. Men looked around for clouds of smoke or warships in the harbor. When neither materialized, they continued to speculate on the cause of the explosions. None of their talk made any sense to Will. He looked toward the end of the pier. Off to the east, beyond Dorchester Heights, a dirty grey plume began to rise slowly in the sky. Will thought it must be from Castle Island. The Americans still occupied The Heights and the British had assembled and left from Castle Island. He kept his opinion to himself as others pointed in the direction of the short thick cloud. What a waste of good powder. He smiled to himself. You are beginning to reason like an artillery man, he thought.

Returning to the barracks late in the afternoon, he found himself again on the narrow street of the coal warehouse. He passed a line of waiting women, their shawls tied tightly over their hats to ward off the chill, baskets on their arms, gossiping amicably with each other. Two different sentries stood in front of the broken doors, flirting with the women at the beginning of the line.

At the top of the street, after he turned the corner, he heard the women scream and shriek in panic. He ran back toward the warehouse, as some women rushed up the hill and others scattered in terror down the street. Several of the Essex Militia, led by a Sergeant, emerged from the brick building adjacent to the warehouse.

"You men search the buildings below as well. You others, those across the street," he ordered. "What do you want?" he asked Will gruffly, looking up and down the hastily deserted street. Two militiamen lowered their bayonets at him.

"Nothing, sir" Will replied quickly. "If I can be of help, I am willing."

"No need. I have men enough to do the job. The gentleman who owns this building," he gestured to the open door behind him, "now the British are gone and we are on patrol, bravely returned to inventory his property. He found a train of powder hidden under straw leading to a number of loaded shells against the wall with the warehouse." He looked about angrily. "The damn fool ran screaming into the street, yelling 'run for your lives!' and panicked the women. At least they have an excuse for fleeing," he said contemptuously.

Will hesitated for a moment. "I am with Colonel Knox's Massachusetts Artillery Regiment. I was returning to the barracks." The Sergeant looked askance at him, taking in Will's shabby appearance. "I will inform an officer," Will continued. "The Regiment could use the powder and shells."

"You tell who you have to tell," the Sergeant said, still skeptical that Will really was with the artillery. "There may be more in the other buildings. It only needed a flame from a British spy or bloody Tory to ignite an explosion."

"Or an accidental spark," Will said. "You should break the powder train in several places, working backwards from the shells," he suggested.

The Sergeant nodded and turned to the soldiers returning from having scouted the other nearby buildings. Will hunched his shoulders against the wind coming from the harbor and strode back the street up toward the Commons.

That night in the nearly deserted barracks, Will took stock of what he had accomplished since entering Boston. In two and a half days he had made inquiries from Hancock's Wharf at the northern end to Bull's Wharf past the South Battery and Fort Hill, and found not a single soul who had even heard of his brother. Tomorrow, he hoped to start at Sea Street near Winchmill Point and work his way down toward The Neck. If he hadn't found Johan, Sergeant Merriam would be back from leave by then. He would ask for his help.

On Friday he started his search later than he had intended. Most of the morning had been spent hauling planks of lumber the British had cached, but not destroyed, from a field near the powder tower below Mt. Whoredom to the Commons. He left some of the gunners and local carpenters repairing the wooden barracks, fed and brushed Big Red, and started out just before noon. The sun was pleasantly warm and the sky a crisp blue. He stuffed the scarf his mother had made for him into his coat pocket and loosened Elisabeth's scarf, feeling the breeze cool on his throat. Walking briskly past the Common Burying Ground, he inquired of a passerby how to get to Winchmill Point and was directed down Frog Lane and Essex Street to the harbor.

As he approached the water, the clean salt smell of the sea air was overpowered by the strong stench of human piss and excrement. Broken bricks impeded the flow of the open drains carrying human waste downhill to the harbor, forming small cesspools that made the adjacent cobblestones slippery with filth. He glanced down a narrow alley between the low wooden buildings. The stink was worse, and he thought he saw the body of a man, sleeping, drunk or dead, curled up against a wall. Will noticed that the warehouses were outnumbered by stillhouses, grog shops, taverns and brothels.

After inquiring unsuccessfully at the few warehouses, he began asking laborers on the wharves, those who seemed to belong to the few boats tied up, and fishermen repairing nets, boxing their catch of fish, or sorting mussels or oysters onto wheelbarrows. No one knew of Johan, many were gruff in their response and some simply ignored him. He did attract the attention of several of the harbor whores, eager for business in the early afternoon. They quickly lost interest when he made clear he was not interested in their services. Some of the women

were garishly dressed with mismatched shawls over what he thought
were tops of ballroom gowns, or pieces of taffeta or silk hastily stitched
onto old worn dresses.

By late afternoon he was near Arbuthnot's Wharf, where, from
Nook's Hill, Sergeant Merriam had pointed out the men loading bales
on wagons. He recalled Merriam had said his tannery was nearby. He
wandered around until he found it, hoping to find the Sergeant. It
was a small two-story brick building. Above the entrance, a weathered
simple sign for Merriam's Tannery swung in the wind, hanging askew
by a chain from one hook. The doors had been torn off and the ground
floor was empty. Before entering he called out, "Sergeant. Sergeant
Merriam." There was no answer. A few slats and occasional iron rims
were all that remained of the wooden tanning vats. He noticed several
unfinished hides piled up in a corner, covered with shattered glass
beneath what had been a window with panes. The long flat work tables
had been smashed with sledgehammers and axes. The looters seemed to
have taken all of the tools of the trade, scrapers, leather cutters, sewing
awls, as well as the finished hides. These would have been useful to the
army, to be made into boots, belts, shoes, harnesses, haversacks and
saddle bags.

As he left the tannery, he reached up and for no reason touched
the swinging sign with his hand. He noticed a man dressed in the work
clothes of a dockhand staring at him. Will smiled, as if embarrassed
by being caught in the act of doing something silly. The man scowled
at him, rubbed his index finger over his bulbous red nose and kept
staring. Will shrugged and continued down Short Street to the harbor.

He stepped through the mud and ducked his head to clear the
doorway of a grog shop at the junction where the unpaved street met
the wharf. The one room was noisy and dark. It smelled of stale beer,
piss and vomit. The low ceiling kept the smoke from the poor draft of
the narrow fireplace from escaping. It made Will's eyes burn. The room
was crowded with men, some already in a drunken stupor, their heads
either lolling back or resting on the rough wooden tables. Will waited
until his eyes adjusted to the dank gloom. A man stood behind three
flat boards resting on two stools, which served as the bar.

He was ladling mugs of rum from an open vat and appeared to be in charge, if not the owner.

Will pushed his way past some men to the front.

"Excuse me, sir," he said. "I am looking for my brother, Johan Stoner."

The man focused his beady eyes on Will and rubbed his chin.

"I do not give anything away for free. That includes what I may know."

"If I buy a drink, would that help?" Will asked.

"It might make me more favorably minded to think about your question. Beer or grog?"

Will thought both were probably diluted, the rum perhaps more so.

"A mug of rum."

"Twenty pence first."

Will knew he was being overcharged but didn't want to argue. He reached inside his pocket. He didn't want to bring his purse out and show anyone in the grog shop how much money he had. He pried open the pouch with his fingers, felt around and pulled out two ten pence coins. He dropped them in the man's extended dirty hand and took the mug in return. It was barely half filled, which suited Will. He took a sip. He had guessed correctly. It was slightly more rum than water but not by much.

"Well," he asked, and waited.

"Another cup might help my memory," the man said.

Will shook his head. "Twenty pence for this one mug is more than enough for your watered drink and your information."

The man shrugged as if to say you get what you pay for.

"Never heard of your brother or any other man of that name. Of course, those who come here don't usually tell me their names." He laughed, revealing his brown stained teeth. "You might ask some of the whores," he said loudly. "All the men they know are called John or Tom." A few of the men at the bar laughed in hopes of ingratiating themselves with the owner.

Will put his unfinished drink down. As he turned to leave, the man to his right grabbed Will's mug from the table and emptied it before Will was out the door.

Once on the street, Will was undecided how to proceed. He pulled Elisabeth's scarf closer around his throat to protect against the cold wind blowing off Roxbury Bay. Going from grog shop to stillhouse did not seem very promising, and there were more shops than he had money. He stood there in the gathering dark. There were no street lights in this part of town. The only dim light came from the narrow doorways and the small windows covered with thin sheets of horn rather than more expensive glass. From the alley next to the grog shop he heard a woman's laugh, a man's insistent whisper, the clink of coins and the rustle of clothing. Probably not the time to ask that whore if she knew Johan Stoner, he smiled to himself.

"Hey you," someone shouted. Will turned and saw the man with the bulbous nose, from outside Merriam's Tannery, approaching. "I heard you asking about your brother. I have a friend who may be able to help," the man said in an ingratiating manner.

This was the first piece of good news Will had heard since he began his search. It was either perseverance or luck, but no matter, he thought, as long as he found Johan. "Where is your friend," he asked eagerly.

"Up the street. At Child's Stillhouse. A larger and more friendly place than the grog shop you have just come out of." The man touched Will's elbow and guided him along the harbor. They passed the street to Merriam's Tannery. Will wanted to hurry along, run if possible, but did not know the way and he could not compel the man to walk any faster. In answer to his questions about his friend and what he knew about Johan, the man offered vague tidbits that gave Will hope he would soon find his brother. Yes, his friend had seen Johan, within the past two weeks. Yes, he knew who employed him but no, he didn't think his friend knew where Johan was now. And here they were now and Will could ask the man himself.

Child's Stillhouse was more like the Roxbury Tavern than a harbor grog shop. Although the ceilings were low, it was well-lit with candles and the fireplace was large and warming. It was crowded with benches and tables, it smelled of stale beer, the serving women looked more like whores than country maids, but Will saw none of that. The man with the bulbous nose led him to a crowded table, and like a horse breeder presenting his prize stud for examination, introduced Will to his friend, Christian Brackett.

Brackett studied Will for a minute before standing up. He was taller than Will, big-boned and more muscular, with a broad face and hooded dark eyes. A rough wool scarf hung loosely around his neck. He took Will's hand in his and after shaking it, pulled him on to a hastily vacated chair on his left. The man with the bulbous nose, now introduced simply as Tom, squeezed in next to Will. Brackett wrapped one large callused hand around the mug handle and put his left arm around Will's shoulder.

"So," he said, studying Will's face. "You are John Stoner's little brother." It was more of a statement than a question. "He changed his name you know. From Johan to John. Said it sounded more English." Tom laughed, although Will did not understand what was funny. "There is a family resemblance," Brackett continued. "John, of course, was a bit more refined and better dressed than you are. No offense of course," he said, squeezing Will's shoulder and smiling.

"You have seen my brother. Where? How is he? How can I find him?" Will's questions tumbled out.

"Patience. All in due time, lad. First, I have some questions for you."

Will was puzzled. "For me. I am more than willing to be of any assistance."

"Hear that," Brackett said to the men at the table. "He is more than willing to assist us." A few of the men snickered.

"Look around the room, Will, and tell me what you see."

Will had not taken any notice before. He swiveled in the chair. Hanging above the bar was an ornate coat of arms, painted on what appeared to be a broken carriage door. The rectangular table they were sitting at was made of mahogany and cherry with intricate filigree carvings around the tabletop. A few of the chairs had fabric seats, now stained with beer, and matched the long table. A large portrait in an ornate gilded frame hung askew from a peg across the room. From around the edges, shards of broken glass stuck out like stubs of broken teeth. The painting was of some wealthy, elegantly dressed English gentleman, his hunting dogs at his feet, standing with one foot on a large dead stag, Someone had thrown a knife at the painting. The blade had struck him in the crotch and the handle remained protruded between his legs.

"Well," Will said slowly, uncertain of the purpose of the question. "This does not look like any other tavern I have ever been in. The furniture and decorations appear to me to have been taken from elsewhere."

Brackett let out a deep laugh. "Do you hear that, men" he said loudly. "Will Stoner thinks our stillhouse has been furnished with the property of others?" The room was silent as the men waited to see what Brackett would do. He laughed again. "It has been, Will. Taken from the homes of the bloody bastard Tories who thought they were better than us." He glanced around the room.

"One more question, Will," Brackett said amiably. "You ask him, Tom," he gestured with his chin.

"Yes, Christian. I will ask him. Will," Tom said a bit too eagerly. "Do you know a man named Timothy Ruggles? Brigadier General Timothy Ruggles?" [3]

Will felt Brackett's large left hand tighten on his shoulder before Brackett hit him full force with his right fist on his cheekbone slightly below his eye. The blow knocked him off his chair. Stunned, he lay on the floor as Brackett bent down and hit him again on the back of his head. He grunted in pain as a booted foot connected with his kidney. He vomited. Strong hands dragged him from under the table, and he was kicked from all sides. His right eye was swollen closed and his left, pressed to the floor, had a limited view. Funny, he thought groggily, as he tasted his own blood oozing from his mouth. These table legs don't match the carvings on the other table. A chair smashed down on his shoulders. He wondered if his collarbone was broken. As he lay there on the floor, in his own blood and vomit, the blows and kicks continued. I am truly going to die here by drowning in my own fluids, he thought. And Elisabeth's scarf is sopping with my vomit. How will I ever get it clean? No need, a voice in his brain said. You are never going to see her again anyway. He groaned as another kick landed on his side.

He was grabbed by his collar and propped up against the wall. Brackett leaned down and pulled Will's head up by his hair.

"Now, you fucking Tory asshole. You will be sorry you came back. We are going to tar and feather you and parade you in front of every warehouse and shop in the harbor that your bastard of a brother and the rest of his buggering Loyal American Associators looted and plundered. Then we are going to cart your whore-mongering ass to the stump of the Liberty Tree and leave your carcass to rot where all can see." He hit Will across the face backhanded. If that didn't break my nose, it must have relocated it, Will thought. "Your prick of a brother worked with Crean Brush and his sorry sons of bitches. Terrorizing people. Stealing. Smashing windows." Each statement of Johan's offenses was accentuated by Brackett banging Will's head against the wall.

"Why did you come?" Brackett shouted at him. "After your brother left. Was it to spy on us?" He slapped Will's face hard. "Or was it to light the powder and shells those fucking Redcoats left behind?" The last question was punctuated by another blow, this one a fist to his forehead. His head hit the wall and he almost passed out.

"He was seen near the coal warehouse," a voice said. "Yes, but I was there to help, Will thought.

"Get some boards," he heard Brackett say but it sounded far away. "Some of you run ahead and build the fire under the tar vats." That would be helpful, Will thought. Wouldn't want the tar to be cold on such a frigid night.

What is wrong with my hearing, he thought. Everything sounds distant. He tried to raise a hand to his ear. It felt as though it was on fire. He couldn't move the arm on the same side as his ear. And it was too much of an effort to try and use his other one and reach across. I must crawl away from here, Will thought. Before they come back. But they haven't left, the voice inside his head said. Maybe if you explain who you are, they will let you go. Yes, he would do that. But he couldn't speak. The only sound he made was a gurgle before he vomited again. I should have taken declamation like Colonel Knox or Lieutenant Hadley, he thought.

He was lifted to his feet. "Drag him by the armpits. You do not want bloody Tory vomit on you." That was Brackett's voice, Will thought. He tried to raise his head so he could see out of his left eye. It was dark out. There were men with torches on the street in front of the still house. The light of the flames blinded him. Well, so much for seeing, he thought. He felt the planks shoved roughly between his legs as he was lifted up. He tried to stay upright but kept falling to one side or the other. Each time provoked a sharp pain in his chest. Must have broken ribs, he thought.

"Shit. We are going to have to build the Tory prince a fucking sedan chair." Brackett again, Will thought, as he was dumped on the cobblestones. His head struck the ground. When he came to, he was strapped to a board behind his back with the long planks between his legs. They were carrying him somewhere, the torches on his left side bobbing up and down. Nothing but blackness on his right side. Ah yes, he remembered. His eye was swollen shut. I hope I see again with it, he thought. No need, the inside voice said again. You'll be dead. Nothing to see from either eye. He heard a roar of voices, shouting about tarring and feathering, calling him a Tory bastard and Loyalist prick. Not the way he anticipated being received in Boston. Didn't anyone recognize him as the one on Big Red, pulling the twelve-pounder? Big Red. What would happen to him? Who would take care of him. Not to worry, the inside voice said. The gunners will keep him. He's a good artillery horse now. That is true, Will thought. I trained him myself.

Still strapped to the upright, he was dropped onto the stones. He groaned from the pain in his ribs. As he tipped over on his side, he noticed that it was Elisabeth's scarf binding his chest to the board behind his back. Not how she intended it to be used, he thought, lying on his left side in a puddle of frigid, muddy water.

"Prop him up, strip him down and pour the tar on the bloody little bastard." Brackett again. Better to close his eyes. He didn't want the tar to burn them. One eye is already closed. They did it for you, his inner voice said, as first his coat and then his shirt were roughly torn off. Right, he thought. I only have to concentrate on closing the left eye. I should be able to manage that. He felt himself slipping into unconsciousness.

In the distance, which seemed to Will miles away from where he was, he heard a pistol shot. He tipped over, still tied to his board, shivering on the cold cobblestones, his teeth chattering, his bare skin freezing to the icy wet street. He was aware everything had stopped, the rough hands pulling his clothes off, the men off somewhere nearby with the vat of tar and the brushes, the vengeful crowd milling about cursing him. He heard voices speaking, more likely shouting but he could not make out any words. He recognized Brackett's voice, angry and defiant. His good eye, his left one, stared at a wet stone and beyond that, booted feet standing in place. He closed his eye and almost drifted off, hearing deep in the groggy mists of his mind a familiar call, "Marblehead Mariners to me." He almost sobbed out-loud, "Here, over here, I'm over here on the ground," but no sound emerged from his broken lips. When he was gently lifted up, he moaned in pain. He was slung over someone's broad shoulders and carried away, each step sending a jolt of sparks to his brain from every part of his body. He felt a cloak thrown over his bare back and opened his one good eye to see his own wrists clasped by the hands of the man carrying him. They were black. Adam, he whispered to himself. Will you really take me fishing before I die? He stopped fighting to remain aware and accepted unconsciousness as welcome relief to his unbearable pain.

When he awoke, Will's first thought was he had died and was already in heaven. Or, at least, somewhere bright, airy and warm. He moved and felt the pain course through his body. If he were in heaven, he reasoned, he would have been healed without pain. So he was still on this earth. He could only see out of his left eye. He tried to move his head and winced. He lay still and let his good eye roam around the room. Sunlight flooded through two windows, their lace curtains tied back, one facing a street, the other an alley. In a fireplace on the far left wall, the logs were slowly burning, casting off welcome heat and warmth. He was lying in a bed under a flowered quilt. Gingerly, he moved the fingers of his left hand and felt the linen beneath. His fingers brushed against a nightshirt he was wearing. His chest felt tight and his right arm was immobilized. When he moved one leg, a lightning bolt of pain shot up his back. The same happened when he tried to move his arm to feel his face. He licked his lips, feeling the split skin with his tongue, and sank back against the pillow, exhausted by all of his efforts.

He must have fallen asleep, because when he opened his eye again, it was dark and the room was lit by candles. And there was an angel in a chair next to the bed. She had long brown hair, which fell in curls on to her shoulders. Her complexion was fair, her face petite with delicately arched eyebrows, a pert little nose and a beautifully dimpled chin. She was concentrating on her embroidery and was unaware he was awake. He studied her with his one eye. She sat straight in the chair, a light blue shawl around her shoulders covering a sturdy white linen dress. She looked vaguely familiar although Will was certain he had never met her. He felt as if he were spying on her, taking advantage of her being unaware he was awake. He closed his left eye, shifted under the covers, groaned and opened his eye again. She looked at him with concern and sympathy.

"Would you like some water?" Her voice was soft and clear. He recognized the Boston accent. So she was from the town. He nodded and watched as best he could as she walked to a side table and poured water from a pitcher into a china cup. She sat so lightly on the bed, it was as if she were a feather, he thought. He tried to sit up and this time genuinely groaned in pain. She tilted the cup to his lips, and he sipped a few swallows. He signaled he was done by barely shaking his head.

"How long have I been here?" His words were hoarse and came slowly, as if they had to be forced through a narrow opening. If he hadn't known he had spoken, he wouldn't have recognized his own voice. He was surprised the effort to speak cost him so much of his strength.

"You have been here two full days, not counting the night my brother brought you home." She smiled at him. "Wait. I will fetch him for you." He turned his head to watch her leave the room. She moves so gracefully he thought, closing his eye and sighing.

"Priscilla. You told me Will was awake," Lieutenant Hadley said peering down at him. Will opened one eye, smiled at Hadley and immediately winced from the pain in his cheek around his right eye.

"I am," he whispered. I have a half-sister named Priscilla, he thought. She must be seven by now. Try as he might, he couldn't remember what she looked like, other than that she had been small and a quiet serious child.

With Hadley standing next to his sister, Will could see the family resemblance. They both had the same bright, inquisitive brown eyes and curly hair. Strange how the high cheekbones on Hadley made him look more masculine, while Priscilla's made her appear more feminine, even regal.

"Dr. Thaxter said if you are going to be a regular patient of his, he will have to start charging you," Hadley said, sitting down on the bed. His weight caused Will to shift slightly, and he winced again.

"Now, brother. Be gentle." Hadley sprang up in consternation, causing the bed to move. Will groaned again. Priscilla motioned sternly to a chair on the left side of the bed. Duly chastised by his sister, Hadley pulled it closer and sat down. Will turned his head slowly and grinned.

"Tell me what. . ."

"It seems your brother was quite the well-known Tory in Boston. One of Crean Brush's favorites," Hadley said, raising his eyebrows. "And a member of the Loyal American Associators as well." Will noted he was freshly shaven. The brass buttons of his clean jacket sparkled in the candlelight.

"General Howe's orders were to confiscate all linens and woolen goods so as to deny them to our army," he continued. "After breaking into people's homes and giving worthless receipts for the goods taken, your brother John, together with the Associators, took anything else they wanted. Most of it went to Brush, that slimy New York Tory, as if we did not have enough of our own homegrown variety," he muttered. "Of course, his minions lined their own pockets as well."

Will closed his eye and sighed. He tried to picture Johan when he had last seen him. How many years ago had it been? Johan leaving the farm, sometime in the early fall, after the hay had been cut, baled and stored, waving goodbye from the wagon seat. As brothers growing up, they had wrestled and fought, kept secrets and told each other lies. They had their own secret signals to protect them from their father's temper and each one felt for the other when their father singled one of them out for a beating. All those brotherly ties gone, broken by John's misconduct. No, it was more than misconduct, Will corrected himself. He acted criminally, against innocent people. Relatives and friends of Will's friends.

"Where is he now?" Will asked, licking his lips.

"All we know is that he was among the Loyalists who fled Boston under General Howe's protection. There were almost two thousand of them, including Mrs. Knox's entire family," he added. "You knew her father was Secretary of the Province." Will nodded.

"They lay off King's Road below Castle Island for a few days before putting to sea with the fleet. Their destination is most likely Nova Scotia. Halifax, I suppose. Like the verse in the song Nat brought us," he said smiling. "After that, General Washington anticipates the fleet and troops will attack the port of New York."

"You are tiring him, brother," Priscilla said, putting her hand on Hadley's arm. Will shook his head and compressed his lips to stifle another groan.

"Priscilla is right, as always. Besides, the Colonel is hosting a dinner for his officers tonight. His first one in Boston since liberation. He is in a fine fettle. We have recovered more than one hundred and forty cannons, some of large caliber. The trunnions have been knocked off some. The British spiked others. The Colonel is confident they can be repaired. He is planning to expand the Regiment. Unfortunately," he said, "we still suffer from an extreme shortage of reliable powder."

Will tried to smile but imagined it was more of a grimace.

"You are continuing to tire him," Priscilla said, "with your military information. He needs rest and quiet, not an inventory of arms. Go. Go to your Colonel's dinner."

Hadley stood up to leave. "The good news, Will, is that Dr. Thaxter opines you will recover. You are young, he said, and the young heal quickly. Still, you have taken a brutal beating and it will definitely be awhile before you are up and about. Rest, gather your strength and we can talk more another time."

"Convey my best to the Colonel and Mrs. Knox," he managed to say softly.

After Hadley departed, Priscilla spoon-fed him some beef broth. He finished the cup and shook his head when she asked him if he wanted more.

"Where am I?" he asked.

"You are in the home of my mother and me. Samuel and some

other soldiers brought you here. This is his bed. My brother is staying with the Regiment at the barracks." Her voice was soft and the tone very matter of fact. Will imagined the commotion there must have been when the two women had been disturbed by his arrival. Suddenly he wondered, if he was alone in this house with the two women, who would attend to his bathroom needs and clean him up afterwards? He blushed to think that the Lieutenant's demure sister was nursing him in that way.

"You are flushed," she said, feeling his forehead. Her hand felt cool and he sighed with pleasure. "I do not believe you are feverish," she continued, unaware the color in his cheeks was due to embarrassment.

"We must wash you and attend to your needs before you sleep," she said matter-of-factly. Will barely had time to think. He was more afraid of this than the threatened tar and feathering. He started to protest, but Priscilla swiftly glided from the room. He was helpless. He couldn't attend to his own needs. He could not even move without pain, let alone use a chamber pot. He closed his eye and tensed with anticipated shame and embarrassment.

Priscilla returned with a soldier in uniform and discreetly left, closing the door behind her.

"How are you feeling, lad?" the soldier asked. Will looked at him through his one good eye. He was from the Massachusetts Artillery. The man removed his regimental coat, hung it on a peg, and unbuttoned his waistcoat. "Since I am going to handle your privates, you would probably like to know who I am before I do so. Right?" He gently folded down the quilt and moved the chair so he could reach the basin in the small wooden table.

Will nodded, more than grateful it was the soldier and not the sister sitting next to him.

"Isaiah Chandler," he said by way of introduction. In the confines of the small room, he seemed older to Will than other soldiers of the Regiment. His brown hair, which he wore long and fluffed out on the sides, was tinged with grey at the temples. His arms lacked the thick muscle of one accustomed to constant physical labor. "No need to tell me who you are. I was up on the Heights, the night you and Lieutenant Hadley delivered food for us. Saw you standing in the back of the wagon, unmindful of the driving sleet of that terrible storm, handing down boxes of meat and kegs of rum." He continued chatting as he pulled up Will's nightshirt and cleaned him with a wet linen. "That food and drink sustained many of us through that cold night and into the day beyond." He washed Will's arms and chest and put the linen back in the basin.

"This is going to hurt a bit lad," he said, putting an arm under Will's waist and rolling him on to his side. Will gritted his teeth but emitted a soft groan anyway. "It was easier to do when you were unconscious." He quickly folded a clean linen on the bed underneath Will and then rolled him back.

"Were you here after they brought me?" Will managed to say once he was lying flat again.

"Here afterwards? I was down at Child's Wharf when the Lieutenant rescued you," he said emphatically. Isaiah took a clean linen and began washing Will's legs.

"Tell me what happened."

"Well," Isaiah said, leaning closer to examine the strips binding Will's ribs. "Doctor told me to look for blood seeping through," he said by way of explanation.

"Is there?" Will asked, unable to see for himself.

"No. They are as white as when you were bound up," he replied before continuing with the story. "We had begun that morning. Early. At Hancock's Wharf. The Redcoats had dropped a large mortar off the pier and the Colonel wanted to salvage it. That took most of the morning." He described how squads of gunners, throughout the afternoon, had gone from wharf to wharf with block and tackle and tripods of sturdy poles loaded on wagons, hoisting cannons from the muck of the harbor. He and several gunners had been trying without success to raise a brass twelve-pounder near Child's Wharf. It was getting dark.

"The British must have tossed it overboard from a sloop and not off the pier because it was a ways out. The trunions were broken and we were having trouble getting chains around it. Then, this flat bottomed boat comes up, rowed by some men in sailor like uniforms." He lifted Will's head and washed the back of his neck.

"Marblehead Mariners," Will whispered hoarsely, noticing smallpox scars on Isaiah's face for the first time.

"Yes," Isaiah confirmed. "And all the better for you, as it turned out, friends of yours." Will nodded and smiled.

Isaiah continued with the details of how two of the Mariners had stripped down and dived into icy waters to fasten the chains on the cannon. The gunners erected the hoist on the flat-bottomed boat, and together the two groups of men pulled the twelve-pounder out.

"The Redcoats had stripped it from its gun carriage. But that is no matter. There are plenty of skilled Yankee carpenters in Boston town," he said. "By now it was dark, but Lieutenant Hadley wanted to finish the work that evening." Will lay quietly in the bed, warm again under the quilt. "Let me take these linens out. We do not want the room smelling like a latrine. Not with the Lieutenant's mother and sister about." He threw his coat on, carefully tucked the dirty linens under his arm and disappeared for a few minutes. When Isaiah returned, he stoked the fire, added another log and pulled the chair closer to the bed.

"Where was I," he asked himself.

"The twelve-pounder was . . .," Will reminded him, unable to finish the sentence.

"On the boat. Yes. Right. So we stayed at the wharf, unloaded the cannon from the boat and hoisted her on to our wagon. The Lieutenant had been talking to this young Lieutenant of the Mariners. They seemed to know each other. Then Lieutenant Hadley mounted the wagon. He was standing on the wagon seat and noticed this commotion on the street. Good thing our Lieutenant has sharp eyes. Later, he told us he recognized you in the light of their torches." Isaiah shook his head in disbelief. "Given the beating they gave you, I would have thought your own mother would not have known you in broad daylight."

Will stifled a sob at Isaiah's words. It was he, Will, who wouldn't recognize his own mother, her face lost to him in his dreams and memory.

Isaiah misunderstood Will's sound. "You have been through a good deal, lad. I know that. Sorry to take you through it again but you asked."

Will shuddered at the memory of being carried on the planks. When Hadley fired his pistol, that was when they dropped him. He stiffened, as if he were going to be thrown to the cobblestones again.

"Our Lieutenant jumped down from the seat and dashed down the pier, shouting for us to follow. We had no muskets. We were on work detail. Myself, and the rest of the gunners grabbed whatever was handy, chains, poles, ropes, even block and tackle and raced after him as fast as we could."

Will kept his one good eye on Isaiah. He began to see how it happened, as Isaiah continued his account. Lieutenant Hadley had arrived at the scene, fired a pistol in the air and ordered them to release Will. Brackett, ever the bully, had challenged the Lieutenant, asking him what he was going to do now that he had discharged his piece. Hadley pulled another pistol from his belt and aimed it at Brackett's broad forehead, saying even one as stupid as he would not risk a ball in the head.

"There were only eight of us, armed as I said with our work implements. There were almost one hundred of them," Isaiah observed. "It was dicey for a minute there. Like when a cannon is primed with the quill in the touch hole but the powder has not yet caught fire. You understand," Isaiah said, more as an affirmation than a question.

Will nodded. "I have been on the lines . . .," he said, his voice tighter, as his recollection of the night's events came back.

"Of course you have. That is when your other friends, the Mariners arrived. There were ten of them, armed with muskets and fitted with bayonets. Smarter than we were," Isaiah chuckled. "Gunners without guns we were and they were sailors without sails." Will smiled numbly but didn't see the humor.

"They came down the pier at a run, shouting all the while, 'To me! Marblehead Mariners to me!' As they came up the crowd was quiet. From all about from the darkness, it seemed every direction of the compass, there were answering cries of 'Mariners are coming!'" He nodded to Will. "The Mariners had other work crews out and they were converging on us. The crowd did not know how many, but there were no heroes in that bunch of misfits ready to find out. One of the Mariners, a strong stocky African fellow handed me his musket, and parted the crowd as if he were taking a Sunday stroll after church. Next thing I saw, he came back carrying you over his shoulders as easily if you weighed less than a sack of flour. We cushioned you on the wagon with some canvas and, at the Lieutenant's order, brought you here."

Will felt exhausted, as if he had relived the terrible night again. Nat, he thought, with tears in his eyes. You have been such a good friend to me. And Adam. It is a good thing for me that Dr. Thaxter put your dislocated shoulder right. And if it hadn't been for the Lieutenant, standing up to the mob. He felt the tears trickle down his cheeks.

"If I cry from my bad eye, does that mean it will get better?" he asked Isaiah, with a weak smile.

"I have seen worse," Isaiah replied. "It should begin to open in another day or two. It appears to me the swelling has gone down some. Time for me to leave before I am reprimanded by Miss Priscilla for depriving you of your healing rest." He stood up.

"Isaiah. Why are you here taking care of me?"

"Oh," he shrugged, putting on his coat. "The Lieutenant asked for a volunteer. It seemed like easy duty. No hauling salvaged cannons about. I sleep in the shed attached to the house, instead of the barracks. And I get to eat Mrs. Hadley's cooking instead of that of the Regiment's cooks." He gave Will a wink and a goodbye wave. "Sleep and get your appetite back. You will soon see the benefits of healing here."

After he left, Will could not fall asleep. He saw the Mariners in the harbor hoisting the cannon. Nat and Adam had been there for certain. Were Solomon and Jeremiah? And Titus? Was he back? Well, if his right eye never healed, he and Titus would be a pair, wouldn't they? Titus without his left and Will without his right.

He awoke before dawn to the smell of freshly baked bread and muffled noises from the kitchen. He lay quietly, testing his body, assessing what he could do and what he dare not try. He knew from prior beatings, at the hand of his father, the few days after the beatings were the worst. The bruises, battered muscles and open wounds tightened, making every step, twitch and gesture painful. There was not much he could do about his face. He imagined he looked terrible with his right eye still swollen shut. The lump on the back of his head still throbbed, although he thought, not as much as the day before.

It was his ribs and shoulders that caused him concern. Every breath caused sharp pain in his chest and side. Very carefully, he made an effort to raise his arms, first one and then the other. He could barely move either one higher than a hand's breadth above the bed before the pain warned him to go no higher. It was bearable when he shifted his weight or bent his legs at the knee. He was encouraged by being able to make such small movements and surprised at how exhausted he felt from the effort.

The bread was the first solid food he ate, biting off small warm chunks from the large slice Isaiah held for him and eagerly taking the spoonfuls of broth to wash it down. It was another clear day, as he could see out the ground-floor windows. Isaiah pulled the curtains back, and when Will was not asleep, he amused himself by watching people passing by. He slept on and off most of the day, and when he awoke in the late afternoon he was both slept out and bored. He tried to compose a letter to Elisabeth but had trouble telling her either too little about the entry into Boston or too much about Johan. As he struggled to find the correct balance, there was a sharp knock at the door and Nat came in.

Will smiled and instinctively started to sit up and shake hands. The pain in his ribs made him gasp. Instead of greeting Nat with a broad smile, he uttered a groan and fell back on the pillow. He did manage to smile wanly.

"I am lucky you were there on the wharf. They were about to tar and feather me."

"How are you healing?" Nat asked. "You do look awful."

"That is what everyone either tells me or I can see it in their eyes. And you look very well and fit. I gather married life is appealing to you."

Nat grinned. "I am as happy as I could be. Anna and I have dined with Colonel Glover, whose wife is still unfortunately in poor health, and earlier this week with Colonel and Mrs. Knox. And you. What does your body tell you?"

"That it is sorely smashed and broken." He chuckled, careful not to bring the laugh from too low down in his chest. "I am both bored and depressed. I wish I could see with my right eye. That would serve to cheer me up. Follow that with being able to walk and use my arms, and then I will know I am on the mend."

"Well. That is too much to expect so soon. Perhaps, I can dispel your boredom with some news."

Will nodded eagerly. It was rumored General Washington would move the army to the port of New York to defend against the anticipated British attack there. While the troops would march the two hundred and fifty-plus miles, the Marblehead Mariners would proceed by ship. "A much more pleasant way to travel than jolting along on your hard wooden wagon seat," Nat added. "For me, it fulfills my father-in-law's prediction that I would be gone more than at home. But it matters not now. We are married and Anna understands I must go." He was silent for a moment.

"Another bit of news is not rumor. I have seen the orders." There was disappointment in his voice. "General Washington has asked the Colonels of each of the established regiments to recommend four men to form a personal guard for the General and his baggage. They must be between five foot eight and five foot ten inches tall. And 'neat and spruce' were the words used in the order." [4]

Although Nat looked unhappy, Will could not help laughing. He did so with difficulty. "Well, it seems to me," he said, "in General Washington's judgment, the Mariners were short pitch pines instead of taller spruce trees."

Nat scowled at him, before breaking into a grin. "If your sense of humor is returning, then I would say you are on the mend," he said, acknowledging Will's joke. "Colonel Glover told the men it is better procedure to draw the General's guard from among the soldiers of the different regiments than to choose a single regiment for that honor. It can create friction among the units, as we have seen." They both were silent, remembering the bloody riot at the General's headquarters in Cambridge. It seemed so long ago to Will. "And yet," Nat continued, "it would have been more courteous if the General had told Colonel Glover in advance."

"In advance of what?" Will asked.

"In advance of our Colonel finding out when the orders of the day were delivered, to be read to all Regiments," Nat replied simply.

Will had no answer, although he thought General Washington might have been too preoccupied with everything he thought commanding generals did, to have time to forewarn Colonel Glover.

"And, as for Regiments, the Mariners are being reconstituted as the Fourteenth Continental Regiment."

"You will no longer be called the Marblehead Mariners?"

Nat shook his head. "All militias are being made over into Regiments of the Continental Army. General Washington is restructuring the entire army. We will keep our distinctive uniforms," he added hastily.

Will looked at his friend mischievously. "Somehow, the cry, 'Fourteenth Continentals to me' does not sound the same rallying note as Marblehead Mariners."

Nat nodded in agreement before realizing Will was teasing him.

"Nat. If you had not called out for the Mariners on Child's Wharf, I would have suffered much worse at the hands of those men."

"Even though you do not wear our uniform, we consider you one of us. Remember, you earned our friendship and respect. It was not an act of charity, so do not think you owe us anything."

"If not my life, at the very least you saved me from being tarred and feathered," Will said gratefully. "It is the truth."

Nat seemed embarrassed by this turn of the conversation. "Here is a piece of news you may find satisfying. None of the Rifles, including Morgans, were allowed to enter Boston. Too ill-disciplined was the word. General Washington is sending some to Albany to join General Schuyler's forces in opposing the British Army coming down from Canada."

"To Albany?" Will said, shocked. He sat up abruptly, his face pale and drawn. Nat assumed it was from pain.

"Will. You should not move so suddenly."

"Do you not see what that means? Colonel Knox now has a reason to adhere to the agreement he made with my father. Without Johan in Boston, there is no longer a need for me to remain." He shook his head in despair. "Indeed, there is a need for me to be a teamster, and transport the supplies accompanying the Rifles to Albany."

Nat thought for a moment. "Whether the Riflemen go to Albany or not is of no consequence. Your brother is not here. You are free now to decide whether to return or not. Make your wishes known to the Colonel. I am sure he will be sympathetic."

Will shook his head. "No, Nat. It is finished. Colonel Knox will use me as a teamster to help move the troops and supplies to western New York." Nat continued to argue with him, but Will had ceased listening. He saw himself on a wagon, one of many on the thawing, muddy roads passing through Springfield, heading west to the border with New York and north to Albany. And then back to the farm.

Nat stood up, unhappy he had made Will depressed. "I have to go. I leave you with this one encouraging thought." Will licked his lips and waited, ready to reject Nat's words. "You recall you once believed your journey would end when the artillery train crossed from New York into Massachusetts? I told you my belief was Providence had a different plan. Now you think Boston will be the end. I think not." He tugged at his short blue jacket and pointed a finger at Will. "You are destined to continue on. Keep that thought as your North Star and speak up for yourself with the Colonel." He paused in the doorway. "And for the love you claim to have for Elisabeth, write the dear girl quickly, now that you know there are troops and dispatches bound for Albany."

After Nat had left, Will raised his right hand and flexed the fingers, practicing the motions he would need for writing. His arm was stiff and his right elbow ached, but he knew he could hold a quill. After dinner he started mentally composing his letter to Elisabeth and felt better for it.

The next morning, Isaiah helped him sit up and swing his legs over the side of the bed. Together, Will accomplished three firsts since being brought to the house: he walked around the room with assistance, he sat in a chair, and he used the chamber pot. By afternoon, he was back in bed, propped up by two pillows and anxious to do something. He was at a stopping point in his letter to Elisabeth. He had composed the part about the entry into Boston and his impressions of the city. He was unsure of what to say about Johan. He certainly was not going to write anything about the beating and his rescue. And he had nothing more to tell her since he had done nothing but lie in bed and recuperate.

He heard horses and a carriage stop in the street and the sound of women's voices in the hall. After the briefest of pauses, Mrs. Knox waddled into the room, bundled up against the cold in a long coat with a cloak around her shoulders. She was accompanied by Priscilla and another young lady. Lucy was extremely pregnant. Her face was slightly fuller since he had last seen her, and she exuded the radiance and glow of expectant motherhood. She stood at the side of the bed, smiling down at him. From his prone position, Will had little choice but to stare at her protruding belly. He shifted his position as best he could so that he could see her face. Her shock at his appearance was evident.

"Will Stoner. I am pleased to see you are for the most part in one piece," she said with her distinct English accent. "Harry assures me Dr. Thaxter is confident you will be fully mended."

"Thank you ma'am for coming," Will said in a hoarse voice.

"Now, Will. Remember the dinner we had in Cambridge. I feel frumpy and unglamorous as it is with my condition. Do not go adding years to my age by addressing me as ma'am." Priscilla offered her the chair and she gratefully accepted, billowing out over it like a hauled-in sail.

"I hope you are not in any discomfort," Will said, politely, still unable to call the Colonel's wife by her given name.

"Our baby is due within the next few weeks," she said, patting her stomach under her dark grey cloak. "I expect to travel with Harry as he has been ordered to examine the coastal defenses of Rhode Island and Connecticut. He will be with me when our first child is born." She seemed lost in thought. "Although it would be comforting to have Dr. Thaxter in attendance, should I remain in Boston."

Will nodded, not knowing what to say.

"Goodness, I have forgotten my manners. Will, this is Anna Holmes, the lovely young bride of Lieutenant Nathaniel Holmes."

Will smiled at Anna. She was slightly shorter than Priscilla, which made her shorter than Nat. She had taken off her bonnet and her straight light brown hair was tied in one braid, which she wore fetchingly over one shoulder. Her skin was very pale and fair, almost translucent. With her wide brown eyes and delicate figure, she reminded Will of a doe or young fawn.

"I cannot tell you how much Nat spoke of you during our journey to bring the cannons to Cambridge."

"And I cannot tell you how much Nat spoke of you since his arrival," she responded vivaciously with a smile. "I felt I knew you before we met."

"I looked better when Nat spoke of me than now," he said ruefully.

"You will be well again, soon enough" Lucy said confidently. "Now, I have brought you, at my Harry's direction, the latest broadsides and a few sheets of writing paper. I am led to believe, from our last conversation," Mrs. Knox said coyly, "there is a certain young lady awaiting your letters."

Mrs. Hadley came and invited the ladies to the dining room for herbal tea, the patriotic substitute for British teas. Mrs. Knox was tiring. Nevertheless, she made the effort to bend over him and kiss him on the forehead simultaneously patting him gently on his cheek. "Come see Harry, when you are up and about. I know he would enjoy such a visit. He is so busy these days with military matters. And he worries about my condition, the poor dear," she said.

Will tried to read the broadsides with one eye. He read all of the bold type, but became frustrated with the small print and put them away. When Isaiah came later in the day, Will felt strong enough to walk around the small room and stand for a while in front of the fireplace. "I would like to walk more, perhaps in the hall or kitchen, but I am not dressed," he said to Isaiah.

"I doubt the ladies would mind," Isaiah replied, guiding Will to a chair. He knelt down and eased Will's worn boots over his bare feet. Will winced as Isaiah pulled him up, but he followed him out of the room, his boots scraping across the wooden floors. It felt good simply to be able to move about.

He shuffled behind Isaiah toward the sounds of women's voices at the back of the house, a blanket wrapped around his shoulders for warmth against the draft in the corridor. He walked cautiously so as not to bump into the furniture despite being unable to see on his right side. The kitchen had a low ceiling with a brick fireplace at the back wall. Pots hung from hooks over the flames. Mrs. Hadley and Priscilla were seated at the table, sewing. Will wrapped the blanket more closely around him, conscious of his bare legs sticking out from under the nightshirt.

"Well, well," Mrs. Hadley said cheerily. "It is good to see you up and about."

"I am indebted to you and the Lieutenant for letting me stay here." He lowered himself gingerly on a bench near the fireplace on the right, so he could see the two women with his good eye.

"Nonsense," Mrs. Hadley replied.

"We were hoping to surprise you," Priscilla said, holding up a pair of brown pants. "These were my brother's before he joined the artillery. I am shortening them for you. My mother has taken in one of Sam's jackets. There are two shirts yet to be done." Mrs. Hadley held up a shirt she was sewing.

"My clothes?" Will asked turning his head to see Isaiah.

"All torn or gone," Isaiah replied. "Nothing worth keeping except for the boots you have on."

"Colonel Knox gave me them," he said. "And a scarf? A dark blue one? And a red one. Are they also lost?"

"When you were brought here, you were wrapped in a cape, with nary a shirt nor coat upon your back," Isaiah said. "There were no scarves." He looked to the ladies for confirmation.

"Were the scarves out of the ordinary?" Priscilla asked.

"The red one was made by my mother when I was a young boy. She has since died. The other was given to me by the young lady Mrs. Knox referred to," Will said quietly. "It was dark blue and reminded me of her."

"Then you will have to write and ask her for another," Mrs. Hadley said. "Most young ladies enjoy making scarves for men they are fond of." She looked at her daughter. Priscilla blushed, smiled prettily and concentrated on sewing the pant leg on her lap.

In his mind, Elisabeth was now Priscilla, sitting in the kitchen making a scarf for him. Did Elisabeth even knit? He didn't know. There was so much about her he didn't know. Lulled by the warmth from the hearth, and tired from his first real exercise, he thought back to the moment on the east bank of the Hudson when Elisabeth had given him her scarf. Lost in the memory, he didn't hear Mrs. Hadley speaking to him.

"Will?" Isaiah said loudly. "Mrs. Hadley asked if you would stand.

She wants to measure the shirt." Will mumbled an apology and stood, clasping the blanket tightly to his chest with both hands.

Mrs. Hadley laughed. "No need to be so modest," she chortled. "I have had children of my own. Besides, you do have on a nightshirt." Cautiously, Will let one arm fall to his side, holding the blanket more firmly with his other. She measured the sleeve length and clucked approvingly. "The tails are long but maybe you will grow and the extra fabric will add more warmth," she said.

He ate his dinner with Mrs. Hadley, Priscilla and Isaiah at the table in the kitchen, instead of being fed in his bed as an invalid. He mopped the remains of the beef broth from the bowl with a piece of bread.

"Samuel ate just like that when he was hungry," Mrs. Hadley said, beaming at him.

Isaiah walked him back to his room and bathed his right eye with warm water. After he had left, Will lay snug and stretched his legs under the quilt. Instead of revising his letter to Elisabeth, he marshaled his arguments to Colonel Knox. The Colonel was a man of his word. He had promised George Stoner he would send his son and the team of eight horses, wagons and sleds back to Scholarie. It would be a matter of honor for him. Try as he would, Will could not overcome this point. A bargain is a bargain, the Colonel would say. He fell asleep unable to resolve the matter.

Will walked reluctantly down Common Street toward the harbor. He ignored the passerbys staring at his still bruised and battered face. The swelling had receded and his right eye had opened again. As far as he could tell, his vision was unaffected. He had finally seen an image of himself in Mrs. Hadley's looking glass. It was the look of a ruffian. If it were not for his clothes, meaning Samuel's, clean and of much better quality than the ones he had lost, the people he passed might have given him a wider berth. He was conscious of the cold, and pulled the collar of his cape up around the back of his neck and Sam's old slouch hat down lower. He missed the wool scarf around his throat.

It was now more than ten days since he had been beaten, almost the end of March. His ribs ached but he was no longer brought up short by sharp pains every time he took a deep breath or moved suddenly. Will had decided, although he had no desire to go anywhere near the wharves, to make a personal pilgrimage of sorts before meeting with Colonel Knox.

He had asked Isaiah about the Liberty Tree, where Brackett had threatened to leave him, tarred and feathered. It had been a large American Elm, Isaiah said, where he and other patriots in Boston had met, rallied and condemned the various oppressive acts of the British.

"When they imposed their bloody Stamp Tax in '65, I was a young bookbinder, just starting out in the trade. Merriam was still apprenticed at the tannery where my master binder bought his leather for binding.

Thomas and I were among those who hung two tax collectors in effigy"
he explained hastily, "from the Liberty Tree." He smiled at the memory
and rubbed the stubble on his chin. "We called it a 'knowledge tax'
in those days. It was the Crown's attempt to restrict what we, as free
Englishmen, could read and write. Oh, Merriam and I were young
hotbloods back then."

"And what would you call yourselves now? " Will had asked,
without thinking.

Isaiah had paused a long time. "Sober patriots and tradesmen,"
Isaiah answered thoughtfully, "with families who depend upon us. We
are not demonstrating against the Crown's representatives anymore.
We are in armed rebellion and fighting against the King's Army, which
is treason." He looked grimly at Will. "Punishable by hanging."

Will easily found the intersection of Essex and Orange Streets.
There was a large round stump in an open field, already weathered
from half a year's exposure. When the Redcoats occupied the town,
Isaiah told him, the Loyal American Associators had chopped it down
and used it for firewood. [1] Further down the hill Will could see the
wharves. He thought Merriam's Tannery was also nearby. He shuddered
both from the chill wind and his proximity to Child's Wharf. Ignoring
the others on the street, he stared at the stump, a bare two feet above
the frozen ground. Will imagined his brother taking part, wielding
an axe to the cheers of his newfound friends in the Loyal Associators.
Johan had been good with an axe, although Will, with his longer arms
and broader shoulders, had developed into a better woodsman.

Well, Will said to himself, glancing at the stump one more time.
This Stoner is no Tory. If the Colonel talks to me about honor, our
family honor requires me, regardless of my father's attachment to
money, and my brother's support of the King, to assist a cause I have
come to believe in. I must offset the actions of my brother and rebalance
the scales, he thought to himself. Resolutely, he turned his back on the
wharves and walked up Essex toward the Commons.

Colonel Knox's headquarters had belonged to Dr. Amos
Fairweather, a prominent Tory physician. It was located beyond Beacon
Hill, an imposing three story brick building on a narrow street facing
Mill Pond. Beyond that, lay the ruins of Charlestown.

Will was ushered into a small anteroom, occupied by two clerks who were busily copying orders and dispatches. He sat down on the only empty chair in the room and ignored the clerks' curious stares. Another larger room was filled with officers of all ranks, waiting impatiently for an audience with Knox. The Colonel had made the front parlor into his office and, although the thick wooden doors were closed, Will could hear his booming voice from within. One of the clerks glanced at Will and shrugged, as if to say that the Colonel is incapable of speaking softly. If the clerk had asked, Will would have said he well knew it, having been with the Colonel on the Hudson, in the Berkshires and on the Heights.

Initially, on the trek across New York and Massachusetts, it had been the Colonel who had educated Will by speaking eloquently of the justice of the patriots' cause. Since arriving in Cambridge, Will realized it was men like Nat and Hadley, Merriam, Adam, Solomon, Jeremiah, and now Isaiah who had shown him what risks they were willing to take, what sacrifices they would make and hardships they would endure to oppose British tyranny. If Providence had thrust him into contact with such men, he must take advantage of it. He would have to trust he would find the proper words to express himself and convince Colonel Knox not to send him back to Albany.

From the anteroom, Will could see the central stairwell leading up to the living quarters. The woodwork of the banister was so intricate Will had trouble believing it had been made by human hands. The first three posts were the same, a round acorn shaped carving at the bottom, topped by a solid cylinder with a spiral pattern, another acorn, with the banister resting on the carved cap of the acorn. The fourth post, and every fourth one thereafter, was a marvel of airy spiral. In place of the solid cylinder, a highly burnished wooden coil corkscrewed between the two carved acorns as if it had been pulled from them as a thread.

By late afternoon, the crowd of officers had dwindled to a few. Will became nervous about his meeting with the Colonel, still unsure of what he would say. The Colonel's brother emerged through the double doors. He recognized Will and smiled broadly.

"Master Stoner," he said, elongating the syllables. "It has been a long time." He shook Will's hand and held it while he tilted his head to examine Will's face. "Bruised in body but not in soul, I hope."

"No, sir," was all could think of to respond.

"My brother is finishing with his meetings. All these Captains and Majors to deal with, wanting to be in the Regiment. You know the Regiment is expanding."

Will nodded. "I had heard so from Lieutenant Hadley."

"Not expanding exactly. It would be more accurate to say we are recruiting up to our designated strength." Billy gestured to the stairwell. "Come upstairs to the Colonel's private office. I know he wants to talk with you."

As they mounted the stairs, Will could not resist running his fingers along one of the intricately carved posts, tracing the clever pattern of the acorn shell and the smooth spiral of the wood.

"Elegant, isn't it?" Billy said. "I knew this doctor. Indeed, he treated Henry when the fowling piece exploded in his hand." He shook his head sadly. "And now he has fled his home, his town, his neighbors, to who knows where, afraid for his safety as a Tory in patriotic Boston." [2]

"He has due reason to be concerned," Will replied. "I was beaten and almost tarred and feathered for merely being the brother of a Tory."

Billy nodded. "There is a difference however," he said, pausing at the landing. "Your brother was a newcomer and directly involved in terrorizing decent citizens. Dr. Fairweather was from an old established Boston family and well respected by one and all. We will miss him and his learned practice of medicine."

He thought people like Brackett, and others who avoided military service and preferred to loot Tory homes, would consider the good doctor's property fair game. They would not be deterred by the doctor's pedigree or his past contributions to the well-being of the citizenry.

It was as if Billy had heard his thoughts. "Will, I was as eager as the next man to return to liberated Boston. But it is not the same place as I left. People are mean-spirited, divided and suspicious of one another. Neighbors, nay even relatives are on opposite sides." He sighed. "There is no longer the grace of living which characterized this city. It is inhabited by the ghosts of those who fled and it will be marked by the empty hearths of those who serve our cause."

"Such as you and the Colonel," Will said softly.

"And many more. Boston will become a town of old men, women and children until this struggle is over."

And men like Brackett, Will thought angrily.

Billy led him to a room on the second level at the back of the house, knocked and opened the door. Colonel Knox was seated at a desk with neat stacks of paper on one side, writing in a large notebook.

"Will, my lad. How good to see you." He rose ponderously from his chair, came around the desk and grasped Will's outstretched hand in both of his, shaking it warmly. "Lucy gave me an honest account of how terrible you appeared when she visited. I must say, whatever you think, seeing you in person is an improvement over her description."

"You look well," Will said. The Colonel had taken off his blue uniform which lay on a chair, the white cloth lining facing up. His unbuttoned waistcoat showed he had not lost any weight since Will and Nat had dined with him.

"Indulge me for a moment. I must complete this letter to Mr. Hancock, assuring him his home is intact, his possessions accounted for and his library unmolested." He returned to the desk and took up his quill. "However, General Grant, who used the home as his quarters during the occupation," the Colonel said, glancing up at Will, "apparently had an inclination to avail himself of the contents of Mr. Hancock's wine cellar. There is nary a bottle left." [3]

Puzzled, Will watched Knox continue writing in the notebook.

"Sir. Are you sending the entire notebook to Mr. Hancock?"

The Colonel sat up in his chair, studying Will's face for a sign of impudence. He decided Will was sincere and laughed. "Will. Sometimes you ask the most peculiar questions. This is my letter book. Why would I send all of my correspondence to Mr. Hancock?"

"What is a letter book?"

"Why, a book for both drafting a letter and having a copy of what you have written and sent." He turned the book around for Will to see. "This is my letter to Mr. Hancock and I have crossed out and amended portions as I have composed it. I will copy the final version in my own hand and send it as my correspondence. Do you not have a letter book?"

Will shook his head. "I compose the letters to Elisabeth in my head. I make the revisions and memorize the letter. When I transcribe it to the paper you and Mrs. Knox have given me, there are no changes to be made." He shrugged. "I have no copies of course, only what I remember."

The Colonel stared at him. "You amaze me Will. You truly do." He glanced over at Billy. "Have you ever heard of such a feat, brother? If I had to rely on my memory to recall the content of my letters I would confuse the ones to Mr. Adams with the ones to Mr. Hancock and vice versa."

"But not the ones to your beloved wife, and Will is writing only to his lovely acquaintance," Billy remarked. Will blushed and said nothing.

"Well, Billy. See to this and provide Master Stoner with his own letter book. He will have to write his father soon if I am not mistaken and explain his situation. And he may have other letters to write. He cannot remember all of them."

The Colonel reread the last line he had written to Mr. Hancock, mouthing the words silently, then wrote another line and put his quill in the inkstand. "In addition to the fine cannons, His Majesty's forces left behind, they also abandoned several bottles of high quality ink. I was struggling with our ink. It has too much oak gall and too little iron and glycerin in it. Not surprising though, given the shortages we all must endure."

Will nodded, still trying to digest what the Colonel meant by telling him he would have to write his father.

"Now brother, do we have the final figures of what is owed to Mr. George Stoner for the use of his teams and sleds?"

Billy took a ledger from the shelf, opened it and searched for the appropriate entry. "Since Will arrived in Cambridge, I was able to rent out all six of the horses and both sleds, almost continuously." He paused to run his finger down another column, nodding to himself. "Subtracting for the cost of feed, we owe Mr. Stoner seven pounds, fourteen shillings and fifteen pence."

The Colonel clasped his big hands together. "There you have it. A tidy sum that I will forward to your father. How old are you, Will?"

"Sixteen, sir," Will replied.

Knox sat at the desk, his chin resting on his folded hands. "When I was your age, I was supporting my widowed mother and little brother over here," he said gesturing toward Billy.

"These are perilous times," the Colonel continued. "We are at war against a merciless foe who will not refrain from any measure to suppress us. But for the intervention of Providence, you would have been involved in a bloody battle on the Heights. We have shared dangers together, not to mention your service with the Mariners and the misadventure on the wharf with that cowardly riffraff. I count myself a good judge of men. You are no longer a lad incapable of deciding his own course of action. I do not wish to hold you to your father's bargain. Indeed, I would prefer you enlist as a private in our regiment."

Will started to interrupt. The Colonel thought he was going to object. He held up his left hand, the white handkerchief on the stumps of his end fingers waving loosely like a small flag.

"Once the cannons we have captured are restored to working order, I have enough artillery for more than one thousand men. The Regiment at present has less than half that number. I have fewer than forty officers. That is the reason I spend my time interviewing officers in my office downstairs, or beating back those who want to join our regiment." He removed his reading glasses and pinched his eyes with fatigue. "Can you believe it, Will? One candidate gave as his reason for wanting to become an officer in our Regiment that we are the smartest-dressed unit in the army." He shook his head in disbelief and laughed deeply, the loose flesh of his neck shaking from the effort.

"Sir," Will said. "Your offer is beyond anything I had hoped for. I was rehearsing how to ask for something, some work or assignment to keep me in Boston." The words came to him now without hesitation, although he had no idea or plan as he spoke. He told the Colonel of how inspired he had been by his speech to the teamsters in the Berkshires. How the Colonel's words and the examples of sacrifice of Massachusetts men at Lexington, Concord and Bunker Hill had enabled Will to persevere and pull the heavy cannon through the winter storm. He told of his gratitude for the Colonel's kindness and that of Mrs. Knox, their obvious concern for him, their efforts to educate him, their gifts of paper, clothing and of course his boots. He even told the

Colonel of how he had recited his teamster speech to the Mariners at their mess. When the Colonel raised an eyebrow, Will hastily added he had not attempted to mimic him but had only repeated the words so the Mariners would likewise be inspired.

"Those men are stalwart and true patriots," Knox said. "They are in no need of any inspiration for our cause from me."

"I was in need of such inspiration and you provided it," Will responded. "I will gladly and enthusiastically enlist for however long it takes."

"Well said, Will," Knox said. "You see, Billy. I told you we would get the better of the bargain with George Stoner." He turned to Will. "My brother thought we paid your father too much. Do you still think so, Billy?"

Billy shook his head. "No, brother, I do not. Congratulations and welcome," Billy said extending his hand.

Will turned back to the Colonel. "If possible, sir, I would like to keep Big Red. He pulled The Albany to the Heights and the twelve pounder to Nook's Hill and, as you yourself have seen, he stands calmly when the guns are fired. It would be useful to have him in the field." He looked expectantly at the Colonel.

Knox smiled. "It is true we need trained horses as much as trained men. In addition to your soldierly duties, perhaps," he winked at his brother, "Will could be assigned to work with the other horses." He nodded to Billy. "Write out a requisition to Mr. Stoner for Big Red. He will be compensated for his horse when the war is over. The other seven of his horses and the two sleds shall be sent on to Albany and returned to him." He raised himself from the chair. "And, Billy, see if you can arrange for the horses and sleds to be gainfully used in carrying supplies for the Army to Albany. The additional monies may assuage Mr. Stoner's disappointment in the changes in our arrangement."

The Colonel threw his coat over his arm. "Now, Will. I must devote what little remains of this day to Mrs. Knox. She will be pleased to know of your enlistment." He left, and Will heard the stairs creaking as he went to the third floor.

"Write the letter to your father and bring it to me here, tomorrow morning," Billy said, walking him to the door. "It is almost the end of the month. Your service will begin the first of April. Please, no more scrapes between now and then," he called after him as Will exuberantly went down the stairs two at a time.

Once outside, Will walked briskly past people hurrying home in the dark. He was oblivious to their presence and the way some looked at his bruised face. I will write a letter to my father, he thought. I will tell him of Johan becoming a Tory and my enlistment. Father will only care that Johan is no longer in a position to make money to send to him. He will regret I am no longer at the farm to do his work and bidding, he thought bitterly, but will not have a care for my well-being. My letter will be the last I write to him.

Tomorrow, he promised himself, I will seek out Adam and ask him, despite the cold, to row out in the harbor so I can feel the rhythm of the water he spoke of. Perhaps, he will teach me to catch fish from the ocean.

Prologue

1) All of the cannons, gun carriages, shot and flint were first ferried by boats from Fort Ticonderoga to Fort George, a distance of thirty-three miles down Lake George. The loading was completed on December 9, 1775. The scow carrying most of the cannons went down off Sabbath Day Point. Fortunately, its gunnels remained above water. It was William Knox, Colonel Knox's younger brother, who organized the soldiers and volunteers to bail out the scow and continue on to Fort George. (North Callahan, Henry Knox-General Washington's General, p. 43).

In Nathaniel Holmes' mind, the cannons were needed to bombard the British and force them to abandon Boston. In reality, Washington already had artillery in Cambridge. The addition of the 59 guns, including 18 and 24 pounders, howitzers and fortification guns, enabled him to keep his existing batteries in place and construct new ones on Dorchester Heights to menace the British fleet in the harbor.

Chapter 1 - The Ghosts of Bloody Pond

1) The battle of Bloody Pond was the last of three encounters on September 8, 1755. On the morning of the 8th, near Lake George,

French forces, consisting mainly of Canadians and their Iroquois allies, ambushed Colonial militias from New England and New York (or provincials, as the British called them) and their Mohawk allies. The Colonials had marched out of their camp near the bottom of Lake George and were heading to reinforce Ft. Edward. The French, firing from behind trees and bushes, crumpled the lead column and drove the Colonials back to their camp. The combat that morning was called "Bloody Morning Scout."

The French followed the retreating English and attacked the camp, located on raised ground, and hastily reinforced by a barricade of logs and overturned wagons and boats. The Canadians and Iroquois fired from the protection of the woods near the camp as French regulars made a frontal assault. Their ranks were decimated by English cannon, firing grape shot. The French forces retreated, leaving behind their wounded commander Baron Dieskau, who was captured. This engagement, sometimes called the Battle of Lake George, took place about three miles south of what is today the town of Lake George.

The third engagement of the day was the Battle of Bloody Pond. Certain facts are uncontested. Others are disputed. English provincial reinforcements from Ft. Edward marched up the military road toward Lake George. One account states they surprised Canadians and their Indian allies, who had left the ongoing fight before the English camp and had returned to the morning's battle site to strip and scalp the dead. The English ambushed them and, after killing many of the French forces, threw their bodies into a pond that ran red with their blood for several days. Another version is the English reinforcements surrounded the French encampment after the entire force had retreated from the battle at the camp. As the French forces were washing themselves in a pool, the English opened fire, and many of the French and Canadians fell dead in the water, discoloring the pool with their blood. In either version, the place became known as Bloody Pond.

The end result of the day's three bloody battles was a stalemate between the French and British forces in northern New York. The French retreated from the field and the British claimed victory. They built a fort near the site of the battle and named it Ft. William Henry. The French built a new fort at Ticonderoga and named it Ft. Carillon.

The two forts were approximately forty miles apart. The French used Ft. Carillon to conduct raids of colonial settlements in western New England. It was captured by the British in 1759 and renamed Ft. Ticonderoga.

For further reading about the three battles of September 8th, see Following in the Footsteps of William Johnson and the Mohawks: From Johnstown to Lake George to Kanatsiohareke, by Jerry L. Patterson, a colloquially written discovery tour of the battlefields. Chapter 13 of History of Saratoga County, New York, by Nathaniel Bartlett Sylvester gives a straightforward account of the battles, with reputed quotes by the Mohawk Chief, King Hendrick, who was killed in the morning's ambush. The entries from The Lake George Mirror about Bloody Pond, available on the Lake George Historical Society website, www. lakegeorgehistorical.org/bloodypond, are interesting, with a local flavor of pride in the Pond's location and righteous indignation at tourists who whiz by the historical marker in their cars.

One author, describing the colonial militias at Lake George in 1755, characterizes them as farmers who had volunteered for a summer campaign and brought their own muskets. In place of bayonets, not a common farming implement, they carried hatchets attached to their belts and slung powder horns over their shoulders. When there was leisure time, these "rustics" carved "quaint devices with the points of their jack-knives" in their powder horns. The Great Republic by the Master Historians-Sir William Johnson: The French and Indian War, Volume I, edited by Hubert H. Bancroft.

2) The French and Indian War was part of the worldwide conflict between the British and French known as the Seven Years War. Basically, it pitted the British and their German Hanover allies (plus Prussia and the German State of Hesse–Kassel whence the Hessian mercenaries later came to North America during the American Revolution) against the French, Spanish, the Russian Empire, Sweden and Austria. An estimated 900,000 to 1.4 million people died in the war. It raged throughout Europe and the colonial empires of the warring parties, in India, West Africa and the Philippines. Naval battles were fought in the Caribbean and Atlantic and Pacific Oceans. Winston Churchill called

it "the first world war." The part of it fought in North America, from the frontier areas of the British colonies and west of the Alleghenies in the Ohio River Valley to the Plains of Abraham outside the walls of Quebec, was only one arena in the vast theater of operations of this global conflict.

The war's impact on the American colonialists was crucial in three major respects. First, it provided military experience for many of the principals and participants in the American Revolution. Second, because they fought against Catholic France, it reinforced the colonialists' Protestant beliefs in a non-hierarchical church, an antipathy to an official State Church, and a nasty streak of anti-Catholicism. And third, it strengthened the colonialists' concept of themselves as free Englishmen entitled to certain rights, including the right of representative government. One historian characterized the French and Indian War as "the war that made America." (Fred Anderson, The War That Made America: A Short History of the French and Indian War).

Many of the prominent officers of the American forces during the Revolution gained their experience either leading colonial or provincial troops or serving with the British during the French and Indian War. First and foremost, of course, was George Washington. He was Colonel of the Virginia provincial regiment, appointed by British Lieutenant Governor Robert Dinwiddie, charged with building a fort at the Forks of the Ohio. On July 3, 1754, he suffered a disastrous defeat at the hands of French Regulars, Canadian militia and their Indian allies at Ft. Necessity. The battlefield is located 11 miles east of Uniontown, Pennsylvania on U.S. 40. Hopelessly outnumbered, surrounded, and trapped in a poorly chosen position in an open meadow, Washington by the end of the day accepted a French offer to capitulate. The terms allowed Washington and the remains of his regiment to keep their arms and personal property and to leave the Ohio River Valley and not return for a year.

Slightly more than a year later, on July 9, 1755, Washington, a member of General Edward Braddock's staff with a rank of Captain, was present at a major British defeat, this one costing the British Commander his life. At the Battle of Monogahela, about seven miles south of Pittsburgh, now the town of Braddock, Pennsylvania, almost two thirds of Braddock's 1,500-man army were killed or wounded. General Braddock was hastily buried in an unmarked grave along what is now U.S. 40, as the remnants of his army retreated to Ft. Cumberland in Maryland.

Among the surviving officers, Captains Horatio Gates, Charles Lee and William Mercer all became Major Generals in the American Continental Army. In addition to other prominent officers on both sides in the American Revolution, many of the ordinary soldiers gained their combat experience in the French and Indian War. One historian estimates a minimum of 28 to 33 members of the Lexington militia in 1775 had seen active service in the French and Indian War. (David Hackett Fischer, Paul Revere's Ride, Appendix O, p. 320).

New England preachers were proud of their Protestantism. They treated the British victories over the Catholic French, particularly the capture of Quebec by General Wolfe and the defeat of the French General, Montcalm, as proof of the superiority of their religion to be "practiced [throughout North America]. . in far greater purity and perfection, than since the times of the apostles." The Colonialists celebrated British victories with sermons, songs, church bells and even commemorative shoe buckles. (Anderson, The War That Made America, pp. 207-209).

3) General Thomas Gage, who was Chief of His Majesty's forces in North America from 1763 until 1775, had served with General Braddock at the Battle of Monogahela. He enforced the Coercive Acts of 1774, which allowed Gage to ban town hall meetings held without his permission. He also attempted to limit the Congregational Churches while promoting the Anglican ones. His attacks on their churches raised the Colonists suspicions as to his motives. Gage's family in fact had been Catholic and supported the Catholic side in British dynastic disputes until the early 1700s. General Gage's grandfather only converted to the Protestant Church of England in 1715.

On March 17, 1775, the raucous St. Patrick's Day celebration by Irish Catholic soldiers deeply offended the Calvinist, Puritan morals of Bostonians. It followed disruption by other British soldiers of a Fast Day, on March 16th, called by the Congregational clergy. The

Massachusetts newssheets, gazettes and magazines accused General Gage of all manner of vices and even worse, of being a Papist, whose aim was to convert all of North America (the French of British Canada having been allowed to retain their Catholicism) to Catholicism. (Hackett-Fischer, Paul Revere's Ride, pp. 70-71,73-74).

Chapter 2 - The Road to Albany

1) When Knox's artillery train arrived in Albany on January 5, 1776, the ice on the Hudson River was not solid enough to hold the cannons' weight. Colder weather followed and the river froze. Knox's hired teamsters transported all of the cannons successfully across to the eastern shore. However, since each sled followed the same tracks as the preceding one, the constant weight and wear and tear weakened the ice. The last cannon, an eighteen pounder weighing one ton, fell through the ice and was left until it was raised the next day with the help of the people of Albany. Knox, in recognition of the local citizens help, christened the "drowned" cannon, "The Albany."

Chapter 3 - A New Bargain at Great Barrington.

1) Massachusetts was in open rebellion long before Lexington and Concord. General Gage, in implementing the Coercive Acts, appointed judges to the various Crown Courts. The Colonialists refused to recognize them. In many cases, the newly appointed members of the judiciary were threatened by the Colonialists and were fearful of serving. In other cases the Colonialists refused to sit on juries in such courts, Paul Revere being one of them. On September 4, 1774, Revere wrote a friend in New York:

". . . our new fangled Councellors are resigning their places every day,[due to threats of the people against them]; our Justices of the courts, who now hold their commissions during the pleasure of His Majesty, or the Governor, cannot git a jury to act with them, in short the Tories are giving way everywhere in our Province." (Cited in Hackett-Fischer, Paul Revere's Ride, p. 48)

The incident in Great Barrington in August 1774, prevented

the King's Sessions Court from sitting and exercising its authority. It also underscored the point that General Gage's writ, and the King's authority, extended only so far as it could be enforced by British troops.

Chapter 4 - "Never Was a Road There Before or After"

1) Knox kept a diary of the trip hauling the cannons from Lake George to Cambridge, Massachusetts. Unfortunately, he failed to make daily entries and there are none for some of the crucial days, particularly the struggle through the Berkshires in the dead of winter. However, the diary is useful for the details Knox does note, such as the specifics about the cannons, howitzers and mortars, their weights, and the amounts Knox paid the teamsters he had hired. (See Drake, Life and Correspondence of Henry Knox).

There are discrepancies as to the route. Until recently, the generally accepted version was that the "Noble Train of Artillery," as Knox called it, went south from Albany, after crossing the Hudson, through Kinderhook down to Claverack, before turning east toward Great Barrington. (See North Callahan's biography, Henry Knox, General Washington's General, pp 44-45.)

However, more recent research concludes that Knox cut the corner, not proceeding as far south as Claverack, and headed southeast from Kinderhook toward the New York-Massachusetts border. You can view the route and the Knox Trail markers in New York and Massachusetts by taking the Knox Trail –Heritage Tour Guide at www.nysm.nysed.gov/services/KnoxTrail/kktour. By either route, Knox and his men struggled across the Berkshires in the midst of a brutal winter. The road from East Otis to the summit at Blandford and down toward Westfield, now Mass. State Highway 23, a distance of approximately 17 miles, is a hellish series of steep inclines and descents, without any switchbacks. Callahan claims the artillery train climbed toward the Blandford Summit passing between the two Spectacle Ponds and a mountain pass. There is no road there today. Callahan's version rules out Knox's route as the present Highway 23. (Callahan, p. 51). The Knox Trail markers follow Highway 23 to the Blandford summit and down to the valley and river leading to Westfield.

On January 13, 1776, before the ascent to the Blandford summit, some of the teamsters refused to proceed any further. Again, according to Callahan, it took "about 'three hours of persuasion' by Knox to get them to go on." (Callahan, p. 52). What Knox said to convince them to continue is unknown. I have used actual incidents of the Battles of Lexington and Concord as part of Knox's fictitious speech to the Massachusetts teamsters to inspire them to continue on the trek and deliver the cannons to General Washington. These stories about the battles were well publicized by the Whigs, through sermons, gazettes and news sheets.

For example, as the British retreated from Lexington, they passed through the town of Menotomy, now Arlington, a part of greater Boston. David Hackett-Fischer describes the stand there by an old patriot. Samuel Whittemore, who was 78 years old and badly crippled, "an old soldier and a strong Whig,. . . armed himself with a musket, two pistols and his old cavalry saber and took a strong position behind a stone wall. . . . [When the retreating British came within range] Whittemore got off five shots with such speed and accuracy that a large British detachment was sent to root him out. As the Regulars assaulted his position, Whittemore killed one soldier with his musket, and shot two more with his pistols. He was reaching for his saber when a British infantryman came up to him and shot away part of his face. Others thrust their bayonets into his body. After the battle he was found barely alive, bleeding from at least fourteen wounds. Friends carried him to Dr. Cotton Tufts of Medford, who shook his head sadly. But Samuel Whittemore confounded his physician. He lived another eighteen years to the ripe age of ninety-six, and populated a large part of Middlesex County with a progeny of Whittemores. . . (Hackett-Fischer, Paul Revere's Ride, p. 257.) The description of the bashing out of the brains of two Colonialists at Cooper's Tavern by British Regulars appears on the same page.

Chapter 5 - The Muddy Slog to Cambridge

1) Surprisingly, despite Knox's own accounting, historians differ on how many cannons were part of his "noble train." Knox's specific

inventory "of Cannon &c., brought from Ticonderoga, December 10, 1775, and instructions for their transportation," lists 43 cannon and 16 mortars for a total of 59 guns with a total weight of 119,900 tons. (Drake, pp. 129-130.) Knox originally estimated it would take him sixteen days to get to Cambridge. Instead, it took more than forty days to cover approximately three hundred miles. The entire train arrived after fifty-six days. He paid for the costs from his own funds, although General Washington had given him a warrant to the Paymaster General of the Continental Army for a thousand dollars, "to defray the expense attending your journey and procuring these articles, an account of which you are to keep and render upon your return." (Washington's Instructions for Henry Knox, Esq., dated December 16, 1775 at Cambridge).

Knox indeed did keep an exact accounting that came to 520 pounds, 15 shillings and 8 and ¾ pence, including expenses for himself, his brother and a servant. (Drake, p. 23.) In today's money the cost of bringing 59 cannons, mortars and howitzers, one barrel of flint and twenty- three boxes of lead was roughly $50,735 (converting the 1780 value of 520 pounds, 15 shillings to the 2005 value of more than 32,731 pounds, converted at $1.55 to one British pound as of January 2012).

Chapter 6 - In the Employ of Colonel Knox

1) Immigrant gunsmiths, primarily Germans who settled in the area around Lancaster, Pennsylvania, originally made what became known as the long rifle. Daniel Boone carried such a rifle with him when he explored the area west of the Cumberland Mountains. At the time that area was generally referred to as Kentucky, and the name Kentucky rifle stuck. By the 1750s, long rifles were commonly used in the frontier areas, including the western parts of Maryland and Virginia. (For more on the origin of the Kentucky long rifle, see Alexander Rose, American Rifle: A Biography).

2) On June 14, 1775, Congress voted for "six companies of expert riflemen [from] Pennsylvania, two in Maryland and two in Virginia" to

join General Washington's Army in Cambridge. These rifle companies were composed of frontiersmen. They generally wore hunting shirts and moccasins, and otherwise, dressed and acted like Indians. Many carried sinister-looking hunting knives or tomahawks. They put on shooting exhibitions for the other troops and notables from Boston. One Dr. Thacher stated "their shot have frequently proved fatal to British officers and soldiers, who expose themselves to view, even at more than double the distance of common musket shot." (Rose, American Rifle, p. 45-46).

The musket was neither suited nor designed for accuracy. The standard army practice was to mass enough men with muskets so the volume of their fire would strike the opposing force. It was calculated that "a skilled musketman, who fired five shots a minute, and who often had just five minutes of firing time before a charge, could participate in up to nineteen battles before he actually killed a man using his [musket]." (Rose, American Rifle, p. 25).

The frontiersmen and their accurate long rifles were certainly a novelty among the other soldiers. They were also a source of envy and resentment. The riflemen were excused from normal camp tasks, such as guard duty and working parties, and they lacked discipline. General Thomas, headquartered in Roxbury, complaining about the southern riflemen wrote they "deserted to the enemy, were mutinous, repugnant to all kinds of duty and exceedingly vicious."

3) Rumors about an attack across the ice were not idle camp gossip. Washington contemplated such a move in January 1776, even before the ice had frozen. By early February it was solid enough to walk on. On February 16, 1776, Washington convened a council of war and proposed that the American troops cross the frozen Roxbury Bay or attack across the ice from Lechmere's Point. Washington was anxious to take action. The Continentals outnumbered the British and Washington wanted to strike before reinforcements arrived by sea. His Generals, by unanimous vote, opposed Washington's plan. They objected on several grounds: there were not enough soldiers, guns or gunpowder for the assault, and the British had strong fortifications and more artillery on land as well as a strong supporting navy. What

did evolve from the council's discussion was a plan to seize Dorchester Heights, thereby threatening the British troops and fleet. The objective was to draw the British Army out of Boston to attack the Continentals on the Heights. (See David McCullough, 1776, pp. 86-87; and "Washington's Attack That Never Was," posted on the fascinating, detailed and lively history blog "Boston 1775" on February 18, 2008. (Boston1775.blogspot.com.)

Chapter 7 - With the Mariners

1) A Google search for Emmanuel Leutze, Washington Crossing the Delaware yields many images of the familiar painting of the Commander-in-Chief on his way to surprise the Hessians at Trenton. The painting is wildly inaccurate: the crossing occurred at night, not at sunrise, the American Flag being resolutely held by two men was not designed and approved until later in 1777, the boat is not a high-sided Durham boat, and the entire party seems to be going in the wrong direction. Nevertheless, it is accurate in that at Washington's right knee is an African American wearing the short blue jacket of the Marblehead Mariners.

The Marblehead Mariners were organized as a militia in April 1775. On January 1, 1776, they were reorganized as the 14th Continental Regiment. They were sailors and fishermen from Marblehead, other Massachusetts North Shore fishing towns and Salem, where their Colonel, John Glover, was born. And they were the first integrated militia or regiment in the Continental Army. Freed Negroes worked on board Marblehead fishing vessels, lived in the same towns, attended the same churches and enlisted in the same militia as did their white counterparts. The Mariners were Washington's amphibious troops, "sailors who could handle oars as well as muskets." (See George Billias, General John Glover and His Marblehead Mariners). They carried General Putnam's men in bateaus from Cambridge into Boston in March 1776, when the British abandoned the city. Throughout 1776, the fatal first harrowing year of the War, the Mariners were the men who saved the Army. They ferried the trapped Continental Army across the East River to Manhattan. They carried the Army in retreat across the Delaware and back again on the offensive to attack Trenton. In 1776, they were the most essential troops for the very survival of the Continental Army.

2) For the names of the fictitious African Americans in the Marblehead Mariners, I have drawn upon the Massachusetts portion of Forgotten Patriots-African American and American Indian Patriots in the American Revolutionary War published by the National Society, Daughters of the American Revolution. Many of the soldiers and sailors designated as African American, and listed as having served during the Revolution from 1775 to 1783, have first names such as Plato, Julius, Titus, Nero, Pompey, Scipio, Primus, Prince, and Fortunatus, coupled with well-established and familiar New England last names such as Abbot, Adams, Everett, Fairweather, Fuller, Gage, Glover, Mason, Mead and Miller. Presumably, their former masters, with their knowledge of Greek and Roman history, saddled their slaves with these pompous-sounding first names. Others have Portuguese or Spanish-sounding names and are designated in the pension rolls as having been of Iberian, Azorean or mixed African descent.

3) During much of the siege of Boston, the Marblehead Mariners served as General Washington's Headquarters troops at Vassall House and were housed on the grounds. There was an actual race riot between a regiment of Virginia riflemen and the Mariners. I have placed it on the grounds of Vassall House, where the Mariners were stationed. I have also assumed it was between them and Morgan's Rifles. Although it could have been provoked by each group making fun of the other's uniforms or frontier dress, it was more likely caused by the presence of freed African Americans among the Mariners, which aroused the racist emotions of the riflemen.

Here is how David Hackett-Fischer describes the event:
"Many of the Virginians were slaveholders and some of the Marblehead men were former African slaves. Insults gave way to blows, and blows to a 'fierce struggle' with biting and gouging.' One spectator wrote that 'in less than five minutes more than a thousand combatants

were on the field.' [This is probably an exaggeration because the Marblehead Mariners Regiment at full strength were only 405 men].

Washington acted quickly. A soldier from Massachusetts named Israel Trask watched him go about it. As the fighting spread through the camp, Washington appeared with his 'colored servant, both on horseback.' Together the General and William Lee rode straight into the middle of the riot. Trask watched Washington with awe as 'with the spring of a deer he leaped from his saddle, threw the reins of his bridle into the hands of his servant, and rushed into the thickest of the melees, with an iron grip seized two tall, brawny, athletic, savage-looking riflemen by the throat, keeping them at arm's length, alternately shaking and talking to them.'" (Hackett-Fischer, Washington's Crossing, p. 25).

4) At the end of the War, the Continental Army was the first integrated institution of the new United States of America. Again, according to Hackett-Fischer, Washington's views on African Americans serving in the Continental Army evolved. At first, free Negroes were allowed to continue in service but no new recruits were permitted. Then, new enlistments were tolerated but not approved. By the end of the War, the Americans were actively recruiting African Americans, including slaves and promising them freedom in return for their service. (Hackett-Fischer, Washington's Crossing, p. 22). An estimated 6,611 African Americans and other minorities, (of which roughly 1,000 were Native Americans) served in the Continental Army or Navy. See, Forgotten Patriots, Appendix D, p. 706.)

The British, on the other hand, from the beginning of the war, openly recruited slaves and enticed them with the promise of their freedom if they fought for the Crown. Virginia Governor Lord Dunmore (who had fled from Williamsburg after a skirmish with the local militia prompted by an effort to impound their gunpowder) issued a proclamation offering slaves their freedom if they fought for the British. An initial 500 slaves were recruited into the British Army and misnamed the Ethiopian Regiment. Lord Dunmore's proclamation had the unwanted effect of making revolutionary supporters out of the landed gentry in Virginia and in the other slaveholding colonies. The

Virginians saw the prospect of armed African Americans as a serious threat to the slave holding plantation owners, as well as the loss of valuable property. Thomas B. Allen, Tories: Fighting for the King in America's First Civil War, pp. 154-155).

Chapter 8 - The Bombardment from Lechmere Point

1) Henry Knox and Lucy Flucker were married on June 16, 1774. She was the second daughter of Thomas Flucker, Royal Secretary of the Province of Massachusetts. Knox was a simple bookseller. After the battles of Lexington and Concord on April 19, 1775, Knox, an avid patriot, fled Boston in disguise, accompanied by Lucy. She never saw her family again. When the British evacuated Boston on March 17, 1776, Lucy's mother, Hannah Waldo Flucker, and Lucy's brothers and sisters left with them. According to David McCullough, her father, Thomas Flucker, appears to have departed earlier. (McCullough, 1776, p. 103.) Ultimately, the entire family returned to London where Thomas Flucker continued to be paid as Royal Secretary to the Province. In a letter written in July 1777, Lucy informed her husband, "By a letter from Mrs. Tyng to Aunt Waldo (Lucy's aunt on her mother's side) we learn that papa enjoys his 300 pounds a year as Secretary of the Province. Droll, is it not?" (Noah Brooks, Henry Knox, A Soldier of the Revolution, p. 46.)

2) According to Dr. David Robarge, Chief Historian at the Central Intelligence Agency, Washington employed subterfuge throughout the War to confuse the British and mislead them as to his intentions. One such ploy was turning barracks into hospitals and bringing wheelbarrows to the front lines in Cambridge, moves designed to deceive the British into thinking he was preparing to attack their fixed positions in Boston. In reality, he was planning a stealth operation to occupy Dorchester Heights overlooking the city and harbor. (Dr. David Robarge, "Secret Revolution: How the Patriots Used Intelligence to Help Win American Independence," Lecture to The Society of the Cincinnati, July 26, 2011.)

3) The story Will read in the Salem Gazette actually appeared, but in April on the anniversary of the Battles of Lexington and Concord, not in March. The sermon of Reverend Jonas Clark was also preached on April 19, 1776, to commemorate the anniversary of the battles, and not earlier. Clark's sermon was printed and widely distributed, as the Whigs wished to whip up patriotic fervor. The "Coffin Broadside," with its two rows of twenty coffins each, and the names of those who had been killed by the British at Concord, was also reissued and widely distributed by the Whigs.

The Whigs were also expert at getting their version of the Battles of Lexington and Concord to members of Parliament and the British public. A letter from Dr. Joseph Warren, "To the Inhabitants of Great Britain," dated April 26, 1775 (one week after the battles), was hurried across the Atlantic and arrived before the official dispatches from General Gage. Warren, who was President of the Provincial Congress of Massachusetts, described some of the atrocities as follows:

"To give the particular account of the ravages of the troops [the British Regulars], as they retreated from Concord to Charlestown, would be very difficult.. . Let it suffice to say, that a great number of the houses on the road were plundered, and rendered unfit for use; several were burnt; women in childbed were driven, by the soldiery, naked into the streets; old men peaceably in their houses were shot dead; and such scenes exhibited as would disgrace the annals of the most uncivilized nations."

The women in childbed theme was repeated by the Reverend Jonas Clarke in his famous sermon on the anniversary of the Battles. His account, as referred to in the broadsheet Will read, is as follows:

"Add to all this; the unarmed, the aged and infirm, who were unable to flee, are inhumanely stabbed and murdered, in their habitations! Yea, even women in child-bed, with their helpless babes in their arms, do not escape the horrid alternative, of being either cruelly murdered in their beds, burnt in their habitations, or turned into the streets to perish with cold. . ." (Boston1775.blogspot.com, April 16, 2009).

Chapter 9 - The Taking of Dorchester Heights

1) General Washington planned for the battle for Dorchester Heights to take place on March fifth, the sixth anniversary of the Boston Massacre. He reasoned that the memory of that event would inspire the New Englanders to fight more bravely. Washington visited the Heights sometime on the fifth, fully anticipating a British assault later that day. According to an eyewitness account, General Washington told the troops, "Remember it is the fifth of March, and avenge the death of your brethren." (McCullough, 1776, p. 95).

Chapter 10 - A Providential Storm

1) General Howe did make preparations for an attack on March 5th but the storm that arose prevented his troops from disembarking. Several days later, he called off the operation and prepared to evacuate Boston. That such evacuation did not take place until March 17th was due to the lack of favorable winds and not a ruse on Howe's part.

Chapter11 - Screams in the Night

1) At one point during the siege, with cannon balls scarce, Washington issued an order offering a small cash reward to be paid for those that were retrieved. Many of the brash and brave young soldiers "contended" for cannon balls by running out and placing a foot in front of a slowly rolling ball, some from eighteen-pounders, resulting in crushed feet. Washington rescinded the order to avoid further injury, although soldiers still retrieved cannon balls when they were stationary.

2) I have relied heavily on the historical blog Boston 1775 (Boston1775.blogspot.com) and several articles and reprints of diaries of Bostonians for accounts of the British pillaging, destruction and debauchery in Boston prior to March 17th.

When the British finally did get their favorable winds and departed, they did so in 120 ships in a convoy that stretched nine miles out to sea. Although they threw some of their cannons in the harbor, they left behind thirty cannons which Massachusetts gunsmiths were able to restore. They scuttled ships in the harbor but left usable stocks in warehouses on the wharfs of bushels of wheat, beans and tons of hay, 3,000 blankets and 35,000 wooden planks as well as coal, essential for heating homes and barracks in the remaining days of winter. According to McCullough, the ships carried 11,000 people, 8,900 troops, approximately 1,100 Loyalists, almost 670 women and over 550 children. (McCullough, 1776, p. 105).

3) Crean Brush was a notorious New York Tory. He, together with a Loyalist militia, carried out Howe's Orders to collect linen and other materials which could be of use to the Continental Army when they entered Boston. He did so by smashing and looting homes and businesses and collecting all manner of valuables for his own personal gain. Ironically he, along with his booty, was captured by American privateers harassing the retreating British fleet.

4) The song, "Some say they sailed for Halifax," and others were composed after General Howe called off the attack on Dorchester Heights around March 6th but before the British evacuated Boston on March 17th. The quoted verses combine the exhilaration of driving the British out of Boston with the realistic fear of being on the receiving end of their artillery.

Chapter 12 - The Search for Johan

1) Washington did not enter Boston with the first American troops on March 17th, which was a Sunday. Instead, he spent the Sabbath with Knox's unit in Cambridge. The Chaplain of the Artillery Regiment chose for his text Exodus 14:25: "And they took off their chariot wheels, that they drove them heavily; so that the Egyptians said, 'Let us flee from the face of Israel; for the Lord fighteth for them against the Egyptians.'" McCullough, 1776, pp. 105-106.
As per Washington's instructions, only those troops who had been inoculated against smallpox were ordered into Boston. On March 17th, led by General Artemus Ward, they marched across the Boston Neck,

while soldiers under General Israel Putnam crossed the Bay from the Cambridge side by boats manned by Marblehead Mariners.

It may seem surprising that such an order was necessary, but Washington's Order of the Day for March 18, 1776, promised the severest punishment of American troops for any pillaging or looting of Boston. "The inhabitants of that distressed town have already suffered too heavily from the iron hand of oppression. Their countrymen surely will not be so base enough to add to their misfortunes."

2) Knox did ride with Washington when the Commander-in-Chief entered the city by crossing the Boston Neck on Monday, March 18th. Knox's artillery had done some damage to church steeples. One Boston clergy man, was reputed to have punned, as Knox rode by, "I never saw a (Kn) ox fatter in my life." (Callahan, Henry Knox: General Washington's General, p. 59).

3) Brigadier General Timothy Ruggles, a leading Massachusetts Tory, had fought in the French and Indian War. He was the Commander of three companies of Loyalists, known as the Loyal American Associators. He left Boston with General Howe's entourage and served with the British forces during the invasion of New York. In compensation for the land he lost in Massachusetts, he was given 10,000 acres in Wilmot, Nova Scotia.

His daughter, Bathsheba Ruggles, was not as fortunate. She remained behind in Boston with her husband Joshua Spooner. She had an affair with a young Continental soldier, hired assassins who successfully murdered her husband and was tried and convicted of his murder. In 1778, she was the first woman hung in America by a legal authority other than a British court. She probably was five months pregnant at the time, which should have stayed her execution but did not.

4) Following the taking of Dorchester Heights, while Washington waited for the British to leave Boston, he issued the following General Order on March 11, 1776, from his Cambridge Headquarters, calling for the establishment of a Headquarters Guard: The General being

desirous of selecting a particular number of men, as a Guard for himself, and baggage, The Colonel, or commanding Officer, of each of the established Regiments, (the Artillery and Riffle-men excepted) will furnish him with four, that the number wanted may be chosen out of them. His Excellency depends upon the Colonels for good Men, such as they can recommend for their sobriety, honesty and good behaviour; he wished them to be from five feet, eight Inches high, to five feet, ten Inches; handsomely and well made, and as there is nothing in his eyes more desireable, than cleanliness in a Soldier, he desires that particular attention be made, in the choice of such men, as are neat, and spruce. They are all to be at Head Quarters to morrow precisely at twelve, at noon, when the Number wanted will be fixed upon. The General neither wants men with uniforms, or arms, nor does he desire any man to be sent to him, that is not perfectly willing, and desirous, of being this guard. . .

In the novel I have dated the Order later than when it was actually issued.

Chapter 13 - The New Private

1) The Liberty Tree in Boston was an American Elm. It stood near Essex and Orange Streets near Hanover Square. It was chopped down by the British, both as a gesture of contempt for the Patriot's cause, and probably for firewood. Once news of this spread through the colonies, Liberty Tree flags were designed and flown in many towns and carried by militia units arriving in Cambridge. Most of these flags depicted spruce or pine trees and not an elm.

2) Dr. Amos Fairweather is a fictitious character. I have depicted his home as that of a wealthy doctor, a Tory who for his personal safety was compelled to leave with his British protectors.

Not all loyalists fled Boston. Henry Lloyd, a prosperous merchant and prominent loyalist (he imported tea for the British) left for Halifax with the British when they evacuated the city. However, his younger brother, James, also a loyalist, remained behind and was treated decently because he was a physician and apparently was also well liked. (See, Boston1775blogspot.com, 19 July 2013.)

The doctor who actually treated Henry Knox's injury to his hand when the fowling piece exploded was a surgeon with the British Army then occupying Boston.

3) Shortly after arriving in Boston, Knox wrote John Hancock to assure the wealthy Boston patriot, who was in Philadelphia at the Continental Congress, that his home and possessions were untouched. George Washington also wrote Hancock on March 19,1776, from his Cambridge Headquarters. His letter was more of a report on the goods and materials left behind by the British. It gave Hancock the estimate by the Quarter Master General that the value was 25,000 to 30,000 pounds sterling.

Author's Note and Acknowledgements

Willem Stoner is modeled on John Becker who was born in Schoharie, New York. As a twelve-year-old boy he accompanied his father, serving as a teamster pulling the cannons from Fort Ticonderoga through the Berkshires in the winter of 1775-1776. They went as far as Springfield, Massachusetts, before returning to Albany.

When he was in his sixties, Becker wrote The Sexagenary or Reminiscences of the American Revolution. It was originally published in Albany in 1833 and dedicated to Major General Philip Schuyler. I was fortunate to find a copy printed in 1866.

Becker describes his journey with Colonel Knox and his subsequent encounters and observations of the Revolutionary War in upstate New York. He never joined the Continental Army and did not participate in any military engagements. He was too young. But he was old enough to manage teams of horses hauling cannons over the most difficult part of the trek to Cambridge.

Today, I doubt whether any modern reader would believe a twelve-year-old capable of enduring such hardships and bearing such responsibilities. So I have made Will fifteen, a teenager struggling to get out from under his fictitious father's heavy hand and inspired by those he meets to join the Continental Army in the late spring of 1776. Will's story continues as a private in General Knox's artillery regiment. General Knox was with Washington in every major battle from New York to Yorktown. Will Stoner will be there too, serving until the end of the War. I hope the subsequent books in the series provide both compelling and interesting historical reading.

I could not have written this novel without the encouragement and assistance of numerous friends, who read the manuscript in various iterations and made many helpful suggestions. They know who they are. I treasure their friendship.

Special thanks to Nickola Beatty Lagoudakis who pointed me to source material on the role of free African Americans, Indians and other persons of color in the Revolution.

I am also indebted to Priscilla Drucker who provided editorial assistance and whose keen eye and patient attention to detail eliminated errors in style and punctuation I had missed despite many readings. Any remaining mistakes are my sole responsibility.

Finally, I am the beneficiary of my son's uncompromisingly honest and incisive criticism as well as his artistic abilities and production skills. My beloved wife has given me consistent encouragement, support and willingly and most importantly, the time and space to write. My gratitude to her is exceeded only by my love.

Martin R. Ganzglass
Washington, D.C.
December 2013

Bibliography

The following are books, blogs or websites, I have read for historical background. I found The Sexagenarian in North Callahan's bibliography for Henry Knox, General Washington's General. I hope one or two of my sources similarly pique the reader's curiosity. Since it is easy enough to search a book online by author and title, I have omitted the customary reference to publisher and date of publication.

Allen, Thomas B.,
Tories: Fighting for the King in America's First Civil War
Anderson, Fred,
The War That Made America: A Short History of the French and Indian War
Breen, T.H.,
American Insurgents, American Patriots: The Revolution of the People
Becker, John,
The Sexagenarian or Reminiscences of the American Revolution
Billias, George Athan,
General John Glover and His Marblehead Mariners
(boston1775.blogspot.com)
Brooks, Noah,
Henry Knox, A Soldier of the Revolution

Callahan, North,
Henry Knox: General Washington's General
Crocker, Thomas E.,
Braddock's March: How the Man Sent to Seize a Continent Changed American History
Drake, Francis S.,
Life and correspondence of Henry Knox: Major-General in the American Revolutionary Army
Dwyer, William M.,
The Day is Ours: An Inside View of the Battles of Trenton and Princeton
Fielding, Henry,
The History of Tom Jones, a Foundling
Fitzpatrick, John Clement,
George Washington Himself: a Commonsense Biography Written from His Manuscripts
Grundset, Eric G., Editor,
National Society Daughters of the American Revolution: Forgotten Patriots—African American and American Indian Patriots of The Revolutionary War, a Guide to Service, Sources and Studies
Hackett-Fischer, David,
Paul Revere's Ride
Hackett-Fischer, David,
Washington's Crossing
Hibbert, Christopher,
Redcoats and Rebels: The American Revolution Through British Eyes
Lengel, Edward G.,
This Glorious Struggle: George Washington's Revolutionary War Letters
McCullough, David,
1776
Martin, Joseph Plumb,
Private Yankee Doodle: Being a Narrative of Some of the Adventures, Dangers and Sufferings of a Revolutionary Soldier
Massachusetts Historical Society,
Siege of Boston, Eyewitness Accounts from the Collections
Prescott, Frederick Clarke, and J.H. Nelson,
Prose and Poetry of the Revolution

Puls, Mark,
Henry Knox: Visionary General of the American Revolution
Rose, Alexander,
American Rifle: A Biography
Sloane, Eric,
Sketches of America Past
Sloane, Eric,
Diary of an Early American Boy: Noah Blake-1805

The thrilling saga of our War for Independence
continues with . . .

Tories and Patriots

The hastily constructed gallows was a simple inverted L. The rough hewn, brown weathered upright beam appeared to have been torn out of a stable stall. A thick, dirty rope noose hung from the narrow and newly-planed tail. It loomed ominously on a platform, the freshly made planks interspersed with worn grey ones, expropriated from nearby abandoned sheds. The entire structure stood five feet off the ground providing the people assembled at The Bowery, a clear view of the hanging. Five regiments of regular troops of the Continental Army were lined up in front of the scaffold. Militias held back the vast crowds on the other three sides of the execution grounds.

Will Stoner waited in the third file of the four hundred soldiers of the Massachusetts Continental Artillery Regiment, their backs to the New Yorkers massing behind them. Sweat dripped down Will's shirt underneath his dark blue wool coat. They had been standing in the warm June sun since nine that morning, having marched smartly to The Bowery from their red brick barracks on lower Broadway. Sergeant Merriam marked the end of their line. The tall thin figure of Corporal Isaiah Chandler was to Will's immediate left. Will took comfort from the older man's presence, recalling how he had nursed him back to health in Lieutenant Hadley's home in Boston. That had been only three months ago, he thought. Three months since his beating by a thuggish mob of patriots who thought he was a Tory spy, and his rescue by Hadley with the aid of Will's friends in the Marblehead Mariners.

Their Artillery Regiment, in the center of the line of troops in front of the scaffold, were part of General John Fellows' Brigade. General Washington himself had ordered the entire Brigade to attend the hanging of Sergeant Thomas Hickey, a member of his own headquarters troops, the General's Life Guards. Will was not sure whether the Brigade was there to witness the hanging or to prevent armed New York City loyalists from rescuing the convicted traitor. He held his loaded musket tightly across his chest. He wished he had been issued a pike or at least a bayonet. In these close quarters, he didn't think his musket would be of much use.

The 14th Continentals, the Marblehead Mariners, looking smart in their short blue jackets and white oiled canvas breeches, were drawn up to the left of Will's regiment, at the corner, almost to the side of the gallows. He looked in vain for his friends, Lieutenant Nathaniel Holmes, Adam Cooper and others. The Mariners' Colonel, John Glover sat motionless on his horse in front of their ranks facing the gallows, his red hair tied back with a black ribbon, protruding from the bottom of his blue tri-corn.

The Militia men across from Will and on the sides surrounding the scaffold platform stood in their homespun clothes in an undisciplined lounging stance. They were armed with an odd mixture of muskets and fowling pieces held askew at all angles. Some casually rested the stocks on the ground.

Almost the entire population of the city, said to be twenty thousand, had turned out for the hanging. Ordinary citizens filled the long grassy field closest to the gallows platform and beyond up the slopes of the hill a hundred yards away. Most were men, young and old, some well dressed on horseback, others common laborers and n'eer do wells. Several barefoot boys had climbed the nearby trees for a better view. Here and there, like butterflies among moths, a few women in their colorful bonnets and dresses sat in carriages fanning themselves.

"Oh, the Tory traitor will soon do the gallows dance," a man's voice said from behind Will.

"Why do you say that?" his companion asked.

"Look at the knot on the noose," the first man replied, pointing with his dirt encrusted hand past Will's right ear. "'Tis a gallows knot, they have tied. It will strangle him. The hangman's knot breaks the neck," the man said with authority.

"Serves him right, the treacherous bastard," his companion said. "Trying to poison General Washington and his staff. I heard he put arsenic in the General's food. It could have killed Mrs. Washington too."

"True enough," a third man chimed in. "They say their plan was when the Redcoats landed, Hickey and his conspirators were going to seize the General and his staff, while the Tory traitors among us blew up our powder and then turned the cannons, loaded with grape shot, on our troops."

"I do not see," Sergeant Merriam said in a loud voice to Isaiah and Will, "how one can both plot to poison General Washington and to seize him." He snorted derisively. "General Howe would like nothing better than to take our General back to London for trial."

"And what do you know about our whore-faced New York Tories," the first man responded, noting that Sergeant Merriam's Boston accent marked him as a stranger. "Before you and your fellows arrived, Mayor Matthews and the Royal Governor were entertaining British Naval Officers in their homes with their elegant balls and dinners and such, while the Redcoats and their ass bag sympathizers threatened and terrorized decent patriots in the city."

"Good thing they caught Mayor Matthews," his companion added. "They should hang him next."

"And Governor Tyron too," another man shouted. "I heard he escaped to one of those ships of the line in the harbor. It mounts seventy four guns I am told, ready to bombard and burn New York to the ground."

"Would you not think, the Royal Governor would want a city to govern," Sergeant Merriam said loudly, turning his head to partially look at the men behind them. "If the city is filled with loyalists, why would he burn their homes and property?"

Merriam leaned closer to his friend Corporal Chandler. "If these men were true patriots instead of undisciplined rabble and gossip-mongers, they would either be in the militia or working on constructing the fortifications in Brooklyn. All they are good for is spreading rumors."

"You may make all the smart talk you want," the man who had spoken first yelled at Merriam. "The city is crawling with armed traitors, scheming away in their secret meetings, ready to rise up on a given signal. The only way to rid us of those pockey scum is to hunt them down like rats and ride them on a rail."

"Oh we had some grand Tory rides this past week," his companion said, laughing. "There were so many of the traitors, we almost ran out of tar and feathers."

Will shuddered remembering how close he had come to being tarred and feathered in April and his narrow escape from the mob. Adam, his friend from the Marblehead Mariners had carried him away from the frenzied crowd, while Lieutenant Hadley and others had held them at bay.

"Steady lad," Isaiah said, noticing Will rub the faint scar over his eye. "You are in uniform and one of us now. General Putnam's men made short work of these ruffians, dispersing them and putting an end to their mob justice. These loud mouth patriots are long on talk and . . ."

He was interrupted by a drum roll signaling the arrival of the prisoner and his guards. A uniformed drummer boy, no older than ten, led the troops into the square. A small round snare drum hung from broad white straps that crossed his narrow chest. He bit his lower lip concentrating on maintaining the beat with two hardwood sticks. Behind him, forty soldiers marched ten abreast. The long bayonets on their muskets glinted in the late morning sun. Hickey, bare headed with his hands tied behind his back walked between two Lieutenants of Washington's Life Guards. They gripped the condemned man by his arms, their long unsheathed swords held upright in their free hands. An officer on horseback and another forty soldiers followed. The entire procession came to a halt directly in front of the scaffold and faced the gallows. The officer rode forward, dismounted and climbed the platform. The crowd was quiet as Hickey was led up the stairs.

Commands rang out and the regulars came to attention. The militias behind the gallows shifted into some semblance of military order. Will watched the officer on the platform.

"That is Captain Gibbs, Commander of the General's Guards,"

Merriam whispered. "A Massachusetts man."

Gibbs unrolled a scroll of paper and read it in a loud clear voice.

"By Order of General Washington, with the concurrence of Generals Heath, Spencer, Greene and Putnam, in conformity with the verdict of the Court Martial of the 26th of June of One Thousand Seven Hundred and Seventy Six, duly and properly convened, finding Sergeant Thomas Hickey guilty of mutiny and sedition, said Thomas Hickey shall be stripped of all rank and insignia and hung by the neck until dead." Gibbs tucked the scroll in his waistcoat and nodded to the guards. "Bring the prisoner forward," he commanded.

The prisoner stood bareheaded, his black hair unkempt and his cheeks covered with stubble. He was stocky, about five feet six, with a wide flat forehead, a narrow chin and a tight thin line of a mouth, which seemed mismatched to the rest of his head. He looks so ordinary, Will thought. Like any common soldier. What could have driven him to try and kill the Commander in Chief?

Hickey smirked as Captain Gibbs drew a straight razor from his jacket. He mockingly bared his neck as if preparing to be shaved. Gibbs ignored him and methodically cut the buttons off Hickey's uniform and then his Sergeant's stripes. The sound of the razor slicing through the wool fabric was like a saw rasping through soft wood.

One of the guards lowered the noose and placed it over Hickey's head while the other brought a wooden stool and helped the prisoner, his hands still bound behind him, to climb up. The officer attempted to tie Hickey's feet around the ankles. The condemned man kicked the officer's hand away. He made another failed attempt before Captain Gibbs waved him off.

"Does the prisoner wish to say any final words before the verdict is carried out?" Gibbs asked.

If there were to be an attempted rescue, it would have to occur now. Will felt the tension among the troops around him. He gripped his musket tightly and scanned the people massed on the hills. The crowd shifted forward. Will felt the pressure from those behind his file. He kept his eyes forward and hoped the pushing was from their eagerness to see the execution.

Hickey looked out over those in front of him, their faces upturned, watching him. He swiveled his head slowly within the looseness of the noose, taking in the people to his left and right. He made an effort to look at those behind him, but decided against trying further, given the narrowness of the stool. He smiled, as if pleased with the enormous numbers who were present. He licked his lips, marshaling his thoughts and then bellowed out, "God damn you all. May you all be blown to hell."

"No priest for this one," some one from the crowd yelled back.

"I have no need for one," Hickey shouted back. "They are all charlatans."

Those were his last words. Captain Gibbs kicked the stool out from under Hickey with his booted foot. Hickey's body jerked down, his legs moved wildly as if he were trying to run on air, his neck seemed to stretch up from his violently twitching shoulders as his entire body struggled against the rope tightening around his throat. His eyes bulged frantically and blood trickled from his nose. His death spasms made his body turn and as his back now faced Will and the others, a dark brown stain appeared on the seat of his pants.

"He was a Tory shit all right," someone yelled from the crowd. Others laughed at the now limp corpse hanging from the gallows.

Made in the USA
San Bernardino, CA
14 May 2014